Brenda wyau

1991-C Powers Ferry Rd
MARIETTA

Three Best Loved
Barbara Cartlands

Books by BARBARA CARTLAND

Romantic Novels

The Fire of Love
The Unpredictable Bride
Love Holds the Cards
A Virgin in Paris
Love to the Rescue
Love Is Contraband
The Enchanting Evil
The Unknown Heart
The Secret Fear
The Reluctant Bride
The Pretty Horse-Breakers
The Audacious Adventuress
Lost Enchantment
Halo for the Devil
The Irresistible Buck
The Complacent Wife

The Odious Duke
The Daring Deception
No Darkness for Love
The Little Adventure
Lessons in Love
Journey to Paradise
The Bored Bridegroom
The Penniless Peer
The Dangerous Dandy
The Ruthless Rake
The Wicked Marquis
The Castle of Fear
The Glittering Lights
A Sword to the Heart
Bewitched

Autobiographical and Biographical

The Isthmus Years 1919–1939
The Years of Opportunity
    1939–1945
I Search for Rainbows 1945–1966
We Danced All Night 1919–1929

Ronald Cartland
    (with a Foreword
    by Sir Winston Churchill)
Polly, My Wonderful Mother

Historical

Bewitching Women
The Outrageous Queen
    (The Story of
    Queen Christina of Sweden)
The Scandalous Life of King Carol
The Private Life of King Charles II

The Private Life of Elizabeth,
    Empress of Austria
Josephine, Empress of France
Diane de Poitiers
Metternich—
    the Passionate Diplomat

Sociology

You in the Home
The Fascinating Forties
Marriage for Moderns
Be Vivid, Be Vital
Love, Life and Sex
Look Lovely, Be Lovely
Vitamins for Vitality
Husbands and Wives

Etiquette
The Many Facets of Love
Sex and the Teenager
The Book of Charm
Living Together
Woman—The Enigma
The Youth Secret
The Magic of Honey

Barbara Cartland's Health Food Cookery Book
Barbara Cartland's Book of Beauty and Health
Men Are Wonderful

Three
Best Loved
BARBARA
CARTLANDS

❦

BEWITCHED
A SWORD TO THE HEART
THE GLITTERING LIGHTS

NELSON DOUBLEDAY, Inc.
Garden City, New York

Bewitched

AUTHOR'S NOTE

I am indebted for the facts about the Gypsies, especially about the Kalderash and those in Russia, to the works of Jean-Paul Clebert, C.G. Leyland, John Hoyland and George Borrow.

I know myself how strictly the true Romanys keep to their Moral Code. In 1960 I fought a bitter, lengthy battle for Gypsy Camps so that their children could be educated. I considered it a gross injustice that any race of people should be moved every twenty-four hours or pay exorbitant fines. I was opposed and abused over my championship for three years.

In 1964 I founded the first Gypsy Romany Camp in the world near Hatfield in Hertfordshire, which the Gypsies themselves christened 'Barbaraville.' I was helped by the Earl of Birkenhead and the Earl of Onslow. Entirely due to our efforts the Minister of Housing and Local Government issued a Directive—which then became Law—that all County Councils must provide camps for their local Gypsies. Hertfordshire now has five camps and other Counties are following suit.

The Betting-Book at White's Club still exists. The Bets recorded in this novel, other than the one referring to the plot, are genuine.

CHAPTER ONE

1818

"I must say, Fabius," Captain Charles Collington remarked, "this is the best Port you have ever offered me."

"I am glad you appreciate it," the Marquis of Ruckley replied.

With the candles from two silver candelabra on the polished table lighting his face, it was impossible to imagine any Gentleman of Fashion could be more handsome or more elegant.

His high cravat was tied in the intricate manner which was the envy of the younger Dandies, the points of his collar high against the sharp line of his firm, almost aggressive chin.

"My father was wise enough," the Marquis went on, "to put down a pipe of this particular wine, and in my opinion it is now worth drinking."

Captain Charles Collington laughed.

"At one time," he said, "we would have been prepared to think any wine delectable after that unspeakable rubbish we drank with the Army in Portugal."

"We were glad enough to find a bottle of anything," the Marquis replied dryly. "I was always convinced that the peasants hid their stores from us."

"Of course they did," Charles Collington agreed. "Would you not have done the same if an Army of foreigners was drinking your country dry?"

"I remembered in the summer when we were down on those dusty plains," the Marquis remarked reminiscently, "feeling so damned thirsty that the mere thought of Prinny swilling champagne at Carlton House used to make me grind my teeth with rage."

"A great many thoughts about 'Gentlemen in England now a-bed,' made me do the same," his friend replied.

The Marquis poured himself out another glass of Port and passed the cut-glass decanter.

"All the same, Charles, I often regret we are not still at war."

"Good God, what an assertion!" Charles Collington exclaimed. "After eight years in the Army I do not mind telling you that I have had enough of it!"

"Going to buy yourself out?" the Marquis asked.

"I might," Captain Collington replied cautiously, "but at the same time I have not enough money to do nothing."

"You mean that you might spend what you do possess drinking and gambling?" the Marquis questioned. "There is nothing more expensive than leisure."

"That is just what I have been thinking," Charles Collington agreed.

"I have been thinking about it too," the Marquis went on, "not because I cannot afford to do nothing, but because it is so damned boring!"

"Really, Fabius, that is doing it a bit brown!" his friend protested. "You have large estates, some first-class racehorses, you are the pride of the Four-in-Hand Club and acknowledged to be the best gameshot in England. What more do you want?"

There was a silence and then the Marquis said:

"I am not certain, but I do know it is not enough!"

"Are you hipped in love?" Captain Collington asked cautiously.

"Good God, no!" the Marquis exclaimed. "What you call 'love' is the least of my troubles."

"I thought it seemed unlikely," his friend said with a laugh. "You are too good-looking! That is what is wrong with you, Fabius. You have only to smile at a woman and she is ready to cast herself into your arms or march you up the aisle!"

The Marquis did not reply.

There was a frown between his eyes as he stared reflectively at his glass of Port.

Since he was one of the greatest matrimonial catches in the *Beau Monde*, it was not surprising that a large number of females were, as Captain Collington had put it, ready to throw themselves into his arms if he so much as looked in their direction.

The Marquis, however, was known to be extremely fastidious.

He had, since the war had ended, spent much of his time in London and had therefore become involved in a number of amatory adventures. These had naturally been gossiped about in the smart Social circle in which he moved.

But there had been no open scandal because either the Marquis had been exceptionally discreet, or the ladies in question had complaisant husbands.

As was the fashion, the Marquis kept a mistress in a house he provided for her, and in the more exclusive night resorts he was a familiar figure.

But at the same time there was always something reserved, or perhaps the right word was "aloof," about him which made women of every class feel in some extraordinary way that they were not good enough for him.

Among the members of the Corps de Ballet, who were so attractive that they were courted by all the Beaux and Dandies of St. James's, the Marquis was known, behind his back, as "Lord High and Mighty."

It was perhaps significant that none of his friends had been brave enough to inform him that this was his nick-name.

Looking across the table at him now, Captain Collington thought it was true that the Marquis had, while he was in the Army, appeared to be much happier and more carefree than he was at the moment.

"You know what is wrong with you, Fabius?" he said suddenly. "You ought to get married!"

"Get married?" the Marquis exclaimed, obviously startled at the idea.

"You are twenty-seven," Captain Collington said. "We are the same age and we are both in fact getting on in years. A whole generation of beardless boys has come after us. They are snapping up the heiresses and considering themselves arbiters of fashion."

"Most of them would run a mile if they heard a shot fired in anger," the Marquis said scathingly.

"That is not entirely true," Captain Collington protested. "At the same time I must admit that most of them seem a trifle immature. There is no doubt, Fabius, that war ages a man."

The Marquis smiled. It gave him a kind of raffish, beguiling quality which his face did not have in repose.

"So you think marriage is the cure for all our ills?"

"I did not say that," Charles Collington said. "I merely suggested it as an alternative to your boredom."

The Marquis threw back his head and laughed.

"I think the remedy would be far worse than the disease! Can you imagine what it would be like to be tied to one woman indefinitely?"

"All the same, Fabius, you will have to produce an heir."

The Marquis was suddenly serious.

"You are thinking of Jethro?"

"I am!" Charles Collington replied. "I suppose you know he was borrowing heavily on the chance that you would be killed before the end of the war?"

"I am aware of that," the Marquis said. "If there was one thing which made me determined that Napoleon's troops should not blow a hole through me, it was the thought of Jethro setting himself up at Ruckley as the Sixth Marquis."

"I agree, the idea is quite intolerable."

Charles Collington finished his glass of Port before adding:

"We cannot sit here all night glooming over your unpleasant cousin, or wondering how to solve the problem of your ennui. How shall we amuse ourselves?"

The Marquis glanced at the clock on the mantel-shelf.

"I thought we might go to the Opera House when the performance is ended. There is a rather attractive red-head I contemplated taking out to supper."

"I know the one you mean," Charles Collington said. "She comes from Vienna and she should certainly sweep away your doldrums for tonight at least!"

"She may do that later," the Marquis said. "It is the boredom of talking to those pretty doves, especially the foreign ones, which makes the hours pass slowly. You had best join me at supper, Charles. Is there not someone in the Company who takes your fancy?"

"I seem to have exhausted most of the attractive ones already," Charles Collington said. "I agree with you, Fabius, one really has nothing to say to them."

The Marquis sighed.

"'You think I pretty—yes?'" he mimicked with a broken accent. "'You give me nice brooch? So very hard for me pay ze rent!' Oh, God, I have listened to the whole gamut of it!"

"I expect they think you are a soft-touch!" Charles Collington laughed. "At the same time it is always amusing to speculate if they will be more entertaining than the Fashionable Impure with whom one spent the previous night, or the bit o'muslin one entertained the night before that."

"You know the trouble with you, Charles," the Marquis remarked, "is that you are becoming a regular Casanova! You tell me I ought to settle down! What about you? You are quite warm enough in the pocket, or at any rate you will be when your father dies."

"He is extremely hale and hearty at sixty-five," Charles Collington replied, "and I have no intention of saddling myself with the expense of a wife and family until I can afford them. It is another kettle of fish where you are concerned."

"It is not a question of affording them, it is enduring them," the Marquis said. "A very different thing, Charles."

He pushed back his chair and stood up.

"Come on then, let us hope that this evening will sweep away the dismal idea that we are getting too old to enjoy the fluffy frivolities of the Corps de Ballet."

"The trouble with you," Charles Collington said as he rose from the table, "is that you do not drink enough!"

"I know," the Marquis answered, "and perhaps that is another pointer to the fact that I am getting old. I dislike waking up in the morning with a splitting head."

"We are two decrepit old campaigners from a war that most people are trying to forget," Charles Collington said solemnly. "Before we go to the Opera House, let us look in at White's and see if there are any other veterans of Wellington's Army feeling as we do."

"That is not a bad idea," the Marquis agreed.

In the Hall of the Marquis's house in Berkeley Square, there were a Butler and four footmen in attendance.

One handed the Marquis his high-crowned hat, and he refused the suggestion of a cape to wear over his long-tailed close-fitting evening coat.

Setting his hat firmly on his dark head, the Marquis walked ahead of Captain Collington.

Outside in Berkeley Square a carriage was waiting, and as he appeared a footman hurried to open the door.

A red carpet had been run across the pavement, but as the Marquis stepped onto it he suddenly remembered that he had not told the Butler that he wished to be called particularly early next morning.

He proposed to attend a Mill that was being held at Wimbledon Common and it necessitated his leaving London by eight-thirty at the latest.

He turned back.

"I wish to be awakened at seven . . ." he began.

As he spoke there was a resounding crash behind him.

A large piece of masonry had fallen from the upper part of the house with a deafening noise and in a cloud of dust onto the very spot where he had stood a second earlier.

Splinters from the stone spatted his legs, and there was dust on his immaculate evening clothes.

"What the devil was that?" Charles Collington ejaculated.

The footmen had all jumped and the Butler with a note of deep concern in his voice asked:

"You're not hurt, M'Lord?"

"No indeed," the Marquis replied calmly. "Although if I had not turned back to speak to you, Burton, I might easily have received the full force of that coping stone, or whatever it was."

"Indeed, Your Lordship's had an extremely fortunate escape!"

"It must have been loose and perhaps the wind blew it from the top of the house," Charles Collington suggested.

"I cannot understand it, Sir," the Butler replied. "On his Lordship's orders the roof was overhauled only a month ago. Surely if there had been anything amiss the workmen would have reported the matter?"

"They should indeed," the Marquis said.

He looked down at the heavy stone as it lay broken but ominously menacing on the red carpet.

The noise had frightened the horses and the coachman was having trouble getting them under control again.

The footman who had been about to open the door was looking at the scene with a dazed expression on his face.

Charles Collington walked forward to stand beside the Marquis.

"If that had hit you, Fabius, it would undoubtedly have killed you."

"That is just what I was thinking," the Marquis said.

He stood patiently while a flunkey brushed the dust from his clothes; then he stepped over the debris and went towards the carriage.

He settled himself comfortably inside, putting his feet up on the opposite seat.

"You had a lucky escape, Fabius," Charles Collington said as they drove off.

The Marquis did not answer. He appeared to be deep in thought.

The carriage, a D'Orsay Cabriolet which was the latest fashion amongst the aristocracy, was extremely comfortable and built for speed.

The two horses drawing it were examples of the outstanding horseflesh that was to be found in the Marquis's stables.

It was only a short distance to White's Club in St. James's Street, and the Marquis and Captain Collington entered through a door beside which stood the famous bow-window.

The window had been converted by Beau Brummel into a Holy of Holies and had become the centre of attraction for men in the fashionable world.

An ordinary member of the Club would as soon have thought of taking a seat on the Woolsack in the House of Lords as of appropriating one of the chairs in the sacred window.

In the previous year, however, Beau Brummel had indulged in an unfortunate and ruinous quarrel with his Patron and friend, the Prince Regent.

Socially that did not ruin him, since the Regent had many enemies, and despite the fact that Beau Brummel was barred from Carlton House Society continued to make much of him.

Financially, however, he was in an appalling state of penury and early one day in 1816 he was forced to flee from London to land in Calais without any resources.

It was inevitable that as the Marquis and Charles Collington walked into the Morning-Room at White's they should think of Beau Brummel.

A large number of the friends who had been closest to him were in the room and it was almost as if the ghost of him—elegant, audacious and witty—was amongst them.

The Marquis noticed Lord Alvanley, Prince Esterhazy and Lord Worcester, who were all listening to the somewhat pontifical voice of Sir Algernon Gibbon.

When Sir Algernon saw the Marquis his face lit up.

"Come and support me, Ruckley," he said. "I am having an argument and I am certain you will be in full agreement with my cause."

"Why should you be sure of that?" the Marquis asked, sauntering towards the group standing round the fire-place.

Sir Algernon Gibbon was, as everyone knew, attempting to take the place of Beau Brummel by setting himself up as an arbiter of fashion and deportment.

He was in fact, well qualified for the position, having excellent taste both in furniture and in clothes. He had also, since Beau Brummel's downfall, become a close confidant and associate of the Regent.

He had, however, not the sharp perception nor the impertinent self-confidence which had made Beau Brummel so exceptional.

He was inclined to dogmatise and, although he was very knowledgeable on the subjects about which he spoke, his contemporaries were often more inclined to laugh at him rather than accept his dictates.

"What I am saying," he said to the Marquis now, "is that it is impossible for someone who is ill-bred to disguise such a disadvantage of birth."

"And I am saying," Lord Alvanley interposed, "that if in particular a woman is well-educated and well-instructed it would be quite easy for her to pass herself off as a Lady of Quality."

"She would not convince me," Sir Algernon said obstinately.

"This all started," Lord Worcester explained to the Marquis, "because Prince Esterhazy has queried the antecedents of a very pretty little French pigeon who swears she is an aristocratic refugee. She has a family tree—which she shows to her admiring gentlemen friends—which would make the Emperor Charlemagne's look like a piece of scrap-paper!"

"The whole thing is a complete fake!" Prince Esterhazy exclaimed.

"Of course it is!" Sir Algernon agreed. "And anyone with sensibility or taste is able at a glance to tell the dross from the gold— the fake from the real."

"What do you think, Ruckley?" Lord Alvanley enquired.

"I agree with you," the Marquis replied. "I am sure, if the lady in question was astute enough, she could easily convince the average man that she was who she pretended to be. Surely it is only a question of acting?"

"Well, I can tell you one thing," Sir Algernon said heatedly, "no woman or man would be able to deceive me. I can smell a *parvenu* a mile away!"

"Would you care to bet on it?" Lord Alvanley enquired.

"Of course," Sir Algernon answered.

"Why not?" Lord Worcester said. "We can all set ourselves to deceive Gibbon and make him eat his words. He is getting too pompous by half!"

Everyone laughed and Sir Algernon took it good-humouredly.

"All right," he said, "I will accept your bets. In fact I will go further. I will make it worth your while. I will bet you one thousand guineas to a hundred that you will not find a man or woman who can convince me that they are blue-blooded when they are in fact exactly the opposite."

There was a roar of laughter from the gentlemen standing round him.

"Good for you, Gibbon!" Lord Worcester exclaimed. "I like a man who is prepared to back up his assertions in hard cash. What is more, I can do with some blunt at the moment!"

"Are foreigners barred?" Prince Esterhazy asked.

"No-one is barred," Sir Algernon declared. "But if you fail to deceive me, Gentlemen, then each failure will cost you fifty guineas! I promise you I shall be well in pocket before the year is out."

"I am not sure that he is not betting on a certainty," Captain Collington said in a low voice to the Marquis.

They were both aware that Sir Algernon was very astute, and he had made a fetish of good taste whether it concerned dress, deportment or the furniture which graced his houses.

He was wealthy because his mother had been an heiress, and his family tree, which dated back to Tudor times, was an example of how the great families of England inter-married amongst themselves.

Genealogy was Sir Algernon's main interest in life and the College of Heralds found him a continual thorn in their flesh as he frequently pointed out to them their mistakes.

Now Sir Algernon asked one of the stewards to bring him the Betting-Book.

Bound in leather and dating from 1743, the first record book having been destroyed in a fire several years earlier, it was an amazing record of the Members' personal interests.

The bets were entered in a very irregular manner, the writing showing all too clearly that a great number of the wagers had been made after dinner and entered by a hand that found it difficult to write clearly.

"Now how many of you are challenging me?" Sir Algernon enquired.

He sat down on a chair as he spoke and, putting the Betting-Book on a table in front of him, inscribed their names one after the other.

There were finally five—Prince Esterhazy, Lord Alvanley, Lord Worcester, Captain Collington and the Marquis.

"You have a year in which to confront me," Sir Algernon said. "If you have not been successful by that time in taking a thousand guineas from me, then I will give you all the best dinner that the Club can provide."

"Do not worry," the Prince said. "Long before that I shall be carrying your gold away in my pocket!"

"You are wrong," Lord Alvanley said, "I shall be the first to win because I need the money and therefore cannot wait!"

"Perhaps your luck will change tonight," the Prince answered, "in which case there will not be so much urgency where you are concerned."

Lord Alvanley needed luck, as the Prince well knew. His extravagance had ruined him, and he owed a gaming debt of £50,000.

Yet his courage, like his wit, never failed him, and he enjoyed all the year round a fresh apricot tart on his side-table at dinner.

Lord Worcester, son and heir of the Duke of Beaufort had recently spent a fortune he did not possess on a team of greys which he drove with a panache that excited public admiration.

His liaison with the famous Courtesan, Harriette Wilson, when he was still a minor had forced the Duke to offer her the sum of five hundred pounds a year for life.

When the Duke tried to settle her claim with a huge sum Harriette wrote her Memoirs, a *chronique scandaleuse* which set fashionable London in a turmoil.

Prince Esterhazy, on the other hand, was the Austrian Ambassador and a very wealthy man. On State occasions he was known to wear jewels worth eighty thousand pounds.

The gentlemen were joking with each other while Sir Algernon, having carefully recorded the conditions and date of the wager, set the Betting-Book on one side.

Charles Collington picked it up.

"You know," he said to the Marquis, "anyone reading this book in the future will think that most of the members of White's were half-witted. Look at this, for instance."

He pointed to a page on which was inscribed:

"Ld Lincoln bets Ld Winchelsea One Hundred Guineas to Fifty guineas that the Duchess Dowager of Marlborough does not survive the Duchess Dowager of Cleveland."

"I remember reading that entry," the Marquis said. "It is not as absurd as Lord Eglington's, who wagered he would find 'a man who shall kill twenty snipe in three-and-twenty shots.'"

"Where is that?" Charles Collington laughed.

"You will find it on one of the pages," the Marquis replied. "I once read the book through from cover to cover, and came to the conclusion that the majority of the bets were made either by drunks or lunatics."

"What about this one?" Charles Collington asked.

Turning the pages, he read aloud:

"Mr. Brummel bets Mr. Methuin two hundred guineas to twenty that Bonaparte will arrive in Paris on September 12th, 1812."

"At least Brummel collected on that occasion," the Marquis remarked.

"Poor Brummel, I wish he was here now," Charles Collington said. "If anyone could give an outsider a setdown it was he."

"That is true," the Marquis agreed. "Well, Charles, time is getting on. Shall we proceed to the Opera House?"

To his surprise his friend did not answer. Then after a moment Captain Collington said in a strange voice:

"Look at this, Fabius."

He passed the book to the Marquis and, following the direction of his finger, the Marquis read:

"Mr. Jethro Ruck bets Sir James Copley that he will be in possession of a fortune and a title by the end of the year 1818."

The Marquis read it slowly then he turned to look at his friend.

"That gives you exactly eight months," Charles Collington said quietly.

"Do you really think—you cannot believe—" the Marquis began.

"Do not be a fool, Fabius. It is quite obvious. I told you Jethro has been praying for your death, and I am quite certain that tonight he was doing something a little more active than pray!"

"I have a feeling you are right," the Marquis agreed.

"What are you going to do about it?" Charles Collington enquired.

The Marquis shrugged his shoulders.

"What can I do? I can hardly accuse Jethro of throwing masonry at me from the top of my house unless I have proof."

"But good Lord, Fabius, you cannot just sit and do nothing! He will get to you sooner or later."

"That is rather a challenge, is it not?"

"Now do not be turnip-headed about this," Charles Collington admonished. "I have always detested your cousin, as you well know. I have always known that he is an unmitigated blackguard and it is no surprise to me that he plans to murder you. The only thing is—I could not bear him to be successful."

"I do not particularly care for the idea myself!" the Marquis said dryly.

"Then do something about it," Charles Collington said urgently.

"What do you suggest?"

"There must be something!"

"There is," the Marquis said slowly, but he did not, in spite of his friend's curiosity, volunteer what that might be.

The following afternoon Lady Walden, at her house near St. Albans in Hertfordshire, was surprised to receive a visitor.

"Fabius!" she exclaimed in surprise when the Marquis was announced. "I thought you never came to the country once you had left it for the London Season."

"I wanted to see you," the Marquis replied.

"I am flattered," Lady Walden smiled, "but as it happens I am leaving here tomorrow, for I do not intend to miss the Duchess of Devonshire's Ball which takes place on Thursday."

"I was sure you would be there," the Marquis said.

"And yet you have come all this way to see me today. I am flattered, Fabius."

There was, however, surprise in her beautiful eyes as she looked at him.

Eurydice Walden had been the toast of St. James ever since she emerged from the school-room six years earlier.

She was lovely in the manner of the fashionable beauties of the time, with fair hair, blue eyes and an exquisitely curved body which left no-one in any doubt as to her femininity.

She had been fêted for her beauty when she had burst almost like a comet on the astonished Social World, but she was at the moment even more desirable because as her beauty had increased with the years so had her assets.

She had married at seventeen the wild, attractive and immensely wealthy Sir Beaugrave Walden.

He had, however, been killed in the last month of the war, leaving an immense fortune to his widow who, a year later on the death of her father, inherited together with other assets ten thousand acres of land which marched with the Marquis's own Estate.

Eurydice and the Marquis had known each other since they were

children, and it had always been understood between their fathers
that they should be married and their estates united.

The Marquis, however, had been abroad with his Regiment in
Portugal when Eurydice married, and although his father bewailed
the fact, he himself had felt no particular loss.

He sat down now on an elegant damask sofa in Eurydice's Drawing-Room and regarded her with a scrutinising expression which
she found somehow perplexing.

"What is the matter, Fabius? You appear worried."

She was in fact puzzling her head as to why he should call on her
so unexpectedly.

She was glad that she was wearing one of her prettiest muslin
gowns because, although she was not strongly interested personally
in the man she had known ever since childhood, she was well
aware that he was sought after by the majority of her female
friends.

To capture his interest would be a feather in her cap, for which
she would undoubtedly be envied.

"I want to talk to you, Eurydice."

"You said that before."

"I know, but I am not quite certain how to explain to you why I
am here."

"It is unlike you to be so reticent," Eurydice teased.

"What I have come to say," the Marquis went on in a serious
tone, "is that I think we should do what was always expected of us
by your father and by mine."

"What was that?" Eurydice enquired.

There was a note of astonishment in her voice. She could hardly
believe that the Marquis was in fact going to say, what she half suspected trembled on his lips.

"I think we should get married!"

"Are you serious?" Eurydice enquired.

"Very serious," he answered. "You know as well as I do that it
was what our fathers planned since the moment you were born.
They were close friends, and they both envisaged the day would
come when our Estates would become one because you became my
wife."

"But all that was years ago," Eurydice objected, "and now they
are both dead."

"But we are alive," the Marquis said, "and I cannot help feeling
it was an eminently sensible plan."

"Sensible perhaps, but not very romantic."

"I am sorry if I have expressed myself badly," the Marquis said with a smile most women found irresistible. "I am very fond of you, Eurydice, as you should well know. I always have been."

"That is nonsense!" Eurydice retorted rudely. "You heartily disliked me when you were a small boy!"

"I am sure I did nothing of the sort!"

"You always said you had no use for girls. You used to pull my hair at parties and once when I threw your cricket ball away you actually hit me."

"Good God, Eurydice," the Marquis exclaimed, "you can hardly hold that against me now!"

"Why not? After all, you have not fallen over yourself to show your affection since we have grown up."

"Have I had a chance?" the Marquis asked. "You were married while I was away fighting in Portugal."

"You certainly did not seem very perturbed about it when we did meet!"

"I only saw you perhaps once or twice after you were married," the Marquis said. "Besides Beaugrave was a friend of mine. You could hardly expect me to make love to you under his nose."

"You did not want to make love to me," Eurydice retorted. "You never have wanted to, so why should you now wish to marry me?"

"For one thing, I think it is time I got married," the Marquis said, "and for another, I am quite certain we should deal well together. I would look after you, Eurydice, and you cannot go on getting yourself gossiped about forever!"

"Gossiped about? And who is slandering me I should like to know?"

"Now really!" the Marquis exclaimed with a hint of amusement in his voice. "You know quite well that you have caused one scandal after another ever since you have been widowed. And as if you did not know, everyone in London is now talking about you and Severn."

There was a pause. Then casting down her eyes Eurydice said: "Perhaps with reason!"

"Good God!" the Marquis exclaimed, "do you mean to say the Duke has come up to scratch?"

"I am not answering that question," Eurydice replied with dignity.

"Then he has not!" the Marquis said shrewdly.

"You have no right to come here and cross-question me."

The Marquis rose to his feet.

"I see it all now," he said. "You came down here in the middle of the Season, which I thought was strange, simply because you believed the Duke would follow you. Well, has he?"

"I told you, Fabius, it is none of your business!" Eurydice cried. "Go away and leave me alone."

"I came here to ask you if you would marry me," the Marquis said firmly. "You have not yet given me your answer."

"I need time to think about it."

He looked at her speculatively and the expression in his eyes was hard.

"In other words," he said slowly, "you are waiting to see if Severn makes you a better offer. If he does you will accept. If not, a Marquis is quite a good catch!"

"There are dozens of people who want to marry me," Eurydice asserted rudely, rather like a small girl who wishes to be aggressive.

"I am well aware of that!" the Marquis replied, "but I doubt, apart from myself and Severn, if you would be prepared to accept any of those love-lorn swain who write odes to your lips and leave little *billets-doux* on your doorstep every morning. It is doubtful if the majority could afford to do anything else."

He spoke sarcastically and Eurydice, rising, stamped her foot.

"How dare you speak to me like that, Fabius!" she said. "You always have been odious and I hate you! Do you understand? I hate you!"

"Nevertheless you will marry me," the Marquis remarked.

"I shall do nothing of the sort," she retorted. "I have no wish to marry anyone unless . . ."

She paused.

". . . unless they can give you the position that you want in Society," the Marquis finished. "You have enough money, Eurydice, we are both aware of that, but you want the standing. You want to be a great Hostess. It was always your ambition."

She did not reply and after a moment he went on:

"That narrows the field, does it not? In fact, as I have already said, it leaves Severn in the lead and me a close second. There is no-one else in the race."

"I am not going to answer you," Eurydice snapped.

The Marquis was aware that she was almost shaking with rage.

"Well I would like an answer soon, in fact within two or three days," the Marquis said. "It is a matter of some urgency."

"What do you mean by that?" Eurydice asked curiously. "Why should you suddenly be in such a hurry?"

Then she gave an exclamation.

"I know why you want to get married! I am not a fool, Fabius. It is because of Jethro, is it not?"

"It is now my turn not to answer questions," the Marquis replied.

"But I will answer them for you," Eurydice said. "The whole world and his wife are well aware that Jethro is waiting to step into your shoes. He is banking on it. He was quite certain you would be killed like poor Beaugrave, and when you were not, he has boasted, when he is in his cups—which is most of the time—that he will get rid of you somehow!"

She paused.

"That is true, is it not?"

"Perhaps," the Marquis admitted.

"So you want a wife and you want an heir," Eurydice said almost beneath her breath.

"Well?" the Marquis enquired.

"I suppose if I say no you will find someone else to marry you. Any wife, whatever she is like, will be better than thinking of Jethro setting himself up at Ruckley and sporting a coronet in the House of Lords."

"You express yourself very eloquently," the Marquis said. "I am waiting for an answer, Eurydice."

"I am not going to give you one at the moment."

"So we have to wait for Severn?"

"Per . . . haps."

"Has he given you any intimation as to whether his feelings for you are serious?"

"I do not wish to discuss him with you," Eurydice said. "In fact I have nothing more to say at the moment, Fabius, except that I will consider your offer of marriage. It is of course very flattering!"

She spoke sarcastically, and quite suddenly the Marquis smiled.

"This is not the way I had intended to approach you."

"No?"

"I meant to doll it up with roses and blue ribbons. It is just that I am not very good at that sort of thing."

"I have heard very different accounts from the ladies upon whom you have bestowed your favours!"

"That is rather different."

"Is it impossible to think of love and marriage at the same time?" Eurydice asked in a low voice.

"Not impossible," the Marquis admitted, "but impracticable. You know as well as I do Eurydice, that life is not like a romantic novelette."

"I loved Beaugrave . . . I loved him madly!"

"That was perhaps the exception which proves the rule," the Marquis agreed. "But do you think your love, your infatuation, or whatever it was, would have lasted? We both know what Beaugrave was like."

Eurydice was silent. She was thinking of the wild, raffish young man she had married. They had both been little more than children and their life together had been one escapade after another.

Then because he craved more excitement than she could provide for him, Beaugrave Walden had bought himself into a fashionable Cavalry Regiment and been killed within six months of joining.

"You see," the Marquis said quietly, as if he followed her thoughts, "a sensible marriage could give you security and a husband who will look after you and protect you. I will do that, Eurydice."

"I believe you would," she answered suddenly serious. "At the same time, have you never loved anyone, Fabius, enough to wish to marry her?"

"The answer is no."

"But you have had many love affairs?"

"Not as many as I am credited with," the Marquis answered, "but enough, Eurydice, to know that what people call 'love' is an ephemeral experience which seldom lasts."

"Is that really true?" she questioned.

She walked away from him to look out on the sunlit garden. There were daffodils under the trees and the shrubs were coming into bloom.

She looked very lovely silhouetted against the dark green of the trees outside, and the Marquis, as his eyes rested on her golden hair and clear-cut features, was suddenly perceptive enough to realise that Eurydice would never be content with no more than a great position, however important it might be.

Like all women, she wanted love, a love that was more than passion, more than desire, a love which he knew he was incapable of giving her.

As if her thoughts had brought her some solution to the problems that beset her, Eurydice turned from the window.

"You are right, Fabius," she said. "I do need security, and I intend to wait to hear what the Duke has to say to me tonight."

"Tonight?" the Marquis asked.

"He is coming to dinner."

"In which case I can most certainly wait until tomorrow."

"I may not be able to give you an answer even then," Eurydice said. "The trouble is, Fabius, I do not want to marry you. If I cannot be a Duchess, I want to be in love."

"You are crying for the moon," the Marquis said.

"How I should like to prove that you are wrong," Eurydice retorted almost rudely. "You are so insufferably sure of yourself."

The Marquis laughed.

"I see it is high time I left you," he said. "Besides, you will want to make yourself particularly alluring for this evening."

There was something almost jeering in the way he spoke the words, and Eurydice, tossing her head, walked towards the door.

"I shall not try to persuade you to stay," she said. "Perhaps when you next call on me either here or in London you will be in a more agreeable mood."

"Or perhaps a more amorous one," the Marquis said. "Would you like to kiss me good-bye, Eurydice?"

"I can think of nothing I wish to do less," she retorted, and opened the door before he could do so.

"Good-bye, Fabius," she said. "You annoy me. You always have annoyed me. I can only hope that one day you will find someone who will make you suffer all the tortures of hell. It will be so very good for you!"

"Your solicitude overwhelms me!" the Marquis retorted.

Then he stepped outside Eurydice's very impressive house on which her father had expended an exorbitant amount of money, and climbed into his Phaeton.

He had driven down from London with only a small groom seated beside him and now, as he took up the reins, the boy released the horses' bridles and, as the Marquis started off, he clambered like a small monkey into his seat at the back of the Phaeton.

They drove away down the drive.

As they went the Marquis had a great desire to reach Ruckley as quickly as possible.

He suddenly felt appalled at what he had done—proposed marriage for the first time in his life—and to someone who said quite frankly that she disliked him.

It had seemed last night and again this morning to be an eminently sensible action to invite Eurydice to be his wife.

He thought that he could do no better than fulfil what had been his father's hopes, and to rely on his father's judgment. But now he felt horrified at the step he had taken.

Life would be intolerable with Eurydice, taunting him at every turn, yearning for affection he was incapable of giving her, and taking every opportunity of irritating him because she felt piqued by his indifference.

The Marquis was very experienced where women were concerned, and he was well aware that they could make life extremely uncomfortable simply because they felt they had been slighted.

Many of his love affairs had in fact ended unpleasantly simply because a woman had been so very much more in love with him than he had pretended to be with her.

It was, he was well aware, something that a female found impossible to forgive. That she should lay down her heart for a man to walk on, and he should in fact be immune to every wile and trick with which she had contrived to capture him.

'One cannot fall in love to order,' the Marquis thought almost despairingly.

Then, as he thought it, he realised what a fool he had been to think that Eurydice would not realise immediately that he was simply making use of her.

Yet he could not pretend to love her and he had the feeling he had made a mess of his first proposal of marriage.

Because it made him angry to realise not only that he had made a fool of himself, but also that if the Duke did not come up to scratch there was every chance that Eurydice might accept his offer, he pushed his horses.

He was a magnificent driver—a Corinthian—and was known to be able to control even the wildest or most difficult animal.

Now, because he was in a rage, he took his team of four down the road which lay between the two Estates at a pace which would have made his Head-Groom look at him in surprise.

The horses swung through the gates at Ruckley and proceeded up the oak avenue in a manner which made the fragile Phaeton seem almost to fly through the air.

They swept up a short incline beyond which there was a sharp descent into the valley, where Ruckley House stood. As the Marquis reached the top of the rise he suddenly saw standing on the drive in front of him a lone figure.

It was a woman with her back to him.

Because he was moving so fast, there was nothing he could do but attempt to turn the horses at the very last moment and drag them onto the verge.

He pulled sharply on the reins, shouting to the woman as he did so to get out of the way.

The horses were almost upon her as she turned a surprised face in their direction.

Then even as the Marquis with a superb effort pulled the horses clear of her, she slipped as she turned and the wheel caught her.

The Marquis drew his horses to a standstill and looked back to see a woman's body lying on the ground behind him.

"Oh, God!" he exclaimed. "I must have killed her!"

CHAPTER TWO

The groom ran to the horses' heads while the Marquis jumped down and hurried up the drive to where the fallen woman sprawled limply on the ground.

When he reached her he saw that she was very young. The wheel had caught her on the left side. There was blood on her forehead and the white blouse she was wearing had been torn from her shoulder where the skin was gashed and bleeding profusely.

The Marquis bent down, taking his handkerchief from his coat pocket as he did so. Then realising that the girl was unconscious, he looked around first at his Phaeton and then at the distance to the house. He decided he would carry her.

Vaguely at the back of his mind he remembered that it was dangerous if someone was hurt internally for them to be jolted or even moved, but he could not leave her lying injured on the drive.

She was small and slight and it would obviously be less disturbing if he carried her than if he attempted to drive her in the Phaeton.

Very gently he lifted the recumbent figure in his arms. She was very light.

"Drive the horses home, Jim," he ordered his groom who was watching from the Phaeton. "Tell them at the house that there has been an accident."

"Very good, M'Lord," the groom answered and set off down the drive.

Moving slowly the Marquis followed.

As he walked he looked down at his burden and realised that apart from the bleeding wound on her forehead, she was lovely, but in a strange manner.

She had black hair, so long that the Marquis was certain that when she was standing it would reach below her waist and her closed eyes were perfect half-crescents with long lashes dark against an ivory skin.

She did not look English; then glancing at her clothes the Marquis understood.

The girl he had knocked down was a Gypsy!

There was no mistaking the full red skirt worn, he was sure, over a number of others, the black velvet bodice laced in the front, the sash around her small waist, and the embroidered blouse, low at the neck, leaving the arms bare.

He had always supposed that Gypsies were dirty, but the girl he held in his arms was exquisitely clean, and there was a faint fragrance of some Oriental perfume which seemed to come from her hair.

The Marquis saw that round her neck she wore a necklace of gold coins linked together with what appeared to be small pieces of red glass.

Gypsy women liked jewellery, he remembered hearing at some time or another.

He had an idea that some of the coins the girl wore were of great antiquity. They were certainly old and all of them were foreign. Then he chided himself for being interested in anything except his victim who might in fact be badly injured.

She was certainly not dead, which was one consolation. She was unconscious, but she was breathing evenly and her rather frightening pallor might well, he thought, be habitual.

It did not take him long to traverse the drive and reach the court-yard which lay in front of a great flight of steps leading to the main entrance.

As he drew nearer a number of men-servants came hurrying towards him.

Bush, the Butler, reached him first.

"We heard there'd been an accident, M'Lord. Is the lady badly hurt?"

"I have no idea," the Marquis answered curtly.

Then as he moved on with the Butler beside him, the latter exclaimed:

"It's no lady, M'Lord! She's one of them Gypsies!"

"What Gypsies?"

"There are always some of them in the woods at this time of the year, M'Lord."

The Marquis walked up the steps.

There appeared to be quite a number of people in the Marble

Hall when he entered, but he ignored them and climbed the carved staircase to where on the first landing he found Mrs. Meedham, the Housekeeper, agitatedly bobbing a curtsy at the sight of him.

"Which bed-room is ready?" the Marquis enquired.

"All of them, M'Lord."

Then she looked at the unconscious figure in the arms of the Marquis and exclaimed:

"Why, it's one of them Gypsies! A room in the servants' wing will do for her, M'Lord."

The Marquis walked across the landing.

"Open the door," he said briefly.

After a moment's surprise Mrs. Meedham obeyed him, and he entered one of the large State-Rooms which opened off the first-floor landing.

"But surely, M'Lord . . ." Mrs. Meedham protested, only to be silenced as the Marquis said:

"There could be a risk, Mrs. Meedham, in carrying this young woman any further. Her life may be in danger."

He moved towards the big four-poster bed but Mrs. Meedham hurried after him.

"Not on the cover, M'Lord! The sheets can be washed."

She pulled back the embroidered silk and opened the bed-clothes as she spoke.

Very gently the Marquis set down the girl he carried on the white linen sheets embroidered with the Ruckley crest surmounted by a coronet.

Her head fell back against the pillows, and her hair was jet black in contrast to the white linen.

"Send for Hobley," the Marquis ordered.

"I'm here, M'Lord."

A middle-aged man came hurrying into the room.

Hobley had been at Ruckley House ever since the Marquis could remember. Officially he was his Lordship's Valet, but he was famous for his skill in being able to set bones.

He had in fact set the Marquis's own collar-bone on one occasion and, if anyone on the Estate broke a leg or an arm, it was always Hobley who attended them.

He was far more efficient, far more knowledgeable than any local Physician, and in fact everyone asked for him whatever their injury.

Hobley moved to the bed-side now, looked at the cut on the unconscious girl's forehead and the bleeding wounds on her arm. He then noticed there was blood dripping from beneath her skirts and pulled them aside to show a deep cut on one ankle.

As he did so, the Marquis saw the girl's legs were bare although she wore red slippers cut low and ornamented with little buckles of silver.

"Hot water and bandages, if you please," Hobley demanded, and Mrs. Meedham and several house-maids who were congregated round the door hurried to fetch what he required.

"Are there any bones broken?" the Marquis asked.

"I can't tell as yet, M'Lord," Hobley answered. "Did the wheel pass over her?"

"I cannot be sure," the Marquis replied. "It happened so quickly."

He paused and added:

"It was my fault, Hobley. I was driving too fast."

"'Tis not often you have an accident, M'Lord," Hobley said, and added reassuringly: "I've an idea this is not as bad as it looks!"

"But she is unconscious."

"That is because of the wound on her head," Hobley replied. "Leave her with me, M'Lord. I'll find out what is wrong and let Your Lordship know if it is necessary to send for the Doctor."

"Thank you, Hobley," the Marquis said with a note of relief in his voice.

He left the room.

As he crossed the landing it was to see Mrs. Meedham and the house-maids hurrying down the passage carrying jugs of water, bandages and towels in their hands.

He went downstairs and, ignoring the Salon where he knew the Butler would have laid out wine and refreshments, he walked instead down the passage which led to the Library.

One of the most impressive rooms in the house, it had been completely renovated in his father's time, who had also added two or three thousand volumes to the books already collected by his grand-father.

Seated at a desk in the centre of the Library was an elderly man with white hair.

He looked up indifferently as the Marquis opened the door, then rose with an exclamation of surprise and pleasure.

"I was not expecting you, My Lord. Why did no-one tell me you were coming?"

"It is a surprise," the Marquis said. "I only decided last night it was necessary for me to visit the country."

He was speaking to the man who had been his Tutor, friend and companion for many years.

The Reverend Horace Redditch had been employed by the late Marquis to tutor his son before he went to Eton.

He had fitted in so well and been so liked by the whole family that in time he became the Marquis's personal Chaplain, as well as being Librarian and Curator.

He was known by everyone in the House and on the Estate as "The Reverend," and enjoyed the familiarity which made it a term of affection.

He had accompanied the present Marquis as a young man on many visits around the country. They had once spent a delightful holiday in Ireland combining learning with the pleasure of salmon fishing.

"It is nice to see you, Sir," the Marquis said, with a note of affection in his voice which few people evoked from him.

"Are you enjoying London?" The Reverend enquired.

"Not particularly!" the Marquis admitted. "As a matter of fact I have just had an accident. I knocked down a Gypsy girl. She is upstairs and Hobley is attending to her."

"A Gypsy?" The Reverend repeated. "Well, that is not surprising. It is the time of year when they visit us."

"Tell me about them," the Marquis said.

"It was your grand-mother, I believe, who gave them permission to camp on the Estate. She was always sorry for everyone who was homeless and I think too she was very interested in Gypsy people who wander over the earth with no settled abode."

"I really know very little about them," the Marquis said.

"They came originally from India," The Reverend replied. "Which of course accounts for their dark hair and dark skins."

"And they have been nomads ever since?"

"There are of course numerous legends and explanations as to why they can never settle down."

"Are there many Gypsies in England?"

"Quite a number, I believe," The Reverend replied. "But they are to be found in every country. If you are interested I must see if we have any books about them."

The Marquis shrugged his shoulders.

"I seem to remember that the Game-keepers dislike them, thinking that they poach the pheasants."

"It has been a tradition on this Estate that they should not be harassed or driven away," The Reverend said, "and as I think there is something picturesque about them, I hope you will not refuse them the hospitality which they have found at Ruckley for nearly a century."

"I will certainly not do that!" the Marquis said. "After all, I feel responsible for the girl I have just injured. Do you think I should get in touch with her tribe, or whatever they call themselves?"

"Maybe she is not as badly hurt as you suspect," The Reverend said soothingly. "Anyway Hobley will deal with it."

"Yes, I am sure he will," the Marquis replied.

He talked for a little while longer to his old Tutor, then went into the Salon to find as he had expected there was wine and a whole assortment of sandwiches and other delicacies laid out on a silver tray.

The Marquis had stopped for luncheon at an Inn on his way down from London before he had called on Eurydice. So, while he sipped a glass of excellent wine from his cellars, he was in fact not hungry.

He had only been in the Salon a short while before Hobley came to find him.

"How is she?" the Marquis asked.

"There're no bones broken, M'Lord, but the blow on the head has undoubtedly caused concussion. I should not be surprised if tonight she runs a fever!"

"It is not serious?" the Marquis asked.

"No, M'Lord, the cuts and bruises are only superficial, and when the Gypsy regains consciousness we shall know how much she has been affected in the head."

"Then she must stay here until she is better," the Marquis said.

"Mrs. Meedham is anxious to move her to another part of the house, M'Lord. She feels it is unseemly that a Gypsy should occupy one of the State bed-rooms."

"Seemly or not, she is to remain where she is," the Marquis said sharply. "It is my fault the girl was hurt and I will have her treated with all possible consideration. Make that clear, Hobley, to the rest of the staff."

"I will, M'Lord, but Your Lordship understands they are afraid of Gypsies."

"Why are they afraid?" the Marquis asked.

"They fear they might put the 'Evil Eye' upon them, steal their children or curse them."

The Marquis laughed.

"All the more reason for them to be polite to our guest! She does not seem to me a kind of creature who would curse anybody."

He thought as he spoke of how light the girl had been as he carried her in his arms, and it seemed to him, although he might have imagined it, that the strange fragrance from her hair still lingered on his coat.

"Well, if there is nothing more I can do, Hobley," he said, "I am returning to London."

"We thought you might do so, M'Lord. The horses have been changed and are ready the moment Your Lordship asks for them."

"Then have them brought round," the Marquis said, "and when our guest is ready to depart, see that she is recompensed for the damage I have inflicted on her."

"What would you consider a reasonable sum, M'Lord?" Hobley asked respectfully.

The Marquis considered a moment.

"I should think about five pounds would cover it, Hobley. Ask Mr. Graystone for the money."

"I will, M'Lord. When shall we see Your Lordship again?"

"I have no idea," the Marquis replied. "The Season is at its height, Hobley, and I am sure you would not wish me to miss any of the endless extravagant and exhausting entertainments which take place night after night."

The Marquis spoke sarcastically, then smiled almost apologetically at the old servant who he knew had loved him since he was a child.

"Anything wrong, Master Fabius?" Hobley asked.

It was a question that seemed to the Marquis to have echoed all down the years. It was always Hobley who had understood if things went awry or if he was upset.

"No, Hobley, not really," he said quietly. "It is just that Captain Collington and I were saying only last night we are getting older. Things do not seem as amusing as they were when I was young."

"You're still young enough to enjoy yourself, M'Lord," Hobley said with a twinkle in his eye, "and if Your Lordship takes my advice you won't waste one minute of the years as they pass."

"Are you having regrets about your own lost youth?" the Marquis enquired.

"No, M'Lord, I've no regrets, and that's something I pray that Your Lordship'll never have. In my experience there's always something to look forward to and there's always adventures when we least expect them."

"You have cheered me up, Hobley!"

The Marquis was smiling as he walked across the Hall and ordered his Phaeton to be brought round immediately.

No-one was more surprised than the Marquis to find himself a week later travelling the same road from London to call on Eurydice.

He had expected to see her at the Duchess of Devonshire's Ball, and he had searched for her during the next four nights at Assemblies, Balls and dinner parties given by their mutual friends, to which he was quite sure she had been invited.

But there was no sign of her and, as the Duke of Severn was also missing, it was not difficult to imagine where they could both be found.

He had confided to no-one that he was waiting for Eurydice's answer to his proposal of marriage, but his friend, Charles Collington, was aware that he was restless and unusually inattentive and uninterested in the succession of parties they attended.

"What is the matter, Fabius?" he asked. "You are like a bear with a sore head!"

"I will tell you about it later," the Marquis promised.

"Jethro has not been up to his tricks again?" Charles asked suspiciously.

"If he has, it was as ineffectual as the falling masonry from my roof!" the Marquis said.

"I hardly think that is a joking matter," Charles Collington replied severely.

"As a matter of fact it is not," the Marquis said. "I had the roof inspected the following day and the stonemason I employed informed me that it was quite impossible for such a large piece of the parapet to have broken away accidentally."

"You mean—as we suspected—it was deliberate?" Charles Collington asked incredulously.

"I was thinking," the Marquis said, "how it would have been quite easy for someone to have hidden in the garden in the centre of the Square. Then when I appeared in the doorway—with the lights behind me—they had only to signal to whoever was on the roof."

"That of course is exactly what happened!" Charles Collington exclaimed. "It was just fortunate that you turned back to speak to Burton."

"Very fortunate!" the Marquis agreed.

"Well, for God's sake—be careful!"

"How can I?" the Marquis asked irritably. "If I have to go about with an armed guard, stay at home, or live eternally on the alert expecting to be poisoned, shot at or struck to the ground—all I can say is—let Jethro try and get it over!"

"If we had taken up that attitude where Bonaparte was concerned, we would have lost the war!"

The Marquis was about to make some quite heated reply, when he burst out laughing.

"I cannot allow you, Charles," he said, "to compare Jethro with Napoleon! It is giving him an undue importance!"

"I never thought it mattered if a man was important or not, if it was his gun which blew a piece of lead through me," Charles Collington retorted, and for a moment the Marquis had no reply.

Driving to the country now, he thought he had taken an unwise step in his effort to circumvent Jethro's plan for securing the inheritance for himself.

He knew, if he was honest with himself, that he did not really wish to marry Eurydice.

In theory it had seemed a good idea. In practice he knew they had no chance of real happiness together and little hope of even getting on reasonably well.

He was quite sure that the reason Eurydice had sent for him was to tell him that Severn had not proposed as she had expected, and she was therefore willing to become the Marchioness of Ruckley.

It had seemed, as he had told her, a practical and sensible idea and one that could be a surprise to neither of them.

But when he thought of Eurydice being permanently at his side either in London or at Ruckley House, the Marquis knew that never had his freedom seemed more attractive.

However what had been done could not be undone. He had offered Eurydice marriage, and if she accepted him he must put a good face on it.

It was with a sense of depression and an ominous feeling of foreboding that the Marquis stepped down outside the pillared portico of Eurydice's house and was ushered with due ceremony into the Drawing-Room where she was waiting for him.

He could not help appreciating that she was looking exceedingly lovely. The sunshine haloed her fair hair as she turned from the window and as she moved towards him with a smile he thought he had never seen her face more radiant.

"You have come, Fabius! I am so glad to see you!"

The Marquis raised her hand to his lips.

"I am honoured by such a warm welcome," he said in his deep voice.

"You must forgive me for dragging you away from London for the second time," Eurydice said, "but what I have to say is of the utmost importance."

The Marquis drew in his breath and waited for the blow to fall.

"Shall we sit down?" Eurydice suggested.

She indicated a chair with her hand and as the Marquis settled himself she sat down on the sofa.

"I have much to tell you, Fabius, but I will start with what is most important to you."

The Marquis nodded his head.

His eyes were on her face and he thought that she was in fact in a completely different mood from the one in which he had last seen her.

"I have first to ask you," Eurydice said, "if you will take over this Estate and run it with your own?"

"But of course. That is understood," the Marquis replied. "It would be a waste of time and money for us both to employ separate Managers, Overseers and Agents. It will just be a question of which of our employees are the most dependable."

Eurydice smiled.

"What I am really saying, perhaps not very clearly, is that later I may sell you the Estate, but at the moment I would rather that you ran it for me. You can rent it if you would prefer."

The Marquis looked at her in a puzzled way.

"I do not understand."

"Why should you?" Eurydice asked and she gave a little sigh.

It seemed to be an expression of almost rapturous satisfaction.

"I am going away, Fabius, and I cannot just leave the Estate with no-one to look after it. It would seem a betrayal of my home."

"Going away?" the Marquis repeated. "Are you telling me that you have accepted Severn?"

"No, I refused him."

The Marquis was very still.

"Then . . ."

"I am to be married," Eurydice said quickly, "but not to the Duke, nor to you."

"There is someone else?" the Marquis asked incredulously, "but who?"

"Someone of whom you have never heard," Eurydice replied. "His name is Silas Wingdale."

The Marquis raised his eyebrows.

"Silas Wingdale?" he repeated. "Who the devil is he?"

Eurydice jumped to her feet and she was laughing.

"I thought you would be astonished," she said. "He is an American. He lives in Virginia and I love him! Yes, I love him! And so I am going to marry him, Fabius."

"Are you telling me the truth?" the Marquis asked in astonishment.

"I do not care a fig for the Ducal strawberry leaves or the Ruckley diamonds or any of the things you thought were so important to me," Eurydice said in an ecstatic voice. "I am in love as I have never been in love for years! Not since I first knew poor Beaugrave. But this is different! Silas is older and he loves me in a very different way. In fact being with him is like reaching Heaven itself!"

The Marquis put his hand up to his forehead.

"Are you quite certain this is not just a joke?" he asked. "You are serious, Eurydice?"

"I have never been more serious in my life," she answered. "Silas and I are to be married quietly tomorrow morning and then we are taking a ship to America from Plymouth and Heaven knows if I shall ever return to this country."

"Do you know what you are letting yourself in for, or the sort of place where you are going to live?" the Marquis asked.

"I have seen sketches of Silas's house and it is delightful. Very like a large English manor, for that matter. But it would not matter to me if he lived in a shack. I love him, Fabius, and he loves me! That is more important than anything else . . . but I have only just realised it!"

It was an hour later that the Marquis, still feeling bemused and astonished by what he had heard, drove his horses to his own house.

He could hardly credit that anyone, least of all Eurydice, would throw up everything which before had seemed important in life to set off across the ocean with a man of whom she knew little, though in her eyes he seemed endowed with all the virtues.

The Marquis had in fact argued with her, and asked her at least to delay her marriage and her departure until her friends had a chance to meet Silas Wingdale.

"It would not matter what you said about him so why should I delay my marriage?" Eurydice asked, with a touch of her old aggressiveness. "I am not asking you to marry him, Fabius, so whatever your opinion might be, it is of no consequence."

Then she had reached up her hand to touch the Marquis's cheek.

"When you fall in love, as you undoubtedly will one day," she said softly, "you will understand why there are no arguments that could change my mind, and nothing that anyone could say would influence me. It is Silas I want and Silas I intend to have."

Eurydice had spoken with such warmth that the Marquis realised she was a very different person from the hard, scheming young woman she had become after her husband's death.

He had thought she was out only for social advancement and for making herself the most notorious and the most talked about figure in the *Beau Monde*.

It was astonishing that she could have changed so quickly from a determined schemer into a gentle, feminine creature whose eyes shone and who seemed to glow at the mere mention of the name of the man with whom she was in love.

'Dammit,' the Marquis thought, as he drove down the drive towards Ruckley House, 'why cannot I feel like that?'

Then he laughed at himself for imagining that such a thing was possible.

The servants were surprised to see him.

"This is a pleasure, M'Lord," the Butler said, hurrying into the Hall.

"Where is Hobley?" the Marquis enquired.

"I'll send for him, M'Lord. The Reverend's in the Library."

"Then I will go and talk to him."

The Marquis opened the door of the Library and saw that his Tutor was not, as he had expected, sitting at the big desk in the centre of the room, but that standing at a bookcase was a slim figure he had seen once before.

She turned round to face him, and his first impression was that her eyes were far too big for her face.

Fringed by the dark lashes he had noticed before, they were very unusual eyes but only as he drew nearer did he realise that while the pupils seemed unnaturally large, the colour of the Gypsy's eyes was not black, as he might have expected, but a very dark green.

She did not speak, but waited as the Marquis advanced towards her. When he reached her he held out his hand.

"I am the Marquis of Ruckley and I owe you an apology."

Almost reluctantly it seemed to him she laid her fingers in his.

They were cool and as he held them for a moment he had the unaccountable feeling that some strange vibration passed between them.

"You are better?" he asked.

"I have recovered, thank you."

The voice was low and musical with a faint foreign accent.

The Marquis glanced at her forehead.

The wound where the wheel of the Phaeton had hit her was still red, and the skin around it was discoloured the purple and orange of a deep bruise.

She was wearing the same attractive Gypsy dress that she had done when he first saw her, but he could see that the blouse was not the one which had been torn from her shoulder. On her arm he could see a bandage.

"I need not tell you how sorry I am that I should have hurt you," the Marquis said.

"It was my fault," the Gypsy answered. "I was looking at your house and I forgot everything else because it was so beautiful."

"I am glad you think so," the Marquis replied. "As I expect someone has told you, it was built in the reign of Queen Elizabeth and there are very few Tudor houses in the whole country to equal it."

There was a note of pride in his voice because Ruckley had always meant so much to him.

"I did not think English houses would be as fine as they are," the Gypsy said.

"You sound as if you have not been in England long."

"No, this is the first time."

"What is your name?"

"Saviya."

"That is a very unusual name."

"It may seem so to you," she replied, "but it is quite a common name amongst my tribe."

"And what is that?" the Marquis enquired.

He thought for a moment she would not answer him. Then she said:

"We are the Kalderash."

She saw that he was ignorant of what this meant and she added:

"The metal-workers, the farriers, the healers, the musicians and the magicians!"

"Magicians?" the Marquis exclaimed, then added: "Oh, you

mean fortune-telling and that sort of thing. I believe the Gypsies are very good at that!"

Saviya gave him a faint smile that had a hint of mockery in it before she said in a low voice:

"I must thank you, My Lord, for having given orders that I was to be well treated in your house and restored to health. It has been a very interesting experience for me."

"I can believe that!" the Marquis said. "Perhaps you have never slept under a roof before?"

Again she gave him that strange smile which made him feel as if he had said something rather ridiculous. But he told himself it was just a trick she had.

"Where have you come from?" he asked, "I mean, from what country?"

She hesitated and, before she could reply, the door opened and The Reverend came in.

"Ah, there you are, My Lord!" he exclaimed. "I heard you had arrived. It is a pleasure to welcome you back so soon, and I see you have made the acquaintance of my new pupil."

The Marquis shook hands with The Reverend and asked in surprise:

"Your new pupil?"

"Saviya has the most intelligent brain and the most remarkable memory I have ever encountered," The Reverend said enthusiastically.

The Marquis looked astonished.

"All in one small person?" he asked.

"You may not believe it, My Lord, but she absorbs a new subject in a manner which I consider phenomenal," The Reverend said, almost as if Saviya was not present.

She was listening, but still, the Marquis noted, with that faint smile on her lips.

"I had an idea," the Marquis said slowly, "although of course I must have been mistaken, that Gypsies could not read or write."

"That is true," Saviya agreed, "and they do not wish to do so. They memorise what they hear and there are story-tellers who translate our legends into poem or song. Besides, for a Gypsy who is always on the move, there is no room for books."

"And yet," the Marquis said, "from what I have just heard, you can read!"

"I am the exception!"

And then, still with that faint mocking smile on her lips, she added:

"But you see, I am a witch!"

"A witch?" the Marquis echoed in astonishment.

"But naturally!" she answered. "Otherwise I should not be able to qualify for the very flattering report the Reverend Gentleman has just given of me."

The Marquis was intrigued.

"You will both have to tell me much more about this," he said. "First of all I want to know where Saviya has come from, and why her tribe has visited Ruckley—it seems, for the first time."

"I have learnt, not from Saviya, but from other people in the neighbourhood," The Reverend answered, "that the Gypsies have certain places which they visit in rotation. Ruckley is one of them, as I told you, My Lord, by arrangement with your grand-mother."

"I had not forgotten," the Marquis said briefly. "What interests me is that we should attract not only English Gypsies but foreign ones."

"All Gypsies are foreign," Saviya said. "We have no place that we can call our own."

"And why is that?"

"We are condemned to wander the earth," she answered, "perhaps for the expiation of past sins, perhaps because for us that is happiness."

The Marquis sat down on the edge of the desk.

"Will you please answer the question I have already asked you?" he said. "Where have you just come from?"

"Germany."

"And before that?"

"We came across Poland from Russia."

"Now let me think," the Marquis said. "I have a feeling that the Russians treat their Gypsies in a different way from other countries. Is that true?"

"All countries at some time or other have persecuted the Gypsies," Saviya answered, "with the exception of the Russians. There we have a different status altogether."

"Why?" the Marquis enquired.

"Because of our music and because the Russians appreciate our dances."

The Marquis looked at her slight figure and realised that even standing still, she had a grace about her that he had not noticed in other women.

"You are a dancer?" he asked.

She nodded her head.

"I have been taught by my mother, who was the daughter of one of the greatest of all Gypsy dancers in Russia. Grand Dukes and Princes fought with each other so that she should appear in their private theatres, and on several occasions she danced before the Tsar."

"It is fascinating, is it not?" The Reverend exclaimed. "These are the things I always wanted to hear, and never until now have I had the chance of learning anything about the Gypsy race."

"Tell us more," the Marquis said to Saviya.

"So that you can laugh at us?" she enquired.

"You know I would not do that," he answered seriously. "I am as interested as The Reverend is, because we both realise how lamentably ignorant we are where your race is concerned."

"The Gypsies prefer people not to know about them," Saviya replied. "It is good that they should be mysterious, so that when they leave there is little to remember."

A footman came into the room to inform The Reverend that someone wanted to see him.

"Do not leave before I return, My Lord," he begged.

"I am in no hurry," the Marquis replied.

As the door shut behind him, the Marquis said to Saviya:

"Come, sit down and talk to me."

He walked to the window as he spoke where in the summer there were comfortable chairs arranged so that from the Library one could look out on the velvet green lawns which ended in a yew-hedge beyond which was the Herb-Garden.

The Marquis seated himself in an arm-chair and Saviya sat on the end of the window-seat, her face turned from the Marquis so that he could see the exquisite outline of her profile.

He tried to think of what she reminded him, but it was hard to say if there was a characteristic from any other race to be distinguished in her features.

'She is beautiful!' he thought suddenly, and yet her beauty was neither classical nor did it belong to any one artistic period.

She was simply unique, with green eyes slanting up a little at the corners, an oval face which ended in a small pointed chin below lips which, when she smiled, curved in that strangely mocking manner.

Her hair hung as it had the first time the Marquis had seen her, straight down her back to below her waist, and now he saw that she wore earrings also made of coins to match her necklace, and they glittered in the sunshine as she moved her head.

"Has Hobley given you the money as I instructed him?" the Marquis asked suddenly.

Saviya turned her face from the window to look at him.

"I do not want your money," she answered.

As she spoke, the Marquis realised that the coins around her neck and in her ears were worth a hundred times more than the five pounds with which he had thought to recompense her for her injuries.

He also had an uneasy suspicion that the red stones he had supposed were glass were in fact rubies.

Then he told himself he must be in a state of stupidity. How could Gypsies be expected to own anything so valuable?

"Tell me about your tribe, the Kalderash," he said.

"I have told you that we are the metal-workers," Saviya answered in a tone that was almost reproving, because she must repeat herself.

"And what metals do you use?" the Marquis enquired.

"Copper, silver or gold. Whatever is necessary for the work we have to do," Saviya replied.

"Gold?" the Marquis questioned.

"The Nobles in Hungary use goblets for their wine and vessels of every description to ornament their tables. It is the Kalderash who fashion them."

"You liked being in Hungary?" the Marquis said, and added before she could answer:

"I have the feeling the Hungarians call you something rather special."

"In Hungary and in Germany our Chiefs are 'the Dukes of Little Egypt.'"

"An important designation! Does it please you?"

"Sometimes we are Kings, in Germany the 'Zigeuner,' in France 'Bohemians,' in Turkey the 'Tchinghanie,' and in Persia 'Karaki.' What does it matter? We are still Gypsies."

"But more appreciated in some countries than in others."

"King Sigismund of Hungary gave the Gypsies letters of protection. James V of Scotland gave one of our patrons, Johnie Faur, Lord and Earl of Little Egypt, juridical rights over his own Gypsy Bands."

"How do you know that?" the Marquis asked.

"Our history is passed by mouth from tribe to tribe so that we know where we may find friends," Saviya answered.

"That is good sense," the Marquis said. "I would very much like to meet the rest of your tribe. May I come to your camp?"

"No!"

The refusal was positive.

"Why not?"

"Because if they see you, I shall not be able to come here again."

The Marquis was surprised.

"But why?"

"You would not understand."

"What would I not understand?"

Saviya hesitated before she said:

"My Father, who is the Chief of the Kalderash, or, as we call him, the 'Voivode,' allowed me to come here and read your books because you were not at home. If he knows that you are back, then I cannot come again."

"But what has your father got against me?" the Marquis asked incredulously.

"You are a man!"

"Explain what you are trying to say," he begged.

"Perhaps another time," Saviya said, rising to her feet. "It is getting late. I must return or they will come in search of me."

"Return where?" the Marquis asked.

"To where we are camped in your woods."

"But I thought you were staying here in the House!"

"Only for the first two days when I was unconscious," Saviya replied. "But because Mr. Hobley was so kind and treated my wounds, I was allowed to return to have them dressed. Then, because I begged and besought my Father to let me read some of your books, he agreed. But there must be no other reason for me to visit your house."

"But you will come tomorrow?" the Marquis asked.

"I think it will be permitted."

"Then do not tell your father that I am here."

She gave him a glance from under her long lashes.

"Please come tomorrow," the Marquis begged. "There is so much I want to learn about you. Why you are a witch, for instance, and what strange enchantments you can perform."

Saviya smiled but did not answer.

Instead she moved away from the Marquis and, as she crossed

the floor of the Library, he thought he had never seen a woman move with such grace—she seemed to float rather than walk.

As she reached the door she looked back at him.

"You will come tomorrow?" the Marquis insisted.

"If it is possible," she replied.

Then she was gone.

The Marquis stood quite still for a moment staring at the closed door.

"A witch!" he said aloud. "That is certainly a being I never expected to encounter!"

CHAPTER THREE

The Marquis rose early the following morning, as he realised he must go over to Eurydice's house and arrange about taking over the management of her Estate.

As Hobley helped him put on riding-clothes, he said:

"You did a good job on our Gypsy, Hobley."

"The wound healed quickly because she was so healthy," Hobley replied, "and it was in fact, M'Lord, a pleasure."

The Marquis raised his eyebrows and asked:

"Did the rest of the household get over their fears of what she might do to them?"

"Yes indeed, M'Lord," Hobley answered. "She captivated all of them before she finished. Even Mrs. Meedham spoke well of the young lady!"

The Marquis was amused to notice that Saviya had changed from being "one of them Gypsies" to a "young lady," and he realised it was indeed a compliment.

There was no-one more snobbish or more rigid in their sense of propriety than the servants in a Nobleman's house.

The slightest infringement of their privileges or of their recognised order of precedence would cause almost a revolution in their ranks.

That they were no longer frightened of Saviya but had accepted her was, the Marquis thought, a very unusual and unpredictable change in their attitude.

He did not, however, express his thoughts to Hobley but merely remarked:

"The Reverend seems to think very highly of her intelligence."

"The Reverend is a good judge of character, M'Lord," Hobley said stoutly.

The Marquis found himself thinking of Saviya as he rode across the Park and then through the woods towards Eurydice's house.

Trees covered many acres of land in that part of Hertfordshire, and as the Marquis moved through them he realised that it would be easy for not one band of Gypsies but dozens to hide themselves away so that it would be difficult for anyone to find them.

He, however, had a vague idea as to where they would be camping, and he thought that when he had the time he would perhaps visit them unexpectedly and see what they were like.

At the same time, if Saviya was to be believed, that would mean her visits to the House would be stopped. At the moment that was something which he had no wish to happen.

He wondered if she was speaking the truth.

He had always believed Gypsies were free and easy, and the women dispensed their favours to whomever they fancied.

If they did, the Marquis thought with a faint smile, they would be behaving just like the more aristocratic members of their sex in the *Beau Monde*.

There was no doubt that sexual morality in the Social World was very lax.

The raffish Society which was centred round Carlton House had since the very beginning of the century, set an example that was, to say the least, regrettable, while London itself was, as the Marquis well knew, a hot-bed of vice.

A man would have had to be blind not to notice the ever-increasing numbers of painted wantons who haunted the streets at night.

Some of them were but children, and the Flash Houses, where boys were taught to steal, pick pockets and commit every other minor crime in the calendar, grew more uncontrollable every year.

There were so many evils that should be denounced and reformed, the Marquis thought, and wondered if he himself should speak on the subject when the opportunity arose in the House of Lords.

Then, he thought with a wry smile, he was hardly the person to take a stand against immorality or to constitute himself a champion of good morals.

He could see the faces of many alluring women looking at him with a fire burning in their eyes, their white arms reaching out, their lips surrendering themselves with an ease which told him without words he was by no means their first lover—nor would he be their last.

And yet he was prepared to bet quite a considerable sum that the Gypsy girl he had knocked down with his Phaeton was intrinsically pure.

At the thought he laughed aloud.

'Really, I must be besotted to imagine such a thing is possible,' he told himself.

After all, Saviya admitted, if she was to be believed, to having visited Russia, Hungary, and Germany. To reach these countries she must have passed through many others. Was it likely that on her travels she had not with her strange beauty aroused attention?

And what about the men of her own tribe? They would have eyes in their heads and warm blood in their veins!

The Marquis emerged from the woods to see in front of him Eurydice's house, and at the sight of it he deliberately put the thoughts of Saviya and all the other women he had known out of his mind.

He was certain that ahead of him lay a great deal of hard thinking and perhaps quite a considerable amount of work.

He was not mistaken.

When he arrived home at luncheon time, he knew that there was no chance of his returning to London for at least a week.

He was in fact appalled at the mess in which Eurydice had left her properties.

Her instructions were very clear.

They were to be handed over to his administration, and all future orders and of course the payment of employees was to come from Ruckley.

Anyone else, the Marquis thought, might have resented having such a problem—and an expensive one—thrust upon him without notice, but he guessed that Eurydice had known that her decision was in a way his triumph.

His father had always wished to acquire the neighbouring land and make it a part of the Ruckley Estate. Now, to all intents and purposes, this had happened!

The Marquis interviewed the Agent, the Farm-Managers and Eurydice's Attorney, who was waiting with a number of papers which required his signature.

As he rode home, the Marquis told himself that it was essential that he should give the new land his personal and immediate attention in order to rectify the loss of revenue he had discovered.

He was still debating who he would put in charge and how to

dove-tail the management of the two Estates when he reached home.

It needed a quarter of an hour to luncheon time, and the Marquis handed his hat and riding-whip to a footman and walked automatically towards the Library.

As he expected, The Reverend was there and so was Saviya.

They were so interested in what they were reading that the Marquis was half-way across the room before they noticed him.

Then they turned round and there was no mistaking the expression of gladness in their eyes at the sight of him.

"Here you are, My Lord!" The Reverend exclaimed. "You left very early this morning, before I had time to tell you of my new discovery."

"Good-morning, Sir," the Marquis said, "and good-morning to you, Saviya."

She smiled at him, and he thought how lovely she looked: her hair very dark against the brilliant bindings of the books; the movement of her hands even more graceful than he had remembered.

"Good-morning, My Lord."

Then, like a child that has something exciting to relate, she added:

"The Reverend Gentleman has found a book which he is sure will please you."

"What is it?" the Marquis enquired.

"It is a book on Gypsies by one John Howland," The Reverend replied, holding it out to the Marquis. "I had no idea it was in the Library, but actually it was only published two years ago in 1816. It relates all you wished to know about the origin of the Gypsies."

The Marquis took the book from him.

"I suppose my father must have bought it."

"That is so, and because he died that same year it must have been overlooked," The Reverend replied, "which was why I had not included it in the Catalogue."

The Marquis opened the book, turned the pages and remarked:

"I see it has a comparative list of the Gypsy and Hindustani language. Some of the words seem very similar."

"That is true," Saviya said. "For instance I would describe you in English as a very important man, or Prince. The word is Rajah in Hindustani and Raja in Romany."

"I shall have to study this," the Marquis said, "but at the moment I am extremely hungry and also thirsty. Will you join me in a glass of wine, Reverend?"

"I shall be delighted, My Lord."

"And I hope, Saviya," the Marquis said, "that you will have luncheon with me."

She hesitated for a moment, then answered:

"I would like that."

"It is no use my inviting you, Reverend, is it?" the Marquis asked.

The elderly man shook his head.

"You know with my poor digestion I can eat only once a day."

"I had not really forgotten," the Marquis replied.

They went into the Salon, and after The Reverend had accepted a small glass of Madeira, he returned to the Library.

Saviya looked at the Marquis's shining riding-boots and said:

"You have been riding. I have admired the magnificent horses in your stables."

"I imagine that you ride?"

She smiled and answered:

"It is something I enjoy doing more than anything else except dancing."

"I hope to see you do both."

They went into luncheon and the Marquis wondered how she would eat. Surely, he thought, a Gypsy would not know either the etiquette or the proper behaviour expected at a Gentleman's table.

But it would have been impossible, he realised, for Saviya to do anything that was not graceful or elegant. He noticed, however, that she did not pick up a knife or fork until she could follow him.

Yet it was cleverly done and anyone who had not been observing her closely would not have noticed that she was imitating not only his choice of cutlery but also the manner in which he used it.

But after a time the Marquis forgot to watch Saviya for any faults she might commit. He was too much interested in what she was saying to think of anything else.

He had little difficulty in persuading her to talk of her travels.

The Marquis was an expert at drawing a woman out, obtaining her confidence and making her feel so secure and happy in his company that she could trust him with her innermost secrets.

Usually he did not exert himself unduly in this way, but he knew without consciously thinking of it that he had the power at his command.

Because he was quite certain that Saviya had never had luncheon alone with a man before, and certainly not in such agreeable circumstances, it was easy to make her talk.

She told him of how the Gypsies trekked across Europe, moving from country to country, often having to flee from cruel persecutions by the Authorities, but usually welcomed by the ordinary people, because of their special crafts, sorcery and horse-dealing.

"My father is a great authority on horse-flesh," Saviya said, "and he has often been commissioned to buy animals in one country and send them to another."

"How big is your tribe?" the Marquis asked.

"When we left Hungary for Russia, there were two hundred of us," Saviya replied, "but usually we number but forty to fifty as we are here in England."

"Do you sleep in tents?"

"We used to," she answered, "but now we have something new."

"What is that?"

"We have acquired caravans. There are not many in England yet, but in Europe a number of Gypsies have them. Caravans have always been used by the Circus people, but they are so attractive and comfortable that now all the Gypsies that can afford it wish to own one."

When luncheon was over the Marquis and Saviya went to the stables and he at once realised, as he might have expected, that she had a special way with horses.

"What magic do you use on a restless or savage horse?" he asked, when she had entered the stable of a stallion of whom even the Marquis's grooms were wary.

"It is a secret which belongs only to the Gypsies," Saviya answered, "and must certainly not be imparted to a Gorgio."

"Is that what I am?" the Marquis asked.

"Anyone who is not a Gypsy is a Gorgio or Gadje," she replied.

"And what do you call yourselves?"

"We are the Rom," Saviya replied proudly.

When they had finished inspecting the stables, the Marquis took Saviya round the old part of the House, showing her the Priests' holes, where the Catholic Priests had hidden from Queen Elizabeth's soldiers, who would have burned them at the stake.

The hiding-places had been used later in the history of the Ruckleys, when Cromwell had defeated the Royalists and hung many of them on Tyburn Hill.

As the Marquis showed Saviya round his home, he found himself recalling family stories and legends that he had known as a boy.

He liked the concentrated attention she gave to everything he said: the light in her eyes; the way her lips curved differently from the mysterious mocking smile she had given him yesterday.

Finally, they reached the end of the long Picture Gallery where he had shown her paintings of his ancestors, and the Marquis stood at the casement window looking out into the garden.

There was a fountain just below them where a stone cupid held a huge fish in his hands. From its mouth a jet of water spouted high, which glittered iridescent in the sunshine.

"You are very lucky," Saviya said in a low voice.

"Am I?" the Marquis asked.

"You do not always think so," she said, "but one day you will realise how important this House and everything it contains is to your happiness."

"I think I realise it now," the Marquis said. "Are you telling my fortune, Saviya?"

"No, not really," she answered, "but at the same time there is something I do not like."

It seemed to the Marquis that her voice had changed.

Now she turned her head to look at him and he had the strange feeling she was not actually seeing him but looking through and beyond him.

"Yes, there is danger," she said in a low tone. "You must be careful! You have an enemy. It is a man and he is trying to injure you."

"How do you know that?" the Marquis asked sharply. "Has Hobley been talking to you?"

"I know it because he is there," Saviya answered. "I can see him quite clearly. He is dark, he has a long nose, and his name has the same first letter as yours. You must be careful . . . very careful where he is concerned!"

"How do you know this?" the Marquis asked again.

As he spoke, his voice almost harsh, Saviya shook her head as if she would dispel something that was hurting her and from which she would be free.

Then she knelt on the window-seat and looked out into the garden.

The Marquis did not speak for a moment and then he said:

"What you have told me is true, but I cannot understand how you can be aware of something which concerns only my private life."

"I told you I am a witch."

"I thought you were joking."

"Magic is not a joke to the Kalderash. It is a part of us and part of our destiny; we cannot escape it."

"What you have told me is true," the Marquis repeated, "but you did not say if my enemy would be successful in what he is attempting to do to me."

There was a silence, and then Saviya, still not looking at him, said:

"I have warned you of danger. That is enough. A man prepared is already armed."

"I hope you are right!"

She turned her face suddenly.

"Be careful! Please be very careful!" she pleaded.

Her eyes met his and for a moment it seemed as if something passed between them and it was impossible for either of them to move.

Almost without meaning to, the Marquis put out his arms towards Saviya.

It was an instinctive gesture—something he had done so often in his life, when he had been attracted by a lovely woman, that he did not even consider what her reaction would be.

He just followed his impulse.

Then as his hands touched her, as he would have drawn her close against him—and had already bent his lips towards hers, she gave a little twist of her body.

She was free of him, and he saw incredulously that she held in her hand a long, shining dagger—a stiletto such as the Italians carried.

She held it firmly in her hand between her breasts, the sharp point directed at his chest.

Slowly the Marquis dropped his arms.

For a moment neither of them spoke, and then Saviya said:

"You are a Gorgio. You must not touch me. It is forbidden."

"Why?"

"No Rom can associate with a Gorgio. If she does she is exiled from the tribe."

"Do you really mean that?" the Marquis asked in genuine surprise. "Tell me about it, Saviya, and put away that dangerous weapon. I promise I will not touch you without your permission."

She looked at him searchingly, as if not sure whether she should trust him. Then so swiftly that he hardly saw it happen, the stiletto disappeared into her bodice and she sat down on the window seat.

"I am very ignorant of your rules," the Marquis said, "so you must please forgive me if I offended you."

He spoke beguilingly and a very much more experienced woman than Saviya would have found it hard to resist him.

"If you had been here with a . . . lady of your own race," she asked hesitatingly, "would you have . . . kissed her?"

"I have a feeling," the Marquis said, "that she would have been very disappointed if I had not attempted to do so."

He smiled as he spoke, but Saviya's face was serious.

"If she had been unmarried, would you not have felt obliged to ask her to be your . . . wife?"

"If she were unmarried," the Marquis answered, "it is most unlikely that we should be here together unchaperoned."

"And had she been married?"

"Then in most cases the lady in question would have expected me to show my admiration for her charms."

"If she had been a Gypsy, her husband would have beaten her for such behaviour," Saviya said sternly, "and in France her head would have been shaved."

"Shaved!" the Marquis ejaculated. "Is that really true?"

"It is a common punishment among Gypsies," Saviya answered, "and for many months a woman who has aroused her husband's jealousy becomes an object of shame in the eyes of the tribe."

"Then Gypsy husbands beat their wives!" the Marquis said.

"There are worse punishments if they behave improperly," Saviya told him. "But it does not happen often. Gypsy marriages are very happy and they last forever!"

"Even if they do not get on together?" the Marquis enquired.

"We are a happy people," Saviya answered. "Family life is sacred and anyone who offends against the sanctity of their marriage deserves the punishment they receive."

She spoke with some conviction, and the Marquis knew that what she was saying must be the truth. Nevertheless he was astonished.

"Who will you marry, Saviya?" he asked.

"I shall not know that until he approaches my father."

"You have no choice?"

"In the Kalderash a marriage is always arranged between the fathers of the bride and bride-groom. A betrothed girl has no right either to visit or to talk to the man she will marry, even when other people are present."

"Surely that is very strange?" the Marquis said.

"I think perhaps it is something we have inherited from our Indian ancestors," Saviya replied. "Whatever the origin of the custom, a gold coin is placed on the girl's neck and this marks her as *Tomnimi*—promised."

"What happens," the Marquis enquired, "if a Gypsy man or woman falls in love with a Gorgio?"

"In either case it brings exclusion and exile from the tribe," Saviya said.

"For life?" the Marquis enquired.

"The woman or the man, is held in contempt, indeed hated, and no-one will speak to the offender. They are *Poshrats, Didikais,* they no longer exist."

"It is a very harsh code!"

Then the Marquis asked:

"Does not the idea of marrying someone you have never seen, whom you do not know and whom you may not even like, frighten you?"

Saviya looked away, and he had the feeling that he had touched on some secret that she had kept hidden, perhaps even from herself.

She did not reply and after a moment he said in his deep voice:

"Tell me. I want to know, Saviya."

"Yes," she said hesitatingly, "the idea does . . . frighten me."

"Do you not think," the Marquis asked, "that love is more important than anything else? Is there no place for love among the Gypsies?"

"A woman should love her husband," Saviya answered.

"And if she finds it impossible?" the Marquis insisted. "If for instance she falls in love with another man before marriage, would that not seem to her more important than tribal laws and regulations?"

"I do not know," Saviya replied, "it has never happened to me."

"And yet you have thought about it," the Marquis persisted. "Perhaps too, Saviya, you have dreamt of a man that you could love, a man who could capture your heart and make it his."

His voice was very deep and now, as she turned her eyes to look at him, he thought there was an expression in them like that of a very small and frightened animal.

Then she said after a moment:

"But the laws of the Kalderash are just and my people believe in them."

"But you—you are different," the Marquis said. "You are a witch and so perhaps more sensitive and capable of deeper feelings than the others."

"Why do you say such things to me?"

"Because you are so beautiful," the Marquis replied. "Because you are not only unbelievably lovely, but because you have a brain. It is the intelligent people in this world who suffer the most, Saviya."

She did not answer, but he saw a little quiver run through her.

"It is the difference between a race-horse and an animal that draws a cart," he went on. "You know as well as I do that the one is far more highly strung, far more sensitive to pain than the other."

Saviya was silent and then she said:

"It is best not to think of . . . love."

"But you do think of it," the Marquis replied. "And something that you cannot control yearns for it."

His words seemed to vibrate between them. Then, as he waited for her answer, there was the sound of footsteps at the far end of the Picture Gallery and a familiar voice cried:

"Ah, here you are, Fabius! I was told you were going round the House."

The Marquis turned his head to see Charles Collington advancing toward him.

"I received your note," the Captain said as he walked over the shining oak floor. "I felt there must be some very unusual reason for you to stay in the country, so I have ridden to the rescue, if that is the right word!"

"I was merely informing you that I could not dine with you to-night," the Marquis said.

"Nevertheless I felt it was important for me to be with you," Charles Collington replied.

He reached the Marquis's side to stand with a look of surprise on his face, staring at Saviya.

"Let me introduce you," the Marquis said. "Captain Charles Collington—Saviya, a very lovely Gypsy whom I ran over with my Phaeton."

"That was an original way of getting yourself introduced!" Charles Collington exclaimed.

He put out his hand to Saviya and went on:

"It is delightful to meet you, Miss Saviya."

She dropped him a small curtsy.

"I must go now," she said to the Marquis.

"No, please do not leave us," the Marquis begged. "This is my great friend, and I know when I tell him about you, he will not believe a word I say unless you assure him that I am speaking the truth."

"Did His Lordship say that you were a Gypsy?" Charles Collington asked Saviya with undisguised interest.

"She is indeed!" the Marquis answered, "and she has opened my eyes to a whole new world I did not know existed."

"I have always been a great admirer of the Gypsies," Charles Collington said. "When we were fighting in Portugal, the Ciganos, as they were called, were extremely useful. They could move between the two Armies without fear. They were neither friend nor foe, and in consequence they carried messages and spied for both sides!"

"Now that I think about it, I believe you are right!" the Marquis said. "I never paid much attention to the Portuguese Gypsies myself."

"Gypsies do not wish you to pay them attention," Saviya said with a smile. "What they would like most would be to be invisible. To come and go with no-one troubling about them."

"Well, I am very glad that you are not invisible!" Charles Collington said with a look of frank admiration in his eyes. "No wonder His Lordship is in no hurry to return to London. Having seen you, I find it a most compelling reason for preferring the country!"

"I expect you would like a drink, if you have ridden here from London," the Marquis interposed. "How long did it take you?"

"An hour and thirty-five minutes," Charles Collington replied. "It is not a record, but I did not hurry myself. My horses are not as good as yours, Fabius."

"It usually takes me an hour and fifteen minutes," the Marquis said. "That is, across country. It takes longer by road."

"I do not mind how long it has taken. I am delighted to be here," Charles Collington said, his eyes on Saviya.

The Marquis noticed that she drew a little away from him, as if she felt he was encroaching upon her.

When they went downstairs for Charles Collington to have a glass of wine after his ride, it was to find tea had been laid in the Salon.

They sampled a few of the vast selection of sandwiches, cakes and small delicacies for which the Chef at Ruckley House was famous.

As they ate and Charles Collington described in graphic detail a Ball he had attended the night before, he said to the Marquis:

"By the way, Sir Algernon was there and sneering because none of us had yet attempted to win his wager of the thousand guineas."

"A thousand guineas for a wager?" Saviya exclaimed. "What a huge sum!"

"It is nothing compared to what some fools lose gaming," Charles Collington replied. "Over twenty thousand pounds changed hands last night at White's alone. Needless to say, none of it came my way!"

"You are poor?" Saviya asked sympathetically.

"Absolutely starving!" Charles Collington replied.

The Marquis laughed.

"Do not believe him, Saviya. He is quite warm in the pocket, but he is extravagant, like all the gay young men who frequent the gambling Clubs of St. James's."

"Gypsies like to gamble," Saviya said, "but it is usually on cock-fights or sport of some sort."

"And very much more sensible," Charles Collington approved. "When you come to think of it, it is exceedingly silly to throw away money on the turn of a card. No-one ever ends up a winner."

"That is true," the Marquis agreed.

"All the same," Charles Collington said, "I should like to confound Sir Algernon with his own words. He is so certain that he is infallible that it irritates me."

He paused before he said slowly:

"Do you suppose that Gibbon would ever think that Miss Saviya was a Gypsy?"

"It is something I am sure I would never have thought of myself," the Marquis said, "except for the fact that she was dressed like one."

"If she were gowned like a Lady of Quality," Charles Collington cried, "I am convinced that Gibbon would never suspect for a moment that she was anything else."

"It is certainly an idea," the Marquis replied.

"What are you talking about?" Saviya enquired in a bewildered voice.

They told her the details of Sir Algernon's bet and she laughed.

"He must be very sure that you have no chance of winning, for him to wager so much money!"

"He is too sure!" Captain Collington said. "That is why we have to show him up for the pompous snob he is! The whole contention is baloney, if you ask me! Everyone's blood is red if you prick them!"

"Or knock them down with a Phaeton," the Marquis said, looking at the mark on Saviya's forehead.

"Now do take this seriously, Fabius," Charles Collington said. "We have found the ideal person to confound Gibbon and make him eat his words."

"It might succeed," the Marquis said, "but one of the difficulties would be how to persuade Gibbon to come down here and meet Saviya. I have a feeling she would not be allowed to come to London with us."

"I am quite certain my father would say no," Saviya agreed.

"Then somehow we have to inveigle Sir Algernon to Ruckley without his becoming suspicious," the Marquis said.

"That is a real problem," Charles Collington said reflectively. "What are his interests?"

"Shooting, for one thing," the Marquis said. "He has shot here in the past, but it is not the time of year for pheasant or partridge."

"No, of course not," Charles agreed. "What else?"

"I have it!" the Marquis exclaimed.

His friend waited expectantly and he went on:

"The one thing Sir Algernon really cares about, besides his Family Tree, is his collection of ancient coins."

"Something I have always found extremely boring," Charles Collington said. "So where does that get us?"

"Quite a long way," the Marquis replied.

As he spoke he looked at the necklace of coins around Saviya's neck.

"Tell me," he said, "has your tribe any loose coins that we could borrow for a day? I see that some of those you wear round your neck are Roman. Have you any more?"

"A large number," Saviya replied.

"If we could tell Sir Algernon that we have found half a dozen coins in one of the fields," the Marquis went on, "and we want advice as to whether we should dig for more, I am certain he would be extremely intrigued."

"That is brilliant!" Charles Collington exclaimed. "Sit down and write a letter now and I will carry it back to London with me."

"I will send a groom," the Marquis said. "He might be suspicious if you were my messenger. He might guess we were collaborating."

"Which we undoubtedly are!" Charles Collington said. "But do not forget we have to find a suitable gown for Saviya, decide who she is to be, and where she comes from."

"The whole thing will be quite a Drury Lane production by the time we have finished," the Marquis laughed.

"Why not?" Charles Collington answered. "A thousand guineas is a thousand guineas."

"May I remind you," the Marquis remarked, "that we have not yet obtained Saviya's agreement to assist us in the masquerade?"

"I feel that I might let you down," Saviya said in a soft voice. "I am a Gypsy, and it is very unlikely that anyone would take me for an English Lady of Quality."

"Who said anything about your being English?" the Marquis asked. "That would be ridiculous."

"You mean . . . I do not sound like an English woman?"

"I hope you will not be disappointed," the Marquis replied, "but you have an unmistakable foreign accent. It is very attractive—in fact it is enchanting—but it is definitely foreign!"

"It is because I have been in England for only a short time," Saviya said. "When we have lived in a country for six months or a year, everyone tells me I speak their language perfectly."

"The phenomenal memory of which The Reverend spoke," the Marquis smiled.

"Then she must be a foreigner," Charles Collington said. "It does not matter—and we can give her a high-sounding name and title. In fact it will make it even more difficult for Sir Algernon to suspect that she is not who she pretends to be."

"Which country do you fancy, Saviya?" the Marquis asked.

She thought for a moment.

"My mother was Russian and I have lived in St. Petersburg and Moscow for nearly ten years of my life. It is obvious that I should be Russian."

"You are right!" Charles Collington cried. "And you look mysterious and excitingly Russian with that black hair and that ivory skin!"

There was a flirtatious note in Charles Collington's voice which the Marquis did not miss.

"I think perhaps you should go now, Saviya," he said. "I would not wish your father to be incensed because you are late, and it is important that you should not be forbidden to return to the house. Will you enquire if we may borrow the coins?"

"I will bring them tomorrow," Saviya replied.

She made a deep curtsy to the Marquis and a very brief one to

Charles Collington. Then she moved away from them down the Long Gallery, and they both of them watched her graceful figure until she disappeared through the doorway at the far end.

Charles Collington gave an exclamation.

"My God, Fabius," he said, "you are a dark horse! Where did you find anything so entrancing, so fascinating, so incredibly beautiful?"

CHAPTER FOUR

The Marquis, dressing for dinner, thought with satisfaction that so far everything had gone well.

Sir Algernon Gibbon had arrived early in the afternoon, and the Marquis and Charles Collington had taken him out to a newly-ploughed field to show him where they said they had found seven Roman coins.

He had become extremely excited, saying that they were not only of great antiquity but in his opinion very valuable, and he strongly advised the Marquis to dig deeper in the immediate neighbourhood of the find in case there were other treasures as yet undiscovered.

He went into a long dissertation on the way the Romans built their Amphitheatres and the construction of their villas, and pointed out with reason that there were many Roman remains at the neighbouring town of St. Albans.

The Marquis had listened with flattering attention, being more punctilious in this particular than he would have been otherwise, because he knew that Charles Collington was restless.

What occupied his friend's mind were the plans they had made for the evening. The Marquis thought with a smile that no-one could have taken more trouble to ensure that their campaign to deceive Sir Algernon was mapped out down to the last detail.

He also told himself that never had he spent a more amusing time than he had the last few days, when they had been teaching Saviya her part.

She had been, as the Marquis expected, a quick-brained and tre-mendously receptive pupil.

They only had to tell her something once: never did she forget or fail to carry out their instructions to perfection.

What had pleased the Marquis was that, while Charles Colling-ton had taken upon himself the role of producer, it was to himself that Saviya regularly looked not only for confirmation of what was said but for approval when she did what was asked of her.

He found himself waiting for that half-shy and yet trusting little glance she gave him.

It was as if she realised that he was a greater authority than Charles Collington and, what was more, she valued his opinion more than anyone else's.

Charles Collington could not praise her enough!

"She is fantastic!" he kept saying over and over again. "No-one would believe she was a Gypsy or that she had not been born into one of the highest families in the land! She is a living example of our contention that it is not blue blood which makes a lady, but education."

"And sensitivity," the Marquis added.

"Of course," his friend replied, "Saviya is unusually sensitive and receptive to everything one says or does."

"You are a born actress," the Marquis said to her once and she replied:

"I think that good acting depends on experiencing one's rôle emotionally as well as mentally. A dancer has to feel deeply everything she portrays, so perhaps it is not as difficult for me as for other people."

It was this remark which had given the Marquis an idea for another way in which they could confound Sir Algernon Gibbon, and this was something which concerned Saviya and him more than Charles Collington.

What made everything so much easier—Saviya told them with a note of surprise in her voice—was that her father had withdrawn his objection to her coming to the house even though he knew the Marquis was in residence.

What was more he approved of their plan that Saviya should act the part of a Russian Noblewoman.

"Why has your father changed his mind about me?" the Marquis enquired.

"I do not know," Saviya answered. "I expected he would be angry and forbid me to take part in your Masquerade, but he was amused by it and only admonished me to act so well that you would win your wager."

She paused and then she added:

"I think perhaps he feels it is the same as performing in the private theatres in Moscow and St. Petersburg."

"You have done that?" the Marquis asked.

"Only in a very small way," Saviya answered. "Amongst the Gypsies who live in both those cities there are many very famous dancers and prima donnas, and because I was my mother's daughter, I was occasionally allowed to take part, not particularly through my own merits."

"I want you to tell me about it," the Marquis said.

But they had been so busy preparing for Sir Algernon Gibbon's arrival that there had been no time to continue the conversation.

Now Hobley finished tying the Marquis's white cravat and, stepping back to look at his handiwork, he said:

"I think I ought to tell you, M'Lord, that Mr. Jethro has been in the village."

"When?" the Marquis asked sharply.

"He was there yesterday, M'Lord," Hobley replied. "I understand from one of the footmen who went to the post office this morning before luncheon that his curricle was outside The Green Man."

"What is he doing in the village, Hobley?" the Marquis enquired.

"I can't understand it, M'Lord. I should have thought that if Mr. Jethro was in the vicinity he would have called upon Your Lordship, but I understand he was making enquiries."

"About what?" the Marquis asked.

"Your Lordship's prolonged stay in the country, and also about Miss Saviya."

"Why should that interest him?" the Marquis asked almost to himself.

Then as Hobley did not reply he asked:

"How did you learn this?"

"Henry—he's the third footman, M'Lord—was in The Green Man yesterday when Mr. Jethro came in. He had two men with him, rather rough types, Henry thought."

"And he listened to their conversation?"

"It was not hard for him to do so, M'Lord. I understand Mr. Jethro was talking to the Landlord about Your Lordship, and then this morning he was in conversation with Bob."

"And who is Bob?" the Marquis asked.

"The new Pantry-Boy," Hobley replied. "Mr. Bush had difficulty in finding one and he took on this boy who said he came from St. Albans. I've discussed it with Mr. Bush, M'Lord, and we thought, in the circumstances, it would be best if we dispensed with Bob's services."

"You think," the Marquis said slowly, "that he is relaying information about the household to Mr. Jethro?"

"I should not be surprised, M'Lord. There was talk of money changing hands."

"Then dismiss him at once!" the Marquis said sharply. "I will not, as you well know, have any of my staff accepting bribes."

"We can't be sure, M'Lord," Hobley said, "that Bob knew Mr. Jethro before they got into conversation in The Green Man, but Mr. Bush did mention that the reference Bob brought with him was from Lord Portgate, who Your Lordship well knows is a close friend of Mr. Jethro."

The Marquis recalled a dissolute, drunken young peer who was frequently in his cousin's company.

"Dismiss the boy!" the Marquis said briefly and, having been helped into his perfectly fitting evening coat, he went downstairs to the Salon.

There were only three for dinner—Sir Algernon Gibbon, Charles Collington and the Marquis.

The Chef had excelled himself, and the wine served with every course was superlative. The Gentlemen lingered over their Port in the Dining-Room for a while and then repaired to the Salon.

They had not been there long before Bush came across the room to say in a low voice to the Marquis:

"There has been a slight accident to a lady's coach, M'Lord. Apparently the leading horse broke its rein. The grooms say they can have it repaired within half of an hour. I thought Your Lordship should know that the lady is outside."

"Then of course she must not wait there," the Marquis said. "Invite her in, Bush."

"Very good, M'Lord."

As the Butler left the room the Marquis turned to his friends and remarked:

"It appears we have company. I wonder if it is anyone we know."

"It is extremely annoying when a leading horse breaks its rein and one cannot control it," Charles Collington said. "It happened once to me on the way back from Brighton. I damned nearly had an accident."

Before anyone could reply, the door opened and Bush said in an impressive tone:

"Her Highness, Princess Kotovski, M'Lord."

The three gentlemen looked round to see a very elegant figure enter the room.

The lady had obviously discarded her wraps and was attired in a dazzling evening gown of emerald green silk ornamented with tulle, caught with satin bows.

The new tight waist had just been re-introduced into London and there was no doubt that as she advanced towards them down the Salon she had the most exquisite figure.

Her face was even more arresting. She had black hair, with blue lights in it in the very latest fashion on top of her head, and her lovely eyes seemed very large in her oval face.

There was a necklace of emeralds from the Ruckley collection round her neck, and the same stones glittered in her small ears and in a bracelet which was clasped over her long kid-gloves.

The Marquis advanced to greet her.

"May I welcome you, Highness, to my house? I am the Marquis of Ruckley and deeply regret that you should have had an accident on the high road."

"I was fortunate in that I was just passing your gates," the new-comer replied in a musical voice, with a fascinating foreign accent. "Your grooms have been most obliging, My Lord, and I am extremely grateful."

"I am delighted we can be of service," the Marquis replied. "You are in fact, Ma'am, relieving the monotony of a bachelor party. Allow me to introduce my friends—Sir Algernon Gibbon and Captain Charles Collington."

The lady dropped two extremely graceful curtsies and, having been seated on the damask sofa in front of the fire, accepted a glass of wine.

The Marquis offered her dinner, but she declared that she had already dined before she left Brochet Hall where she had been staying.

"Is your Highness proceeding to London?" Sir Algernon enquired.

The Princess smiled at him.

"My husband has just been appointed to the Russian Embassy," she replied. "It will be my first visit to your famous capital and I am looking forward to it enormously."

"We must make sure you enjoy yourself, Ma'am," Captain Collington said. "I am sure you will, as the parties at the Russian Embassy are the gayest and most amusing given by the whole Diplomatic Corps."

"That is true," Sir Algernon agreed, "but then no country in the world can entertain better or more lavishly than your countrymen, Ma'am."

"I am glad to hear you say that," the Princess replied.

"I remember when I was in Russia," Sir Algernon went on, "being astonished at the magnificence of their hospitality."

"You have been to Russia?" the Marquis exclaimed. "I had no idea of that."

"It was a long time ago," Sir Algernon replied. "In the last year of the last century. I was but twenty at the time and doing a grand tour of the countries in Europe which were not at war."

"And you enjoyed my country?" the Princess enquired.

"I have never forgotten the beauty of it, the charm of its people, and of course its incomparable dancers," Sir Algernon replied.

The Marquis saw Saviya's eyes light up and hoped in her enthusiasm she would not forget the part she had to play.

"You speak, I suppose, of the Imperial Ballet, Sir Algernon," she said.

"Not only was the Imperial Ballet a delight beyond words," Sir Algernon replied, "but I was also entranced by your Gypsy dancers. In fact my Host, Prince Paul Borokowski, with whom I stayed, married some years later a dancer of the Gypsy race."

"Surely that was very unusual?" the Marquis asked, remembering what Saviya had said to him about a Gypsy marrying a Gorgio.

"Not in Russia," Sir Algernon replied. "There the Gypsy dancers and singers have a special position that is quite different from anywhere else in the world."

The Marquis looked incredulous and, turning to the Princess, Sir Algernon went on:

"You will bear me out, Ma'am, when I say there are some Gypsies who inhabit stately houses, go abroad in their elegant equipages, and are not at all inferior to Russians of the highest rank in appearance or in intellect."

"Yes, that is true," Saviya admitted.

"And you will also agree," Sir Algernon continued, "that it is due not only to their amazing and magnificent dancing, but to the power of song."

He saw both the Marquis and Captain Collington were listening and said:

"Did you not know, Ruckley, that some of the best singers in the world have come from the Russian Gypsies? They have been acknowledged not only by the public of their own country, but by the most fastidious of foreign critics."

"I must admit that such a phenomenon had escaped my notice," the Marquis replied.

"Did you never hear of Catalani?" Sir Algernon enquired. "She was an Italian—one of the greatest Operatic Sopranos the world has ever known. She was so enchanted by the voice of a Moscow Gypsy when she heard her sing, that she tore from her shoulders a cashmere shawl that had been given to her by the Pope as the 'best singer in the world.'

" 'It is no longer mine by right,' the Italian declared, wrapping her shawl round the Gypsy."

"I must thank you for the kind things you say about my country," the Princess said, as Sir Algernon paused for breath.

"It is because what I found in Russia was so unique, so unforgettable," Sir Algernon replied, "that I really believe that it altered my life."

He paused for effect and went on:

"I have ever since cultivated the Arts, but I can never surpass or even equal the magnificent treasures to be found in your Palaces, in the homes of your Princes."

"You make me envious, Gibbon," the Marquis remarked.

"It is true," Sir Algernon said.

He then went into a long discourse about the pictures he had seen in Moscow and the wonderful collections of Objets d'Art to be found in the Palaces of St. Petersburg.

He appealed to Saviya for confirmation of all he contended, and was delighted when she flattered him for being so discerning and knowledgeable on such matters.

When finally Bush came to say that the rein had been repaired and the carriage was now ready to convey her Highness to London, the Princess rose with a murmur of regret.

"You have been so kind!" she said to the Marquis. "What appeared at first to be a disaster has been changed into a delight!"

"I hope you will allow me to call on you as soon as I return to London," the Marquis replied.

"My husband and I will be delighted," the Princess answered, "and I know he will want to add his thanks to mine for your hospitality."

"We shall meet in the very near future," Sir Algernon said as she held out her hand to him. "The Russian Ambassador and his wife, Princess Lieven, are great friends of mine, and you must permit me to give a dinner-party in your honour as soon as you have had time to settle down."

"You are more than kind," the Princess said softly, and held out her hand to Captain Collington.

The Marquis escorted the Princess from the room and out into the Hall.

"You were magnificent!" he whispered, as soon as the door shut behind them. "How long do you want before I take Sir Algernon onto the terrace?"

"A quarter of an hour," she whispered.

Then the Marquis left her and went back into the Salon.

"What a beautiful woman!" Sir Algernon was exclaiming as he entered, "but then the Russians when they are young are unbelievably lovely. I am telling you the truth when I say there are no more beautiful women in the world than those of noble blood."

"I was interested in what you were saying about the Gypsies," Charles Collington remarked casually. "I have always thought of Gypsies as poor, ragged creatures wandering barefoot along the roads and sleeping under hedgerows or in tattered tents."

"Russian Gypsies are different," Sir Algernon replied. "Some of them are, of course, under the protection of the Grand Dukes and Princes."

"I always understood that Gypsies are very moral," the Marquis protested.

"They are never promiscuous," Sir Algernon replied. "My friend, Prince Paul explained to me that no real Gypsy ever becomes a prostitute. If they accept the protection of a Nobleman the liaison lasts for many years. The women in fact look on it as much the same as a marriage."

"And yet, you say some important Russians actually do marry Gypsies?" Charles Collington questioned incredulously.

"Many famous Gypsy singers and ballerinas have become Princesses," Sir Algernon answered. "He told me that it is not the aristocracy that objects to such a mésalliance but the Gypsies themselves who disapprove. They are a strange people who have no wish to intermix with other races."

The Marquis made sure that his guests' glasses were well-filled and then said:

"As it is a warm night, in fact surprisingly warm for the time of the year, I want you to come out onto the terrace. I have something to show you, Gibbon, which I think you will find unusual and very interesting."

"My visit to you has already been full of surprises," Sir Algernon replied. "I am therefore quite prepared for another."

The gentlemen walked out through the long French-windows which opened onto a flagged terrace. In the centre of it there was a flight of stone steps leading down to the lawn.

At the top of those were three arm-chairs.

The Marquis invited Sir Algernon to sit down in the centre while he and Charles Collington took a chair on either side of him.

The garden was quiet and mysterious under a star-strewn sky with a full moon just climbing up the Heavens.

In front of them the green lawn swept away to where there was a small Grecian Temple which had been brought to England by the Marquis's grand-father at the beginning of the eighteenth century.

It gleamed pearly white in the moonlight flanked by the darkness of the shrubs and trees.

Then as they waited, and the Marquis knew that Sir Algernon was anticipating the next surprise, there came the faint, sweet sound of violins from the direction of the Temple.

At first indistinct in the distance, they could now see more clearly coming towards them a number of musicians, playing as they moved a music which seemed compelling and to have a strange, stimulating note which made the pulses begin to beat quicker.

There were not only violins, which Saviya had told the Marquis they called '*bas*' *alja*—the king of instruments—there were also the notes of the violas, the cymbals and the sitar.

They drew nearer until they were just on the edge of the lawn, and then they divided so that as a background there was the white perfection of the Greek Temple.

The music intensified, and suddenly a dancer appeared. She seemed to emerge through the music and be a part of it.

The Marquis had expected Saviya to be a remarkable dancer, but it was difficult to put into words the sheer beauty of her movements.

She was dressed in Gypsy clothes, not those she habitually wore, but those which he knew instinctively belonged to the theatre—white, embroidered with vivid colours, the sleeves of her muslin blouse puffed out almost like wings from her shoulders.

Her skirt flew out from her tiny waist and the Marquis knew it was not one skirt but seven which frothed, rustled and shimmered with every movement she made.

There were jewels around her neck which glittered in the moonlight, and on her head there was a wreath of flowers with trailing ribbons of every hue flying out behind her.

It seemed almost impossible that her feet touched the ground as she flew like a butterfly over the green grass.

Then from behind the musicians there came men and women carrying torches, which lit the garden with a strange, pagan light.

Now the music changed. It was no longer soft and entrancing but wild yet sweet; violent and yet tender; and while Saviya accelerated the speed of her movements, the Gypsies with the torches began to sing.

There was a bewildering beauty in the melody of their voices and a charm in their words, even though those listening could not understand them.

Sometimes the tone was delicate and liquid like the sound of silver bells, at other times it was a wild, invigorating and exciting tone which seemed to draw the heart of those who listened from their bodies and make them one with the music itself.

Quicker and quicker the sound rose; quicker and quicker Saviya danced. She leapt until she almost seemed to hang motionless in the air and she twirled until she no longer seemed human.

Yet everything she did had such an unbelievable grace, so much beauty, so much haunting loveliness, that she became the embodiment of a dream.

Quicker and quicker, louder and louder the music, the dancing, until it aroused an elation that was a part not only of the body but of the very soul.

Then when it seemed that no human being could hold such intensity any longer, slowly the violence of the music was replaced by a soft rippling melody as of a quiet sea after a storm.

First the flaming torches moved away towards the Temple, then the musicians, and finally Saviya herself, dancing like a bewitching will-o'-the-wisp only half-seen in the shadow of the retreating singers—until as the music faded into the distance she stood for a moment silhouetted against the pillars of the Temple, her slight figure hardly human in its grace.

As the last lingering note of the violins died away, she too disappeared.

For a moment there was complete and absolute silence. Then Sir Algernon jumped to his feet clapping and cheering.

"Bravo! Unbelievable! Exquisite! Tremendous!" he exclaimed.

Almost as if he moved in a dream the Marquis, too, rose to applaud, but he felt somehow as if his voice was constricted in his throat.

It had been, although he hardly dared admit it to himself, an emotional experience which he had never encountered before.

Because it was difficult to find words to express what they had all felt, they moved back into the Salon almost as if the silent beauty of the night was too poignant for the commonplaces of conversation.

A little later Saviya came in.

She was still wearing the beautiful embroidered Russian dress in which she had danced and, as she entered the Salon, the Marquis crossed the room towards her and taking her hand lifted it to his lips.

"I expected you to be good," he said quietly, "but I have no words to tell you how superlative you were in every way."

She smiled at him without replying and accepted the congratulations of Sir Algernon and Charles Collington.

"You realise now," the latter said to Sir Algernon, "that you owe us a thousand guineas."

"It is a price I will pay willingly just to see this lovely lady dance," Sir Algernon said. "May I know her real name?"

"It is Saviya," the Marquis answered, "and she is, as you have guessed, a Gypsy. But her mother is a Russian and a dancer."

"Tonight you recaptured for me my lost youth!" Sir Algernon said.

He smiled and added to the Marquis:

"Now you understand why, when I was talking to you after dinner, I sounded perhaps exaggeratedly enthusiastic, but even so I was under-estimating, as you must admit, the brilliance not only of the Russian singers but their dancers."

Then he asked with a note of curiosity in his voice:

"You must explain to me, Ruckley, where you found this fascinating creature. How does it happen that she is here in England?"

"An introduction was thrust upon me," the Marquis smiled.

He explained how he had run Saviya down with his Phaeton.

"If it had not happened," he finished, "I should have had no idea that the Gypsies were encamped on my land. It was not until tonight that I had even seen a sign of them."

"They are a secret people," Sir Algernon said, and turning to Saviya he asked, "Are you all right after your accident? You might easily have broken your leg, and that would have been a tragedy beyond words."

"I was fortunate it was no worse," Saviya answered. "All that is left now is a small scar on my forehead and the few marks on my arm."

"It still looks rather bruised," Charles Collington said, looking down at her arm as he came and stood beside her.

She laughed.

"That is the wrong arm."

"But you do have a bruise there," he persisted.

"No," she replied. "That is a birth-mark, and it is a sign much respected by my tribe."

"Why?" Charles Collington enquired.

"Because," she replied, "it is the head of a hawk. A hawk has very sharp eyes, and this indicates that I am in fact a 'Seer.'"

"Yes, you are right," Charles Collington said, "the mark does look like a hawk's head—can you see it does, Ruckley?"

It was a birth-mark about the size of a florin and Sir Algernon looked at it. But the Marquis went to fetch Saviya a glass of wine from the side-table.

"You must be both tired and thirsty after that incredible performance," he said as he handed it to her.

"I seldom feel tired when I am dancing," she answered. "What was much more frightening was playing the part of a Lady of Quality."

"Which you did as to the manor born," Charles Collington said. "Do you not agree, Gibbon?"

"Of course I agree! It was faultless," Sir Algernon answered. "I am only so disappointed that I shall not be able to give you dinner in London next week."

"I must say, Gibbon, you are taking the loss of a thousand guineas like a sportsman," Charles Collington said irrepressibly. "I almost feel embarrassed at winning the money."

They all laughed at this. Then the Marquis raising his glass said:

"I want to drink to Saviya. There is no-one who has surprised us more with her amazing talents, or who could have been more modest about them. She told me she was a dancer, but not for one moment did I expect a performance such as the one we have just witnessed."

"What I cannot understand," Sir Algernon said, "is why you are here; why do you not stay in St. Petersburg where your talents would be appreciated?"

"My father, like all Gypsies, has a wanderlust," Saviya answered. "After a little while—however comfortable we may be, however happy—he wants to move on. We wandered all over Russia from the North to the very South, then he had a yearning to see England again."

"He has been here before?" the Marquis asked.

"Yes, but many years ago," Saviya replied, "before I was born, or when I was only a baby. I do not remember it."

They talked for some time and then Saviya said:

"I think I must go. My father will wonder what has happened to me, since the rest of the tribe will have long returned to the camp."

As she spoke the door opened and a footman came into the Salon. He carried something in his hand and went up to stand at the side of the Marquis waiting for him to finish speaking.

"What is it?" the Marquis asked.

"This has just been left at the front door, M'Lord. A man gave it to me saying I was to present it to Your Lordship in your bed-room, but seeing that you had not retired, I thought I should bring it here."

"A man?" the Marquis questioned.

"I think he must have been a Gypsy, M'Lord. He said, 'Tell His Lordship this is a gift from the Gypsies.'"

The Marquis glanced at Saviya.

"It sounds as if your father is being unexpectedly generous."

The footman put the parcel into his hands and Saviya saw it was a round wicker basket, not very large, the lid fastened down at each side with a small wooden peg slipped into a cane loop.

"Do you know anything about this?" the Marquis enquired.

She shook her head.

"I cannot imagine what it is. I do not think it can be from my father. It is not the sort of thing he would do without telling me."

"A gift from the Gypsies . . ." the Marquis repeated. "Well, I shall expect something unusual, Saviya."

He pulled out the two small wooden pegs as he spoke.

Then, just as he was about to raise the lid, Saviya suddenly seized it from his hands, and with a swiftness that took him by surprise, ran down the room, put the basket on the floor and pushed it away from her.

It slid across the polished parquet floor, where there were no rugs, to come to rest almost in front of the door.

"Whatever are you doing?" the Marquis asked in astonishment.

As he spoke, the lid of the basket slipped to one side, and through the aperture came first a long, forked tongue, then the head and finally the body of a snake!

It moved so quickly there was hardly time for anyone to ejaculate before on reaching the floor it raised itself and its hood expanded to reveal that it was a cobra.

"Good God!"

The Marquis could hardly say the words, while Charles Collington exclaimed:

"A pistol! Where do you keep a pistol, Fabius?"

The cobra darted its head first right and then left. It was hissing, its long tongue licking in and out of its mouth, obviously angry and annoyed at being moved about.

Charles Collington started to walk cautiously along the side of the room in an attempt to reach the door behind the snake. With a little gesture of her hand, Saviya stopped him.

"Keep still!" she said in a very low voice. "Do not move or speak."

There was an authority in her tone that was unmistakable, and while the Marquis would have expostulated, he bit back the words even as he started to say them.

Moving a little nearer to the hissing, angry reptile, Saviya started to make a strange sound.

It was not exactly singing, it was like the notes of the reed-pipe used by the snake-charmers in India. Yet it came from between her lips and was at first so faint that the three men listening could hardly hear it.

But the cobra heard and now its tongue no longer flicked out, and it turned its head curiously, first this way, then that, regarding Saviya with its yellow eyes.

He was still poised for the attack, his head with its inflated hood high in the air.

Slowly, making that strange music which seemed to consist of just three notes repeated over and over again, Saviya drew a little nearer.

Firstly, she sank down on her knees just a short distance from the cobra, her eyes on his, her body very still.

There was complete silence in the room except for her voice, and the three men watching hardly seemed to breathe. They stood as if turned to stone.

Then slowly, almost imperceptibly, in time to the notes, Saviya began to move her shoulders a little to the left and then to the right, swaying rhythmically, her eyes all the time on the cobra.

Now he too began to move, swaying as she did, turning his

yellowish head with the black and white spectacle-shaped markings on its wide hood to the right, to the left, to the right, to the left.

Still she intensified her tune and her movements until, its hood subsiding, the cobra sank little by little, lower and lower until finally his head was flat on the ground and he appeared to make an obeisance to her.

Then her tune altered and, almost as if she gave a note of command, the sound was abrupt yet still melodious.

Unbelievably, as it seemed to the men watching, the cobra obeyed, and turning he slithered slowly, moving in a very different manner to the quickness with which he had left the basket, back into it.

He slipped over the edge of the basket and, as they watched, his long dark body slithered after his head until finally the tip of his tail disappeared.

Still singing, Saviya very gently moved forward. She pressed the lid back into place and slipped the wooden pegs into the cane loops, which held it firm.

As soon as the basket was secure she ceased her song, and it seemed for a moment as if she would collapse.

The Marquis was at her side and put his arms around her to lift her to her feet.

"Are you all right?" he asked.

"I . . . I am . . . all right."

But he saw that her face was very pale and was afraid that she might faint.

He helped her across the room to settle her down into a chair.

"Do not talk!" he commanded and poured her out a drink.

She took two or three sips, then gave him back the glass.

"I do not need it," she said.

"How could you charm that snake?" Sir Algernon enquired. "I have heard of it being done, but would never have believed it was possible for anyone without an enormous amount of training, and certainly not for a woman!"

"I have seen it done many times," Saviya replied. "But it is the first time I have actually tried it myself."

"Then it was even more miraculous," the Marquis said. "We can only thank you very gratefully, Saviya. I do not need to tell you that you saved my life!"

Saviya gave a deep sigh.

"I suddenly realised that the basket was not of the type used by Gypsies, but by the Circus people. For a moment I could not think where I had seen one before, then I remembered the snake-charmers that we have encountered on our travels."

She paused for a moment before looking up at the Marquis and said:

"Their snakes usually have the bags of venom in their fangs removed, but this was a young cobra and had not been treated. If he had bitten you, it would have been fatal. The venom acts quickly on the nervous system."

"But who can want to murder you, Ruckley?" Sir Algernon enquired.

"The answer to that is quite easy—" Charles Collington began, only to be silenced as the Marquis interposed:

"There is no point in discussing it, Charles. Again we have no proof."

"What is going on? You must tell me about it," Sir Algernon asked curiously.

"I think it is time that Saviya went to bed," the Marquis suggested.

"Yes, I must go," she agreed obediently.

She curtsied to Sir Algernon and to Charles Collington. The Marquis walked with her across the Hall and out through the main door.

She turned to say good-night but he shook his head.

"I will come with you to the wood," he said. "I do not like to think of your going alone."

"I will be quite safe," she replied. "It is you I worry about. Who is the man who wishes to kill you? If you do not tell me I shall lie awake all night trying to see his name as I have seen his face."

"You told me when we were in the Picture Gallery that his name began with the same letter as mine," the Marquis replied. "You were right, Saviya, he is my cousin, Jethro Ruck. If I am dead he will inherit the title and the Estate."

"This is not the first time he has tried?" Saviya enquired, as they walked across the Court-Yard side by side.

"He attempted to destroy me in London, by dislodging a piece of masonry from the top of my house in Berkeley Square," the Marquis answered. "It missed me by a hair's breadth, and tonight if I had, as he thought, retired to bed I would have opened the basket when I was alone."

Saviya shivered.

"He is dangerous! Very dangerous!" she said. "I beg you to be careful."

The Marquis smiled.

"You sound very like Charles. You tell me to be careful, but I should require to be as clairvoyant as you are to anticipate the strange and unusual ways in which Jethro is attempting to exterminate me."

The Marquis was silent for a moment and then he said:

"It was clever of him to pretend it was a present from the Gypsies. He must have learnt about you when he was making enquiries in the village, and he knew, I dare say, without being told that if I did in fact receive a present from you I would open it personally."

"I will never send you anything that you do not anticipate," Saviya promised.

"I doubt if Jethro will repeat the same trick twice. What shall I do with the snake—kill it?"

"No!" Saviya said. "I think it is wrong to take life unless it is absolutely necessary. But the Kalderash celebrate the Feast of the Serpent on March fifteenth. On that day, if anyone kills a snake, he will be fortunate throughout the year."

She paused before she continued:

"I have heard there is a Circus at St. Albans. That was where your cousin must have obtained the snake. Send them back the cobra with your compliments. I think they will understand and not make the mistake another time of selling their stock to an outsider."

"I will do that," the Marquis said. "At the same time I think it is being very magnanimous. If I had any sense I would send it back to Jethro himself."

He gave a short laugh.

"The trouble is, if it killed him, I should have a lot of explaining to do, and there is no proof that it was his idea in the first place."

"You must be on your guard."

"I have a feeling I shall be safe as long as you are here with me," the Marquis answered.

By this time they had reached the edge of the wood and Saviya stopped.

"There is no reason for you to come any further."

"There is every reason I should protect you," the Marquis replied, "but if you would rather go alone, I will respect your wishes."

"Thank you!" she said softly.

"I have so much to thank you for. First for the moments of unbelievable beauty you showed me tonight—and secondly for saving my life!"

He put out his right hand as he spoke and she laid her left hand in it.

Their palms touched. Then a sudden streak of ecstasy, a thrill such as he had never known in his whole life, swept through the Marquis and he knew as he looked down into Saviya's eyes that she felt the same.

For a moment neither of them could move, and yet it was almost as if they lay close against each other and were one.

"Saviya! You know what I feel about you?" the Marquis said hoarsely.

She did not answer and he saw her eyes were searching his.

"I want you!" he said. "I want you more than I have ever wanted anything in my life. Come with me, Saviya! I will give you everything you can ever desire and we will be very happy together."

She did not answer until at last she said in a low voice he could hardly hear:

"Are you asking me to be your *Piramni?*"

The Marquis had no need of a translation of her meaning.

"Must we have words for something that is so wonderful, so beautiful?" he asked. "We were made for each other, Saviya. I have known these past few days that you were aware of me. I could feel it whenever we were near each other. I could see it in your eyes."

She turned her head a little away from him and he said:

"It is too late, my darling, to pretend. I think you love me a little, and I can make you love me with all the wild wonder that lies within your exquisite body, and your entrancing brain. Come to me, Saviya! We shall find a happiness which is granted to few people."

She raised her head.

"I . . . cannot! You know I . . . cannot!"

"Why?"

"Because it would be . . . wrong."

"Who is to decide that?" the Marquis asked roughly. "You may have tribal laws, Saviya, but they are not the laws either of this country or of the Church. Forget them! Remember only that you are a woman and I am a man. We belong to each other!"

His fingers tightened as he went on:

"I will look after you and you shall never want for the whole of your life. That I swear! But do not let us throw away this wonderful, this perfect happiness which we feel when we are together."

She did not reply, yet he knew without being told she was not convinced.

"Look at me, Saviya!"

She hesitated and then as if she must obey him she threw back her head. Her worried eyes were very large in her small face.

"You love me!" the Marquis said. "I know you love me and you thrill me in a way I have never known in my whole life before! My body aches for you! I desire you, Saviya, but there is so much more to it than that. I want to be with you; to know you are there; to listen to your voice. I want to watch the movement of your lips; to see that strange, lovely, melting expression in your eyes which tells me that you love me."

Saviya drew in her breath. Her lips were parted a little, her eyes were pools of mystery and the Marquis knew she was trembling.

"God, I want you!"

It seemed with the words as if something broke within him. He swept her into his arms. He held her crushingly against him.

His lips were on hers and then as her head fell back against his shoulder, his kiss was not only demanding and possessive, but gentle, as he realised how soft, small and yielding she was.

It was a moment of magic such as he had never imagined. It seemed as if the whole world stood still and they were alone in an eternity where there was nothing but themselves.

"I love you!" He remembered even as he spoke, that he had never in his life said that to a woman.

"*Me hamava Tut!*" she whispered.

He knew that she was saying the same words as he had said to her, but in Romany.

"I love you!—I love you!"

Now he kissed her eyes; her cheeks; the little pulse throbbing frantically in her throat; and then again her lips.

"Come back with me now!" he begged. "Why should we wait? I want you with me! I cannot wait until tomorrow to see you again!"

Very slowly she drew herself away from him.

Her face in the moonlight was radiant. Then he saw her expression change.

"No!" she said. "No! No! It is . . . wrong not only for me but for . . . you. I love you too much to . . . hurt you!"

"Why should it hurt me?" the Marquis asked roughly.

She stood looking at him and he felt once again in that strange way he had felt once before that she was not looking at him, but through and beyond him.

"It is you who . . . matters," she said softly.

Then before he could stop her, before he could take her again into his arms, she had moved away from him amongst the tree trunks and vanished!

"Saviya!" he called desperately. "Saviya!"

But there was no answer from the darkness. He was alone.

CHAPTER FIVE

The Marquis walked slowly back to the house, and after a short conversation with Sir Algernon and Charles Collington he retired to bed.

He gave orders to Bush before he did so that, as Saviya had suggested, the snake should be sent over to the St. Albans Circus the following morning in charge of a groom.

When Hobley left him he sat for some time in an arm-chair before getting into bed, and found himself recapturing the incredible magic of the evening.

He had known as he watched Saviya dance that his whole being responded, and she made him feel as no woman had ever done before.

Then when he touched her and was aware of a new rapture and ecstasy within himself, he knew he was in love.

There had been many women in his life whom he had found amusing, entertaining and at times irresistible, but never had they fulfilled his first expectation. Always he had found, however enticing they might be, they could not give him what he really wanted from a woman.

This was something he could not express even to himself. He just knew there was some hidden part of his being that remained untouched by even the most alluring and attractive woman, so that in some inexplicable manner she failed him.

He had laughed at love, mocked it and declared it was the infatuation of fools, but there was nevertheless an idealism that told him that true love was possible, even if he had not met it.

He understood now why Eurydice had been prepared to give up everything that was familiar and cross the world to a strange land with a man of whom she knew little, but whom she loved.

She had warned him that one day he would feel the same, but

even as he thought of her words, he knew it was impossible for him to offer Saviya marriage.

It was what he should do. Even while to her he was a "Gorgio," she would wish him to want her to be his wife. Yet how could he make her the Marchioness of Ruckley?

He told himself that, where only he was concerned, he could not think of anyone more suitable and indeed more perfect to be his wife and the Chatelaine of his house.

But he would have been a fool if he had not realised the difficulties, and indeed the unhappiness such a position would entail for Saviya herself.

However lovely she was, however competent, however charming, she would have to endure the sneers, the innuendos and the insults that she would receive not only from his friends but, in a way far more important, from those he employed and who were part of his background.

Saviya might have charmed the servants when she stayed in the House, but would they accept her as their Mistress?

And even if the servants could be captivated, what about the keepers, the other employees on the Estate, the people in the village, the farmers, the tenants and everyone who lived in the immediate neighbourhood of Ruckley, who had looked up to the family and respected them for generations.

Hatred and fear of the Gypsies lay deep in the roots of almost all Englishmen, but why it should be so the Marquis could not understand.

Ever since the Gypsies had first come to the country in 1512, there had been people who not only disliked them but who attempted to persecute them.

In the book by John Howland which The Reverend had found in the Library, the Marquis had read that even in the reign of Henry VIII a number of outlandish people calling themselves Egyptians had been reshipped to France at public expense.

In the "31st yeare of the Raigne of our Souraigne Lady, the Queen's Majestie, Acts were passed for the punishinge and suppressinge of Roags and Vacabonds," mentioning particular parts of the country where the Gypsies congregated.

Under Scottish laws in 1609, "Sorners, common thieves, commonly called Egyptians were directed to pass forth of the Kingdom under pain of death as common, notorious and condemned thieves."

Things had altered very little, the Marquis thought, and despite a number of romantic writers who had glamourised the Gypsies, the country people still believed they could curse their crops or their animals, cast the "Evil Eye," and that Gypsies were, in the main, evil folk.

According to Howland there were some thirty-six thousand Gypsies in Great Britain and yet nothing was done for them.

No attempt was made to educate their children, Clergymen avoided the camps, and they received severe sentences whenever they were brought in front of the Magistrates.

And yet, the Marquis thought, there were Gypsies like Saviya, who was more intelligent than any woman he had ever met and certainly more cultured than the majority of his friends.

It was true she was half-Russian and, according to Sir Algernon, the Russians were different from those in the rest of Europe. But socially she would always be tainted by her Gypsy blood.

He wondered if any marriage could survive when a man must be continually on the defensive to protect his wife, not against violence, but slanderous tongues and evil minds.

No. Marriage was impossible! It therefore remained, the Marquis thought, to persuade Saviya to live with him as his mistress.

He had not missed the contempt in her voice when she had said the word *"Piramni,"* and he had known that to her it suggested much worse sin than it would have to an Englishwoman.

The strict morality of the Gypsies was part of their faith, an intrinsic part of their way of life, and he knew that only a great love utterly beyond self would make Saviya accept a position that offended every instinct in her body.

But what else could he do? He asked himself the question and then, because there was no answer, he at last went to bed.

He found it impossible to sleep, and rose very early.

He had a feeling it was urgent for him to see Saviya as soon as possible. There had been something unsatisfactory and indecisive in the manner in which she had left him last night, after that moment of indescribable wonder when he had held her in his arms and kissed her.

He knew irrefutably it was the first kiss she had ever received.

He was aware as he felt her quivering against him that he had aroused in her a rapture to equal his own and that already, without physical possession, they were one in body, mind and soul.

'I love her!' the Marquis told himself, and he knew it was an expression of the deepest feelings of which he was capable.

He felt sure she would come to the House at her usual time, which was about eleven o'clock.

Invariably when he returned from dealing with Eurydice's Estate, he would find her in the Library with The Reverend.

She would be discussing subjects so erudite he thought them beyond the intelligence of a woman, and looking so entrancingly beautiful that it was hard to believe she could be as clever as The Reverend proclaimed her to be.

Today the Marquis thought he could not bear to miss a moment of the time they might be together. So this morning Saviya would not be waiting for him, but he for Saviya.

As Hobley assisted him into his riding-clothes, he remembered that he had not given Saviya back the coins that she had borrowed from her father for them to deceive Sir Algernon.

He must remember, he thought, to return them as they were in fact extremely valuable.

How strange it must be, he thought to himself, to know that one must wander the world encountering terrible discomforts from the climate, the hostility of the different races and enduring all sorts of privations, when in fact one could well afford to settle down in comparative comfort.

Then with a smile he felt it undoubtedly had its compensations for a man. To battle against tremendous odds was a challenge. It must also be a very successful way of avoiding boredom and social ennui, when the horizon was limitless.

"Do you know what time Sir Algernon and Captain Collington plan to leave for London, Hobley?" he asked his Valet.

"Sir Algernon ordered his carriage for eleven o'clock, M'Lord."

"I will be back long before that," the Marquis said. "There are certain people I have to see on Lady Walden's Estate. But will you assure Sir Algernon and Captain Collington I shall not be long delayed and hope to be with them some time before their departure?"

"I'll give them your message, M'Lord."

"I have discovered a quick way to the new land, Hobley," the Marquis said with satisfaction, as the Valet helped him into his riding-coat.

"Indeed, M'Lord?"

"I have been using it now for the past week. I have timed myself and it takes me not quite twenty minutes."

"Riding the finest horse-flesh, M'Lord," Hobley said with a smile.

"I admit a fine mount is essential," the Marquis replied.

"I think I know the way you mean, M'Lord," Hobley said. "It is through the Ride at the north end of Battle Wood."

"That is right," the Marquis replied. "It takes me directly onto the parkland sloping down to Lady Walden's house."

The Marquis took a quick glance at himself in the mirror and went from the room.

Hobley watched him appreciatively as he walked down the passage.

There was no-one, he thought, who could look smarter than his master in a grey whipcord riding-coat, which had been cut by a master-hand, over a yellow waistcoat above the spotless white of his riding-breeches.

The shine on the Marquis's riding-boots was Hobley's special pride.

He had refused innumerable bribes to tell the secret of their brilliance to the London Dandies who tried to imitate the Marquis's elegance, and who invariably failed in their aspirations.

Outside the front door two grooms were holding with some difficulty a stallion the Marquis had acquired only a month ago from Tattersall's salesrooms.

It was a fiery young horse with a touch of Arab in its pedigree, and as the Marquis swung himself into the saddle he thought with pleasure that his ride was not going to be an easy one. He would have to assert his mastery over an animal that was not yet broken to his touch.

The stallion bucked several times to show its independence, and was checked from starting off at too swift a pace.

Finally he contented himself with shying at several imaginary objects before the Marquis allowed him to trot over the Park towards the woods.

As he went the Marquis thought of how last night he had walked in the moonlight with Saviya.

It was impossible to keep her from his thoughts. Just to think of her eyes raised to his, of her softness as she had surrendered herself into his arms, made his breath come quicker.

Also he felt once again that strange constriction within his heart that he had never known before.

"God, she is beautiful!" he told himself.

It was not only her beauty which held him. There was some indefinable link between them, some union that had made them part of each other from the first moment they had met.

"I want her!" the Marquis said beneath his breath. "Dear God, how I want her!"

The stallion distracted his attention from Saviya by shying at one

of the speckled deer which, startled at their approach, ran from beneath a tree.

Already they had reached the woods which on the north side of
the house constituted a background, and a wind-break had been
planned for the great red-brick mansion when it was first erected.

There was, as the Marquis had told Hobley, a Ride through the
wood which had been cut originally by the tree-fellers so that they
would use it for conveying the chopped wood to the House in their
carts.

Now it was a straight lane through the trees, and the Marquis set
his horse to a gallop putting up his hand as he did so to settle his
hat more firmly upon his head.

The great trees, many of them centuries old, rose high on either
side. As it was so early in the morning, the sun was not yet strong
enough to percolate through the branches and dry up the dew,
which lay like small diamonds on the grass.

There was a scent of pine and of birchwood, and among the trees
there was an occasional glimpse of the vivid blue of bluebells.

Then as the stallion increased his pace the Marquis, enjoying a
sense of satisfaction and well-being, quite suddenly and unexpectedly, even as he reached it, saw something rising from the
ground with a quick movement.

It was a rope! Knee-high it was taut in front of his horse.

There was not even time for the Marquis to tighten the reins
before he felt his mount gallop straight into it, heard himself shout,
and knew, even as he fell, there was nothing he could do.

He was conscious of the violent impact as his head hit the
ground, then he thought he heard the bone snap as his collar-bone
broke . . .

Someone was speaking very softly and there was a touch on his
forehead that was soothing and somehow hypnotic.

"Go to sleep!" the soft voice said. "You are dreaming. Go to
sleep!"

The cool fingers were comforting, and yet vaguely the Marquis
remembered that someone had been crying out . . . There had
been darkness and pain . . .

But he could not ignore the compelling movement on his forehead, and he fell asleep.

Slowly he came back to consciousness . . .

He thought for a moment he was with his mother. He was in

someone's arms and his head was against the softness of a woman's breast. Then he was aware of a fragrance.

He was very comfortable. He felt secure and there was a strange happiness in knowing he was loved.

Again he thought of his mother, but the fragrance haunted him.

He remembered now he had smelt it first in the hair of a Gypsy he had carried in his arms after he had run her down with his Phaeton.

He felt very weak. It was too much trouble to open his eyes. Then he felt whoever held him move, and he wanted to cry out because his cheek no longer rested against the softness of a breast.

Instead his head was on a pillow, and he felt as if he had been deprived of something very precious.

"How is he, Miss?"

The Marquis thought he would have known Hobley's voice anywhere, even though he spoke in a whisper.

"He was not so restless in the night, but he has not yet regained consciousness."

It was Saviya who spoke. Who else could speak in that soft, melodious tone with just the trace of a foreign accent?

With an effort, feeling as if his eyelids were weighted down with lead, the Marquis opened his eyes.

She must have been looking at him, for with a little cry Saviya knelt beside him. He felt her hand against his cheek.

"You are awake!"

The Marquis looked at her. Her face was very near to his, and he could see the worry and at the same time a glint of excitement in her eyes.

"What—happened?" he asked.

Even as he spoke he remembered the rope across the ride. He had fallen!

"I do not think you ought to talk."

"I want to—know what—happened," the Marquis repeated and now his voice was stronger.

As he spoke, he realised that he was lying on a bed that was almost on the floor and that he was enclosed by curved walls so that he thought for a moment he was in a cave.

It was so small there was hardly room for himself, for Saviya kneeling beside him, and for Hobley with his head bent just inside what appeared to be an open door.

"Where am—I?" the Marquis asked.

"You're all right, M'Lord, and that's thanks to Miss Saviya,"

Hobley replied. "It's worried we've been about you and that's the truth."

With an effort the Marquis turned his head a little, realised that his shoulder was bandaged. He remembered breaking his collar-bone.

"I fell, but it was not my horse's fault. Is he all right?"

"He went home," Saviya said. "There was a rope stretched between two trees. The men raised it just as you reached them."

"What men?" the Marquis asked, and knew even as he spoke it was an unnecessary question.

"Mr. Jethro's men, M'Lord," Hobley said bitterly, "and 'twas them that swore false witness in front of the Magistrates against Miss Saviya."

The Marquis suddenly felt more awake. He tried to raise himself a little and then was conscious of a sharp pain in his back.

"Do not move," Saviya said quickly, "they stabbed you!"

"They'd have killed you, M'Lord, if Miss Saviya hadn't come along when she did," Hobley said.

"I have to know what happened," the Marquis said, with some of his old authority back in his voice. "Start at the beginning."

Saviya looked at Hobley as if for guidance.

"It'll worry His Lordship," he said to her, "if we don't tell him."

"It will indeed," the Marquis affirmed. "All I can remember is feeling myself fall, and knowing it was a rope against my horse's knees that had been the cause."

"'Tis an old trick, M'Lord, but a clever one," Hobley said. "They must've known Your Lordship went that way every morning and were lying in wait for you."

"I had a feeling that something was wrong," Saviya said. "We were packing up ready to move on . . ."

"You were leaving?" the Marquis interrupted.

He looked at her and her eyes fell before his.

"I had to . . . go," she murmured, and he thought the colour rose in her cheeks.

"But you stayed!"

"I felt that you were in danger, and then to make sure it was just my imagination, I told one of the Gypsies to bring me a horse and to come with me on another."

She gave a little sigh.

"I thought as it was so early that you would not yet have left the House, and I intended merely to watch you cross the Park, pass into the Ride and out the other side."

"You have watched me before!" the Marquis said with a sudden perception.

Again the colour seemed to tinge her cheeks.

"Almost . . . every morning," she answered.

"It was fortunate, M'Lord," Hobley interposed, "that Miss Saviya saw you just as you disappeared into the Ride. If she hadn't done so, you wouldn't be lying here at this moment!"

"What happened?" the Marquis asked.

As he spoke, he covered Saviya's hand with his own and felt her fingers tremble beneath his.

"As I reached the Ride," Saviya said, "I actually saw your horse tripped and you shoot over its head. Then when you were on the ground, two men emerged from behind the trees. One of them held a long knife like a dagger in his hand. Before I could move nearer or shout, he drove it into your back."

The Marquis understood then the reason for the pain he had felt a few moments before when he had tried to raise himself.

"The man drew out the knife and would have stabbed you again," Saviya said, "if I had not urged my horse forward, shouting at the top of my voice. And the Gypsy boy with me did the same. The noise we made frightened the two men and they ran away into the woods."

She drew in her breath before she said:

"When I reached you I thought at first you were dead!"

"It's lucky you aren't, M'Lord," Hobley said. "An inch or two lower and there's no doubt those murdering devils would have achieved their object."

"What did you do?" the Marquis asked, holding Saviya's hand a little more tightly.

"Yerko—the Gypsy who came with me—and I carried your body away into the trees in case the men should return to try to finish murdering you."

She smiled.

"You are very heavy, My Lord."

"How did you manage it?" he asked.

"Yerko is strong and I wanted to save you," she said simply.

"When a Gypsy came to the House to tell me I was urgently needed by Miss Saviya in the wood, I'd a suspicion that something like this had happened," Hobley said. "I was sure, M'Lord, that Mr. Jethro was up to something when he was seen at The Green Man."

"Is there any proof that it was Mr. Jethro who tried to kill me?" the Marquis asked.

Saviya looked at Hobley and neither of them spoke. The Marquis knew they were wondering whether they should tell him the truth.

"Dammit all!" he said, "I am not a child. Tell me what has happened."

Saviya put her hand on his forehead.

"You have been running a very high fever for a long time," she said, "and we do not wish to agitate you."

"It will agitate me a great deal if I think you are keeping something from me," the Marquis said.

"Very well, M'Lord, you'd best know the worst," Hobley said. "There is a warrant out for Miss Saviya's arrest for having killed you. The knife that them murderers used on you is in the hands of the Magistrate, and Mr. Jethro has moved into the House!"

"God dammit!" the Marquis ejaculated.

He attempted to move again but there was a sharp pain in his back which brought beads of sweat onto his forehead.

"This is too much for you," Saviya said. "You should have waited. There is no hurry for you to learn these unpleasant things."

"No hurry?" the Marquis enquired. "How long have I been here?"

"For over a week," Saviya answered.

"For over a week?" the Marquis could hardly repeat the words.

"Time enough, M'Lord, for Mr. Jethro to assert that you've been murdered by Miss Saviya, that the Gypsies have buried your body, and that he's entitled to assume both the title and the ownership of the Estates!"

The Marquis lay for a moment in silence trying to digest the enormity of what Hobley had told him.

Then he asked:

"Why has no-one searched for me?"

"Because if you had been taken back to the House in the state you were in," Saviya said, "I am certain that your cousin would have found some way of disposing of you when you were too weak to resist him."

"Besides," Hobley said, "with a warrant out for her arrest, if Miss Saviya is seen she will be taken to prison."

"Where am I hidden?" the Marquis asked.

"In my caravan in the very depths of the forest," Saviya answered. "If it seems dark, it is because the Gypsies have draped it with shrubs and ivy so that it is almost impossible for anyone to see it, even if they are just outside."

"That's true enough, M'Lord," Hobley agreed. "When I come

here I often wonder whether Miss Saviya has whisked Your
Lordship away in the night, even when the caravan is almost right
in front of my face."

"And your people, they are all right?" the Marquis asked.

"They have moved so that it is more difficult to find them,"
Saviya replied. "But, as you can imagine, your cousin is not making
too close a search for you . . . or for me. The last thing he wants is
for anyone to contend that his bribed confederates are not telling
the truth."

"I will not have him taking my place!" the Marquis said in what
he meant to be an angry and determined tone.

But even to himself his voice sounded very weak and before he
could say any more he fell asleep . . .

It was two days later before the Marquis could grasp all the details of the drama that Jethro had planned so cleverly, or appreciate
that had Saviya not been watching him ride through the wood, he
would in fact have been found dead in the Ride with a Gypsy's
knife between his shoulder-blades.

"The knife even had Gypsy characters on it," Saviya said, "and I
think that either it must have come from the Circus folk from
whom your cousin obtained the cobra, or he bought it in a Curiosity Shop in London."

"But is it a Gypsy knife?"

"A description of it was in the newspapers," Saviya said, "and
my father thinks it is a Spanish dagger such as the Gitanos carry
and use in their quarrels."

"Good circumstantial evidence," the Marquis remarked.

It was Hobley who told him how arrogant and autocratic his
cousin was being at Ruckley House.

"Sir Algernon went back to London, M'Lord, after Mr. Jethro
had arrived, saying he'd heard a strange story in the village that
two men had seen you brought down by an ambush and then being
stabbed by a Gypsy woman."

Hobley's voice was contemptuous as he continued:

"They had the rope as evidence, and said they were walking
through the Ride as they were looking for work at one of the adjacent farms. They had their story very pat, 'twas difficult to fault
them."

"Jethro would have seen to that!" the Marquis murmured.

"Mr. Jethro's clever, M'Lord. Make no mistake about that!"

"I am not!" the Marquis answered. "Go on, Hobley."

"Mr. Jethro was obviously so pleased to relate such a gruesome tale that Sir Algernon, while expressing his deep concern that Your Lordship had disappeared, said he thought the whole thing a bundle of lies and, from what he'd seen of Miss Saviya, she'd murder nobody, least of all you."

"Yet he did not wish to be involved," the Marquis said with a smile.

"That was obvious, M'Lord. But Captain Collington argued fiercely with Mr. Jethro."

"I can imagine him doing that!" the Marquis remarked.

"He stayed one more night, saying he was going to search for you. In fact he came looking in the woods, and then Mr. Jethro ordered him out of the House."

"He actually did that?" the Marquis ejaculated.

"Yes, M'Lord. He said as the new Marquis of Ruckley he wasn't standing for the Captain's impudence, and he certainly didn't intend to offer him any further hospitality!"

The Marquis would have expressed himself forcefully but Saviya interposed:

"You promised you would not get angry. It is bad for you. If you do not listen quietly, we will tell you no more."

"Are you bullying me?" the Marquis enquired.

"I am trying to look after you for your own good," she replied.

The frown on the Marquis's forehead was replaced by a smile.

"Once again I have to thank you for saving my life," he said.

"It was Miss Saviya, M'Lord," Hobley went on, "who insisted I shouldn't join you here as I wished to do, but come backwards and forwards from the House."

"I thought that when you were better Hobley would be able to keep you informed as to what was happening," Saviya explained. "But I could not have set your collar-bone as he did, and I have to admit that the healing herbs and balms he has used on your wound were more efficacious than those we Gypsies have used for centuries."

"Mine are also based on country lore and, like the Gypsies, I'm aware that Nature knows best," Hobley said.

"I am well enough now to go and confront my cousin and expose his lies," the Marquis declared.

Both Saviya and Hobley gave a cry of disapproval.

"You will not move from here until we are sure you are strong enough," Saviya said. "Remember, he will not give in easily. He will try again to kill you."

There was so much distress in her tone that the Marquis replied: "I will be sensible. I will not attempt anything fool-hardy—that I promise!"

"You do not know how frightened we have been about you," Saviya murmured in a low voice, and the Marquis saw the sudden glisten of tears in her eyes.

"I will not do anything stupid," he promised, "but once I am strong I intend to teach my cousin a lesson he will not forget, and I have also to clear your name, Saviya."

"That is not important," she said. "The fact that I am a murderer is just what people would expect from a Gypsy."

"There's no-one in the House as would believe that of you, Miss Saviya," Hobley assured her.

She flashed him a smile.

"Thank you."

"Mr. Jethro is not making changes in the household?" the Marquis asked and his voice was sharp.

"Not yet, M'Lord," Hobley answered, "though he threatens to do so. But the Trustees have told him that they are not prepared as yet to presume Your Lordship's death. I think it is Captain Collington who has persuaded them that there may be a chance of your survival."

"Captain Collington would never believe that Miss Saviya was capable of killing me, and he knows of the other two attempts that Mr. Jethro has made on my life."

"I believe he has informed the Trustees of what happened in Berkeley Square and about the cobra, M'Lord."

As Hobley spoke, he drew his watch from his pocket.

"I'd best be getting back, M'Lord. I've to be careful in case Mr. Jethro is suspicious or gets someone to watch my movements."

"Then do not let him suspect you," the Marquis said.

"It's why I usually take a circuitous route to get here, M'Lord," Hobley replied, "but unfortunately it takes longer."

"I am sure the exercise is good for you!" the Marquis said with a smile.

"I'd be willing to climb mountains, M'Lord, to see you back on your feet again. We miss you up at the House."

"Thank you, Hobley. It will not be long now," the Marquis smiled.

Every time he came, Hobley brought with him everything which could be carried in a basket. Food, bottles of the Marquis's favourite wine, clean linen, lotions to heal the Marquis's back, and of course the toilet requisites His Lordship always used.

The Marquis's gold hair-brushes bearing his monogram under a diamond coronet looked strangely out of place in Saviya's caravan. Yet he had not imagined how comfortable such a small place could be.

Because he was so tall, his bed took up the whole of one side of it but there were hooks, shelves and small cupboards on all the walls, and things were stored away ingeniously in a manner which never ceased to amaze him.

The walls were painted with skilful artistry and in gay colours depicting flowers, birds, and butterflies.

The work was, however, more Russian than English, and Saviya told him that the exterior of the caravan was decorated in the same manner.

There were two windows through which, unfortunately, little light could percolate, because the caravan was draped with greenery so that it would not be seen.

But sunlight came through the open door, and at night the Marquis could see shafts of silver moonlight, which somehow reminded him of Saviya's dancing, penetrating through the thick branches of the trees.

Since he had regained consciousness, Saviya did not stay with him at night but disappeared.

He imagined she went back to her family or perhaps slept in the wood, but she was not very communicative on the subject and he did not press her.

After she had given him supper and they talked for a little while, she would merely say softly:

"It is time you went to sleep."

He would kiss her hand then she would leave him alone with his thoughts. At first he was usually so tired that he fell into a deep slumber and did not awake until the following morning, when she brought him breakfast.

Hobley washed, shaved and attended to him two or three times a day. Sometimes, if Mr. Jethro was not at the house, he would remain in the vicinity without returning home, but on other occasions he would slip in for an hour in the morning, again at luncheon time, and back again in the evening.

It was for the Marquis an unusual, strange mode of existence and yet he knew he had never been happier.

He did not feel restless and was not in the least bored.

Sometimes he would lie for a long time without speaking, watching Saviya's face as she sat in the doorway of the caravan.

He thought that her beauty was like some exquisite, exotic flower that every day unfolded more of its petals to reveal a hidden loveliness which grew more and more entrancing.

The Marquis had been in the caravan for over two weeks, when one afternoon after Hobley had returned to the house he said to Saviya:

"Soon I shall be strong enough to confront Jethro, and then you will be unable to stop me."

"You are very much better," Saviya said with a smile.

"Hobley is delighted with my collar-bone, the bandages come off tomorrow and I have very little pain in my back."

"The wound is healing quickly because you were so well," Saviya murmured, "an unhealthy man would have taken much longer."

"Before I leave this idyllic existence," the Marquis said, "we have to talk about each other, Saviya."

She stiffened and the expression on her face changed.

"You have not yet told me why on the morning that you saved my life you were leaving."

She hesitated and looked away from him.

"I told you how much I wanted you," the Marquis said. "How could you leave me, Saviya, knowing it might have been impossible for me ever to find you again?"

"It would not have been right for me to stay with you," she answered.

"Right for whom?" the Marquis asked almost angrily. "I thought you understood that I cannot live without you, Saviya. I knew it then, but now there is no doubt in my mind that we are in fact a part of each other. How can you deny anything that is so perfect; so utterly and completely wonderful?"

She looked away from him and he saw that she was trembling.

"Come here, Saviya!" he said, "I want you."

He thought she would refuse him but, almost like a child who obeys the voice of authority, she moved from her seat near the door to kneel at his bedside.

"Look at me, Saviya!"

She raised her face to his and the Marquis saw that her eyes were very wide and a little afraid.

"I love you!" he said. "Do you not understand, my darling, how much I love you?"

"I love you too!" Saviya answered, "but because you are so important . . . of such consequence in the . . . Social World . . . an association with a Gypsy will shock and perhaps disgust your friends."

"If it does, then they are not my friends," the Marquis said, "and besides does anything matter but ourselves? We do not want the gay life in London, Saviya. We can stay here at Ruckley or go abroad for part of the year. I have a yacht that will carry us along the coast of France to anywhere that you fancy. To me it will not matter where as long as we are together."

She drew a deep breath and he knew that she was deeply moved. Then she said on a sudden note of despair:

"You do not understand!"

"What do I not understand?" he asked gently.

"That you cannot set aside the prejudices, the beliefs, the hatreds of centuries," she answered. "We are, as you say, two people who love each other, but there is a great gulf between us and nothing you can say or do can bridge it."

"That is ridiculous!" the Marquis said sharply. "There is one thing that can bridge it, Saviya, one thing which is stronger than any of the things you have mentioned."

"What is that?" she asked wonderingly.

"Love!" he replied.

As the Marquis spoke he put out his arms and pulled her close against him.

He was sitting up against his pillows and she did not resist him. Her head fell back against his shoulder, and now she was half-sitting, half-lying on the bed.

"Could anything in the world be more important than this?" he asked and then his lips were on hers.

He kissed her fiercely and with a passion which he had been too weak to feel for the past two weeks, but he knew as his mouth took possession of hers that his desire was like a fiery flame burning through his whole body.

Yet at the same time he worshipped with what was almost a reverence the gentleness and sweetness of her.

"I love you!" he said. "Believe me when I tell you, Saviya, there is nothing else in my life except my love for you."

He kissed her again until she trembled and quivered in his arms and then he asked:

"Shall we go away together now and forget that I have any other existence except that I belong to you? Let Jethro be Marquis of

Ruckley and own the Estate and everything else. All I want is you and your love."

Saviya put her arms around his neck and now as her lips responded to his he could feel her heart beating against his breast.

Then, when it seemed they had reached the very peak of ecstasy and human nature must break under the strain, very gently Saviya drew herself from his arms.

"I love you," she whispered, "but you must still rest."

The Marquis protested but she put her finger-tips against his lips.

"Rest," she said. "You are tired, and this is not a moment to make decisions."

"Tell me one thing," the Marquis said, "that you love me as I love you. Tell me, Saviya! I have to hear it as well as know it when I touch you."

"I love you!" she whispered.

Yet there was somehow almost a note of despair in her voice.

CHAPTER SIX

"I'll be going now, M'Lord if there's nothing else Your Lordship requires?" Hobley said.

The Marquis looked up at his Valet from where he was sitting outside the caravan in the shade of the trees.

"Nothing, thank you, Hobley," he said, "but do not forget to ascertain if Colonel Spencer, the Chief Constable, will be at home tomorrow."

"I'll do that, M'Lord."

"Without arousing suspicion," the Marquis admonished. "I do not want anyone to be aware that I am alive until I confront Mr. Jethro."

"I've got it quite clear in my mind, M'Lord," Hobley said with just a touch of rebuke in his voice that the Marquis had thought it necessary to repeat himself.

"Then good-bye, Hobley, and thank you."

"Good-day, M'Lord."

Picking up the empty basket in which he had brought food from the house, Hobley moved between the trees and almost immediately was lost to sight.

It was certainly, the Marquis thought, a perfect place for concealment.

The caravan, with its wooden sides painted in gay colours, was completely hidden by trailing-ivy, shrubs and long strands of convolvulus so that it blended in with the branches of the trees and was, as Saviya had told him, almost invisible.

The trees themselves were very thick in this part of the wood. The Marquis wondered if he had ever actually been there before, and decided if he had, he did not remember it.

It was now three weeks since he had been thrown from his horse and stabbed by Jethro's men.

His wound had healed, his collar-bone had knit and he was in fact, as he had protested for some days now, in perfect health.

At the same time his brave words a week earlier that he wished to rise from his bed and confront his cousin had proved too optimistic.

He had no idea how weak he was until when, for the first time, he was on his feet again and could step from the caravan into the wood.

"I am ashamed of being such a weakling," he said to Saviya.

"You ran a very high fever and you also lost a lot of blood."

"I still expected to feel more like a man than a child," the Marquis averred.

"You must be strong to face what lies ahead," Saviya said in a low voice, and the Marquis knew she was still afraid.

"I expect you to give me courage," he said, "and not go on molly-coddling me as you and Hobley have been doing these past weeks."

Nevertheless, after his first sortie into the open air, the Marquis found he was glad to creep back into bed to fall asleep as soon as his head touched the pillow.

Yet every day he had grown stronger and could do more.

Saviya took him for walks through the woods, and he learnt much that he had never known before about the birds and the animals they saw and also the flowers.

She told him strange legends that were connected with Gypsy lore.

About the squirrels—the *romen morga,* or Gypsy Cats, who are a lucky mascot and particularly effective in the realms of love.

"But the weasel brings ill-luck," Saviya said. "If by chance a Gypsy should kill a weasel the whole tribe will be unfortunate for a long time."

"Superstition about the weasel is very ancient," the Marquis remarked. "It existed in Ancient Greece."

Saviya described how the Gypsies in the Balkans captured young bear-cubs and trained them so that they could dance to amuse the peasants in the villages.

She related that there were groups of Gypsies who were hunters, and who, apart from their skill, had a deep knowledge of the magic rites associated with hunting.

"The Balkan Gypsies," she went on, "will never allow a woman in any circumstances to go near the hunters before they depart in search of game."

One thing Saviya told the Marquis fascinated him: it was the Gypsies who invented lures for line-fishing.

"They were the first to make artificial baits," she said, "such as little wooden fish decorated with tufts of coloured feathers, in the middle of which hooks are hidden."

"I had no idea of that!" the Marquis exclaimed.

"And my father told me it was the Gypsies in Britain," Saviya went on, "who invented the artificial fly for trout fishing."

She looked at him from under her eye-lashes and said with a smile:

"You will doubtless think it un-sporting, but they know how to make magical bait!"

"How do they do that?" the Marquis enquired.

"They are generally made with the gums of resinous plants whose attraction for fish was known centuries ago in Persia," she replied. "But there is another way of coating stones with sweet-smelling oils."

Most of all the Marquis wanted to learn about the Gypsies' proficiency with horses.

"We never say, 'I hope you will live happily,'" Saviya told him, "but, 'May your horses live long!'"

"All Nomads have revered the horse," the Marquis remarked. "The Great Khan of the Mongols had a postal service of three hundred horses."

"Gypsies are strictly forbidden to eat horseflesh," Saviya went on, "as they believe it will send them mad. The Gypsy tribe of Zyghes saddle the horse of a dead man for three days after he is buried and lead it to the Grave."

"What happens then?" the Marquis enquired.

"The man who leads the horse calls the owner three times by name and asks him to dine."

"I believe the Gypsies excel in being able to pass off an old horse at a Fair by making him appear young and spritely," the Marquis remarked with a twinkle in his eyes.

Saviya laughed.

"That is true, and among some tribes there is a great deal of magic connected with the trading in horses."

"And love?" the Marquis questioned. "Is magic necessary to love?"

"Many Gypsies think so," Saviya answered, "but to me love . . . is magic."

"And to me, my darling," the Marquis told her.

It seemed to the Marquis as they walked together or sat outside the caravan that Saviya's knowledge was inexhaustible, and every moment they were together he found her more and more fascinating.

The food she cooked for him, even though Hobley brought most of it from the House, was different from anything he had tasted before. Berries, mushrooms, herbs, nettles, and wild vegetables were all part of the soups and stews she made over a fire in the pot that was supported from a tripod of sticks.

"Why does what you cook taste far more delicious than the food prepared by my extremely expensive and renowned Chef?" the Marquis enquired.

"I think one reason is that the herbs which I add to the meat or the chickens that Hobley brings, are fresh," Saviya replied. "Everything you have eaten today I picked this morning."

"It certainly tastes different," the Marquis said appreciatively.

"The Gypsies use few spices and very little salt," Saviya told him. "In fact the only condiment we like is wild garlic."

Sometimes the Marquis felt he was almost like a child asking for "another story." He found an inexpressible delight not only to listen to what Saviya told him, but also to watch her as she talked.

'It is not only her beauty,' he thought.

But it was impossible not to realise that because she was in love she was more beautiful than she had ever been.

Also the strength of her character and her personality shone like a spiritual light and made him feel at times that there was an aura about her that was not of this world.

In the evening when the Marquis had eaten the supper she had prepared for him and Hobley, having got him ready for bed, had gone home, Saviya would sit beside him and they would look through the open door of the caravan into the mystery of the wood outside.

There would be the rustle of the leaves in the evening breeze; the hoot of an owl; the soft scuffle of some animal through the undergrowth. Otherwise there was an indescribable peace.

"You make me very happy," the Marquis said one evening in his deep voice.

"Do I really?" Saviya asked.

"I have never before known real happiness," the Marquis answered.

He raised her hands to his lips and knew as his mouth touched her skin she quivered with the sudden ecstasy.

"I thought what I wanted in life was to be amused," he went on, "to listen to witty, bright conversation; to be made to laugh; to attend the parties given by my friends. But now I want only to be alone with you."

"Perhaps if we were together for too long, you would be . . . bored," she suggested, a little catch in her breath.

"You know that is not true!" the Marquis replied. "Always before, when I have been with a woman and have not actually been feeling passionate about her, I have been restless."

He kissed Saviya's hands again before he said:

"I think too I have been afraid of being alone."

"And now?"

"I feel," the Marquis replied, "as if a whole new world was opening before me; a world of discovery, not only of people, places and things, but of myself and you."

Saviya turned sideways to lay her head against his shoulder.

"You are my world," she whispered.

Then the Marquis had put his arms around her and held her close.

He knew now, sitting outside the caravan, that Saviya was worried. He had grown to know only too well without words what she was feeling and especially when she was perturbed.

She was afraid for the morrow, and what might happen when he confronted Jethro and threw him out of the House.

The Marquis on the other hand was filled with a sense of excitement. He knew that something fierce and primitive within him wished to do battle with his cousin and punish him for the attempts he had made on his life.

"Why are you worrying, my darling?" he asked Saviya.

She moved from the stool on which she had been sitting to come and kneel beside his chair.

"I cannot help it," she answered.

"Are you being clairvoyant, or merely human in that you are apprehensive?"

She smiled a little forlornly.

"You know that because I love you so deeply I can no longer see the future where you are concerned, but I can feel that you are in . . . danger. Otherwise my love blinds me and I am no longer a witch, but a . . . woman!"

The Marquis laughed.

"Do not sound so tragic about it," he begged, "that is what I want you to be—a woman! My woman! Now and for all time!"

He rose from the chair as he spoke and drew Saviya to her feet to put his arms around her. Tipping back her head, he looked down into her dark, troubled eyes.

"Trust me," he said, "I know what is best for both of us."

Then he kissed her, and they could not think of anything but the rapture which consumed them both and transported them into a world where there was no treachery, no fear, but only love.

Nevertheless, that night before the Marquis went to bed he held Saviya close to him and knew that she was trembling in his arms, but not because she was afraid.

"This is our last night here together," he said slowly. "But after tomorrow we shall never be apart from each other. As soon as I have rid my House of my disreputable cousin and set my affairs in order, we are going away in my yacht."

Saviya gave a little murmur and hid her face against his shoulder.

"We are going away for the rest of the summer," the Marquis said, "and by the time we come back, all the talk, excitement and gossip about us will be over, and some far more amusing scandal will have taken its place!"

He stroked Saviya's head with a gentle hand, feeling her hair like silk beneath his fingers.

"Whatever people say, they will say it behind our backs," he went on, "and why should that worry us? We will cross the Channel and move slowly along the coast of France. I am going to take you to Spain, Saviya."

His arms tightened around her for a moment and he said:

"Anywhere we go together will be like Paradise, but I want to show you the golden beaches and the magnificent Palaces."

Saviya made no answer but the Marquis knew she was listening.

"I have friends in Spain," he said, "who will welcome you because you are beautiful."

"They will think it strange that you are consorting with a Gypsy," Saviya said in a low voice. "The Spanish Gitanos are very poor. They are treated with contempt and have been persecuted by every succeeding Monarch."

"You have been to Spain?" the Marquis asked.

Saviya shook her head.

"Then it will be somewhere new that we can explore together."

The Marquis felt that Saviya was still uncertain, and he said gently:

"We are starting a new life together, Saviya. The prejudices of the old must not encroach on or overshadow our future."

She slipped her arms round his neck and drew his head down to hers.

"I love you!" she whispered. "I love you so desperately! You know that all I want is your happiness?"

"Which is to be with you," the Marquis replied. "There are so many things for us to do. I want to take you to Greece, to the Islands of the Mediterranean. But what does it matter where we go? You hold my whole happiness in your little hands."

Then he was kissing her again, kissing her until she could no longer think, only feel that she was a part of him and that there was no gulf between them.

The Marquis would have kept her with him much longer, but Saviya insisted that he must rest because of what he had to do the following day. Finally he gave in to her insistence, climbed into the small caravan and went to bed.

He slept peacefully without dreaming, but with a sense of happiness which lingered with him when he awoke.

Saviya had already lit the fire, before Hobley arrived with fresh eggs, newly baked bread and a pat of golden butter from the Marquis's own dairy.

He helped the Marquis to dress while Saviya cooked the eggs and brewed the coffee.

As the Marquis came down the steps of the caravan he saw there was a faint flush on her cheeks from the heat of the fire. In her pretty Gypsy clothes, she looked like the heroine of a theatrical melodrama and far too glamorous to be practical.

Yet the eggs were cooked perfectly and, because she had added a few special herbs to the dish, the Marquis thought it tasted better than any breakfast he had ever eaten at Ruckley House.

"Tell me, Hobley," he said as Saviya poured him a second cup of coffee, "has Mr. Jethro any plans for this morning?"

"I ascertained, M'Lord, that he is rising late," Hobley replied.

"Was he drinking deep last night?" the Marquis enquired.

"He was, M'Lord. Two of his friends left after midnight and a third was posting back to London the very moment that I myself left the House."

"Then Mr. Jethro will be alone?"

"Yes, M'Lord."

"That is what I wanted to know," the Marquis said. "You have ordered the horses?"

"They followed me here," Hobley said. "I left them about fifty yards away, M'Lord. I thought it best for the grooms not to see the caravan."

"Quite right," the Marquis approved. "And now, Hobley—be off with you! Collect the Chief Constable and bring him to the House. We will meet you there in an hour. Will that give you enough time?"

"Plenty of time, M'Lord."

Hobley turned to go and then said:

"Good luck, M'Lord! It will be a pleasure to have you back again."

"Thank you, Hobley."

The Valet disappeared and the Marquis resumed his breakfast, eating everything that Saviya offered him with a calmness which bespoke an iron control over his emotions.

"You will be careful?" she said suddenly, as if they had been talking instead of eating in silence.

"I will be careful for your sake," the Marquis replied. "But after all, what can Jethro do? He has announced to the whole world that I am dead and that you are my murderer . . . When I return very much alive with you beside me, it will be difficult for his lies to be treated with anything but contempt."

"All the same, he is like a snake or a rat," Saviya said. "I do not believe that he will give in so easily."

"I have decided," the Marquis told her, "to give him a choice. Either I will bring charges against him for attempted murder, or he leaves the country."

He paused and added:

"I would of course prefer the latter course. It would be unfortunate from the family point of view that there should be a scandal, or for anyone who bears our name to be accused of intent to murder."

"I wish you had taken my advice and asked Charles Collington to be with us this morning," Saviya sighed.

"I am not proud of the manner in which my cousin has behaved," the Marquis answered, "and the fewer people who know what has occurred, the better."

"I can understand that," Saviya murmured.

"There have been few scandals in our family over the centuries, very few. My father and my grand-father were respected here in the county and in the House of Lords where they each played their part. When I die, I hope that men will also speak well of me."

It was only as he said the words that the Marquis saw the expression in Saviya's face and knew perceptively that she was thinking that it would not add to his prestige to associate with her.

He put out his hand and caught her wrist as she turned away.

"Do not look like that, my darling," he said. "My private life is my own and no man shall interfere with it. In public we will be very circumspect."

Even as he spoke he realised how difficult it would be to have Saviya living at Ruckley House without everyone being aware of it.

He knew too that he could never insult her by keeping her as he had kept his previous mistresses, in a small house in the less fashionable part of Mayfair where he could visit her at his convenience.

There were, he knew, very many obstacles ahead, but for the moment he thought it best to take one fence at a time.

When he had disposed of Jethro, then he and Saviya could go abroad, and when they returned in the Autumn, they could face the other problems concerning their association.

He tried to draw Saviya to him but she slipped away.

"You have to get ready," she said. "We must be leaving in a few moments and you must think now of what you have to say to your cousin. But watch him! Please, My Lord, watch him carefully!"

There was a little sob in her voice, but the Marquis ignored it.

"I have said before, you must trust me," he replied. "I have been a soldier, Saviya, and I have learnt never to underestimate the enemy."

The horses that Hobley had brought for them were the best in the Marquis's stables and as he lifted Saviya into the saddle he said softly:

"I have always wanted to see you ride."

He knew by the sudden light in her eyes that she too was excited by the magnificence of the horse-flesh, and the fact that she held the reins in her hands.

The two grooms who had brought the horses were astonished at seeing the Marquis, and when he greeted them there was no mistaking that they were sincerely pleased to see that he was, contrary to what they had believed, alive!

They had their own horses, and as the Marquis mounted they followed him.

It was, Saviya thought, quite a cavalcade that set off through the woods to emerge finally into the Park.

Ruckley House was looking exquisite in the sunshine, its red bricks warm against the flashing diamond-paned windows, the curling chimney stacks silhouetted against the blue sky.

As Saviya raised her eyes to the gabled roofs of Ruckley House, she saw that the flag was flying.

The Marquis saw it too. His lips tightened and his eyes were angry.

It was only when the owner was in residence that the flag flew from the mast on top of the house. That Jethro had ordered it to be flown indicated that he already considered himself the new Marquis of Ruckley.

They moved across the Park, scattering the deer who were clustered under the trees, and moved without undue haste towards the court-yard in front of the main entrance.

'Never,' the Marquis thought, 'has my house looked more beautiful.'

The lilacs had come into bloom since he had last seen it, purple and white; their blossoms as lovely as the showers of golden laburnum and the pink and white petals of the almond trees.

The daffodils were over, but now the rhododendrons were crimson, pink and purple beside the sweet-smelling yellow azaleas.

'It is worth fighting for,' the Marquis thought to himself.

He knew he would struggle with every breath in his body to prevent Jethro and his dissolute, drunken friends from ruining the peace and beauty that was Ruckley.

Saviya was looking over her shoulder as they drew their horses to a standstill outside the front door.

"There is no sign of Hobley," she said. "We must wait for him."

"I am waiting for no-one," the Marquis replied, and there was a note in his voice which told her he was very angry.

It was as if seeing the house again had brought home to him all too forcefully what he might have lost. Now the calmness with which he had started the day had changed to a deep fury.

He dismounted, and lifted Saviya to the ground.

She wanted to beg him to wait a little longer for the Chief Constable. But knowing that nothing she could say would make any difference, she moved silently beside the Marquis as he strode up the steps towards the front door.

It was opened immediately and, while the footmen in their livery stared in astonishment, Bush gave an exclamation of joy.

"Your Lordship! You are alive!"

"Very much alive!" the Marquis replied.

"We were all sure, quite sure, M'Lord, that you could not have died as they said, but we were afraid, sore afraid when you did not return."

"I am back," the Marquis said. "Where is Mr. Jethro?"

"In the Salon, M'Lord. He has just finished breakfast."

The Marquis strode across the Hall and Saviya followed him.

A footman hurried to open the door of the Salon.

Jethro was standing at the far end of the room in front of the fireplace and the expression on his face made Saviya tremble.

He looked exactly as she had seen him the first time, when she had read the Marquis's fortune and known that he was in danger.

Dark-haired, with a long nose, Jethro Ruck could have been good-looking had it not been for his dissolute way of life and an expression on his face which was so shifty, so sinister, that it made people instinctively shrink from contact with him.

His eyes, under heavy eyebrows, were too close together, but it was his mouth, twisted and cynical and perpetually sneering which made him appear so intolerable.

"So you have returned!" he said in a harsh voice before the Marquis could speak. "I saw you coming across the Park and I am therefore ready to welcome you, dear cousin."

The Marquis advanced further into the room.

"How dare you behave in such a manner!" he said slowly his voice completely under control. "Three times you have tried to kill me, Jethro, and three times you have failed. Now I have had enough!"

"You were born under a lucky star," Jethro Ruck replied and somehow he made it an insult. "Any other man would have died as you should have done by the accidents I contrived, but you have survived."

"Yes, I have survived," the Marquis said, "and now we will have no more of them."

"So you think to prevent me inheriting?" Jethro Ruck asked. "But I am not defeated, Cousin Fabius—not yet!"

"I am afraid your plots, ingenious though they may be," the Marquis said scathingly, "have become too insupportable for me to tolerate them any longer. I therefore intend, Jethro, to give you an ultimatum."

His cousin laughed and it was an unpleasant sound.

"And what are you suggesting?" he jeered. "That you hang me from a gibbet or incarcerate me in the dungeons?"

"Neither," the Marquis said. "You will either stand trial for attempted murder and perjury, or you will go into self-imposed exile on the Continent. I will support you generously, Jethro, so long as you never again set foot in England."

Again Jethro Ruck laughed.

"Well thought out, Fabius!" he said, "a typical 'gentleman's compromise.' You hope I will choose the latter course because it will involve no scandal for the family."

"For once we are in agreement," the Marquis said.

"And do you really think," Jethro Ruck asked, and now his voice was smooth and silky and all the more sinister, "that I intend to go abroad and leave you in possession here with your Gypsy mistress?"

The Marquis stiffened.

"You will leave Saviya's name out of our discussions, Jethro," he said sharply. "You have defamed her enough already."

"You really imagine that I, a Ruck, could defame a Gypsy?"

"I have already said," the Marquis remarked, "we will not discuss Saviya. Let us concern ourselves with your movements."

Saviya was watching Jethro Ruck, and she realised that as he stood almost as if he was at attention facing the Marquis, with his hands behind his back, he had a kind of courage that was a part of his heritage.

She had known that he would not bow to circumstances; that he would not acknowledge defeat; that he would fight, even as the Marquis would fight, to the last ditch.

Vile and wicked though Jethro might be, there was good blood in his veins and whatever happened, he was no coward.

"I want your answer," the Marquis insisted.

Now there was steel in his tone as if he was coming to the end of his patience.

"I will give you my answer," Jethro Ruck replied, "and I will give it very clearly, Cousin Fabius, so that there will be no mistake. You have always despised me. You have always looked down at me, you have always believed I was of little consequence, but now, at last, I have the whip hand!"

The Marquis merely raised his eye-brows to show he did not understand what his cousin was saying, and Jethro Ruck went on:

"You are going to die, Fabius, as I have meant you to do all along. It is better that it should be at this moment, because it will appear, at least to the world, as honourable and in the family tradition."

"I do not know what you are talking about," the Marquis said. "Stop this nonsense and answer my question. Will you face a trial or go abroad?"

"I will do neither!" Jethro Ruck retorted. "I stay here and enjoy myself as the sixth Marquis of Ruckley."

As he spoke, he drew his hands from behind his back and Saviya gave a little gasp of horror.

Jethro Ruck held two pistols and each was pointing at the Marquis's chest.

"If you kill me," the Marquis said contemptuously, "you will be hanged for murder."

"On the contrary," Jethro Ruck replied, "I shall have killed you in self-defence."

He gave a little chuckle.

"You have played right into my hands, dear Fabius. The servants saw you arrive and they will all be prepared to swear that you were in a vengeful mood as you strode up the steps and crossed the Hall. They will have heard us talking, and what could be more understandable than that you should lose your temper at my impertinence and shoot me down with your own dueling-pistol?"

There was so much venom in his voice that Saviya felt as if she could not move and that her breath was constricted in her throat.

She saw now how mad they had been to come to the house without weapons; without any defence against a man more deadly than a cobra; more vengeful than a cornered rat.

"You are thinking," Jethro Ruck said jeeringly, "that your Gypsy strumpet might give evidence against me. Do not blind yourself to the truth. No-one would take the word of a Gypsy against that of the sixth Marquis of Ruckley!"

There was a note of triumph in his tone before he went on:

"You have threatened me, Fabius. No-one can deny that. Unfortunately you have not provided yourself with the means to make your threat effective. My plan, therefore, is quite clear."

He smiled the smile of a man who holds all the trump cards.

"As I will tell the Magistrates, you threatened me, Fabius and, when I would not agree to your preposterous suggestions, you attempted to kill me. This pistol, which has been fired, will be found in your hand. To protect myself, I returned your fire and, being of course a better shot than you, I am the victor!"

There was something horrible and gloating in the way Jethro Ruck spoke.

Then as he raised the pistol in his right hand slowly to bring it down at the Marquis, there was a sudden movement!

Even as his finger tightened on the trigger, a flash of steel shot through the air and entered his throat.

It was so quick that the Marquis could hardly understand what had happened.

Jethro Ruck staggered and then fell backwards. As he did so, there was a deafening report and the bullet from his pistol shattered the ceiling above their heads.

For a moment the Marquis stood shocked and unable to move. And before he could do so there was a voice behind him and footsteps crossing the room.

The Marquis turned his head.

"Colonel Spencer!" he ejaculated.

"I am glad to see you are unharmed, Fabius."

The Chief Constable was an elderly but distinguished figure, and his expression was one of gravity.

"You heard what was said?" the Marquis enquired.

"I was trying to make up my mind what I should do," Colonel Spencer replied. "I had the feeling that if I entered the room unexpectedly Jethro might have finished you off quicker than he intended."

"I threw the dagger which killed him," the Marquis said quickly, putting his hand as he spoke on Saviya's to prevent her from contradicting him.

"It was an act of self-defence," the Chief Constable said as if he understood, "and it is quite immaterial who handled the weapon in question."

"Thank you, Colonel," the Marquis said gratefully. "I would not have wished my—future wife to be involved in this unpleasantness."

As he spoke, he felt Saviya's fingers go rigid beneath his.

"I will congratulate you, Fabius, under more pleasant circumstances," the Chief Constable said. "At the moment I have my duty to perform."

"I understand," the Marquis said. "Do you wish me to send for the servants?"

The Chief Constable walked to Jethro Ruck's fallen body and looked down at him.

There was no doubt that he was dead. Blood was oozing from the wound and there was a stream of blood from between his thin lips.

Looking at the dagger, the Marquis knew that it had been a brilliant throw on Saviya's part. She had pierced Jethro's throat in exactly the most vulnerable spot, and with a force which he knew came from the flexibility of the muscles in her wrist.

"I am sorry your cousin's life should have ended like this," the

Chief Constable said quietly. "I have known you both since you were children, and as you grew up together you appeared to be close friends."

"We were," the Marquis answered, "until when we became men, Jethro was eaten up with jealousy and envy. He wanted so desperately to be in my shoes."

"Hobley has told me," the Chief Constable said, "of the other attempts he made on your life."

"Because you were my father's friend, Colonel," the Marquis said in a low voice, "can you arrange that there is as little scandal as possible?"

"I will do what I can," the Colonel promised. "As I was actually present at Jethro's death, my evidence will be sufficient for the Magistrates. It was a duel of honour and there will be few legal formalities."

"In a duel of honour it is customary for the survivor to go abroad for a few months, and that is what I intend to do," the Marquis answered.

"That is wise of you," the Colonel approved, "and now I suggest you leave everything in my hands, Fabius. As a very great friend of the Ruck family, I promise you that the real truth of what has happened between you and Jethro will never go beyond the four walls of this room."

"Thank you, Colonel," the Marquis said. "I knew I could rely on you, and that you of all people would understand."

He held out his hand and then as they shook hands the Chief Constable said:

"I want above all things, Fabius, to see you take your father's place in the County. I know that a young man who has played a brilliant part in the war needs the relaxation and amusements that only London can give him. But there is work to be done here."

His eyes were on the Marquis's face and he continued:

"With the new lands, which I hear have come into your possession, I hope that Ruckley House will see a great deal more of you in the future."

The Marquis knew that what the Chief Constable was saying to him had a far deeper meaning than appeared on the surface.

He was well aware that without mentioning Saviya she was uppermost in Colonel Spencer's mind.

The Marquis had recognised as Jethro staggered and died from the impact of the dagger that there was only one place for Saviya in his life—and that was as his wife.

She had not only saved his life for the third time, but she had killed a man in his defence.

As he thought of her he realised she was not at his side. He looked round the room, then thought that perhaps, to avoid looking at the dead body of Jethro, she had gone in search of The Reverend.

The Chief Constable had already moved towards the door, and as the Marquis followed him into the Hall he started to give instructions to Bush for the removal of Jethro Ruck's body.

The Marquis began to walk towards the Library. Then as he passed a footman, he said:

"Where is Miss Saviya?"

"She left the house, M'Lord."

The Marquis looked at the man in astonishment and then he strode across the Hall and out onto the steps.

The Chief Constable's carriage was outside and Hobley was talking to the Coachman.

The Valet came towards the Marquis with a question in his eyes.

"Where is Miss Saviya?" the Marquis asked for the second time.

"She came out a few moments ago, M'Lord, and took the horse on which I returned with Colonel Spencer, and rode towards the wood."

"Fetch me a horse from the stables," the Marquis said sharply to a footman who was standing behind him.

The man ran off and Hobley looking up at his master found it impossible to ask the questions which hovered on his lips.

He knew that something had gravely perturbed the Marquis and, with an anxious expression on his face, he went into the house to find out for himself what had happened.

There was a few minutes' delay before a groom appeared from the stables riding the Marquis's favourite black stallion.

He jumped down and almost before he reached the ground, the Marquis had swung himself into the saddle.

Without a word he galloped off across the Park towards the woods.

As he went he was afraid with a fear that was almost like an iron hand clutching at his heart.

CHAPTER SEVEN

The Marquis urged his horse on until he reached the woods, wondering how he could find Saviya's tribe and where they were likely to be.

He remembered she had told him that they had moved, after Jethro began searching for her.

While the Marquis realised that it was impossible to hide fifty people for long, the woods were large enough for him to have to spend several days in searching for them unless he was exceptionally lucky.

He had the inescapable feeling that Saviya had always meant to leave him when he was well enough.

He knew she was deeply conscious of the differences of rank between them, and she was far too intelligent not to realise, as he did, the unavoidable implications were he to set up a lasting liaison with a Gypsy.

Saviya was so sensitive, and they were so closely attuned to each other, that the Marquis knew she was well aware of his anxiety concerning the problems which would arise from their living together. And marriage would arouse even greater difficulties, not only from his point of view, but from Saviya's.

He knew she had not spoken idly when she had said that the most terrible thing that could happen to a Gypsy was to be exiled from the tribe.

Because their society was so close-knit and they kept themselves apart from other people, exile was to them as bad if not worse than excommunication to a Roman Catholic.

Marriage between a Gypsy and a non-Gypsy was universally disapproved by all the tribes that were pure Romany.

Saviya had told the Marquis once that, even though in some exceptional instances a marriage might not bring exclusion from the tribe, the outlaw whether it was a man or woman no longer had the right to the name of Gypsy.

"Sometimes," she went on, "this ostracism extends to the whole family and lineage of the guilty party."

"That sounds to me unfair—cruel!" the Marquis exclaimed.

"It is worse than death!" Saviya had said quietly.

Remembering this conversation now, the Marquis was certain that the fact that he had told the Chief Constable that Saviya was to be his wife had driven her away from him.

"I love you!" he had said to Saviya one evening when she had been sitting in the caravan at the door, and he had been watching her from the bed.

He saw the sudden light in her eyes which illuminated her face and made her almost dazzlingly beautiful.

Then he had asked:

"What is love, Saviya? For I have never known it until now."

She had looked away from him and he knew by the sudden concentration in her face that she was trying to find a serious and sensible answer to his question.

"I think that love," she said after a moment, "is when someone else matters so completely that one no longer has even a thought of self. One almost ceases to exist because only in the other is one alive."

She turned her face towards the Marquis and her eyes shone like stars as she finished:

"One lives for him and one would . . . die for him."

"Is that how you feel about me?" the Marquis asked.

She had risen then to come and kneel beside his bed.

"You know it is. All I want is for you to be happy."

"I am happy as long as you are with me."

He had held her close and yet with a new perception he knew that she was not entirely his.

There was some barrier between them; some reserve that he had felt and not understood. Yet now, he thought with a sense of despair, he knew what it was.

'How can I convince her,' he asked himself, 'that nothing is of importance except our love, except the need we have for each other?'

He remembered how in the past he had never believed that he could fall in love. He had not understood when Eurydice had told him that love was more important than rank.

She had given up being a Duchess for an American whose way

of life was entirely different from her own, and with whom she could in fact have little in common except love.

No! He had not understood.

He had even been inclined to laugh at anyone who could be swept off their feet to such an extent that they would alter their whole way of life—forget the past and all it implied for an emotion so intangible that one could not even explain it.

'I am not laughing now!' the Marquis told himself almost savagely.

He had to find Saviya, but he knew that the sands of time were running out.

If, as he suspected, the Gypsies were in the process of leaving, if they once moved away from the vicinity, how would he ever find her again?

They were wanderers and nomads. At the same time centuries of being persecuted had taught them how to evade detection; how to vanish into a labyrinth of woods and mountains, hills and valleys, so that it was almost impossible to find them.

The Marquis, riding as quickly as he could, guided his horse through the tree-trunks until he came to the place in the wood where he himself had been hidden for three weeks.

With a sudden pang of dismay he realised the caravan was no longer there.

Saviya's own special painted caravan, in which he had known a happiness that had never been his before, was not where he had left it that morning.

Then he told himself that if it had so recently been moved, there should be the marks of the wheels.

His eyes searched the ground but it was not easy. There was either moss on which no marks could be seen or low undergrowth through which the wheels of a cart could pass without leaving an impression.

Twisting and turning, straining his eyes for some clue which might lead him to Saviya, the Marquis had ridden for over half an hour before finally he came to an open space.

He knew immediately that this was where the camp must have been before Jethro had tried to kill him, and Saviya had saved his life. There were the remains of fires but they were only ashes.

It was not a camp-site that had just been vacated, but one on which the woodland flowers were already beginning to hide the fact that it had ever been used by human beings.

But here at last the Marquis had the clue! A wheel mark!

He could see that it would lead him deeper into the forest that stood on the south side of the Estate and was in parts almost impenetrable.

'That is exactly where the Gypsies would have gone if they wished to hide,' he told himself.

He found what appeared to be a bridle-path and knew it was just wide enough to allow a caravan to travel along it.

He followed it, all the time conscious that he must move quickly or Saviya might elude him forever.

He knew then with a pain that was both physical and mental that he could not lose her.

It was not only her beauty that attracted him. It was that she was in all truth the other part of himself.

He knew now why he had always felt lonely in his life and somehow apart from other people. He had not been a whole person—he had not been complete. It was Saviya who was the completion of himself as he was the completion of her.

'I love you!' he said in his heart. 'Oh, my darling, do you not understand how much I love you? How could you do this to me?'

He rode on feeling at times almost frantic as the wood bewildered him, and he felt as if instead of advancing he was going round in circles and coming back to the place from which he had first started.

Then suddenly—so suddenly it was almost a shock—he found them!

There were eight caravans, most of them far larger and more elaborate than Saviya's, and they were on the point, the Marquis knew, of moving off.

The horses were between the shafts, some of the Gypsies were already holding the reins in their hands, others were folding tents and stowing a number of objects away inside and beneath the caravans.

They were talking amongst themselves in their own language, until as the Marquis appeared there was a sudden silence.

He reined in his horse and a number of dark-skinned faces were turned towards him and suspicious black eyes regarded him questioningly.

They were an exceedingly good-looking collection of people, the Marquis appreciated, with their high cheek-bones, black eyes and dark hair. They were in fact more Russian-looking than any Gypsies he had seen in the past.

There were children with small, oval faces and large gazelle-like eyes, and several older women with red handkerchiefs over their heads and huge gold ear-rings dangling from their ears.

The Marquis moved his horse forward a little.

"I wish," he said, "to speak to your Voivode."

The man to whom he addressed his remark did not answer but merely pointed his hand to the far end of the clearing.

As the Marquis rode in the direction he saw a rather more elaborate caravan than the rest and standing in front of it, apparently unaware of his approach, was a tall man talking with Saviya.

The man saw him first and Saviya turned. The Marquis saw a sudden expression of radiant gladness on her face. Then it disappeared as if a cloud hid the sun.

The Marquis rode up to them and dismounted.

He found the Voivode was almost as tall as himself, and anyone would have known by his bearing and his clothes that he was a Chieftain.

His coat was blue and he wore very high boots. On his short jacket he had a large number of gold buttons and there was a heavy gold chain hung with pendants round his neck.

The Marquis had heard Saviya speak of the Voivode's staff called *bare esti robli rupui,* which was the last remaining relic of a King's sceptre.

It was made entirely of silver and the hilt, octagonal in shape, was adorned with a red tassel. The staff was engraved with the *Semno,* the authentic 'Sign' of the Gypsies comprising the five ritual figures.

The Marquis held out his hand.

"I am the Marquis of Ruckley and you, I think, are Saviya's father."

"I have been expecting you," the Voivode replied.

"And yet you were leaving?" the Marquis said sharply.

He looked at Saviya as he spoke and saw in her eyes raised to his a look of pleading as if she wanted him to understand why she had run away from him.

"What do you want with us?" the Voivode asked. "We are grateful for the hospitality of your woods. Now it is time for us to go."

"I have come," the Marquis said quietly, "to ask your permission to take your daughter, Saviya, as my wife."

"You would marry her?"

There was no surprise in the Voivode's voice. He merely looked at the Marquis as if he was seeking deep into his character and personality to find the answer to his question.

He had a dignity about him which made it not an impertinent act, but simply the summing up of one man by another without a question of class or caste.

"No!" Saviya said before her father could speak. "No, it is not . . . possible!"

Her voice was passionate with intensity.

Then sharply, and in a voice of authority, the Voivode spoke to her in Romany.

The Marquis could not understand the words but the sense was very obvious.

He was rebuking her, telling her it was not her place to speak. Saviya bent her head.

"I am sorry, father," she said in English.

"We will discuss this," the Voivode said to the Marquis, "and Saviya, I wish you to hear what I have to say."

He stepped past the Marquis as he spoke to address the tribe.

He obviously told them they would not be leaving for a little while; for the Gypsy men, who had been watching with undisguised curiosity the Marquis's conversation with the Voivode, now turned away to unharness their horses.

The women began to re-kindle the fire in the centre of the clearing, which was practically extinguished.

The Voivode led the way to his caravan and Saviya brought a chair which she set down beside the steps.

The Voivode seated himself on the steps and Saviya sank down on the grass at his feet.

The Marquis tried to meet her eyes; to re-assure her; to tell her by a look if not by words not to be afraid.

But her head was still bowed after her father's rebuke and her eyes were on the grass.

She looked very lovely but sadly forlorn, and the Marquis longed to put his arms around her and hold her close.

He knew she was unhappy. At the same time she had been unable to repress the sudden radiance in her eyes when she had first seen him riding towards them.

A Gypsy approached the Voivode and the Marquis was offered a glass of wine which he accepted.

It was red and a good quality. He supposed that the Gypsies must have brought it with them on their journey across Europe.

The horses were unharnessed and taken away from the caravan, and now that they were out of earshot of the other members of the tribe the Voivode said with a grave voice:

"You wish to marry Saviya?"

"I want her to be my wife," the Marquis replied.

He saw a little quiver go through Saviya as he spoke, but still she did not raise her head.

"This is what I knew was Saviya's destiny," the Voivode said slowly.

The Marquis looked at him in considerable surprise. Such a reply was far from what he had expected.

The Voivode was a handsome man of about fifty. His face was very thin, his cheek-bones prominent, but he must, the Marquis thought, have been exceedingly handsome in his youth. Even then he would have had an air of authority about him; a man born to lead, perhaps to rule.

"Saviya will have explained to you," the Voivode went on, "that the Kalderash are not only smiths but also have a knowledge of magic. It was this knowledge which guided me here."

"You mean," the Marquis asked, "that you knew by clairvoyance that Saviya would meet me and that we would fall in love with each other?"

"That is a simple way of putting it," the Voivode agreed.

Although his English was good he spoke with a very pronounced accent.

"Then I have your permission?" the Marquis insisted.

"There is something I have to say to you first," the Voivode said, "something which I intended to tell Saviya when she wished to marry."

Saviya raised her head. The Marquis saw there was a look of surprise in her face.

"You do not know anything about our race," the Voivode went on speaking to the Marquis, "but you must have learnt from Saviya that no Gypsy girl would ordinarily have been allowed to behave as she has behaved these past weeks; coming first to your house to read your books, and then being constantly in your company."

"I did not understand it, father," Saviya said.

"You were permitted such behaviour," the Voivode explained, "because I knew that this, Saviya, was your only chance of finding yourself a husband—otherwise you would have remained un-wed!"

Saviya was puzzled.

"But why?"

"Because I could not have sanctioned your marriage to any member of our tribe or to any Romany," the Voivode replied.

Saviya looked utterly bewildered. The Marquis with his eyes on the Voivode's face was listening intently.

"I have a story to tell you," the Voivode said.

It was obvious as he began to speak that he had a command of words which the Marquis would not have expected from a Gypsy, even a tribal Chief.

Perhaps it was his Hungarian blood which made him not only eloquent but able to speak with the culture of a man who had lived a very different life from the majority of Gypsies.

It was true also there was magic in the way he made the story seem so real.

Zindelo was the son of the Voivode of the Kalderash in Hungary, and their particular tribe was under the patronage of one of the great Hungarian nobles. Their music gave them a special prestige and they were widely respected.

They were rich; they were accepted as part of the community; and Zindelo was acknowledged one of the most attractive young men that could be found anywhere in the country.

Great ladies smiled on him, but he was exceedingly proud of his Romany blood and he would not seek love outside his tribe.

Nevertheless, at twenty-one he had not found any girl whom he wished to marry and had refused all suggestions from his father that he should settle down.

It was then the Hungarian nobleman, on whose ground they were encamped, was sent by the Tsar of Russia some dancers from St. Petersburg for his private theatre.

A great fête was arranged for their entertainment, and when they arrived Society from all over Hungary gathered to see them dance.

The majority of the dancers were from the Imperial Ballet, but the Tsar had included a number of Gypsy dancers and singers who were widely famed in Russia.

Among them was a young dancer called Tekla with whom young Zindelo fell in love the moment he saw her, and she with him.

They were married and she did not return to St. Petersburg. The tribe wandered around Hungary, Rumania and into Austria, for there was much that Zindelo, now the Voivode, wished to show his bride.

It was when they were in Germany and had suffered some minor attempts at persecution that Zindelo decided they should visit Britain.

They went to the coast and found a ship that was sailing for Aberdeen.

Some thirty of the tribe, mostly young and adventurous like Zindelo himself, decided they would like to visit Scotland and then trek south through England and back to the Continent.

It seemed a great adventure, but unfortunately the passage was very rough.

By this time Zindelo and Tekla had been married for nearly three years and a child born before they left Hungary had now reached the age of fifteen months.

Gypsy children are proverbially strong, but the baby Saviya sickened during the voyage, as did her mother.

The ship nearly foundered, and while Zindelo was exhilarated by the storm, he realised that his wife, never having been to sea before, was distraught not only by her own sea-sickness but with worry for her child.

By the time they reached Aberdeen, Tekla was in a state of collapse.

Highly-strung, her Russian blood made her more prone to melancholy and depression than the other women, and by the time they set foot on Scottish soil, he was desperately worried about his wife and his child.

The baby had refused to eat or drink during the whole of the voyage and was now emaciated and very weak.

Tekla was hysterical with anxiety and her own health had suffered to the point that she was running a fever.

They camped not far from the sea. The weather was cold but invigorating, and soon the other members of the tribe began to recover and take an interest in their surroundings.

There was plenty of wild game to be found on the moorland, and hot stews cooked over a peat fire soon had them laughing and singing again.

But Tekla grew worse and the baby weaker.

"I was sitting beside my tent one evening almost in despair," the Voivode recounted, "when one of the tribe came to tell me that a woman wished to speak with me.

"She was standing under the darkness of the trees outside the light thrown by the fire.

"When I reached her I saw that she was elderly with strong features.

"'There is something I wish to say to you,' she told me, 'but we must not be overheard.'

"We moved a little way into the shadow of the trees.

" 'What is it?' I enquired.

"I thought perhaps she wanted her fortune told. It is the usual reason for which women approach us Gypsies in whatever part of the world we travel.

" 'I have known Gypsies for many years,' she said. 'For all their faults they are kind to their children and good parents. I want you to take this child and bring her up as your own."

"I had had many strange requests made to me, but this was extraordinary.

" 'I am sorry,' I replied, 'we are Romanies. We do not want other people's children and we do not steal them, despite the stories that are told about us.'

" 'If you do not take this child,' the Scottish woman said, 'it will die!'

" 'Why? What is wrong with it?' I asked.

" 'There is someone who wishes to kill it!'

"I looked at her incredulously.

" 'It is the truth,' she said, seeing the disbelief in my eyes. 'This child belongs to a nobleman but the poor bairn's mother died in child-birth and her father has married again.'

"She spoke with such sincerity," the Voivode explained, "that I knew she was telling me the truth.

" 'And who wishes to kill the child?' I enquired.

" 'The Master re-married. She was determined to get him almost before my poor mistress was cold in her grave,' the Scottish woman said with venom in her voice. 'And now she herself has had a premature baby. It is a girl, and she is told she can have no more.'

" 'Is that such a tragedy?' I asked jokingly, 'the world is full of women as it is.'

" 'In Scotland,' came the reply, 'if there is no son, a daughter will inherit—the eldest daughter!'

"I began to see what the woman was trying to tell me.

" 'So you mean,' I enquired almost incredulously, 'your master's new wife intends to kill this child so that her own can be their heir?'

" 'She will kill her, make no mistake of that,' the Scotswoman replied. 'This evening I found her in the Nursery with a pillow in her hands. If I had not come in at that moment, she would have suffocated this poor wee girlee in her cot.'

" 'It is sad—very sad,' I commiserated, 'but I am afraid I can do nothing. If I were to take the child of a Gorgio, people would say it was stolen. Can you imagine the hue and cry there would be?'

" 'Please,' the woman pleaded with me. 'Please, save the bairn's life. I would not have brought her to you had not somebody said to me only yesterday that she is dark enough to be a Gypsy. Take her away with you. Who will notice one more baby in your camp?'

"She pulled the child's shawl away from its face as she spoke. I saw it was very small and had dark hair, thicker than was usual for a child of that age.

"I looked down at it, feeling sorry it must die, and knowing there was nothing I could do about it.

"Then I heard a sudden cry. It came from my tent.

"Turning, I ran away without a word, knowing it was my wife's voice that called me.

"She was sitting up in bed and she was half delirious. I caught her in my arms.

" 'What is the matter? What has upset you?' I asked.

" 'It was a . . . dream,' she cried. 'I dreamt that Saviya was . . . dead! Dead!'

"She seemed to scream the words, and holding her close I reached for a potion of soothing herbs that had been made for her earlier in the day by one of our women.

"She drank it and seemed immediately to grow a little quieter.

" 'It was only a foolish dream, Tekla,' I said. 'Go to sleep.'

" 'You will look after Saviya?' she begged.

" 'I will look after her, I promise. She is asleep. Even the noise you have made has not awakened her.'

"I put my wife down against the pillows, saw her eyes close, and then I looked in the basket on the other side of the caravan where my child was sleeping. She was dead!"

The Marquis saw Saviya had been unable to move while the Voivode was speaking. Her eyes were fixed on his face, and the Marquis felt as if every nerve in his own body was tense for fear he should miss a word of what was being related.

The Voivode went on to say how he picked up his baby daughter in an agony of grief, and as he had done so he wondered how he could tell his wife.

Already she was almost mentally unhinged by the dangers of the voyage and her anxiety over her child.

"I knew then," the Voivode went on, "that Fate had brought me the answer. I returned to the Scottish woman."

"You exchanged the babies!" the Marquis exclaimed.

"The woman changed their clothes," the Voivode replied, "and as she did so she kept repeating how little difference there was between the two children. Both were small and rather under-sized. Both had dark hair.

" 'I told you my bairn looked like a Gypsy,' she said, when I held the living child in my arms and my little dead daughter was in hers."

"Your wife did not note the difference?" the Marquis asked.

"She was very ill for a long time," the Voivode answered, "and because I thought it was wise we did not linger in Scotland, we set off south immediately."

He drew in his breath as if he remembered how anxious he was to leave Scotland.

"Saviya—the new Saviya—never left my arms, and no-one in the tribe had any idea that she was not the same baby that had crossed the sea with us.

"By the time we were back in Europe, I had almost forgotten myself that there had ever been another child, and that it had died because I had been foolish enough to take my tribe to Scotland instead of remaining in Europe."

"Then I am not your . . . daughter!" Saviya murmured, and there was a little throb in her voice as she said it.

"Not of my blood," the Voivode answered, "but you know that you have always held a part of my heart."

Saviya's face was very pale.

"I cannot . . . believe it!" she cried. "I cannot grasp the fact that I am not a . . . Romany."

"Now you understand," the Voivode told her, "why I could never have allowed you to marry into the tribe. Our blood must remain pure, and even while to save my wife's sanity and your life I adopted you, it would have been against my every instinct to allow you, a Gorgio, to marry one of us."

"You still feel that about . . . me after all these . . . years I have been with . . . you?" Saviya asked.

"You know that it is the code by which we live," the Voivode said simply.

The Marquis did not speak. He wanted to reassure Saviya, but at the same time he knew what a shock this had been to her, and at the moment he was an outsider.

She must grapple alone with something which concerned only herself, because it involved her whole past.

Now the Voivode in a different tone of voice, as if he now set aside past events, said:

"You wish to marry Saviya. Because I cannot insult my tribe by letting them know they have been deceived, I will ask you to marry her according to Gypsy law, and to make this possible I will, if you agree, make you my brother by the exchange of blood."

"I have heard of such a ceremony," the Marquis replied.

"It is not often performed and not universally acceptable," the Voivode said. "But on this occasion, because I must not lose the respect and authority that is mine by right, I shall present you to the tribe. Afterwards you will be married."

He glanced at Saviya with a little smile on his lips before he added:

"Before a wedding there are of course preparations to be made. Go now, My Lord, and return a little later in the day."

"I know it is traditional," the Marquis said slowly, "for the bridegroom not only to give a gift of money to the parents of the bride, but also to contribute to the feast that follows the ceremony. I trust that you will allow me to do both?"

"It is allowed!" the Voivode said with an inclination of his head.

"Then may I suggest that two or three of your tribe wait at the edge of the wood. This will make it possible for my servants to find you," the Marquis said. "And may I also ask that at the time appointed for my return I have an escort. I had great difficulty in finding you."

"It shall be done," the Voivode agreed. "And now while I speak to my people, you may have two minutes speech with Saviya. But not more. It offends our custom!"

He walked away as he spoke and Saviya rose to her feet.

"I cannot . . . believe what my . . . Father has told us," she said miserably. "I am a Gypsy! I have always been a Gypsy!"

"I think we both know that he was speaking the truth," the Marquis said in his deep voice.

He looked down at her white, unhappy face and said very gently:

"Do not be afraid, my darling. Everything will work out for the best! The only thing that really matters is that we have each other."

"Do you still want . . . me?" she whispered with a little catch in her throat.

"Need you really ask me that question?" the Marquis enquired.

She looked into his eyes. It seemed for a moment as though they were close against each other and he held her in his arms.

"I love you!" he said softly. "Remember nothing else except that I love you and tonight you will be my wife."

He raised her hands to his lips, then walked to where his horse was being held by a Gypsy boy. He mounted it.

As he rode away he heard the Voivode calling his people round him, and knew that he was going to tell them that tonight Saviya would marry a Gorgio.

It was nearly six o'clock when the Marquis drove across the Park in his Phaeton.

The Gypsies had shown him a quick way from the camp to where the cart-track made by the Foresters ran into the wood.

The Marquis was dressed as elegantly as if he was about to attend a Reception at Carlton House.

His cravat, intricately tied by Hobley, was snowy white against his chin and a jewelled fob hung from his waist-coat over pantaloons the colour of pale champagne.

He had been extremely busy since he had left the camp in the morning, writing numerous notes which he had dispatched to London by grooms.

One of them was to Charles Collington to tell him that Jethro was dead.

He was well aware that his friend Charles must have been desperately perturbed all the time he had been missing, and he knew that if anyone would be glad to think Jethro no longer threatened him it would be Charles.

There were several other letters the Marquis found urgent. Then he went to the Library to find The Reverend and have a long conversation with him.

He sent to the Gypsy camp an enormous amount of food and several cases of champagne, although he could not help thinking that the Gypsies would prefer the rich red wine to which they were accustomed.

It was with a feeling of almost indescribable happiness that the Marquis drove towards the woods.

He was no longer overshadowed by the problems that lay ahead. He was no longer apprehensive about what the future might hold. All he could think of was Saviya: her beauty, her softness, her sweetness, and her love.

He knew that while many women had loved him in their own way, what they had felt for him had never been the same as the mystical wonder that he saw in Saviya's eyes, or felt in the trembling of her lips when he kissed her.

'I will make her happy!' he told himself.

Then as he reached the shadow of the trees he saw the Gypsies waiting for him.

They were two young men, dark-haired, eloquent-eyed, finely-built and as beautiful in their own way as any Greek god.

They were dressed in a very different manner from the nondescript clothing they were wearing when the Marquis had entered the camp that morning.

Now there were red sashes around their waists and round their heads. There were ear-rings hanging from their ears, and the jewelled hilts of long knives were gleaming in their waistbands.

They led the Marquis's Phaeton a little way into the wood and then invited him to alight.

He knew that they wished him to go the rest of the way on foot so that his groom sitting on the back of the Phaeton could take the horses home and would not therefore be a spectator of anything that was to happen.

The Marquis gave the order. The horses were turned and were driven back the way they had come.

Then, with a Gypsy on either side of him, he walked on through the trees to the camp.

There was a huge fire blazing in the centre of it, and the caravans were drawn round it in a circle, with the exception of Saviya's which stood a little apart from the rest.

This the Marquis saw with a quick glance was decorated with flowers and greenery.

The Gypsies were clustered round the Voivode. He looked even more magnificent in a coat ornamented with gold buttons and a necklace which flashed with jewels. He held his staff in his hand and beside him stood Saviya.

She was wearing a dress not unlike the one in which she had danced for Sir Algernon, but now her head-dress was more like a crown and glittered with jewels set in gold.

There were gems around her neck and at her wrists, and her skirt was richly embroidered. There were coloured ribbons falling on either side of her face almost in the semblance of a veil.

Slowly, the Marquis advanced towards the Voivode while Saviya looked down only at the ground, her head bent.

Earlier in the day the Marquis had sent, as he knew was correct, a small casket filled with gold coins, and he saw that it now stood on a small table behind the Voivode.

As he reached the Voivode the Gypsy cried in a loud voice:

"You have asked that you should marry my daughter who is one of this tribe and a Romany."

"I have requested your permission to do so," the Marquis replied, feeling that was the answer that was expected of him.

"I cannot give my only child to a Gorgio," the Voivode went on, "but are you prepared to become one of us—to become in fact my brother, because my blood is your blood and your blood is mine?"

"I should be honoured," the Marquis answered.

The Voivode obviously repeated in Romany what had been said. Then taking the Marquis's hand in his, he made a small incision on his wrist with a jewelled knife.

When there was a mark of blood, he cut his own, then pressed his wrist against the Marquis's and their blood intermingled.

As he did so the Voivode proclaimed the new relationship between them, saying it was the Marquis's duty to live from then on in accordance with Gypsy Law.

When he had finished, Saviya came nearer, and now she and the Marquis stood facing the Voivode, the Marquis on the right, Saviya on the left, holding hands.

The Voivode spoke some words in Romany and one of the tribe came forward to hand him a bunch of twigs.

"These twigs," the Voivode said to the Marquis, "come from seven different kinds of trees."

Then reverting to Romany, he made an incantation as he snapped the twigs one by one and threw them to the winds.

"This is the meaning of the marriage bond," he said to the Marquis and Saviya, "and it is wrong to break your pledge to one another until either of you have died.

"As man and wife," he went on, "you will have to give and to share. Go Saviya, and fetch bread, salt and water."

Saviya left the Marquis's side and brought back from her caravan a basket with a loaf of bread in it, a small bag of sea salt and an earthenware jar filled with water.

She put down the bread and salt on the table beside the Voivode and, lifting up the earthenware jar, invited the Marquis to drink.

When he had drunk she too drank from the earthenware jar and the Voivode took it from them and smashed it at their feet.

"As many pieces as there are there," he said, "will be the years of your happiness together. Keep one piece each. Preserve it carefully and only if you lose it will misery and loneliness come upon you."

"I will never lose mine, my darling," the Marquis said in a low voice to Saviya.

She looked up at him and he saw there was an expression of ecstasy in her face.

The Voivode again picked up his jewelled knife and took the Marquis's right hand in his. Saviya held out her left hand.

He cut both their wrists just enough so they should bleed, then he held their wrists together so that their blood would mingle and bound them with a silk cord making three knots in it.

"One knot is for constancy," he said, "the second for fertility, and the third for long life."

Then the Voivode cut two pieces of bread from the loaf, sprinkled a little salt on them and handed them to the Marquis and Saviya.

They ate them and when they had done so, the Voivode undid the silk cord which had held their wrists together.

"Keep the cords," he said. "They will remind you that you are tied to each other for all time and you can never be divided."

As he finished speaking, the Gypsies, who had been standing around in silence listening, gave a loud cheer.

Even as their voices rang out the music started—gay, wild music from the violins and the instruments which the Marquis had heard played while Saviya danced.

The Voivode led the bridal couple to the fire where there were a number of cushions and rug-covered seats.

The men all sat down but the women busied themselves with bringing on the feast.

Whatever the Marquis had sent from the house was very different from what they ate. There were stews so delicious he thought it was a pity he could not ask his Chef to taste them.

There were strange sweet-meats of Russian or Persian origin, of which he knew the main ingredients were honey and nuts, and the wine that he had sent was served in goblets which made him stare in astonishment.

"We fashioned these ourselves," the Voivode said as he handed the Marquis a goblet of gold set with semi-precious stones— amethysts, turquoises and cornelians.

There were others ornamented with pink quartz and rock crystal which could be found in the mountains of Russia and the Balkan countries.

"Is it safe to travel with such valuable objects?" the Marquis asked.

The Voivode laughed.

"It would be a brave man who would attack the Gypsies, unless he had a number of soldiers with him!"

The Marquis, glancing at their jewelled-hilted knives, thought that in fact there was good reason for the Gypsies being left severely alone except by the Civil Authorities, backed by the Military.

They ate and drank and, while the men talked amongst themselves, the women said very little and the Marquis realised that Saviya too was silent.

He took her hand in his and raised it to his lips.

He felt her quiver but still she said nothing, and it was in fact difficult to talk because the Gypsies were singing.

Their voices, melodious and compelling, seemed to raise the tempo so that there was a vibration and excitement in the air.

It grew dark, the stars came out overhead and the moon was creeping up the sky.

The light from the flames of the bonfire, the music vibrating between the trees, the strange clear-cut features and high cheekbones of those who sang, made a picture that the Marquis thought he would never forget.

Finally the women began to dance.

They were not as graceful or as ethereal as Saviya, but still they were amazingly proficient by any standard.

The Marquis realised that their dances were mostly Russian. Sometimes they were slow, sensuous and as lovely as swans moving over the smooth silvery water of a lake.

At other times they were wildly exhilarating, so that once again he found his heart beating quicker and a strange excitement making him feel as though he danced with them himself.

The music grew wilder, the voices louder, the violins seemed to be a part of the night itself. Then the Voivode rose to his feet.

"You go now," he said to the Marquis.

Saviya put out her arms towards him.

"Shall I ever see you again?" the Marquis heard her whisper.

"It is unlikely," the Voivode answered in English, "but you will be in my thoughts and in my heart, as you have always been."

He held Saviya close to him for one moment. Then he released her, taking her arms from round his neck and gave her hand to the Marquis.

"She is yours," he said. "Keep her safe."

"I will do that," the Marquis said.

The two men shook hands. Saviya led the Marquis to her caravan.

There were two white horses to draw it, and he climbed up and sat beside her on the front seat. But there were no reins: the horses were led by the Gypsies.

The men playing the violins went ahead and they were followed by the women carrying what looked to the Marquis like bundles and baskets.

The caravan followed and, just as they turned out of sight amongst the trees, the Marquis looked back to see the Voivode standing alone by the fire in the deserted camp.

He leant on his staff and looked very distinguished and at the same time lonely—a King of a very small community, but nevertheless—a King!

The procession wended its way through the trees where it was too dark for the Marquis to see the way. Then finally they came to a stand-still.

The horses were taken from the shafts and, still sitting in the front of the caravan, the Marquis and Saviya watched the women light a small fire.

Those who were carrying the bundles laid them down on the ground beneath the leafy branches of a tree, just out of reach of the heat from the flames.

They laid rugs over the bundles and scattered the flower petals which filled their baskets. They were in every hue of red, pink, white, orange, yellow, and mauve.

Then the Gypsy women danced around the fire, at first slowly and then their movements growing wilder, and more ecstatic.

In the light of the flames their figures had a strange primitive beauty until, to the music of the violins, they moved away into the wood.

The musicians went last and then they too vanished into the darkness of trees.

Saviya stepped down from the caravan to stand beside the fire staring after them.

The Marquis joined her.

The last notes of the violins seemed to hover on the air and then there was silence.

"Did you notice," Saviya asked, her voice very low and lost, "they did not . . . look at me? They will no longer . . . speak to me."

There was so much unhappiness in her voice that the Marquis put his arms around her.

She no longer wore the crown of jewels in which she had been married, and her hair was against his shoulder. He put his hand up very gently to stroke it.

"I am . . . nobody!" she murmured, "I am not even a . . . witch!"

"You are my wife," the Marquis said in a deep voice, "and you have bewitched me, Saviya, from the first moment I saw you. I am caught in your spell and now I can never escape."

He heard her give a deep sigh. She raised her face to his and her eyes were very dark and mysterious in the light of the moon.

"Are you quite sure that it is . . . enough?" she asked. "I have so little to give you. I do not even now know myself."

"But I know you," the Marquis answered. "I know that you are everything I wanted in a woman; everything I desire in my wife. Everything I shall love, adore and worship for the rest of my life."

His words made her quiver and very gently, just as the music had started, soft as the ripple of a raindrop on a smooth pool, he kissed her, holding her against his heart.

Then as he felt a sudden flame rise within her to echo the flame in himself, his lips grew fierce and more demanding.

Wildly, with an elation that was indescribable, he was kissing her until it was impossible to think of anything save that they were one with each other.

Then as the moon rose higher over the trees and the embers of the fire were red, they lay together on the flower-petalled couch and there was only the whisper of their love.

CHAPTER EIGHT

The Marquis rose very quietly so as not to awaken Saviya.

Asleep she looked very young, and he saw the expression on her face was one of intense happiness.

He looked down at her and thought that no-one could be more breathtakingly lovely.

Her eyes were dark half-crescents against the ivory of her skin and her black hair with its blue lights fell over the pillow and her naked shoulders.

They had moved into the caravan just before dawn. A slight breeze had broken the warmth of the night and rustled in the leaves of the trees.

It had been a night of enchantment such as the Marquis had never believed possible.

There was magic in the moonlight, making Saviya look very ethereal, yet also a siren, a Lorelei.

And as their desire for each other swept them away into the heights of ecstasy where there were only the peaks of passion, they were no longer humans, but as gods.

The Marquis put on the long robe which Hobley had brought him when he had been ill in the caravan, and walking through the open door he descended the steps.

The sun illuminated the small clearing and he realised that it was a part of the wood that he had not visited since he was a boy.

Just beyond where the caravan was resting there was a forest pool surrounded by trees. There were willows overhanging the still water, their leaves almost gold against the dark fir and the silver birch.

Kingcups and wild iris were brilliant yellow on the edge of the pool, and the mosses and lichen beneath the trees were saffron and jade.

It was as lovely in the sunlight as it had been mysterious and unearthly beneath the moon.

Now the Marquis saw that Hobley had already relit the fire which had died away during the night, and it was burning brightly, while beyond it was the flower-strewn couch which the Gypsies had made for them.

On it, thrown negligently among the petals, were the jewelled necklaces he had taken from Saviya's neck.

He had loosed her hair, to kiss the scented silk of it and she quivered at the touch of his hands on her body.

'Had there ever been such happiness?' the Marquis asked himself now.

"Good-morning, Hobley," he said aloud.

"Good-morning, M'Lord."

"Did you have much trouble in finding us?" the Marquis asked with a smile.

"It took me some time, M'Lord, but I've brought to Your Lordship the wine for luncheon, it is cooling in the pool."

"Is the water cold?" the Marquis asked.

"Just fresh, M'Lord."

"Then I think I will try it."

He walked towards the pool as he spoke and pulling off his robe, plunged in, finding the water, as Hobley had said, fresh and invigorating and not too chill.

When the Marquis had finished swimming Hobley shaved him, and when finally the valet was no longer required, he went back to the House.

The Marquis sat for a little while staring into the flames of the fire and then he rose and went to go into the caravan.

He sat down on the edge of the low bed looking at Saviya who was still asleep. But after a moment she opened her eyes.

There was no mistaking the radiance that lit up her face and as the Marquis bent towards her she made an inarticulate murmur and put her arms round his neck.

"It is . . . true!" she whispered. "I was afraid last night must be only a . . . wonderful dream!"

"Was it wonderful for you, my darling?"

"It was such unbelievable happiness, I did not know that even love could be so completely perfect."

His lips found hers. Then as he felt her soft and yielding beneath him, his kiss grew more passionate and more demanding until everything was forgotten except their need of each other . . .

It was a long time later that Saviya hurried down the steps of the caravan towards the fire.

"You must be hungry," she said. "Only the worst type of wife would allow her husband to be so long without food."

"I was hungry for something less material!" the Marquis answered and he smiled as Saviya blushed.

She busied herself breaking the eggs Hobley had brought them and cooked them skilfully over the fire.

But all the time she was aware that the Marquis was watching her, and she was conscious that she wore only a silk wrap and her hair was falling loose on either side of her small face.

"You make me shy," she protested.

"I adore you when you are shy."

She waited on him and he ate all she gave him. Then as she laid aside the plates and the cooking pans he said:

"Leave those for Hobley, Saviya. I want you."

She smiled at him provokingly.

"Are you commanding me?"

"Of course! Are you defying me?"

"What would you do if I did?"

"Carry you away into the dungeons of my Castle and torture you until you surrendered yourself completely and unreservedly. I love you to distraction, my lovely, but I will be your master."

She looked at him uncertainly, not quite sure if he was joking or serious.

"Come here, my precious," he said softly.

And then she ran into his arms like a child seeking safety.

As the hours passed they lay in the sun-shine talking of themselves and their love.

Late in the day when it grew hotter, the Marquis persuaded Saviya to swim in the pool.

As she moved across it he thought that nothing could be more lovely than the perfection of her white body beneath the silver ripples.

It made her seem part of the trees, the irises and the darkness of the woods. When finally she came from the pool, the water glistening on her body like dew-drops, he held her close as if he was afraid of losing her.

"I am convinced now," he said in his deep voice, "that you are a wood-nymph and if I do not hold on you will vanish like the morning mist, and I shall never be able to find you again."

She pressed herself against him, her arms round his neck and he kissed her at first gently, then fiercely, demandingly, until finally he picked her up in his arms to carry her back to the flower-strewn couch on which they had spent the night.

It was late in the afternoon when the Marquis said:

"We must go now, my darling."

"Go? Go where?"

"Home," he replied. "We are to be married."

"We are married!"

"We are, I agree, joined together irrevocably," the Marquis answered. "But at the same time I wish to marry you, Saviya, according to the Law of England, and receive the blessing of the Church —my Church, which I hope one day will also be yours."

She was silent for a moment, her head bent a little as if she searched for words. Then she said:

"As you know, the ceremony yesterday when we intermingled our blood is to me sacred and unites us in a manner which means that I belong to you and could never belong to anyone else. But for you it is different?"

"There is no difference," the Marquis said firmly.

"But there is," she answered. "You do not acknowledge the Gypsy laws which for me are binding, even though I am no longer a Gypsy. And because of your position in the world, because you are of such importance, it is best that you could, if you wished it, be free to marry a woman of your own class."

"You are my class! We are both equally well bred," the Marquis said. "I always believed it even before the Voivode told us his tale."

He lifted her chin with his fingers until she was looking up at him.

"Have you forgotten," he asked, "that when you were exchanged for the dead baby, the Voivode said that you were the child of a nobleman?"

"I am still nameless—still nobody!" Saviya replied miserably. "Let me stay with you because I am yours, but it is best if I do not become your wife according to English Law, so that your friends must acknowledge my position even while they despise me for myself."

"No-one will despise you as far as I am concerned," the Marquis said with a hard note in his voice.

"I can never forget," Saviya said, "the way your cousin referred to me. He was only speaking aloud what your friends and acquaintances will have been thinking even though they are too tactful or too frightened to say it to your face."

"I have told you before, and I must say it again," the Marquis said, "that I am not in the least interested what anyone should say behind my back. I honour and respect you. You are, in every way, all I have ever wished my wife to be."

He saw the troubled expression in Saviya's eyes and added:

"I am not prepared to argue about this, Saviya. You obeyed the Voivode and you will obey me. You are mine and it is for me to make the decisions which affect our lives."

Her eyes were on his and he felt that she was glad that he was so masterful, and that she must obey his authority as she had obeyed the Chief of her tribe.

"I will do . . . anything you ask of me," she said softly after a moment.

And because she was so pliant and so sweet, the Marquis crushed her against him and kissed her until the world whirled around them and once again everything was forgotten but themselves.

When they were dressed they walked a little way through the wood and found on the bridle-path the Marquis's Phaeton.

He helped Saviya into it, took the reins from the groom who jumped up behind. They moved forward.

The Marquis could only drive slowly until they were clear of the trees, but when they reached the Park he tooled his horses swiftly with an expertise that made Saviya look at him appreciatively.

He knew she was delighted with the horse-flesh he kept in his stables, and he planned that as soon as they returned from their honeymoon he would buy her some horses for her own. He knew exactly the type of Arab-bred animal which would suit her.

Ruckley House looked exquisite in the late afternoon sunshine. Already the shadows were growing longer on the green lawns and the flowers were great patches of colour. The house itself glowed warm and welcoming as a jewel.

The flag was flying on the roof-tops and Saviya looked up at it with a little smile.

"Your flag!" she said, remembering how angry he had been when Jethro had flown it in his absence.

"Our flag!" he corrected, "over our house, my darling."

"Can I really own a part of anything so beautiful?" Saviya asked.

"Everything I have is yours," the Marquis replied.

"I think I have always longed for a house of my own," Saviya told him. "Perhaps it was some forgotten instinct or a part of my blood, but for me home has always meant a place where I could stay and not have to move on."

She gave a little laugh that was half a sigh.

"Perhaps really I have never been a Gypsy at heart. I only thought I was. I am beginning to understand now so many things about myself which puzzled me."

"I want to know everything you feel and everything you think," the Marquis said. "I cannot bear that any part of you should not be mine."

"It is all . . . yours," Saviya whispered.

The Marquis drew up at the front door with a flourish.

As they both alighted from the Phaeton he held out his hand to Saviya and they walked up the steps hand in hand.

She was wearing the elaborate, exquisitely embroidered Gypsy dress in which she had been married, and the Marquis had fastened the jewelled necklaces around her neck and the jewelled ear-rings in her small ears.

Only her head was bare, because the crown in which she had married was part of the Kalderash treasure and was used for every wedding which took place within the tribe.

"There are three gentlemen waiting for Your Lordship," Bush said, as they reached the Hall. "They are in the Salon."

"Visitors?" the Marquis asked sharply.

"Captain Collington brought them, M'Lord. They arrived just after luncheon and I told them that Your Lordship was expected later in the afternoon."

The Marquis smiled.

"Charles is here!" he said to Saviya. "I wrote to him yesterday to tell him I was alive. I felt that he would be unable to resist coming to make sure for himself."

Still holding Saviya's hand the Marquis walked towards the Salon, and as the door was opened for them by a footman, they entered.

There were three men at the far end of the room and as the Marquis and Saviya entered they sprang to their feet.

"Fabius, I have never been so glad of anything in my whole life, as I was to get your note!" Charles Collington exclaimed.

He hurried across the room to the Marquis as he spoke, both hands outstretched.

"You are all right?" he added, the Marquis's hand in his.

"I have completely recovered, thanks to Saviya," the Marquis answered, "but it was a near thing."

"His Lordship told me how wonderful you have been," Charles Collington said to Saviya.

She smiled at him as he lifted her hand to his lips.

"I and all of Fabius's friends owe you a great debt of gratitude," he said with great sincerity.

While he was speaking, the Marquis went towards the two other gentlemen standing in front of the fireplace.

One of them was Sir Algernon Gibbon—the other, the Marquis realised, was a man he had never seen before.

"I have heard the amazing story of your preservation from death!" Sir Algernon said. "When your cousin told me you had been ambushed in the wood and murdered by Saviya I could not credit it was the truth, but there was nothing I could do to refute his assertion."

"All is well that ends well," the Marquis said briefly, as if he had no wish to go on discussing what had happened in the past.

He looked enquiringly at the stranger standing beside Sir Algernon.

"I want to introduce," Sir Algernon said pompously, "the Earl of Glencairn whom I have brought here for a very special reason."

The Marquis held out his hand, but to his surprise the man who had just been introduced was not looking at him but at Saviya who was approaching them across the room talking animatedly to Charles Collington.

He was staring at her in such a strange manner that the Marquis's hand fell to his side.

Then, as if everyone realised that something strange and untoward was happening, there was silence until the Earl of Glencairn exclaimed in a voice that was somehow constricted:

"It is incredible!"

Then to Saviya he said:

"You are exactly like your mother!"

Saviya stared at him wide-eyed until Sir Algernon, feeling that the onus for explanation was on him, said:

"Saviya, the Earl of Glencairn wishes to see your birth-mark—the head of the hawk that you showed me when I was here before."

"There is no reason for her to show it," the Earl of Glencairn said before Saviya could reply. "This is my daughter, who I thought was dead but about whom I only learnt the truth six years ago when my second wife died."

"I . . . I am . . . your daughter?" Saviya asked in a voice that was hardly above a whisper.

"You are my daughter," the Earl of Glencairn said firmly.

"Then . . . I have a . . . name?"

"You have indeed," he answered. "You are the Lady Conchita McCairn, and my eldest child who I believed had died when she was fifteen months old. When I learnt you had been given to the Gypsies I believed that you were lost to me forever."

Saviya was very pale and, almost as if she was afraid of what was being revealed, she put her hand on the Marquis's arm.

He covered her fingers reassuringly with his own and said:

"As you are Saviya's father, My Lord, I think it right that you should know we have already been united by a Gypsy marriage. Now I would ask your permission for her to be my wife according to the laws of this country."

"Must I lose my daughter having only just found her?" the Earl asked, but he smiled as he spoke.

"How did you find me?" Saviya asked.

"You can thank me for that," Sir Algernon Gibbon said proudly. "When the Marquis and Charles Collington thought they had won a thousand pounds from me because they had passed off a Gypsy as a Lady of Quality, I was prepared to acknowledge myself the loser and pay my debt."

"You were indeed very sporting about it," Charles Collington said irrepressibly.

"I am glad you thought so," Sir Algernon Gibbon replied, "but I was also quite certain that my contention was right, and that Saviya was in fact the possessor of blue blood."

"How could you have thought that?" the Marquis said.

"Because," Sir Algernon answered, "I knew in the back of my mind, when it was first mentioned, there was one family somewhere in the Kingdom whose members carried somewhere on their person the mark of the hawk."

"I thought it . . . showed that I was a . . . witch!" Saviya murmured.

"On the contrary," Sir Algernon said, "after some thought I remembered that it showed that you were a McCairn."

"It is quite true," the Earl interposed. "The birth-mark occurs all down the ages, not on every member of the Clan, of course, and more often amongst the females than the males. In any case it happens and our crest is the hawk's head."

"We must be very grateful," the Marquis interposed, "for your amazing knowledge of genealogy, Gibbon."

"When I remembered the history of the McCairn birth-mark," Sir Algernon said, "I wrote to the Earl asking to see him. He replied that he was coming to London and would call on me. By the time I received his letter your death was being proclaimed by your cousin, Jethro, and there was a warrant out for Saviya's arrest."

"I should still have wanted to find her," the Earl said.

"Fortunately, I did not have to upset you with such a disturbing story," Sir Algernon replied, "because while I was wondering what excuse I should make for dragging you to London, Charles Collington heard yesterday from the Marquis and I was able to give you good news of your daughter instead of bad."

"It is very good news indeed," the Earl exclaimed and to Saviya he said:

"If you only knew how much I have suffered these past six years!"

"Had you no idea that the baby which was buried was not your own?" the Marquis asked.

"None at all!" the Earl answered. "Actually I was away from home at the time and only returned the very day of the funeral which had been arranged by my wife, Conchita's step-mother."

"And I imagine the old nurse told you exactly what happened," the Marquis said. "We have heard the story from the Voivode, the Chief of the Kalderash, who brought Saviya up as his own child."

"I want to hear every detail," Charles Collington cried. "When did you and Saviya learn that she was in fact not a Gypsy as she had thought herself to be? There is a lot of explaining to do."

"There is indeed," the Marquis answered, "but there is one thing I want to ask before we go any further and I think it is a question uppermost in all our minds."

"What is that?" the Earl enquired.

"Why is Saviya so dark?" the Marquis enquired. "She does not resemble you in the least."

"No indeed," the Earl answered.

His hair was almost white but it was obvious that when he was young it would have been the pale red that was essentially Scottish.

He also possessed blue eyes and a fair complexion. Sturdily built with square shoulders, it seemed almost impossible for the slim, small-boned Saviya with her jet-black hair to be his child.

"The explanation is very simple," he said. "My wife was Spanish."

"Spanish!" Sir Algernon ejaculated, "why did I not think of that?"

"It did not occur to any of us," the Marquis admitted.

"My family has always owned land in Spain," the Earl went on.

"It is near Segovia. When I visited it as a young man I fell in love with a most entrancing Contessa. I brought her back to Scotland but she died when our child was born."

He paused and said to Saviya in a voice deep with emotion:

"When I saw you walk across the room just now you might in fact have been your mother. The resemblance is almost uncanny."

"Now tell us the whole story," Charles Collington insisted. "From the very beginning."

The Marquis related briefly what the Voivode had revealed to him and Saviya only the day before.

"It was Conchita's old nurse who told me the truth six years ago after my second wife died," the Earl said on the completion of the Marquis's story. "What you have just related exactly bears out her tale."

He smiled at Saviya who had been listening wide-eyed.

"There is only one thing I have to add," he went on, "which I hope, my dear, will not disappoint you. It is that you are not my heir."

"Why not, now that you have found her again?" Charles Collington asked impulsively.

"Because," the Earl replied, "I have married for the third time and two years ago my wife, who is a good deal younger than I am, presented me with twin sons. There is therefore a male McCairn to inherit the Earldom."

"I am glad," the Marquis said. "I do not wish my wife to be concerned with any Estate save my own!"

As he spoke he looked at the clock on the mantel-shelf and rose to his feet.

"The Reverend will be ready for us in my private Chapel in exactly half an hour's time. I feel, My Lord, that you would wish to give your daughter away, and what could be more appropriate than that my best man should be my oldest friend?"

He smiled at Charles and went on:

"And that the witness to the ceremony should be Sir Algernon Gibbon, whose exceptional knowledge of ancient family characteristics has brought my future wife and her father together?"

The Marquis took Saviya by the arm and drew her towards the door.

"Upstairs, my darling," he said quietly, "you will find a white gown which I ordered from London yesterday, along with some other clothes which I hope will please you. They come from the same dress-maker who provided the green dress in which we attempted and failed to deceive Sir Algernon."

"I can hardly believe that all this is true!" Saviya told him. "Now I am no longer ashamed to be your wife."

"There was never anything of which you need have been ashamed," the Marquis replied, "but if the knowledge that you are of noble Scottish descent makes you happy, then it makes me happy, too."

He lifted her hands to his lips and kissed her fingers one by one.

She looked into his eyes and for a moment they were both very still.

"I love you!" the Marquis said below his breath, "and I want to be alone with you."

"I want it . . . too!" Saviya whispered.

Then with an effort she drew her hands from his and went up the stairs.

It was nearly mid-night when the Marquis dismissed Hobley.

There had been so much to talk about after the wedding; so much to hear both from Saviya and her father that the hours had sped by.

Their wedding had been very beautiful.

The Chapel at Ruckley House had been built at the same time as the house itself, and the carved pews and beautiful reredos behind the Altar had remained unchanged down the centuries.

There had been the soft music of an organ, very unlike the throbbing melody of the violins, viola and sitar which had been part of the ceremony of the night before.

But there had been an atmosphere of faith and devotion in the small Chapel. The candles glowing brightly illuminated Saviya's lovely face covered by a lace veil that had been in the Ruckley family for centuries.

There had been a tiara of diamonds on her dark hair, diamonds to encircle her neck and glitter in her ears, and her bouquet had been of white lilies.

She had looked beautiful but also so conventional that it was hard to remember they had ever imagined her to be a wild, uncivilised Gypsy.

The Marquis had repeated his vows in a firm, strong voice that seemed to echo round the Chapel.

Saviya's tone had been soft but at the same time there had been such a deep sincerity in the way she spoke which brought, the Marquis thought, a new solemnity to their relationship.

On The Reverend's advice and to please the Earl, Saviya used her real name which had been given her at her Christening and which had also been her mother's.

But because the Marquis would never be able to think of her except as Saviya, she said:

"I, Conchita Saviya, take thee, Fabius Alexander, to be my wedded husband . . ."

Last night the Marquis had not given her a ring, but tonight, his mother's ring was on the third finger of her left hand, and he felt that it bound them even closer to each other than they had been before.

'You are mine, mine by every law and vow that could unite us with each other,' the Marquis wanted to cry.

Instead, when the ceremony had ended, he lifted Saviya's veil and kissed her very gently on the lips.

He knew then that she was as moved as he was.

It had seemed that there was a new dignity and authority in The Reverend that neither of them had known before, and by the sanctity of his office they were now husband and wife, in the real sense of the word, and no-one could ever put them asunder.

"I love you!" the Marquis whispered as, with Saviya on his arm, they walked from the Chapel and down the corridor which led to the more familiar part of the house.

"I am your wife!" she said, "and now I want everyone to know that I am yours and that I am who I am!"

"It shall be in *The Gazette* the day after tomorrow," the Marquis said with a smile, "and then there will be no doubt in anyone's mind as to whom I have married."

"You know I am not thinking of myself," she whispered, "but of you."

"I know that," he answered, "but I am glad for your sake, my beloved, as well as for mine. Now you have a background. Now you have roots. Now you have a whole family and a Clan!"

"You are trying to frighten me!" she said accusingly, but her eyes were shining.

"I am only reminding you that you have taken on many heavy responsibilities," the Marquis said. "There will be no more wandering carefree over the world!"

"If you talk like that I shall run away from you!" she threatened, but he knew she was only teasing.

"You will never leave me," he answered seriously, "because you know I could not live without you. You will be with me always, Saviya, and because we have so nearly lost each other, I will never let you out of my sight."

She laughed a little at that, but she knew that it was true.

She had not only nearly lost him through the murderous intentions of his cousin, but also, believing it was in his best interests, she had attempted to run away with her tribe and break the bond which bound them to each other by some indefinable magic.

After the wedding they had dinner, but it was a very different feast from the one they had enjoyed the night before.

Course succeeded course, served by powdered footmen on crested, silver dishes. There had been champagne to drink, but now it was in crystal glasses and not in the fabulous jewelled goblets from which they had drunk around the fire in the woods.

The Earl of Glencairn told them stories of the McCairn Clan; their fights and feuds and the part they had played in Scottish history.

Sir Algernon related strange signs which other families besides the McCairns bore, and repeated again and again how delighted he was that it was his knowledge which had united Saviya and her father.

There was so much to talk about; so much that was interesting and amusing. But the Marquis did not only wish to be alone with Saviya; he also remembered that the following day they were starting on a journey that would carry them to Spain.

"It is strange that I should have chosen Spain for our honeymoon," he said to the Earl.

"You must visit Conchita's relations," the Earl replied. "I will give you letters of introduction and you will learn if you have not visited Spain before how very beautiful its women are."

"To be aware of that I have only to look at my wife," the Marquis answered.

It had been altogether a very satisfactory day, he told himself, when finally he knocked gently on the communicating door between his own and Saviya's bed-rooms and without waiting for an answer entered.

The room was in darkness save for the light from the flames in the fireplace.

It might have been expected, the Marquis thought, that Saviya would have a fire. It was so much a part of the Gypsy way of life, it was in fact almost a sacred symbol amongst them.

But the heat of the day had passed and tonight there was a chill wind blowing outside, so the fire was in fact a necessity.

He walked across the room and in the darkness the bedposts reminded him of the trunks of the trees which had encircled them last night.

Saviya was sitting on a white bear-skin rug in front of the fire.

The Marquis noticed that she had pulled the cushions from the chairs and placed them around her.

But she was sitting upright, her long dark hair covering her to below the waist.

There was the scent of flowers but now they were in vases on the side-tables. There was also the exotic fragrance of Saviya's hair, that strange, haunting perfume which the Marquis had noticed that first time when he carried her in his arms after he had knocked her down with his Phaeton.

He stood looking down at her, very tall and handsome in his long brocade robe.

As she lifted her face there was a smile on her lips and an expression in her eyes which made his heart turn over in his breast.

"You are very beautiful, my precious."

There was a depth in his voice to which she vibrated.

"I want you to . . . think so."

"Could I ever think anything else?"

The firelight was on her face and he wondered if any other woman could look so alluring, so mysterious and at the same time so utterly and completely desirable.

There was a sudden gust of wind in the chimney and the creeper outside the windows tapped against one of the panes.

"There is a cold wind tonight," the Marquis said in an absent-minded voice as if he was thinking of something else. "I am glad we will sleep in a bed."

"Are you sure of . . . that?" Saviya asked.

Now he saw there was that faintly mocking smile on her lips that had entranced him when they had first met.

He reached down to lift her to her feet but as he did so her arms went round his neck and she pulled him down to her.

"Saviya!" he said hoarsely.

Then he felt her lips seek his and as his mouth took possession of her he could feel her heart beating against his.

"I love you!" he wanted to say.

But he was swept away by an indescribable magic—a spell so blinding, so compelling that they were both lost in an ecstasy and rapture for which there were no words.

A Sword
to the Heart

AUTHOR'S NOTE

The Labourers' revolt in 1830 was extremely serious. Several Counties in the South of England were in a state bordering on insurrection. The Government was in a panic. The rebellion failed completely although there was some improvement in the farm workers' wages. Six men were hanged, four hundred imprisoned and four hundred and fifty-seven transported. Three boats carried the convicts to Van Dieman's Land and New South Wales. The list of prisoners shows they came from thirteen different Counties, but there was no-one from Herefordshire.

There are innumerable legends about the famous "Captain Swing," whose threatening letters spread terror among the landowners of England. It has never been satisfactorily established if he was or was not hanged with several other leaders of the riots.

CHAPTER ONE

1830

"Lord Colwall to see you, Sir James."

A middle-aged man sitting by the fire reading a newspaper rose with an exclamation of surprise.

Advancing towards him across the room was a young man, elegantly attired with a meticulously tied high cravat and a jewelled fob glittering below his cut-away coat.

He was in fact extremely handsome with fine-cut features and dark hair above a square forehead, but there was an expression on his face which at first acquaintance seemed almost repellent.

It was hard to believe that a man so young in years should look so cynical and at the same time so proudly aloof that a stranger might instinctively shrink from contact with him.

But Sir James Parke was an old friend, and the way in which he held out his hand and the smile on his lips showed that he was sincerely pleased by the intrusion.

"Ranulf!" he cried. "Why did you not let me know you were coming? But none the less it is a great pleasure to see you."

Lord Colwall did not smile in response. Instead, he joined Sir James in front of the log-blazing fire and replied in a cold, almost expressionless, voice:

"I made up my mind to visit you only yesterday evening."

Sir James looked at the young man's face a little apprehensively.

"Is there anything wrong at the Castle?"

"No, nothing."

Sir James waited as if for more information, and when it was not forthcoming, he said genially:

"Do sit down, Ranulf. What will you have to drink? A glass of Port? Or would you prefer Madeira at this hour of the morning?"

He put out his hand towards the bell-pull as he spoke.

"Thank you, but I have not long breakfasted," Lord Colwall said before he could ring the bell.

"I have just been reading *The Times*," Sir James said, "about the threatening letters written to landlords in the Southern Counties and signed 'Swing.' It seems extraordinary that no-one knows who this man is."

The two gentlemen seated themselves opposite each other at the fireside.

"When they do discover his identity," Lord Colwall replied, "he will surely be hanged, or at least transported."

"There are all sorts of rumours about him," Sir James said, "that he is a disgruntled Peer or a criminal who has escaped the gallows, or a lawyer who has been barred from practising."

Lord Colwall did not reply and Sir James went on:

"Whoever he may be—and I imagine he is an educated man from the manner in which he writes—he is undoubtedly responsible for the riots around Canterbury. Farm-workers could never organise such a rebellion by themselves. There must be someone behind them."

"That is obvious," Lord Colwall said in a hard voice, "and they have been inoculated with this man's poison. Did you hear what a labourer said to the High Sheriff of Kent?"

"No, tell me," Sir James said.

"Apparently the High Sheriff attended one of the College meetings to remonstrate with the rioters. They listened to his homily with attention. But before they dispersed a man said:

"'This year we will destroy the corn-stacks and the threshing machines, next year we will have a turn with the parsons, and the third we will make war upon the Statesmen.'"

"Good God!" Sir James ejaculated. "That will be Civil War!"

"It will be now if the Government does not use a firmer hand than they are doing at the moment," Lord Colwall remarked.

"Reading some of the letters in *The Times*," Sir James said, "I cannot help feeling that the labourers have a case."

"A case?" Lord Colwall ejaculated sharply. "They have nothing of the sort! They are paid for their work, and to burn ricks and break up farm machinery is sheer anarchy, as you well know."

There was now almost a note of violence in the cold voice and, because Sir James Parke was a man who enjoyed peace and disliked argument, he said in a conciliatory tone:

"Let us talk of something more pleasant. What brings you on this most welcome visit?"

Lord Colwall hesitated as if he was considering his words, then he replied slowly:

"I came to ask you, Sir James, if you would be best man at my wedding."

For a moment Sir James Parke stared incredulously, then he exclaimed:

"At your wedding? My dear boy I can assure you that nothing would give me greater pleasure! I had no idea—no-one told me that you were even contemplating matrimony. Have I missed the announcement of your engagement?"

"There has been no announcement," Lord Colwall replied.

"And who is the bride? Do I know her?"

"No, you do not know her."

As Lord Colwall spoke he rose to his feet and walked across the room to the window to stand staring out at the elaborate garden, to which his host devoted a great deal of his time and thought.

Sir James looked at his broad shoulders in perplexity.

"What is all this about, Ranulf?" he said at length. "As you well know, nothing would delight me more than to see you married."

"I am aware of that," Lord Colwall said, turning from the window. "It is because you were a friend of my father, Sir James, and because until I was twenty-five you acted as my Trustee, that you are the first person to learn of my intended nuptials."

"I am indeed honoured by your confidence," Sir James said, "but why is it a secret?"

"It is no secret," Lord Colwall answered. "It is in fact something I have planned for a long time."

"You have planned?"

Lord Colwall came back from the window to the fireplace.

"When Claris left me," he said slowly, as if he forced the words between his lips, "I swore that I would never marry again."

"You were distraught at the time," Sir James said quietly. "You had been badly treated, Ranulf, as we know, and at the same time you were very young. You had not even reached your twenty-first year, and under such circumstances one says things that one does not mean."

"I meant every word of it!" Lord Colwall contradicted, "but three years ago, when I was twenty-five and came into full possession of my properties, I realised that, whatever my personal feelings in the matter, I must for the sake of the family beget an heir."

Sir James looked at him quickly before he said:

"You are right, of course. There have been Colwalls at the Castle since the twelfth century."

"Exactly!" Lord Colwall agreed. "And that is why the inheritance must continue in the direct line. I intend, Sir James, when I die to hand the Castle over to my son!"

"That of course is what we would all wish to happen!" Sir James agreed. "And I would like above all else, Ranulf, to see you happy."

"I am entirely content as I am," Lord Colwall said coldly, "but since I cannot have a legitimate son without a wife, I have therefore chosen one!"

"Who is she?" Sir James asked. "One of our local belles? Or have you found some 'Incomparable' in London who will bring grace and beauty to our rather dull countryside?"

"I told you," Lord Colwall went on, as if he had not listened to what Sir James was saying, "that I have planned my marriage with care. That is precisely the truth."

There was a note in his voice which brought a little frown between Sir James's eyes.

"What are you trying to tell me, Ranulf?"

"I am attempting to explain what I have done," Lord Colwall replied, "not because I need your approval, but simply because I feel that you, who have always been so closely concerned with my affairs, should know the truth."

"And what is the truth?" Sir James enquired.

"When I decided to get married again," Lord Colwall replied, "I knew that the one thing I could not face was to marry another wife who might behave like Claris. I have learnt, Sir James, by bitter experience that what is loosely called love can be a weapon of self-destruction."

"Now, Ranulf, you are still bitter, still resentful of what happened eight years ago," Sir James interposed. "Surely you can understand now that the emotions through which you passed were unusual, to say the least of it, in fact a disaster which might happen to perhaps one man in a million."

"I can only hope your figures are right!" Lord Colwall said with a cynical twist of his lips.

"Now that you are older and wiser," Sir James went on, "you can forget the past. You have your life in front of you. You have a position that men envy. You have great possessions, a heritage which is steeped in the history of England, and a name which is respected throughout the land."

"Exactly!" Lord Colwall ejaculated, "and that is why, since my name is respected, and since I was fool enough to put at risk both the honour and the pride of my family, I shall not make the same mistake again."

"You could not have known at your age what Claris was like," Sir James said. "You were infatuated with her beauty, and who shall blame you? No-one could have anticipated what occurred."

"You yourself warned me that I was taking a risk in marrying her," Lord Colwall said harshly, "but I would not listen."

"You were in love," Sir James said quietly, "and all must be forgiven if a man loses his head in such circumstances."

"I was besotted, infatuated and bewitched until I behaved like a damned idiot!" Lord Colwall said roughly. "It will never happen again."

"We all make mistakes in our lives," Sir James said soothingly. "We all make jackasses of ourselves at some time or another. But what I had always hoped, Ranulf, is that as the years passed you would forget; your bitterness would pass and one day you would find a woman you could love and who would love you."

"I remember telling you when I learned the truth about Claris, that I would never love anyone again," Lord Colwall answered. "It was not the statement of an hysterical boy, Sir James. It was in the nature of a vow, a vow to which I shall adhere to my dying day."

"And yet you are to be married?"

"I am to be married for the reason I have given you," Lord Colwall answered. "I chose my wife three years ago when she was fifteen. She has now passed her eighteenth birthday and she is at this moment on her way from Cumberland, where she lives, to the Castle. She will arrive next Wednesday and the marriage has been planned for the following day at which I hope you will support me."

"What do you mean—you chose her when she was fifteen?" Sir James enquired.

"Exactly what I have said," Lord Colwall answered. "I made a list of my relations and close connections who had girls of about the right age. I visited them."

There was a faint note of amusement in his voice as he said:

"In Lincolnshire I found that a third cousin once removed had a daughter of the right age, but her mother was a hopeless drunkard!"

Sir James said nothing and Lord Colwall continued:

"Sixty miles further north another relative produced a girl with a

squint and the suspicion of a harelip! Hardly encouraging characteristics!"

There was still no response from Sir James.

"Then at Pooley Bridge in Cumberland," His Lordship continued, "I found my father's second cousin, Lady Margaret Graystoke,
had a daughter aged fifteen."

Lord Colwall glanced at Sir James, who was sitting listening intently, his eyes on his face.

"Lady Margaret's antecedents are impeccable," he continued,
"and Graystoke comes from an old and respected Cumberland family. His brother is the fifth Baronet. They have little money, but
their breeding is faultless!"

"Are you telling me," Sir James asked with an astonished note in
his voice, "that you chose this girl whom you are to marry as if you
were buying a foal?"

"Why not?" Lord Colwall answered. "After all, the reason I
require her as a wife is simply that she should produce children."

"Have you told the girl this?"

"I have not seen her since I visited her father's Vicarage three
years ago."

"You have not—seen her?"

Sir James rose to his feet.

"My dear Ranulf, this is monstrous! This is the most crazy, in-
sane action I have ever heard! You cannot do such a thing!"

Lord Colwall looked at him in surprise.

"What is wrong with it?" he enquired. "If I had met a girl in
London, spoken to her perhaps two or three times under the eyes of
her mother, and then asked if I might pay her my addresses, you
would not have been in the least surprised. But I would know as
much or as little about her as I know about Natalia."

"A girl you saw once as a child?" Sir James insisted. "What was
she like?"

"She was pleasant-looking," he replied, "with no apparent physical imperfections. A little short perhaps, but doubtless she has
grown. As I have already said, she comes of good stock, and I cannot imagine that the daughter of a poverty-stricken Vicar would
not feel honoured to be the Chatelaine of Colwall Castle."

"In other words, you take for granted that she is selling herself
for your title and your position, and you are buying her to act as a
breeding machine!" Sir James said.

For the first time Lord Colwall gave a faint smile.

"You are very dramatic, Sir James, but I assure you that a

mariage de convenance is far more likely to be successful than one which rests upon throbbing hearts, passionate declarations, and that deceptive emotion called love."

"Supposing when you meet the girl again you dislike one another?" Sir James asked. "What then?"

"She will still have her position as my wife," Lord Colwall explained patiently, "and I shall hope to have not only an heir, but several children."

"It is the most unnatural thing I have ever heard," Sir James said crossly. "Now listen to me, Ranulf, for one moment."

"I am listening," Lord Colwall replied.

"You are an extremely attractive young man. There is not a young woman in the whole length and breadth of Herefordshire who would not fall into your arms if you gave her the slightest encouragement. The girls have told me how you seem to rebuff every overture they have made in your direction. That is not to say they would not go on making them!"

"I am well aware of that!" Lord Colwall replied.

"And surely," Sir James went on, "there have been women in London whose company you have enjoyed."

There was a cynical twist to Lord Colwall's lips as he replied:

"Many of them, but they were hardly suitable, either by birth or by education to sit at the top of my table."

"I am not talking about strumpets!" Sir James said sharply. "You have moved in the society of what in my day, when the Regent considered himself a gay Lothario, we used to call 'The Dandy Set.' Surely in that crowd there must have been beautiful women who attracted your attention?"

"Quite a number," Lord Colwall replied frankly, "but they had the great advantage, from my point of view, of already having a husband, even if he was a complaisant one. And while they certainly pleased my eye and, shall we say, excited my interest, I did not find any difficulty in parting from them once they bored me."

"Good God, Ranulf! You must have a heart somewhere in that handsome body of yours?"

"A heart?" Lord Colwall inquired mockingly. "I assure you, my dear Sir James, I tore that vacillating vessel from my breast and replaced it with a stone! I have no heart! No tenderness! No love! And, I hope, no vulnerability left in what you call 'my handsome body.'

"I am a man with the normal passions of a man, but I am completely armoured against the wiles and the deceits of women."

"And you really think you can live the rest of your life in such a state?" Sir James asked.

"I am sure of it," Lord Colwall answered confidently, "and let me tell you that I am absolutely content with myself as I am. People speak of me as a hard man—I am well aware of that! I am hard! I am ruthless! And I intend to stay that way. I do not wish to be beguiled and enticed up the aisle by any designing female, who covets my name."

"It would be easy for a woman to love you for yourself," Sir James said quietly.

"That is where you are wrong!" Lord Colwall contradicted. "No woman will ever love me again because I do not intend that she should do so. I will take her body if it amuses me, but I am not interested in her mind, in her feelings and certainly not in her affections!"

There was a sneer on his lips as he finished.

"Most women, after a few plaintive protestations, are content to take my money or whatever I am prepared to give them and leave me alone."

Sir James gave a deep sigh.

"You were one of the most attractive boys I have ever known. You were a very charming young man. I am not being dramatic, Ranulf, when I say I would have given my right hand to save you from the tragedy which altered your whole character. It should never have happened."

"But it did happen!" Lord Colwall said quietly. "And, as you say, it altered my character and my outlook. There can be no going back. I have therefore made my life my own way! And I can say with complete honesty that it is the way I prefer."

"Perhaps one day . . ." Sir James began tentatively.

"No, no, Sir James," Lord Colwall interrupted. "You are a romantic! This is reality. A man may suffer once from being burnt by a raging fire, but a second time he is too wary to approach it. I have suffered, as you rightly said, but it has made me wise and I shall not make a fool of myself a second time."

"And what about this child that you intend to marry?" Sir James asked.

"Doubtless her parents have explained to her the advantages of such a match," Lord Colwall said loftily. "Incidentally I have paid quite a considerable sum over the years for her education."

"You wanted her educated then?"

"Not for my own benefit," Lord Colwall answered, "but because the mother of my children should be cultured and have a certain amount of learning. After all, a mother is the first teacher a child knows."

There was silence for a moment and then Sir James said:

"It is a pity you did not know your mother. She was very beautiful and very understanding. I have always been convinced that, had she been alive, you would not have been deceived by Claris."

"She died when I was only a year old, and therefore I cannot remember her," Lord Colwall replied. "On the other hand, I remember my father distinctly. I endured eighteen years of his severity and his unmistakable indifference."

"Your father was never the same after the death of your mother," Sir James said. "It was his love for her which made him resent that you were alive, and he blamed you because she never recovered from the very difficult time she had when you were born."

"I know that," Lord Colwall remarked, "and it only proves my point, Sir James, that love, obsessive, possessive and demanding is something to be avoided at all costs."

"Perhaps you will be unable to avoid it," Sir James suggested. "It conquers us all at some time in our lives."

"You are living in cloud-cuckoo land!" Lord Colwall sneered. "Now I must ask you if, having heard the truth about my impending wedding, you will still act as my best man?"

"I will do anything you ask of me," Sir James answered simply, "but I am no less worried and perturbed by what you have told me."

"Leave me to do the worrying," Lord Colwall said. "The marriage will take place in the afternoon, and we shall sit down to what will be a Medieval Wedding Feast at about five o'clock."

"Medieval?" Sir James questioned.

"I found some difficulty in discovering amongst the archives any precedent for a marriage feast of the owner or his son taking place in the Castle," Lord Colwall replied. "Of course, the Reception was usually given at the home of the Bride."

"Naturally," Sir James agreed.

"But in 1496," Lord Colwall went on, "Randolph, the elder son of Sir Hereward Colwall, was married at the Castle to a bride who came to him from Northumbria. It seemed, when I found the reference, an interesting coincidence that my wife comes from Cumberland."

"Were they happy?" Sir James enquired.

"As they had eleven children how could they be anything else?"
Lord Colwall replied mockingly.

"Then let us hope that for your sake history repeats itself," Sir
James said, but he spoke without conviction.

The Dritchka chariot moved along the highway at a quicker pace
than had been possible on the previous days of the journey.

"Look, Papa, it has hardly rained here at all!" Natalia exclaimed.

"I believe it has been a dry October in the South," the Reverend
Adolphus Graystoke replied in a tired voice.

He had found the long journey somewhat exhausting while it appeared that his daughter was fresher and in gayer spirits than when
they had first left their home in Pooley Bridge.

Everything en route was of interest to Natalia; even the rough,
muddy roads that they had encountered on the first part of their
journey had been no hardship.

This was due to the well-sprung travelling chariot which Lord
Colwall had sent for them. When it arrived at the Vicarage, its silver accoutrements and four magnificent horses had evoked the admiration of the whole village.

Even the Vicar had been astonished at the luxury at which they
travelled.

His Lordship's horses had been waiting at every Posting Inn, and
the journey had been made easy by frequent halts, while a courier
in another carriage containing the servants and their luggage left
well ahead to see that everything was in order before their arrival.

"We might be Royalty!" Natalia said in awe-struck tones, at
their first stop.

They had been ushered into a private Sitting-Room by a bowing
Landlord and she found upstairs that a maid had already unpacked
one of her trunks and a valet was attending to her father.

"His Lordship is extremely considerate," the Reverend Adolphus
agreed.

"He thinks of everything!" Natalia said softly.

She had walked across the panelled room to touch a huge vase
of fresh flowers that were arranged on a table.

In front of them lay Lord Colwall's visiting card, and she found
the same attention waiting for her everywhere they stayed.

Each time she admired the flowers she felt that they had a special message for her and she treasured the cards, placing them carefully in her bag.

'Could any man be more attentive to his future bride?' Natalia asked herself.

Lord Colwall had sent not only his carriages, his horses and his servants to Pooley Bridge.

A week before Natalia was due to set out on the journey a trunk had arrived containing new gowns and for the journey a cloak lined with fur!

"Ermine, Mama!" Natalia had exclaimed. "I cannot believe it!"

She was so overcome by the magnificence of the gift that she had not noticed the strange expression on her mother's face.

Lady Margaret had already been informed that Natalia's trousseau from a Bond Street dressmaker would be waiting for her when she arrived at the Castle.

Lord Colwall had written:

"It will not be possible for you to buy in the North the type and variety of gowns Natalia will require as my wife. I have therefore instructed Madame Madeleine to prepare what is required. Kindly send all the measurements necessary to the enclosed address."

"I would have preferred that we should provide Natalia with her trousseau," Lady Margaret said to her husband in private.

"Colwall knows we live in a backwater," the Vicar had replied. "And to be honest, my dear, it would be difficult for us to find the money."

His wife's face was still troubled and he added with a smile:

"Natalia looks lovely whatever she wears, but I would like to see her in an expensive gown like the one you wore the first night we met!"

"Given to me by my godmother, but I at least went with her when she bought it!" Lady Margaret exclaimed and then she added: "Of course I am being nonsensical. Cousin Ranulf is being extremely kind."

But the feeling of uncertainty—with perhaps a touch of resentment had remained.

"If only Mama could be with us," Natalia said now, looking out of the coach window. "Think how thrilled she would have been to see the South again!

"She has often told me how much she has missed the green fields, the apple-blossoms in the spring, and the hedgerows which are so unlike our Cumberland walls."

"It is a bitter disappointment to your mother that she could not see you married."

"Poor Mama, she cried when we left!" Natalia exclaimed with a soft note of sympathy in her voice. "I felt like jumping out of the carriage and sending His Lordship a message to say that, like other brides, I wished to be married from my own home."

"Lord Colwall had not anticipated that your mother would break her ankle just a week before we were due to go South," the Vicar said.

"No, of course not," Natalia agreed, "and, as Mama herself said, it was too late then to alter all the plans."

All the same, there was an ache in her heart as she knew how desperately disappointed her mother had felt at being left behind.

"Never mind," Lady Margaret had said bravely, "I will look after the Parish for your father and at least everything will be ready for him on his return. I shall miss him, as I shall miss you, darling."

Natalia knew this was the truth. Her father and mother loved each other dearly and it was hard for them to be parted, even for a night.

She was well aware that they would both suffer from what would seem a very long time before the Vicar could travel to Herefordshire for her wedding and return to Pooley Bridge.

Natalia had always thought that her home at the end of the Lake of Ullswater was the most beautiful place in the world.

She looked every morning from her bed-room window towards the mountain peaks high on either side of the silver water—their bare, rugged tops silhouetted against the sky.

They always seemed to her to be filled with mystery and a strange enchantment that was part of her dreams.

When she had learned that she was to be married at Lord Colwall's home rather than her own, she had felt a pang of disappointment.

She had thought of him so often that somehow he had become part of the mountains and the beauty of the lake. It was hard to think of him elsewhere.

Although her mother had frequently described to her the wonder and the majesty of the Castle, she found herself always visualising Lord Colwall as she had first seen him.

He had walked towards her through the morning mist rising over the lake. The mountains behind him had made it seem as if he emerged from the insubstantial mystery of her dreams into the reality of her life.

It had been one of those days when everything was very still.

The mountains which round Ullswater changed colour hour by hour had been almost purple, and the sun was attempting to break through the clouds and glint spasmodically on the silver of the lake.

Natalia, who had been visiting a cottage on the outskirts of the village, was returning home. The basket on her arm was empty of the sustaining soup and homemade jam which her mother had sent to an invalid.

Then in front of the Vicarage she had seen a very grand travelling carriage and the four horses which drew it had made her gasp with astonishment.

She walked towards them and then a man who had been standing at the edge of the lake turned from his contemplation of it and moved into the road.

Natalia was so surprised at his appearance that she stood quite still under a tree staring at him. Never in her whole life had she ever seen anyone so handsome or indeed so awe-inspiring.

A cape swung from his shoulders, his dark head was bare because he carried his high hat in his hand.

She watched him wide-eyed but, deep in his thoughts, it appeared he did not see her and he walked directly past her towards the horses.

She thought that he was about to enter the carriage, but instead to her surprise the footman opened the gate to the Vicarage for him.

'Whoever the stranger may be,' Natalia thought to herself, 'he has come to see Papa.'

Still without moving, she watched the footman, the crested gilt buttons on his livery glinting as he hurried ahead of his master to rap sharply on the Vicarage door.

'Who can this visitor be?' Natalia wondered.

Then she realised that the sensible thing to do would be to go home and find out.

She had in fact run back to the Vicarage, entering not through the front door but by the back way to deposit her empty basket in the kitchen. Then she slipped upstairs to change her dress.

At fifteen she had few dresses and there was therefore little choice. But she put on the blue cotton with its full skirt and satin sash that she wore on Sundays, and tidied her hair.

Anxiously she peeped through her bed-room window to see if the horses were still outside.

She was overwhelmed with curiosity, but at the same time she felt a sudden shyness at the thought of speaking to a man who was so impressive, of such obvious importance, and at the same time so handsome.

'Perhaps after all, he is not real,' she told herself, 'but just some-one of whom I have dreamt.'

She smiled as she recalled how often her mother had rebuked her for letting her imagination run away with her, and for peopling the world with the heroes about whom she had read in her father's books.

Always it seemed to her that the Gods and Goddesses of Mount Olympus resided on the mountains that she could see at the end of the lake.

Sometimes as she wandered through the woods which bordered the water, she thought that she saw Apollo pursuing Daphne, or Persephone coming back with the first stirring of spring from the darkness of the Underworld.

"It is all very well for you to stuff the child's head with these mythical characters," Lady Margaret said once to her husband, "but she has to concern herself with Mrs. Warner's rheumatism and Johnny Lovell's measles!

"It really does not help for her to imagine that she is Mercury, the Messenger of the Gods, instead of just little Natalia Graystoke!"

Her father had laughed but had continued to relate to Natalia the legends that he loved and to teach her about Alexander the Great, the Philosophers of Ancient Greece and the achievements of men like Hannibal.

So when Natalia finally met Lord Colwall, his handsome face stirred a chord deep in her memory and she knew who he was.

He was not one of the Gods of Olympus nor one of the great Conquerors of History.

But just as surely as if a voice had spoken to her from the sky, she knew he was to her someone very special and very personal.

He was in fact her Knight.

CHAPTER TWO

It was of course the Reverend Adolphus who had put the idea into Natalia's head.

She had been twelve years old and was walking with her father along the side of the lake. They wended their way through the silver birch trees which were just coming into bud.

A strong wind was blowing the waters into silver ripples and the clouds were heavy on the tops of the mountains.

But Natalia could only listen enthralled to the story her father was telling her about the Crusaders.

It was one of his favourite subjects, and because he had a Scholar's command of words he could make her feel the excitement which fired the noblemen of England and other Christian countries when they decided they must defend the Holy City of Jerusalem from the infidels.

Natalia used to imagine crowds of men assembling in the Castles of their Liege Lords.

There, inspired with the desire and the will to go on the long and dangerous journey, they left behind them their wives, families and everything familiar.

She could visualise the ships setting out in style filled with horses and men, flying pennants and bedecked with flags.

Their Commander, King Richard the Lion-Hearted, led the British contingent on what must have seemed to many a hopeless mission.

It was thinking of the courage of those that attempted such a feat which made Natalia's eyes shine and her blood quicken as she learnt how much over the centuries they had achieved.

Her father told her about the hospital in Jerusalem which had been founded more than a hundred years earlier to care for Christian pilgrims.

He told her how the Knights Hospitallers had been driven out first to Rhodes and from there to Malta.

He described their ceaseless fight from that small island against the Barbary pirates who infested the Mediterranean and who held at one time more than twenty-five thousand Christian prisoners in Algiers alone.

He made Natalia see as clearly as if she had been there the magnificent Auberges built in Rhodes and Malta to house the Knights of each country, men not only of great courage, but of culture, intelligence and breeding.

Then the Reverend Adolphus had said sadly:

"Napoleon overran Malta sixteen years ago, dispersed the Knights and stole all the treasures they had accumulated over the centuries."

"Oh, Papa! But they cannot be vanquished forever!" Natalia exclaimed in concern.

"Certainly not forever," her father replied. "The Order still exists in other European countries and the ideals they stood for and the bravery which has lifted men's hearts all through the ages will survive."

"I am glad!" Natalia cried. "I could not bear all that wonderful courage to be wasted."

"That could never happen," the Reverend Adolphus remarked. "Never forget, my dearest, the desire to combat the forces of evil is something which should animate us all."

Natalia considered what he had said, then she asked quietly:

"You mean, Papa, that we should each of us fight physically and mentally against what we think is wrong."

"And for what we believe is right," the Reverend Adolphus added. "I often think, Natalia, that we are too prone to accept conditions as they are instead of trying to improve them."

He sighed and Natalia said:

"But Papa, you have often said in Church that we must love our enemies."

"Love does not mean accepting what is wrong or refraining from punishing ill-doers," her father replied. "We have to be strong in ourselves, to be upright, and above all, courageous, as the Knights were."

He paused and added with a faint smile:

"I often think that when we tell children that they have a guardian angel to watch over them, we give them the wrong image."

"And what is the right image, Papa?"

"I think that instead of an angel, soft and gentle with white wings," the Reverend Adolphus had replied, warming to his theme, "that we each of us have a special Knight who fights on our behalf against evil and all the dangers that encompass us."

"A Knight!" Natalia echoed softly.

"Yes, indeed," her father went on, "a Knight with a sword in his hand! For love is not only a sentimental and romantic emotion; it is also an unsheathed sword that must thrust its way to victory."

After that Natalia was never afraid when she walked through the woods alone or sometimes had to find her way home blindly through the thick mist which would rise unexpectedly from the lake.

She believed that her Knight—her guardian Knight—was with her, accompanying her and watching over her. Sometimes she would even talk to him and sense rather than hear his answers.

So when she was summoned to the Drawing-Room to meet the tall, handsome stranger whom her mother introduced as a relative, she recognised him!

'No wonder,' she thought to herself after her very first glance at Lord Colwall, 'he seems familiar.'

He was just as she had visualised her Knight would look.

As she stared up at him, her eyes very large in her small pointed face, she had seen not the elegance of his fashionable clothes, nor the crisp whiteness of his frilled cravat, but a shining armour, a plumed helmet and a naked sword in his hand.

"This is Natalia, Cousin Ranulf," she heard her mother say. "She is fifteen, and she is our only child, but even so, we try not to spoil her."

It seemed to Natalia that Lord Colwall looked at her surprisingly searchingly. She felt as if his eyes penetrated deep into her very heart.

She curtsied, then found it impossible to look away from him, or even to drop her eyes modestly as she knew she should do. Never had she imagined that any man could be so handsome!

"I wish to speak with you and your husband alone," Lord Colwall remarked abruptly to Lady Margaret.

Her mother turned towards Natalia.

"I am sure, darling, you have something to occupy you in the Study. I will call you before His Lordship leaves so that you may say good-bye."

With an effort, Natalia found her voice.

"May I please," she asked, speaking to Lord Colwall, "go and look at your horses?"

"You like horses?" he asked.

"I love them!"

"Then I will send you one."

She stared at him in astonishment.

"You will send me a horse?" she questioned. "One like those you have outside?"

"A better one."

She had gone from the room, her head in a whirl, hardly believing that she could have heard him aright.

When a month later, the horse arrived, it had only confirmed her conviction that Lord Colwall was the Knight who had been sent to look after her, to guard her and to bring her an almost inexpressible happiness.

Her father and mother had not told her for two years that her future had been decided that afternoon when Lord Colwall had come so unexpectedly to the Vicarage.

She only knew that her whole life had changed.

From having a few lessons a week with old Miss Grimsdown who lived in the village and who had long retired from teaching, her days were now filled with visiting teachers, two of whom came from as far away as Penrith.

There was a French teacher who spoke with a Parisian accent, which her mother considered most important. There were teachers for Arithmetic, Algebra, Geometry, Geography, the fundamental rules of English grammar, and Music.

There was a teacher of Latin who thought her father's methods were hopelessly out of date and who made what had been a joy and an interest into hours of laborious boredom.

The Vicar, however, had been insistent upon one thing; he and no-one else should teach his daughter History and the Classics, and it was these lessons which Natalia prized above all others.

She did, however, try to learn from the other teachers because, although nothing had been said, she sensed that this new tuition was connected with Lord Colwall and she wanted, above all things, to please him.

"How could anybody be more kind than to give me you as a present?" she asked her horse.

He was a high-spirited three-year-old who had arrived at the Vicarage complete with a groom to look after him.

Inevitably Natalia christened him "Crusader," and sometimes she thought that she herself was embarking on a special crusade. Whom she was fighting or for what cause, she was not quite certain!

"How can we afford all these expensive things, Mother?" she asked her mother once, and was surprised when Lady Margaret did not reply immediately.

"Someone is helping your father and me in this matter," she said at length a little evasively.

Natalia said no more. She had felt sure without being told who that someone was, and when eventually her mother told her the truth, it was what she had always suspected.

Only one person could have thought of her well-being, or cared enough to plan her education.

'I must work hard so that he will be proud of me,' she told herself when she first started on the new regime.

When finally she reached her seventeenth birthday and her mother told her that all this preparation was because Lord Colwall wished, when she was old enough, to marry her, she knew she had worked because she loved him.

She loved him because from the very moment she first saw him she had been sure he was the Knight who had been in her thoughts and her dreams for over three years.

She loved him for his thought of her, for the trouble he had taken in planning her education, and most of all because he had given her Crusader.

"His Lordship told us when he came here," Lady Margaret had said in a hesitant, worried voice, "that when you were old enough, he desired to make you his wife."

Natalia did not answer. It seemed as if the small room in the Vicarage was suddenly filled with a golden unearthly light.

She could feel her heart beating loudly in her breast and yet she could not speak, could not find the words in which to answer her mother.

"Of course, darling," Lady Margaret was saying, "when you meet him again, you may not care for His Lordship. In which case Papa and I would have to explain that despite all he had done, a marriage between you was not possible."

Still Natalia did not speak, and after a moment Lady Margaret went on:

"But if it was not against your wishes, it would be in fact the sort of marriage I had always hoped and prayed you might make. It would be wonderful for me that you should live in the house I always loved and which as a girl was the most exciting place I ever visited."

"You have often . . . spoken of the . . . Castle, Mama," Natalia managed to say.

"It is so magnificent—a dream Castle," Lady Margaret said. "Of course Cousin Ranulf's mother was dead, but his widowed Aunt, Lady Blestow, always played hostess when there were visitors.

"We had very gay parties at Christmas and in the summer. There was a great Ball-Room where we could dance until the early hours of the morning, and lovely gardens where there were endless amusements for young people."

"You have told me about it very often, Mama," Natalia said in a faraway voice.

"I never dreamt in those days my daughter would ever live there! But even so, Natalia, Papa and I have talked it over and we would not compel you to do anything you do not wish to do."

"But I do wish to marry Lord Colwall," Natalia said, feeling as if the words came winging from the depths of her heart.

"I had hoped," Lady Margaret continued, "that he would visit us again, but perhaps it is best for him to wait until you are grown up. He will see then how much you have altered since he first saw you, and I know he will be interested, Natalia, to discover how talented you are."

She gave a little laugh.

"Your Papa has always said that if you had been a boy, he is certain that you would have done very well at Oxford and gained a degree."

"When can I be . . . married, Mama?"

There was a note of impatience in Natalia's tone, and now her mother saw that her eyes were shining as if a light had been lit behind them.

"I do not know exactly, Natalia," she replied. "I write to His Lordship every month telling him of your prowess. I know when he came here he spoke of waiting until you were eighteen. That will mean another year at least, and I can assure you that Papa and I are in no hurry to lose you."

"No, of course not, Mama," Natalia said, almost as if it was expected of her. "At the same time, if I have only a year before I am married, then there is so much more I must learn; so much I must read. Oh, dear! How shall I get it done?"

Lady Margaret gave her a fond smile.

"I do not think, Natalia, that Lord Colwall will marry you entirely for your intellectual abilities. At the same time your Papa has always said that women should be educated as well as men. I must say I have often regretted that I cannot follow his more erudite arguments, or understand everything he tries to impart to me."

Natalia had bent to kiss her mother's cheek.

"Papa thinks you are perfect, Mama," she said fondly, "and I hope that His Lordship will find me as agreeable."

Lady Margaret gave a little sigh.

"I am sure he will, darling," she said, but she sounded almost as if she convinced herself rather than her daughter.

Because she was so anxious to shine in Lord Colwall's eyes Natalia persuaded her father to take not only the *Morning Post* but also *The Times*.

"I shall never have time to read two newspapers, Natalia," the Reverend Adolphus protested.

"But I have!" Natalia answered. "I must be up to date, Papa, with what is happening in the world outside."

She gave a little sigh.

"Pooley Bridge is so isolated that we might be living on an island in the Atlantic."

"Now, Natalia, that is not fair," her father protested. "You and your mother visit Penrith at least once a month and there are some very agreeable people in the neighbourhood, including my own family."

"Yes, I know, Papa, and I am not complaining," Natalia answered, "but I wish that Lord Colwall had thought it part of my education that I should go to London or perhaps even to Europe!"

She paused and said:

"Can you imagine, Papa, what it would be like to see Rome, or Athens?"

"I am sure your husband will take you to both these places when you are married," the Vicar answered. "It would be disappointing for him if you had seen them already with someone else."

A little shadow cleared from Natalia's face.

"Yes, of course, that is what His Lordship intends," she said. "How clever of you, Papa, to realise it. And naturally I would much rather go with him than with anyone else in the world.

"But you must tell me the whole history of the Colosseum, the Forum, and Acropolis and the Parthenon, in case however clever His Lordship may be, he does not know as much as you."

"I am sure he will know a great deal more," the Reverend Adolphus declared modestly.

At the same time he dropped a light kiss on his daughter's hair.

"But however interesting the Ancient World may be," Natalia went on, "and you know how much their histories delight you and me, Papa, I must also be knowledgeable on current affairs."

There was a little frown between her eyes as she said:

"There are more letters in *The Times* today about the cruelty of very young children being employed in the mines. I think you should read them, Papa."

"I will, indeed," the Reverend Adolphus replied. "I suppose they have not published my letter about the iniquity of 'Strappers' being used to whip into wakefulness the children who labour on the looms."

"It has not appeared yet," Natalia answered, "but there is a letter from Lord Lauderdale insisting that climbing boys are essential if chimneys are to be cleaned, and that people who say it is cruel to use children of five or six years old are talking rubbish!"

The Reverend Adolphus gave a snort of sheer fury.

"Lord Lauderdale should be thrust up a chimney himself!" he declared. "I only wish I could meet His Lordship and tell him what I think of him."

He spoke so violently that Natalia gave a little laugh.

"Oh, Papa, I love you in your militant mood," she exclaimed. "If you only could be in the House of Lords I really believe that you would rout Lord Lauderdale!"

As she spoke she remembered that Lord Colwall was a member of the Upper House.

She wondered why she had never seen his name amongst those who spoke on the subjects which interested her and her father, and on which they both felt so intensely.

Journeying now in the Dritchka chariot on the last day of their journey as they passed through the fruitful vale of Evesham, Natalia said almost triumphantly:

"There has been no talk in the newspapers of agricultural trouble in Herefordshire."

"No, I have noticed that," her father replied. "It started early last month in Kent and then spread into Sussex and Hampshire."

"There has been a great deal about the Dorchester labourers in *The Times*," Natalia said. "The men are receiving only 7 shillings per week, but they used no violence beyond breaking up a number of threshing machines."

"I read that," her father said. "They behaved with restraint and actually said: 'We do not intend to hurt the farmer but we are determined that we shall have more wages.'"

"Nevertheless, two of the men were sentenced to death," Natalia said in a low voice.

"It is disgraceful," the Vicar said angrily, "when a man cannot speak up for himself without being tried for his life or transported!"

He pursed his lips before he continued:

"I read the case of one man called Legge who was transported because he was declared by the Prosecutor to be 'saucy and impudent' and to have talked 'rough and bobbish.'"

"I read that too," Natalia said. "Yet his character, which included a testimonial from a clergyman, was said to be exemplary."

"How could they do anything so unjust?" the Reverend Adolphus asked. "Legge had five children whom he supported without Parish help on 7 shillings per week. His cottage was given to him, but no fuel."

"I am sure Lord Colwall would never tolerate such cruelty on his estate!" Natalia exclaimed.

"No, of course not," her father agreed quickly. "But I have noticed that there has been trouble in Gloucester which is not far from Colwall."

"But there had never been one word either in *The Times* or the *Morning Post* about Herefordshire," Natalia said quickly. "I am sure Lord Colwall cannot have a threshing machine."

"Let us hope not!" the Reverend Adolphus said in heartfelt tones. "A landowner near Canterbury wrote that in his parish, where no machines had been introduced, there were twenty-three barns. He calculated that in three barns fifteen men would find good, steady employment threshing corn by hand until May."

"And they make extra money!" Natalia exclaimed.

"A man threshing by hand over the winter can earn from 15 to 20 shillings per week," the Vicar replied.

"It is easy for us to imagine," Natalia said quietly, "what the sight of one of those hated machines can mean to men like that! Are you surprised they destroy what to them is a monster of injustice?"

"I do not think," her father said firmly, "that the labourers over the whole country are getting either a fair deal or a fair hearing."

He added positively:

"You must speak to His Lordship when you are married, Natalia, and see that on the Colwall estate at least there is justice and a living wage for those who work there."

"I am sure His Lordship is most generous," Natalia said softly, thinking of how kind her future husband had been to her.

She could feel the softness of the ermine inside her cloak which had kept her warm against the bitter winds and sleet they had encountered soon after they started on their journey South.

She remembered the gowns of silks and satins that had been sent to the Vicarage at the same time as the cloak.

There had also been nightgowns like gossamer, petticoats and chemises so fine they could pass through a wedding ring.

She then realised her trousseau must have cost an almost astronomical sum of money, and she thought that her mother's quite obvious lack of enthusiasm was due to her feeling that Lord Colwall had been extravagant.

Lady Margaret's reaction was in fact because she considered the gifts had been sent in a somewhat arbitrary manner, but Natalia was overcome by such kindness.

The way they travelled, the flowers that had awaited her at each stopping place, the money that had been expended on her over the years, and above all Crusader could only, Natalia thought, have been provided by a man who was unbelievably generous, in thought as well as in deed.

They stayed the last night of their journey at a black and white Inn in Tewkesbury.

Although she was a little tired after so many miles on the road, Natalia had accompanied her father to the Norman Abbey, which the Reverend Adolphus said he had always longed to visit.

The great rounded arches, the stained-glass windows, and the immensely high Chancel had made Natalia feel that she offered her heart up to Heaven in gratitude for all that was happening and all that lay ahead of her.

As she knelt beside her father, she had told herself she could never thank God enough for the happiness she had known as a child and the happiness that would be hers in her married life.

"Thank You, God, thank You," she whispered, and thought even as she prayed that a voice within herself told her that she was really blessed.

"Tomorrow I shall see him," she said later as she laid her head on the pillow.

She was sure she would be unable to sleep but nevertheless she slept peacefully until the Lady's Maid who had travelled with them came to call her.

" 'Tis eight o'clock Miss, and the Reverend Gentleman has already gone down to breakfast."

For a moment, Natalia could not remember where she was, then she gave a little cry of excitement.

"We shall reach the Castle today, Ellen!" she exclaimed.

"Yes, Miss, and very impressed you'll be with it. They say there's not a Castle in the whole length and breadth of the country to equal ours."

Natalia smiled at her. She had already learnt that Ellen had been at the Castle since she was very young and had in fact been born and bred in Herefordshire.

"I shall see His Lordship," she whispered almost to herself.

"Yes, Miss, and I expect you will find a very grand wedding awaiting for you. When His Lordship organises anything, he always expects perfection."

"That is what my marriage will be," Natalia murmured.

She thought Ellen looked at her in rather a strange manner, then the Maid said:

"I hopes you'll bring His Lordship happiness, Miss. From all I hears he was hard done by in the past, and it's only right he should be happy the second time."

Natalia did not reply.

The thought of Lord Colwall's first marriage was something she had pushed to the back of her mind and which she had not discussed with anyone, not even her mother.

"Cousin Ranulf has been married before," Lady Margaret had said when she had told Natalia the reason for her intensive education.

"He was married!" Natalia ejaculated.

"For a very short time," Lady Margaret said.

"What happened to his wife?"

"There was an accident and—she died." Lady Margaret answered hesitantly.

Natalia had been curious, and yet at the same time something had prevented her from asking questions.

She had not wanted to know. She had not wanted to think that her Knight, the man who was bliss, had ever belonged to another woman.

It had seemed to her as if for a moment some of the light that illuminated the room when her mother had told her of Lord Colwall's intentions, had been dimmed.

Then she told herself she was being absurd! It had happened a long time ago, he had been very young, and by now he would have forgotten his sorrow.

"Yet would one ever forget someone to whom one had been married?" an inner voice questioned.

Natalia tried to think of herself in the same circumstances and failed.

'Perhaps,' she told herself, 'it is different for a man.'

"There were no children of the marriage," Lady Margaret was saying, "and I am praying, dearest, that you will have a son, perhaps more than one, and daughters, too, who will enjoy the Castle as much as I did as a child."

She said reminiscently:

"It is a wonderful place for Hide and Seek with its twisting stairways, turrets and towers! It has all the things which appeal to a child's imagination."

Natalia had thought of her mother's words that night when she had gone to bed.

Yes, she would love to have children. They would play in the Castle, and she would tell them the stories that her father had told to her. Of one thing she was quite certain—she would have more than one!

It had been lonely having no brother or sister to share her games, or, more important, to whom she could confide her dreams of the wondrous characters who in her imagination peopled the woods and the mountains.

"I long to see the Castle," she said aloud to Ellen. "It is I am sure a very fitting home for His Lordship."

She said no more but allowed Ellen to dress her hair in what was a more elaborate style than usual.

A travelling gown of dark blue cashmere trimmed with frills of taffeta and small velvet bows seemed to Natalia after her plain cotton dresses to be the zenith of elegance.

She had no idea until she wore expensive gowns what a tiny waist she had, that her skin was so white or her hair the colour of Spring sunshine.

"How do I look, Ellen?" she asked staring at her reflection in the small mirror.

"Very lovely, Miss," Ellen replied in almost awestruck tones. "You will make a beautiful bride."

That is what Natalia wanted to hear, that she would look beautiful, really beautiful for the man whom she dreamed about, and who had become already an indivisible part of her life.

The Knight who walked beside her through the woods. The Knight with whom she had raced over the fields when she rode Crusader, allowing him in her imagination to beat her because, as a Knight, he must excel at everything, even at the games they played together.

Then finally as they drove round the Malvern Hills they had their first view of the Castle.

Natalia drew in her breath.

She did not believe it possible for any place to be so magnificent! Or indeed so dream-like.

The last leaves of October were still russet and golden on the trees which surrounded it. The great towers emerged above them, grey and stalwart, and the afternoon sunlight seemed to touch the stone walls with a shimmer of fairy gold.

"Look, Papa. The Castle!"

Natalia could hardly breathe the words, and the Reverend Adolphus, who had been sleeping in a corner of the carriage, raised himself to look out of the window.

"Yes, indeed, the Castle!" he exclaimed. "It is a very fine building, Natalia."

"It is wonderful! Glorious! I had imagined it, but it is far, far more magnificent than I thought any place could be!"

There was a river running through the valley below and the Castle, visible for miles away, had been built to stand sentinel over the lush and undulating countryside which surrounded it.

Far away in the distance there were the Welsh Mountains, their barren peaks high in Heaven, purple and mysterious as the mountains at Ullswater.

Now that the moment when she would meet Lord Colwall was near, Natalia for the first time felt nervous.

Supposing, after all, he did not like her? Supposing he had changed his mind in the three years since he decided that she should be his wife, and had found someone else he loved more?

Then she told herself she was being ridiculous.

After all, if he had found someone else, he would not have sent for her. The summons had come immediately after her eighteenth birthday, so perhaps, like her, he had been counting the days until he considered her old enough to be his Bride.

"Do I look . . . all right, Papa?"

The words were a little frightened and the large grey-green eyes in the small face which was lifted towards the Reverend Adolphus were troubled.

"You look very beautiful," her father replied. "Not as beautiful as your mother was when I first saw her! No-one could be as beautiful as that! But lovely in your own way."

"Thank you, Papa," Natalia gave him a little smile, and then bending forward she laid her cheek for a moment against his arm.

"I shall miss you, Papa, and I shall miss more than I can tell you, our talks, our discussions and the clever way you explain everything to me."

"Your husband will talk to you now," the Reverend Adolphus said. "You are not only beautiful, my dearest, but you are very intelligent. It is unusual amongst women, and because God has blessed you, especially as regarding your talents, you must not hide them under a bushel."

"I will try not to do that, Papa."

"At the same time," the Reverend Adolphus said quickly, "no man wants a woman to be assertive, dictatorial, or—shall we say?—bossy. You must be subservient to your husband in everything and do what he says.

"But I would not wish you, Natalia, to waste your powers of intellectual perception, and I feel sure that in the life that lies ahead of you, such qualities can be utilised."

"If in no other way," Natalia replied with a smile, "I should have to be intelligent before I could run a place as big as the Castle!"

"I am sure His Lordship has a very adequate staff," her father replied.

Then he added:

"But you are right, my dear. There will be many things you can do to help your husband to keep the background of his life running smoothly. At the same time, I am sure you can persuade him to use his influence to help those unfortunates about whom we have so often spoken."

"The children, the labourers, the chimney boys," Natalia exclaimed. "There are so many of them!"

She gave a little sigh.

"You cannot expect to work miracles overnight," her father warned. "But a man who loves his wife listens to her. I cannot help feeling that the more people speak out, especially in the House of Lords, against the many injustices and indeed the atrocities that are perpetrated in this country at the present moment, the sooner we can bring to those who suffer both mercy and justice."

"I will do my best, Papa," Natalia murmured in a soft voice.

"I know you will, dear Child," her father answered.

As if he knew Natalia was feeling nervous, he took her hand in his and held it.

Now the horses had reached the valley behind the Malvern Hills and they were proceeding to climb again up the hill on which the Castle was situated.

Because the leaves were still on some of the trees, they only had glimpses of its magnificence through the branches.

They passed through the impressive wrought-iron gates with great heraldic stone lions on either side, and drove up a long avenue of ancient oak trees rising all the time until finally, when they reached the top, there stood the Castle in front of them, a truly awe-inspiring sight.

Built originally on the site of an older Castle which had been erected soon after the Norman Conquest, it had been the focal point of defence for the West of England against the onslaughts of the Welsh.

Its towers and thirty-foot-high Keep stood dramatically on a great conical mound of earth which had been part of the original plan, while other towers had been erected in the succeeding centuries.

For a moment Natalia felt that it was too magnificent, too overpowering! Then she remembered it was in fact the perfect background for her Knight.

'Where else should a Knight live except in a Castle?' she asked herself. 'How many deeds of chivalry, how many great battles against injustice have been planned within these walls?'

It seemed to her that there was an army of servants waiting to assist her and her father from the carriage.

A Major-Domo in resplendent livery stepped forward to say:

"May I welcome you, Miss Graystoke, on behalf of His Lordship, to Colwall Castle, and you too, Sir."

"Thank you," Natalia replied in a shy voice.

She had expected Lord Colwall to be waiting for them in the Hall which, with its Grand Staircase and high Gothic ceiling, was extremely impressive.

Slightly to her surprise, she was immediately escorted up the stairs past the coloured heraldic beasts on each turn of the marble stairway to a bed-chamber on the first floor.

There an elderly woman whom Natalia felt sure was the Housekeeper, and two other maids were waiting for her. They curtsied and explained that they had prepared a bath and a change of clothing after her journey.

"Thank you. That will be very pleasant," Natalia said gratefully.

It was consistent, she thought, with the consideration she and her father had been shown ever since they left home, and she was glad that she was not to see His Lordship until she looked her best for him.

'He thinks of everything!' she told herself once again.

She allowed the Maids to help her undress and enjoyed her bath which had been placed in front of a warm fire. She was aware that the bathwater was scented with roses and the soft towels with which she dried herself smelt of lavender.

The bed-chamber was a fine room. There was a huge four-poster bed hung with embroidered curtains which Natalia learnt had been worked by the ladies who lived in the Castle during the reign of Queen Anne.

There were French Commodes which she knew were priceless and the ceiling had a cornice of brilliantly painted heraldic devices. The carved Medieval fireplace was surmounted by a huge Coat of Arms picked out in gold.

It was difficult to take in everything at once and Natalia was at the moment concerned only with looking her best for Lord Colwall.

There was no need to unpack the bags that had come with her on the journey, for when the Housekeeper opened the wardrobe, it was filled with gowns of every possible material and colour.

"These all came from London, Miss," she explained.

"They are lovely, very lovely!" Natalia said in awe-struck tones. "What must I wear now?"

"It will soon be time for dinner, Miss. I have chosen, if it meets with your approval, a white gown trimmed with Venetian lace."

"You are sure that is the most becoming?" Natalia asked, a worried expression in her eyes.

"I am sure you would look lovely in anything, Miss," the Housekeeper replied. "But I felt that this particular gown was most suitable for this evening. There will be His Lordship and Sir James Parke to dinner besides yourself and your Reverend father."

Natalia smiled. It was perfect that they should be such a small party and she was sure that the reason Lord Colwall had arranged it this way was so that they could have a chance to get to know each other.

But then the Housekeeper went on:

"After dinner, there will be a number of people from the Estate arriving whom His Lordship will present to you. The Agent, the farm managers and some of the more important tenants."

"Of course I should like to meet them," Natalia answered.

She suppressed a feeling of regret that she would not after all be able to talk alone with her future husband.

"Your wedding, Miss, will be exactly the same as the one which took place here in Medieval times," the Housekeeper continued. "His Lordship discovered the details in a book. The food will be the same, the Orchestra will use the same type of instruments that were played here in the Castle hundreds of years ago."

She looked at Natalia's surprised face and said:

"His Lordship is a great one for tradition, Miss. I heard him say that he had searched through all the archives of the family history to find a previous occasion on which a marriage of an owner of the Castle had taken place here."

Natalia did not know why, but the idea that it was all being copied from the past and was not something planned just for her was a little depressing.

Then she told herself she was being nonsensical.

This is why Lord Colwall had wished her to journey to the Castle. It was unthinkable that with his vast possessions and great importance he should be married at Pooley Bridge!

It was completely right and fitting that she should come to him, that their marriage should be traditional and would become in the years that lay ahead another item in the history of the Colwall family.

'I must get His Lordship to tell me all about the previous weddings that took place here,' Natalia thought.

Then with a feeling almost of dismay, she found herself unable to prevent the question which she knew she should not ask.

"Was His Lordship . . . married from here . . . before?"

"No indeed, Miss, of course not," the Housekeeper replied. "He was married from Lady Claris's own home. 'Tis not far away. Only the other side of the hills."

Then as if she felt she had said too much, the Housekeeper turned away abruptly to give an almost sharp order to one of the housemaids to hurry up and remove the bath.

With her hair arranged once again in the more sophisticated manner that Ellen had tried out for the first time that morning, and with her full skirts rustling silkily, Natalia descended the stairs.

Now for the first time she could appreciate the exquisitely moulded arches of the staircase, although the marble itself felt cold beneath the touch of her hand.

The huge tapestries hanging on the walls she knew must be of great antiquity and she realised that they depicted battles. Battles in which, she told herself, the Lord Colwall of the day had fought as a Knight.

There were also faded flags hanging on either side of the chimney piece and swords and shields on two walls.

There were a number of footmen on duty in the hall. Their claret-coloured livery seemed very ornate in Natalia's eyes, and their powdered wigs were splotches of white against the dark panelling.

The Major-Domo was waiting to take her down a long Gothic-arched corridor which was lined with suits of armour, some early English and some French. He threw open the door of a large Salon.

Natalia had a quick glimpse of walls covered with pictures, of a ceiling of carved mahogany, of gilded furniture, of sofas and chairs in tapestry and damask.

There were three Gentlemen standing by the great carved mantel-piece but she had eyes for only one!

A Gentleman so outstanding, so handsome, that he seemed, even as he had done in her mother's small Drawing-Room, to dominate the whole room.

Lord Colwall had not changed!

If anything, she thought, he was more handsome than she remembered.

And because she was so pleased to see him, because everything in her life had seemed to move towards this dramatic climax, she forgot everything, formality, good manners and even her own shyness as she ran towards him.

Her voice seemed to ring out in the silent room.

"You are here! I am so glad, so very . . . very glad to see Your Lordship again!"

CHAPTER THREE

Natalia reached Lord Colwall's side.

She stood looking up at him; her eyes were very large and shone like stars in her small face, her fair hair seemed to gleam like a halo in the lights from the chandelier.

To Sir James Parke, watching them, Lord Colwall's face was entirely expressionless as he said courteously:

"I am delighted your journey was not too arduous."

As if she suddenly remembered her manners, Natalia sank down in a deep curtsey. Then as she rose she said irrepressibly:

"The Castle is magnificent! Even more magnificent than I imagined it would be. And you, My Lord . . . you are just the same as when I first saw you three years ago!"

"I was telling Lord Colwall," the Reverend Adolphus interposed, "how much your mother regrets being unable to accompany us."

"Yes, of course," Natalia said quickly.

She sensed that her father was reprimanding her for not having mentioned her mother at once.

"It is indeed regrettable that my cousin should have sustained an accident at such a very inappropriate moment," Lord Colwall remarked.

"It only happened a week before we left . . ." the Reverend Adolphus began . . .

Natalia's attention was distracted by a big dog which rose from the hearth-rug to approach her tentatively. It was a mastiff and quite one of the largest dogs she had ever seen.

"He is yours?" she exclaimed to Lord Colwall. "Just the type of dog you should have!"

"I should not touch him," Lord Colwall said quickly, but it was too late.

Natalia had knelt down on the floor beside the dog and put her arms around its neck.

"He is magnificent, like your horses," she smiled.

The mastiff's tail was wagging and he was submitting amicably to her caress. Lord Colwall watched them both with surprise.

"Herald does not usually take to strangers," he said after a moment.

"That is true," Sir James Parke agreed, speaking for the first time since Natalia had entered the room. "After all these years, Ranulf, he still never greets me with anything but a low growl!"

"Natalia has always had a way with animals," the Reverend Adolphus remarked proudly.

He looked at the picture Natalia made with her white skirt billowing out over the hearth-rug, her bare arms around the neck of the huge mastiff, her face soft and glowing in the firelight.

There was something like a challenge in the Vicar's voice as he said to Lord Colwall:

"I think Your Lordship will discover that Natalia can charm not only animals but also human beings."

It appeared, however, that Lord Colwall was not listening. He moved to the side of the fire-place where there was a table on which were two leather-covered boxes.

He opened them and said in a voice of command:

"Come here, Natalia."

She rose to her feet immediately and walked to where he stood. The mastiff, as if he did not wish to part from her, walked at her side.

"I have for you," Lord Colwall said, "the engagement ring which has been in my family since the days of Elizabeth I. It was designed by Sir Francis Colwall for one of Her Majesty's Ladies-in-Waiting, whom he married."

He opened the box he held in his hand and Natalia saw a large ring, very different from anything she had expected. It consisted of a huge baroque pearl, set in gold and surrounded by rubies and diamonds.

"It is lovely!" she exclaimed.

"I hoped you would think so."

Lord Colwall held the box out to her, but for a moment she hesitated.

She had expected him to put the ring on her finger, then as he did not do so, she slipped it onto the third finger of her left hand.

"It fits exactly!" she said in surprise.

"I had it altered to the measurements sent to me by your mother," Lord Colwall explained in a matter-of-fact voice.

Natalia stared down at the huge ring which seemed far too big for her little hand.

It was very beautiful and very unusual but it evoked a memory of her childhood.

She had been about ten years of age when she had looked at her mother's engagement ring, which consisted of one very small diamond surrounded by even smaller ones.

"The stones are not very big, Mama," she had said with the frankness of a child.

Her mother smiled.

"It was all that your Papa could afford when we got engaged, but when he gave it to me and kissed my finger before he slipped it on, I felt that every stone was as big as a marble!"

She laughed and held Natalia close in her arms as she added:

"It is not the gift which counts, dearest, it is the love with which it is given. Always remember that!"

Lord Colwall's voice interrupted Natalia's thoughts.

"I have something else for you."

He opened the other box, a much larger one. There on black velvet lay a pendant which Natalia could see was intended to be worn with the ring.

It, too, consisted of a baroque pearl—another very large one. It was suspended from the most brilliant enamel-work, also ornamented with rubies and diamonds.

As she looked closer, she saw that the enamel represented a man on horse-back, a spear in his hand, and the huge pearl was part of the body of a dragon which he was killing.

"He is a Knight!" she exclaimed incredulously.

"I believe it is intended to portray one of my ancestors," Lord Colwall explained. "The pendant was made for Lord Colwall in 1655 when he visited Venice, and every Colwall bride since then has worn it when she first receives the engagement ring."

"They certainly complement each other," Sir James said. "You must show your future bride, Ranulf, the many portraits in the Castle of past Lady Colwalls wearing both these jewels."

Lord Colwall took the pendant from its box, and Natalia saw that it was attached to a long, thin chain which glittered with diamonds.

He held it out to her and once again she wondered if he would put it around her neck, but it was in fact her father who did so.

"Thank you . . . My Lord," she said when it finally lay on her chest, nearly reaching the little hollow between her breasts.

Lord Colwall moved from the table back to the hearth-rug.

"I think, Sir," he said to the Reverend Adolphus, "you will be interested tomorrow to see how a Medieval Wedding Feast can still be produced in modern times."

"Tomorrow?" the Reverend Adolphus ejaculated in astonishment.

Lord Colwall did not reply.

"Are you telling me that Natalia is being married tomorrow?"

Lord Colwall raised his eyebrows:

"It appears to surprise you!"

"I had no idea the ceremony was to take place so soon!" the Reverend Adolphus exclaimed. "After all, we might have been delayed."

"I was not afraid of that!" Lord Colwall answered. "My arrangements are made with the greatest precision, and I would have been extremely incensed with my coachman if you had not arrived today at exactly the time I expected you!"

The Reverend Adolphus looked at Natalia.

"My daughter might have been expected to be tired after the long journey," he said. "I should have thought a few days' rest would have been an obvious consideration."

"But I am not tired, Papa," Natalia protested.

She felt uncomfortable at the note of criticism in her father's voice.

"I felt certain, in view of the quite small number of miles you have had to travel during the last three days," Lord Colwall said slowly, "that you would not be in the least exhausted, and I have in fact made all the arrangements for our wedding to take place tomorrow."

"I am quite happy to agree to anything Your Lordship has planned," Natalia said.

Because she felt there was still a feeling of obvious disapproval emanating from her father, she quickly tried to change the subject:

"Your horses are so splendid that you were quite justified in trusting them to bring us here at exactly the time you had planned."

She looked up at him with a smile on her face and added:

"Of all the wonderful gifts you have given me . . . and I have so much to thank you for . . . the best of them all was, of course, Crusader!"

Lord Colwall looked puzzled.

"Crusader?" he queried.

"My horse . . . the one you sent me. I have ridden him every day, and I was going to ask you later if he could be brought here to the Castle. I cannot bear to be without him."

"But of course," Lord Colwall agreed. "That is very easily arranged. When your father returns tomorrow he can carry my instructions to the groom to bring Crusader home."

"Oh, thank you! Thank you!" Natalia cried. "I knew you would understand how much Crusader has meant to me all these years."

She did not see the look at first of incredulity and then of anger on her father's face.

The Reverend Adolphus could hardly believe that, having travelled all the way from Cumberland to attend his daughter's wedding, he was to be sent back like an unwanted servant as soon as the marriage had taken place.

Then with a Christian-like forbearance he realised that it would be embarrassing for Natalia if he were to protest.

As if Sir James realised what was passing through his mind, he tactfully drew the Vicar on one side to show him a collection of exceptionally fine snuff-boxes which stood on a table at one side of the room.

For a moment they were out of ear-shot of Natalia and Lord Colwall, who remained at the fire-side.

"As I have already said, My Lord," Natalia remarked, "I do not know how to begin to thank you for everything you have given me! My trousseau is so beautiful . . . I cannot really believe it is mine."

"Your trousseau is a replica of the one provided for the daughter of the first Lord Colwall when, in the reign of Charles II, she married the Duke of Wessex," Lord Colwall replied. "I found a complete list in our records and I ordered exactly the same number of garments for you."

He paused and added:

"I knew that as far as good taste is concerned I could trust Madame Madeleine."

His words dulled a little the look of gratitude on Natalia's face.

She had thought that he had chosen himself—and with care—the elaborate gowns which were hanging in the wardrobe upstairs; the ermine-lined, exquisite garments which had been sent to the Vicarage.

Then she gave a metaphorical shake of her shoulders.

How foolish she had been to think His Lordship would actually select her gowns. After all, tradition was part of his life. How could it be anything else when he lived in a Castle like this? When he bore a name which was part of the history of England?

She forced a smile to her lips.

"I am so very grateful."

"There is no need for you to be," he replied. "As my wife you must of course uphold the dignity of your position."

She glanced at him quickly, then before she could speak the Butler announced from the door that dinner was ready.

Lord Colwall offered Natalia his arm, and as they walked through the marble Hall and down the wide corridor, she realised it was the first time she had touched him.

She felt her fingers tremble on his arm at the thought.

'How proudly he holds himself,' she thought admiringly.

As they passed the suits of armour which lined the corridor, she knew exactly how he would look dressed in one of them with a great plumed helmet on his head.

The Dining-Room had a high, Gothic-arched roof, but the cold austerity was relieved by the carvings on the stone capitals.

There was a whole log burning in the great fire-place and the walls were hung with portraits of the previous owners of the Castle.

The high-backed chairs were covered in tapestry which Natalia learned later had been worked by industrious Chatelaines over the centuries.

The table was massed with gold ornaments and lighted candelabra, and as Natalia seated herself on the right of Lord Colwall she felt small and a little insignificant in a room that could comfortably seat a very large number of people.

As if Lord Colwall read her thoughts he remarked:

"Tomorrow we shall hold our Marriage Feast here and will entertain over two hundred guests."

"It sounds frightening," Natalia said. "I had always thought that I should be married in our tiny Church at Pooley Bridge by Papa."

"The Bishop of Hereford will officiate," Lord Colwall told her. "Your father will not be required to take part in the service."

There was a little silence and then, as if Sir James once again sensed the resentment arising in the Reverend Adolphus, he said:

"Have you seen the newspapers today? I read in *The Times* that at Fordingbridge in Hampshire a mob under the leadership of a man who called himself Captain, broke up a factory which manufactures threshing machines."

"Do you think that the Captain in question is the mysterious Mr.

Swing?" the Reverend Adolphus asked, diverted for a moment from Natalia's wedding.

"I should not be in the least surprised," Sir James answered. "They say he definitely started the riot. He was apparently on horseback and his followers addressed him bare-headed."

"I cannot imagine why he was not arrested," Lord Colwall remarked sharply. "I hear that the Prime Minister has sent the Seventh Dragoon Guards to Canterbury and the Fifth Dragoons to Tunbridge Wells to quell disturbances."

"I read," Sir James answered, "that Sir Robert Peel has deprecated strongly the action of certain magistrates in yielding to the mobs."

"I can assure you of one thing," Lord Colwall said sternly. "If there was rioting here, which I cannot believe possible, then I would shoot every rioter myself, rather than give in to their demands."

There was something in his tone which made Natalia look at him questioningly.

Then as if he was no longer interested in the conversation, Lord Colwall again began to speak of his arrangements for the morrow.

He went on to tell Natalia about some of the people she was to meet after dinner. She found it bewildering to take in so many names, or indeed to understand what part they each played on the Estate.

'Later I must make a list of them,' she told herself.

But she would not allow herself to be dismayed at the thought of what lay ahead.

She was sensible enough to realise that while they employed two local untrained Maids at the Vicarage, it would be very different at the Castle.

Here she would find herself confronted with over one thousand employees, comprising the hierarchy, not only of indoor servants, but of those who worked outside for Lord Colwall.

She was to meet only the heads of each department this evening, but even they made up a large number of people.

There were the head men in charge of the farms, the dairies, brewhouses, granaries, stables, laundries, and workshops.

There were also the Chief of the carpenters, of the iron-smiths, painters, masons, and glaziers, besides the woodmen, foresters, gamekeepers and those who held superior positions in the garden.

"The man in charge of my greenhouses," Lord Colwall was saying, "is an artist. I think, Natalia, that you and your father will be astonished when you see how skilfully he has decorated the Chapel and how he will transform this room into what will literally be a 'bower of beauty!'"

"You have everything here on your Estate?" Natalia said in awe-struck tones.

"I try to make it a State within a State," Lord Colwall replied. "I am attempting to achieve perfection. I have, fortunately, the advantage of having had very wise and knowledgeable forbears."

He glanced at the pictures on the walls and continued:

"The Tudor herb garden, for instance, is the most famous in the whole length and breadth of the land, and the man who supervises my Carnation House is unchallenged."

"I shall want to see everything when you have the time to show it to me," Natalia said.

"Of course," Lord Colwall agreed.

Dinner came to an end while they were still talking about Lord Colwall's possessions, and when he said it was time for them to repair to the Baronial Hall where their guests were waiting for them, Sir James took his leave.

"You do not require me tonight, dear boy," he said, "and I will therefore, with your permission, return home. I shall of course be here in plenty of time tomorrow to support you."

"Sir James is to be my Best Man," Lord Colwall explained to the Reverend Adolphus.

"I can imagine nothing that could give me greater pleasure," Sir James said, looking at Natalia.

He took her hand in his and held it for a moment.

"I want to wish both Ranulf and you great happiness," he said, "and, somehow, I feel completely sure that you will find it."

The sincerity in his tone was undeniable, and as Natalia curtsied she said sweetly:

"Thank you, Sir James, I know we are going to be very happy."

She smiled up at Lord Colwall as she spoke but he was not looking at her, having drawn from his pocket a list which apparently required his attention.

"Good-night, Ranulf," Sir James said, and then, having bade the Reverend Adolphus farewell, he departed.

Lord Colwall led Natalia through several passages until finally they came to the Baronial Hall.

This had been built later than the original Castle. It was, however, in the Gothic tradition, if more ornate, and was used for all

formal occasions including that of making, Natalia remembered her
mother telling her, a very attractive Ball-Room.

The Hall was crowded with men who were sitting at long trestle
tables laden with food and pewter tankards filled with beer.

There were several great barrels set at one end of the Hall, and it
was obvious from the applause when Natalia and Lord Colwall arrived that his guests were enjoying themselves.

Their benign humour stemmed however not only from the importance of the occasion, but also because they had been generously entertained.

Lord Colwall made a speech in which he introduced his future
wife, and then, as the cheers of welcome rang out, Natalia went
round the Hall at his side.

Man after man was presented to her until the whole throng
became nothing but a sea of faces, and it was difficult to hear either
their names or the descriptions that Lord Colwall gave her of each
person he introduced.

They did not stop to talk to anyone, although occasionally an old
man having mumbled congratulations and good wishes would start
on a rambling tale of His Lordship's father or grandfather.

It was nearly an hour before the round was completed and Lord
Colwall led Natalia from the Baronial Hall back along the passages
towards the Salon.

The Reverend Adolphus had not accompanied them and Natalia
could not help hoping that, if he had gone to bed, she would have a
chance to speak alone with Lord Colwall.

With a little throb of excitement she wondered if he would kiss
her.

He had not kissed her finger before the engagement ring had
been placed upon it and she wanted more than anything else in the
world that he should kiss her lips.

All the way down from the North, she imagined herself being
held in his arms; of being close to him; of hearing him say that he
loved her and of telling him how much she loved him.

'If only we can be . . . alone,' she thought, and felt herself thrill
at the idea.

She knew that he must love her deeply to have done so much for
her already, and she thought now that the reason the marriage was
taking place so speedily after her arrival, was that he wanted her to
himself.

She felt her heart leap at the thought. Of course, that was the explanation.

Even though it might seem slightly inconsiderate where her father was concerned, she knew it would be a wonder beyond words to be alone with the man she married.

She wanted to talk intimately with him; to know that she was his! She wanted to tell him all the things that she had imagined about him through the three long years when she had thought of him, and of no-one else.

'I love him! I love him!' she cried in her heart as they reached the Salon.

Then, with an undeniable feeling of disappointment, she saw her father was waiting for them.

He rose to his feet as they entered, and before Natalia could speak, Lord Colwall said:

"I am persuaded that you should retire to bed and have a good night's sleep. Tomorrow will be for both of us somewhat of a trial. I am sure you would wish to rest."

Natalia wished nothing of the sort, but she had not the courage to say so. Instead, obediently, she kissed her father good-night, and then turned towards Lord Colwall.

There was a question in her eyes as she looked at him.

'At least,' she thought, 'he might wish to kiss my cheek.'

But he only bowed in response to her curtsey, and she moved away a little forlornly to climb the big stone staircase alone.

She heard a sound behind her and she turned round expectantly. Herald wagging his tail ecstatically was escorting her to her bedchamber.

Natalia was in fact more tired than she had thought.

She fell asleep almost as soon as her head touched the pillow, and when she awoke it was to see a pale sun struggling through the sides of the curtains.

'I am sure it is going to be a fine day,' she thought.

Jumping gaily out of bed she ran across the room to pull open the heavy curtains. It was in fact the loveliest day she could have imagined!

There had been a sharp frost during the night and the grass was white, the air crisp and the sky very clear.

Below in the valley she could see a river winding its way through the fields that were green, and in the forests there was still the red of the beech trees and the golden yellow of the oak.

'Soon it will be winter,' Natalia thought, 'but now it is beautiful— a perfect day for my perfect wedding.'

It was appropriate that the world should wear a semblance of white on her wedding day. Natalia remembered with excitement the wonderful white wedding gown the Housekeeper had shown her before she went to bed.

"Will he think I look beautiful in it?" she asked aloud.

She was sure Lord Colwall would tell her so, and she felt herself thrill with the anticipation of what lay ahead.

A few minutes later the maids came to call her.

"It is a quarter before nine o'clock, Miss," Ellen announced. "The Reverend Gentleman is having breakfast in your Sitting-Room next door. He asks when you are awake if you would join him."

"Is it as late as that?" Natalia exclaimed. "I am usually called at eight o'clock."

"I thought you would wish to sleep later this morning, Miss," Ellen replied. "I did look in a little earlier, but you were asleep."

"Well, now I must hurry," Natalia said, "especially if my father wishes to see me."

She paused and then asked:

"Where is Lord Colwall having his breakfast?"

"Downstairs, Miss," Ellen replied, "but of course today you cannot leave your own rooms. It is very unlucky for a Bride to see her Bridegroom before she meets him in the Church."

Natalia laughed.

"Are you superstitious?"

"Yes, Miss, and so is His Lordship. He has given instructions that on no account must you appear until it is time to proceed to the Chapel."

Natalia gave a little sigh.

"Oh, dear! It is such a lovely day and I would have wished to visit the garden, or perhaps to climb to the very top of the Castle to look at the view."

"I don't think His Lordship would like it," Ellen said.

"Of course I must do as His Lordship wishes," Natalia smiled.

She dressed herself quickly.

It was impossible to find a plain morning-gown amongst the elaborate creations which hung in the wardrobe, but she chose the simplest there was and then hurried into the Sitting-Room to find her father had already finished his breakfast.

"I am sorry to be late, Papa," she said, kissing his cheek.

"It is of no consequence, child," he answered. "You might be expected to be fatigued after such a long journey."

"I think in reality I was just day-dreaming," Natalia answered.

There were two footmen and a Butler to bring her innumerable dishes from which she found it difficult to make a choice.

Then the servants having left the room, the Reverend Adolphus said:

"I want to talk to you, Natalia."

There was a note of concern in his voice which made her glance up at him in surprise.

"What about, Papa?"

"I have been thinking since last night," her father began slowly, "that you are being married at quite an unnecessary speed."

Natalia did not answer. She merely put down the cup she had been holding in her hand, and sat looking at her father wide-eyed.

"Your mother and I had thought," the Reverend Adolphus went on, "that when you arrived at the Castle, you and I would be here for perhaps a week or ten days before the marriage took place."

He paused to continue:

"During that time, your mother asked me to tell you that, if you wished to change your mind, if you decided after all that Lord Colwall was not the man you thought could make you happy, then you were to accompany me on my return home."

"But why should Mama think," Natalia asked after a moment's pause, "there was any chance of my changing my mind?"

"You met Lord Colwall only once when you were but fifteen," her father answered. "If you marry him, Natalia, you will be his wife in the sight of God for the rest of your life. Whatever you may feel about him later, it will then be too late."

"Yes, I realise that, Papa."

"Therefore I should have wished you to have a chance of getting to know him better," the Reverend Adolphus went on. "As your mother suggested, if you had a week together, or even longer, you would be able to exchange your viewpoints on different subjects.

"You would begin to know a little about each other and be quite certain in your own mind he was the man you would love for the rest of your life."

"I am quite certain about that!" Natalia said in a low voice.

The Reverend Adolphus rose to his feet and walked across to the window.

"I have been wondering during the night, and I have not slept very much, if your mother and I did wrong when we agreed to His Lordship's proposal three years ago, when he said he wished you to marry him."

He sighed.

"I thought it strange at the time, and yet to your mother it was understandable seeing you were a distant relative. Then you were educated and brought up in the way which he approved. Now I am not so sure."

"What do you mean, you are not so sure?" Natalia enquired.

There was a silence as her father did not answer.

"Explain to me what you are trying to say, Papa," Natalia insisted. "After all, look at what Lord Colwall has done for me. Look at what he has given me. Can there be any doubt that he loves me as I love him?"

Again there was a silence.

Then in a strained voice her father said:

"I wish your mother were here. Did she talk to you, Natalia, about marriage before you left?"

"We have talked of little else," Natalia said with a smile. "Mama, as you well know, Papa, was very excited that I should live in the Castle she had known as a child."

"I did not mean that," the Vicar said a little uncomfortably. "I mean, Natalia, did she explain to you that when a man and a woman are married they are very close and intimate with each other, and it is love which makes their marriage either a Heaven or a Hell."

There was a little pause and then Natalia said:

"I think I understand what you are trying to say, Papa, and although I am somewhat ignorant on this matter I am sure that I love Lord Colwall in the way of which you are speaking. I want to belong to him! I want to be very close to him!"

Her voice quivered a little as she spoke.

"You are quite certain, Natalia, that you would not rather come home with me today?" her father asked, turning round from the window to look at her. "We could tell Lord Colwall that his plans are too precipitate; that you would rather wait a few months, perhaps until the Spring."

He looked at his daughter pleadingly.

"Then if you are both of the same mind, he can come to Pooley Bridge and you can be married from your own home as I always intended you would be."

"Papa, how could we do such a thing?" Natalia cried. "His Lordship has made all the arrangements! Think of the flowers in the Chapel; the hundreds of people who are coming to the ceremony and the Medieval Feast. How could everything be cancelled at the last moment? He would never forgive me!"

"I suppose not," the Reverend Adolphus admitted dully, "but I am not happy about it, Natalia."

He walked towards his daughter and put his hands on her shoulders.

"You are so very lovely, my dearest, so very intelligent, and so very sweet. I think it would crucify me if I thought that you were unhappy."

"But why should I be?" Natalia asked. "I have told you that I love Lord Colwall, that I want to be his wife, that I want to be with him now and for always."

A smile lit her face.

"I have thought of him so often," she said, "that I feel I know him just as if he had been with me these last three years. I am sure, quite sure he feels the same about me."

There was an expression on her father's face she did not understand.

He dropped his hands from her shoulders and with a heavy sigh turned towards the fire.

"If only your mother was here," he muttered.

And because she did not understand she did not answer him.

As if he felt he could say no more, the Reverend Adolphus deliberately talked of other things—describing to Natalia the Library which she had not yet seen and which he had visited before breakfast.

He made her a list of the books he had seen there which he particularly wanted her to read.

They talked on the many subjects which had always interested them both, and somehow the hours passed until it was time for Natalia to dress for the Marriage Ceremony.

She went into her bed-room to find the Maids and the House-keeper waiting for her.

When they had dressed her in a magnificent gown of white lace which was so elegant that it could only have come from Bond Street, Natalia looked at her reflection in the mirror, she felt sure Lord Colwall would approve.

The boat-shaped neckline of her gown was very becoming and showed the tops of her white shoulders.

Her tiny waist was encircled by a sash exquisitely embroidered with pearls and diamonds, which fell into a long train behind her.

There was a sparkling diamond tiara for her to wear on her head over the cobweb-fine veil of Brussels lace, which had been worn through many centuries by Colwall brides.

She looked unreal—a nymph who might have risen from the lake at Ullswater or stepped out from one of the cascades which poured down the high mountains after the rains.

Behind the veil, Natalia herself felt as if she viewed the world through a dream.

But this was really happening! She was to be married—and to the man who was the human embodiment of the Knight, her guardian Knight who had been her protector for so long.

"Thank you, God," she whispered beneath her breath.

The Housekeeper's voice interrupted her.

"I wonder, Miss, if I might ask a very great favour?"

"But of course, Mrs. Hodges," Natalia replied. "What is it?"

"His Lordship's old Nanny, Mrs. Broom, is too crippled with arthritis to come downstairs to see you, Miss. She didn't wish me to trouble you, but it would be a real kindness if you could step up to the next floor and let her see you in your wedding gown."

"But of course I will," Natalia replied instantly. "Show me the way."

She lifted the front of her skirts and following the Housekeeper went from her bed-room along the passage to another staircase to the floor above.

It was quite a long way along corridors narrower than those on the first floor.

The Housekeeper stopped, knocked at a door, and Natalia heard a voice say:

"Come in."

She found herself in what in one glance she recognised as a Nursery. There was a fire burning behind the high grate, there was a rocking-horse standing in one corner. There was the inevitable nursery screen made from scraps and transfers.

Sitting in a chair by the fire-side was a small grey-haired woman with the kind and gentle face of one who has devoted her life to the care of children.

"I have brought you Miss Graystoke, Nurse," the Housekeeper said.

"How kind! How very kind!"

Nanny made a great effort to rise from her chair, but Natalia moved quickly across the room to prevent her.

"Do not get up," she said in a gentle voice. "I hear you have arthritis."

"I have indeed, Miss, and some days it is worse than others. I think, if you ask me, it is sitting here having nothing to do."

"I am sure it is," Natalia agreed. "The moment I have time, I will make you one of the herbal drinks that Mama always makes for anyone who has rheumatism in the Parish. It really does help to relieve the pain."

"I shall be very grateful for it, Miss," Nanny said. "Won't you sit down?"

The Housekeeper brought Natalia a cane chair and then withdrew from the room.

"You were His Lordship's nurse?" Natalia asked.

"I have been at the Castle since I was fifteen," Nanny replied. "At first I worked in the house as a housemaid, and then when His Lordship arrived, Her Ladyship, his mother, asked me if I would help the old Nurse who had been brought in to look after him.

"When she retired soon after Her Ladyship died, Master Ranulf was so happy with me that I was allowed to look after him all on my own."

"He must have been a very sweet little boy," Natalia said.

"He was the most beautiful baby you ever saw!" the Nurse exclaimed. "So handsome, I thought at the time he looked like an angel, and when he grew older, there was never a happier child.

"He may have been the only one but he never seemed lonely, and there was not a man or woman in the Castle who would not have laid down their life for him."

Natalia smiled.

"I can see you loved him."

"I still do," the old woman replied, "but it is different, very different these days."

Natalia was silent for a moment and then she asked:

"Why is it different?"

"He were badly treated—very badly treated, Miss. I expect His Lordship 'll tell you about it himself, although they say he'll speak of it to no-one—no-one at all."

"Who treated him badly?" Natalia asked—and knew the answer even as she asked the question.

As if she suddenly remembered it was Natalia's wedding-day, Nanny pursed her lips together.

"You don't want to be talking of things that happened in the past," she said. "All I would ask is that you make my baby happy. That's what he needs—happiness!"

"I shall try to make him very happy."

Nurse stared up at Natalia as if her old eyes were trying to penetrate the veil.

"You will love him?"

It was a question.

"I already love him," Natalia answered, "and I know that I will bring His Lordship happiness."

"That's all I ask, God bless you, Miss. May He bless you both."

The words were said in such a heart-felt manner that Natalia felt tears prick her eyes, then realising it must be getting late, she said good-bye.

'If he has been really unhappy in the past I will make it up to him,' she told herself. 'I will make him happy! I must!'

Her father was waiting for her in the Sitting-Room and as she entered he looked at his watch.

"It is time we went to the Chapel, Natalia," he said. "I cannot believe His Lordship would be pleased if we are late."

There was some reserve in his tone as he spoke of his future son-in-law, as if he resented the plans that had been made and the fact that he and Natalia must carry them out.

"No, of course, we must not be late," Natalia agreed. "Do I look all right, Papa?"

"You look beautiful," her father said in all sincerity. "I would have wished above all else that I could have had the privilege of marrying you today, but I promise you one thing—I shall pray for you and, always, that God will bless you."

"I think He has done that already, Papa," Natalia smiled.

Then taking her father's arm, she moved with him across the landing and down the great stone stair-case towards the Chapel.

CHAPTER FOUR

"The last guest has left, M'Lady," Ellen announced, returning to the bed-room from the top of the stairs.

"Then I must go down to His Lordship," Natalia said with a lilt in her voice.

There had only been a few people left in the Dining-Hall when she had gone upstairs to remove her veil and tiara and change from her wedding-gown into another dress.

She had said good-bye to her father knowing he was displeased and resentful at having to return to Cumberland so quickly.

She had a deep affection for him, but at the same time she longed above all things to be alone with her husband.

The wedding had been even more wonderful than she had anticipated.

The Chapel with its high pillars and great Gothic arches had been filled with flowers. The altar was white with them and in every window-ledge and against every wall there were clumps of lilies, carnations, gardenias and other exotic blooms from the greenhouses.

There had been a choir of young boys whose voices had seemed to soar like angels towards the Heavens.

The Chapel was packed with all the distinguished nobility of the County, but Natalia moving slowly up the aisle on her father's arm was conscious of only one person.

Her Knight—waiting for her at the Chancel steps!

When they had said their wedding vows and Lord Colwall had repeated in his deep voice: "With this ring, I thee wed; with my body I thee worship," Natalia had felt it was a moment so sacred and so moving that the tears had come into her eyes.

She was his wife! She was his! This was the moment she had longed for for three years!

The Marriage Feast, as Lord Colwall had intended, was sensational and an astonishment to his guests.

They had exclaimed over the glazed boar's heads, the geese stuffed with oysters, the swans garnished with peaches.

There was even a peacock served with its enormous tail spread fan-like to arouse loud exclamations of surprise from the diners.

Course succeeded course, and the gold goblets from which they drank were kept constantly replenished with champagne.

The Dining-Hall was filled with guests, and yet there appeared to be a footman behind every chair. Natalia had never imagined that anyone could entertain in such luxury.

The flowers in the Hall made it the "bower of beauty" which Lord Colwall had promised.

Natalia thought how wonderful it was to find a man who was so masculine in every way and yet had an appreciation of flowers and gardens.

It would make yet another interest that they could share together, and she longed for the moment when they could exchange opinions on so many different subjects.

'Now I understand,' Natalia told herself, 'why His Lordship wished me to be so well educated! He himself seems to know even more than Papa!'

When the feast was over, Natalia received so many compliments, so many good wishes and so many blessings for her future happiness that it was finally with flushed cheeks and shining eyes that she left the Hall.

She first said good-bye to her father and then she went upstairs to change her gown.

'Now the house will be quiet,' she thought as she descended the stone staircase.

In the Hall, Herald, the mastiff, was waiting for her. He had been shut up during the wedding and he ran towards her playfully, glad to be free again.

She put her hand on his head and he walked beside her into the Salon where she expected to find Lord Colwall.

He was not there, so she moved towards the fire-place, thinking she would sit on the hearth-rug and play with Herald until he appeared.

It was then she heard voices, and realised they came from another room which opened out of the one she was in.

She had learnt by now that the Salon in which Lord Colwall had received them last night was called from the Norman days "Le

Salon d'Or," and the one beyond it was known as "Le Salon d'Argent."

In Le Salon d'Argent she heard Lord Colwall's deep voice and another which she suspected belonged to Sir James Parke.

'He would be the last one to leave,' she thought, 'because he has so ably supported His Lordship all the afternoon and evening.'

The door into Le Salon d'Argent which was to the right of the fire-place was half-open and as Natalia drew near, she heard Sir James say:

"She is enchanting, Ranulf, the most exquisite creature I have ever encountered! So tell me, dear boy, that you have now discarded all those ridiculous notions with which you shocked me the day before yesterday. You will fall deeply in love with this beautiful girl and live happily ever afterwards!"

"Never!"

The exclamation was sharp and loud.

"Listen to me, Ranulf. Natalia is not an ordinary, stupid Society Chit who will be content with a position at the top of your table. She is intelligent, sensitive and will ask more from life than that!"

"I told you when we talked of it before exactly what I want in this marriage," Lord Colwall retorted. "I require, Sir James, in case you have forgotten, a wife who will give me a son! That is all I ask except that she should be pure and untouched. And this time I have made certain of that!"

"Ranulf, have you looked at Natalia? Knowing that she was her mother's daughter, I was expecting her to be pretty and charming, but nothing so unusual, or indeed so breathtakingly lovely."

"You are very dramatic, Sir James," Lord Colwall said scathingly, "but I assure you that whatever Natalia looks like, it will not affect my resolve never again to love any woman—nor, if I can prevent it, to allow her to love me. There is no place for that nauseating emotion in my life."

There was a pause and then Sir James said sadly:

"I can only pray, Ranulf, that time will make you change your mind, or perhaps Natalia will do that."

"In this instance, your prayers will undoubtedly remain unanswered," Lord Colwall said coldly.

"Then I can only say good-bye," Sir James said. "It was a very delightful wedding and the County will talk about the Feast which followed it for years to come. I hope that gives you some satisfaction."

"It does indeed," Lord Colwall said lightly. "It always pleases me when my plans work out in exactly the manner I intended. Good-bye, Sir James, and thank you for your support."

Natalia stood in Le Salon d'Or as if turned to stone.

She had not moved since she first overheard what Lord Colwall and Sir James were saying in the next room, and as Lord Colwall pushed open the door he saw her.

Her face was so pale that he was instantly aware that something had occurred.

"What is it?" he asked. "What is wrong?"

She did not answer because she felt as if her throat was constricted and it was hard to breathe. Then Lord Colwall realised that the door had been open and she must have overheard what was being said.

"I was talking to Sir James," he said and his voice was a little uncertain.

"I . . . heard . . . you."

Natalia managed to speak the words and now she made her first movement. One small hand crept up to her breast.

Lord Colwall advanced a little further into the Salon.

"It was a conversation that was not meant for your ears," he said. "I feel sure you will understand that whatever I said to Sir James does not in any way alter the respect I have for you."

"Re . . . spect?" Natalia could hardly breathe the word.

Lord Colwall walked to the fire-place and stood with his back to the fire.

"I must commend you, Natalia, on the excellent way in which you received my employees last night and my friends today. I am well aware that it was a great ordeal for a girl brought up as quietly as you have been. But let me tell you that you came through with flying colours!"

He spoke heavily, choosing his words with care. But now, looking at Natalia's white face, he realised that what he said had not impinged on her consciousness.

"I did . . . not . . . understand," she said in a very low voice.

"What did you not understand?" he enquired.

"That all you . . . wanted from a . . . wife was that she should . . . produce . . . an heir."

Lord Colwall made a little gesture of impatience.

"Surely it was obvious? I supposed that your mother would have explained to you that our marriage was advantageous to us both."

There was a silence and then Natalia said:

"Did you really . . . think that I was . . . marrying you simply for your . . . title and the . . . position you could give me . . . here?"

"What else?" he asked in surprise. "We did not know each other."

"But we did!" Natalia contradicted. "You came to Pooley Bridge. You saw me and after that everything in my life was changed. You arranged my education, you sent me Crusader, and Mama wrote reports to you of my progress every month. She told me so."

"It was in fact your mother's suggestion," Lord Colwall said. "But surely at such a brief encounter you could hardly expect to engage my affections?"

Natalia raised her eyes to his and he saw they were dark with pain.

"I thought you . . . loved . . . me."

For a moment it seemed as if Lord Colwall had also been turned to stone. Then he looked away from Natalia's eyes to say harshly:

"How could you imagine anything so absurd? So ridiculous? You were only a child when I came to your home."

"I was . . . old enough to fall . . . in love," Natalia answered. "I loved you when I saw you coming towards me through the mist over the lake. You looked as I had always . . . imagined . . ."

She stopped.

"What did you imagine?" Lord Colwall asked curiously.

"It is difficult to . . . explain," Natalia answered. "Papa said once that instead of an angel to . . . watch over us, we each have a Knight . . . like the . . . Knights of Malta to . . . guard and protect us from . . . evil. In my . . . dreams he looked exactly like . . . you!"

There was a little throb in her voice which was extremely moving.

Lord Colwall took a deep breath.

"This is not what I anticipated," he said. "I think, Natalia, the best thing we can do is to sit down and discuss this matter sensibly."

Obediently, as if she was a puppet that must obey his commands, Natalia seated herself on the edge of the sofa. She put her hands in her lap and raised her eyes to his.

She suddenly seemed very small, very fragile—a waif, rather than the glowing, happy girl who had walked down the aisle on his arm.

"I do not know how much you know about my first marriage," Lord Colwall said. "There is in fact no reason for you to learn the details. It is sufficient for me to tell you that what happened then made me determined never again, as long as I live, to be embroiled in the misery, the degradation of what is called love."

"And yet you . . . wished to marry . . . again?" Natalia said.

"I married so that I could have children," Lord Colwall replied. "You know the history of my family. You have learnt that this Castle has been handed from father to son all down the centuries. I want an heir, Natalia, and that was why I chose you."

"Any . . . woman could have served the same . . . purpose," Natalia said in a low voice.

"Not any woman," Lord Colwall corrected. "It had to be someone whom I would be proud to acknowledge as my wife and who would be a fitting mother for my children. You have both these qualities, Natalia."

"But they are external assets," Natalia answered. "They do not affect me . . . the real . . . me. I would never have married . . . anyone I did not . . . love."

"It is unfortunate," Lord Colwall admitted, "that we could not have this discussion before the Marriage Ceremony took place! But I could not be expected to imagine that a girl to whom I had spoken once three years ago would consider herself in love with me or expect me to love her in return."

There was something almost defiant in the way he spoke.

"I see . . . now that it was very . . . foolish," Natalia said in a low voice.

"If you admit that," Lord Colwall said in a brighter tone, "I think the best thing for you to do is to forget that, by an unfortunate chance, you overheard a private conversation between myself and Sir James. You are my wife, Natalia, and I shall always treat you in a manner to which I am quite certain you can never take exception."

He seemed to consider his words and he went on:

"There is much here which I am sure will give you pleasure. The Colwall family jewels are magnificent. You will not find me an ungenerous husband in every other way, and I am sure that our children, when we have them, will make up to you for all the shortcomings of their father!"

Natalia was very still and then she said:

"Are you really . . . suggesting that, now I know you do not . . . love me, I should . . . permit you to give me a . . . child?"

For a moment Lord Colwall looked embarrassed, but he said in an unemotional voice:

"I can appreciate that you are very innocent in these matters, but you will find it not too unpleasant to accept me as your husband—in fact, as well as in name."

There was the slightest twist of his lips as he added:

"I am not inexperienced where women are concerned, Natalia, and I am confident that I can make our association, if that is the right word for it, pleasureable for us both."

Natalia jumped to her feet.

"No! No!"

Lord Colwall looked at her in surprise.

"May I enquire what you mean by that?"

"It means," Natalia replied, "that I could not allow you to touch me . . . now that I know you do not love me!"

For a moment there was an expression of anger in Lord Colwall's eyes, but he managed to say unemotionally:

"That is a ridiculous assertion, as you must well know. For the moment you are upset, but I have asked you to forget what you inadvertently overheard. In fact I order you to do so."

"And you imagine . . . even if I could forget it . . . that I could delude myself into . . . believing that you . . . love me?" Natalia asked.

"I have told you that there is no point in our discussing love," Lord Colwall replied. "But let me tell you in all sincerity, Natalia, that I do appreciate that you will make me a very charming wife, and I cannot believe that in the course of a few minutes the love that you have just professed to feel for me has changed into dislike."

"No, I do not . . . dislike you," Natalia said. "I love you . . . although I was mistaken in thinking you love me. But I . . . cannot give you a . . . child."

"Why not?"

There was no doubt of the irritation in Lord Colwall's tone now.

"Because if we had one without you . . . loving me . . . then it might easily be . . . deformed."

Lord Colwall stared at Natalia incredulously, and then as if he could not prevent himself he ejaculated:

"What the devil do you mean by that?"

Natalia's hand went up to the pendant which she wore around her neck. She felt her fingers touch the cool enamel of the Knight. Somehow she felt that it gave her courage.

"Will you allow me to . . . explain exactly what I mean, My Lord?"

"But of course," Lord Colwall said courteously, the irritation fading from his eyes. "Will you not sit down?"

He indicated the sofa again. But Natalia sank down on the rug in front of the fire.

As if he sensed what she was feeling, Herald came to be beside her and place his great head in her lap.

She stroked him for a few moments until, when Lord Colwall had seated himself in a high-backed arm-chair, she began in a low voice:

"I thought about having . . . children and I wanted above all else to give you a . . . son."

He did not speak and after a moment she went on:

"When I was coming here yesterday and I saw the Castle, I remembered how Mama had told me of the wonderful place it was for the young; a place for children to play Hide and Seek, to run along the broad corridors and to climb the turrets. I knew then I wanted to have not an only child, such as I myself had been, but a number."

She paused and stared into the fire before she said:

"I am well aware that at the moment you are . . . incensed with me for not agreeing instantly to your wishes, but I think when you hear the . . . reason for my refusal, you will . . . understand."

"I am listening," Lord Colwall said.

"I must have been twelve, or perhaps thirteen, when I learned first that a baby could be born out of wedlock," Natalia began in a low voice. "There was a girl living in the village, the daughter of a small farmer, who fell very much in love with one of the farm labourers.

"He was, of course, not of her class and there could be no question of her marrying him. But soon people began to talk of her condition, and I learned from the conversations I overheard in the village that she was having a baby."

The colour rose in her cheeks.

"The man was sent away—no-one knew where he went—and the baby was born the following winter. His mother died in child-birth and the child was brought up by his grandparents."

Natalia paused.

"When Jeremy was three years old, he was the most beautiful child I have ever seen in my life. I remember saying to Papa: 'It seems strange that two quite ordinary-looking people should have such a beautiful child. He looks like an angel!'

"'That often happens with love-children,' Papa told me.

"'But Jeremy was born in what everybody in the village calls "sin,"' I protested.

"Papa looked across the lake before he answered and then he said:

"'When a man and a woman love each other with all their heart, their soul and their body, Natalia, their desire for each other can, I am sure, evoke the Divine Life-Force. It pours through them, and at the moment of conception, they beget a child that is in fact, as we should all be, in the image of God.'"

Natalia's voice died away. Then Lord Colwall said with a cynical smile:

"That is hardly a part of orthodox Christian doctrine."

"But the Bible says that love is more important than anything else," Natalia replied quickly.

He attempted no further argument, and after a moment she went on:

"Now I have another story to tell you."

"I am still listening," he replied.

"You will naturally understand that I often thought about little Jeremy. As he grew older, he had a sweet character which matched the beauty of his face. I do not think there was anyone in the village, however much they disapproved of his mother, who would have said a cruel or unkind word to Jeremy himself."

"I assure you, most bastards are treated very differently," Lord Colwall said almost harshly.

"I have heard that. Yet I have read much about them," Natalia replied, "and there is no doubt that in history, when Kings and great noblemen have fathered illegitimate children, they have all been reported as being extremely handsome . . . like the Duke of Monmouth, for example."

Lord Colwall had apparently no answer for this. Leaning back in his high-back chair, he looked amazingly elegant.

He had not changed from the tight-fitting, long-tailed, cut-away coat he had worn for his wedding, and his frilled cravat was a master-piece of intricate design. A huge emerald tie-pin glittered in the firelight, and his clear-cut features were revealed with every movement of the leaping flames.

"My other story," Natalia went on, "is perhaps a little embarrassing for me to relate to you, but at the same time I want you to understand."

"Needless to say, I am trying to do so," Lord Colwall told her.

"There was another family in the village. The mother had been widowed when her husband was killed in an accident, and she had a daughter—a gypsy-like girl with dark eyes and dark hair.

"Sarah must have been fifteen when her mother decided to marry again. She took for a husband a rough, uncouth man who worked in the gravel-pits and did not belong to the village. I think he was part-Irish, part-Tinker."

Natalia's expression darkened.

"No-one liked him! He drank and was too quick with his fists to make anything but enemies. Not surprisingly Sarah loathed her step-father!"

Natalia glanced at Lord Colwall.

"Everyone was sorry for the girl. Soon after he moved into the cottage her mother occupied, there were stormy scenes and tales that he was knocking her about when he had drunk more than usual! Then one morning the step-father was found dead in bed beside his wife."

"Dead?" Lord Colwall questioned.

"They had both gone to bed the worse for drink," Natalia answered, "and Sarah's mother had heard nothing during the night! When she awoke she found her husband with a long, sharp kitchen knife through his stomach!"

"Good Lord!" Lord Colwall exclaimed.

"Sarah had disappeared," Natalia continued. "There was of course a hue and cry to find her and a warrant out for her arrest. Then people spoke of hearing her scream in the woods the night before."

She made a little gesture with her hand.

"No-one had gone to her rescue because they knew that it was the route her step-father returned home from the gravel-pits, and he was an unpleasant person to encounter at any time. But there was no doubt that Sarah had been screaming for help."

There was a little quiver in Natalia's voice almost as if she was fighting against the horror such memories evoked before she went on:

"All this happened late last summer, and then in the spring of this year, Mama, Papa and I rose early as was usual on Sunday morning to go to Communion.

"We walked through the garden of the Vicarage, which, if you remember, is just beside the church.

"As we entered through the lich-gate we saw something white lying on one of the graves. As I looked, I realised that it was the grave of Sarah's step-father, and I could not imagine who could possibly wish to lay flowers there when he had been so disliked."

Natalia drew in her breath.

"When we drew nearer, we saw there were no . . . flowers on his grave but a . . . naked baby. It was dead! Quite dead, and it was . . . deformed! Terribly . . . obscenely deformed!"

"My God!" Lord Colwall said the words almost beneath his breath.

"They found Sarah two days . . . later in the . . . lake," Natalia continued. "She was very . . . emaciated, I am told, as if she had been . . . starved!"

A tear overflowed onto her cheek and she wiped it away with the first finger of her right hand, then dropped her head low so that Lord Colwall could not see her face.

"I can appreciate," he said after a moment, "this tragedy must have been a great shock for you. But I cannot quite see how either of your stories need concern us."

Natalia's head came up with a jerk.

"I cannot make it clearer," she said, "than to tell you that a baby born in love, in or out of wedlock, is likely to be strong and beautiful, while the one born without love . . . may be . . . deformed."

Lord Colwall rose to his feet.

"Are you really suggesting," he asked incredulously, "that everyone who conceives a child without love will breed a deformity?"

"No, of course not!" Natalia answered. "But it may account for the number of ugly, brainless, under-sized people one finds even in wealthy families."

She saw the expression on Lord Colwall's face.

"Papa told me the Ancient Greeks arranged beautiful statues round the bed of a woman who was about to give birth, believing the new-born child would resemble them."

She considered her words before she continued slowly:

"I am convinced that the thoughts and feelings of a mother affect her unborn child. Therefore, as far as I am concerned, because I saw Sarah's contorted, abnormal baby, it would be impossible, if I was having one without love, not to be haunted by the memory of it."

She spoke quietly, but there was a note of conviction in her voice which Lord Colwall could not ignore.

"It is absurd! Absolutely absurd, without medical foundation of any sort!" he ejaculated.

"That may be your opinion," Natalia replied, "but I have seen with my own eyes what can happen when a woman is forced against her will to . . . have a child from a man who has no feeling for her other than . . . lust!"

Lord Colwall put his hand up to his forehead.

"I cannot imagine how such things can happen in a small village," he said angrily. "I thought that you were brought up in a quiet, decent place, where you would never encounter such horrors."

"In a village one knows all the people and hears everything about them," Natalia replied. "After all, they are human beings. They are born, they live and they die. And they love or they hate— just as people do in grand Society."

She added almost angrily:

"I think Papa is right when he says that too many of the noblemen of England think the labourers are just animals."

"I cannot imagine what your mother was about not to protect you from such unpleasantness," Lord Colwall snapped. "Anyway, these abnormalities occur in not more than one case in a million."

"That is not true!" Natalia answered. "The Orphanages and Workhouses are filled with children who have no idea who their fathers or even who their mothers might be. I read the figures that were given in the debate in the House of Commons barely a month or so ago. The Member of Parliament who spoke on the subject said our rate of illegitimacy was a disgrace to the Nation."

For a moment Lord Colwall looked confounded by her argument, and then he said almost grimly:

"We are not discussing illegitimacy, Natalia, but the question whether you will give me a legitimate son to carry on my name and inherit the Castle and my very large possessions."

"I will not pretend, My Lord, that I should not be extremely afraid of what we might produce," Natalia replied.

She looked up at him as she spoke and saw the glint of anger in his eyes.

"I am . . . sorry," she said, rising to her feet, "desperately sorry to . . . disappoint you. I wanted to make you . . . happy and I promised to . . . obey you. But I know this would be wrong . . . very wrong!"

She gave a little dry sob.

"I know it would not be the right way to have a child, and I could not . . . would not . . . take such a risk knowing, as I do now, that you have no . . . feeling for . . . me."

"Now listen, Natalia—" Lord Colwall began, but without waiting for him to reply Natalia had turned and walked across the Salon.

She pulled open the door and left the room before he could even rise to his feet.

"Good God," he ejaculated. "What a coil! What an incredible, unbelievable tangle."

Upstairs Natalia allowed the Maids who were waiting for her to help her undress. As they did so, they chattered of the wedding, of how beautiful she had looked and the compliments that had been paid to her from every side.

She heard them speaking, but the sense of what they said could not penetrate her mind. It was like the chatter of starlings outside the window. It was a sound, but it made no sense.

There were smiles on their faces when finally she was ready for bed. She knew they were thinking that Lord Colwall would soon be coming to her room.

When she was alone, Natalia did not get into bed but sat down in front of the fire.

It did not seem possible that what had happened was a fact, that she was not waiting, as she had expected, for an ardent bride-groom, but would sleep alone on her wedding night.

She knew that Lord Colwall would have too much pride at this particular moment to force himself upon her.

But she wondered whether, if she had not overheard the conversation between him and Sir James, she would have realised when he touched her that he did not love her, that to him she was only a body that would give him a son.

She felt certain she would have known. It would have been impossible for her to love him so deeply and not realise there was no genuine response on his side.

She recalled so many things which might have given her a pointer as to the real truth about his feelings: the manner in which he had greeted her; his allowing her to place the engagement ring upon her own finger; the cold way he had spoken; the fact that he had never attempted to touch her.

'How stupid! How inexperienced I am!' Natalia said to herself. 'Now we are married, how can I face the future knowing that he does not love me?'

She laid her head down on her arms, her long, fair hair falling over her shoulders.

There were no tears in her eyes. It was as if she was past tears and was conscious only of a terrible heaviness within her breast and a coldness which seemed to penetrate her whole body.

All her dreams, all the imaginings of the past three years had crumbled into pieces around her. They were as unsubstantial as leaves falling from the trees outside as winter set in.

'I love him! I still love him!' she thought. 'But how can I endure to live with him, knowing the reason for the coldness in his voice, the indifference in his eyes?'

She wondered now how she could have ever been so stupid as to imagine it was just a reserve. It must be quite obvious to anyone else like Sir James, or indeed, the servants.

Natalia felt not only depressed and dispirited, but also humiliated. She had been so sure of her happiness.

She could understand now why her mother had not seemed as enthusiastic as she might have been about the marriage, and her father's resentment at the speed at which it had taken place.

'How right they were! How sensible!' But she had not listened to them.

She thought how hard it would be to admit that she was wrong. How could she tell her parents, who loved her so deeply, that her marriage was already a failure before it had even started?

Yet to stay with Lord Colwall, knowing he wanted her for one reason and one reason only, would be an agony almost impossible to contemplate.

'What shall I do? What shall I do?' she asked herself, and then almost as if a voice answered her cry she seemed to hear the word "fight."

Once again she knew she was sensing the answer of her Knight to her problem, sensing it so vividly that as had happened before, it was almost as if he spoke to her.

"Fight! Fight for what is right!"

She could hear her father saying all those years ago as they walked by the lake at Ullswater:

"Love is not only a sentimental and romantic emotion; it is an unsheathed sword that must thrust its way through to victory."

In the darkness and despair within herself, Natalia felt a little glimmer of hope.

Could she fight? Was it possible to fight for Lord Colwall and to gain from him the love for which she longed?

Natalia sat very still, feeling the warmth from the fire on her face. In that moment she grew up!

She saw that her childish dreams were hollow, the delusions of an adolescent, the conceptions of a girl who knew nothing about the world or about men.

But as a woman, she knew that Lord Colwall was suffering. He had admitted his first marriage had been disastrous, and she knew now that it must have hurt him to the point where he would allow himself to be hurt no further.

That was the key to the problem—she was sure of it!

"I will fight," she said aloud. "I will fight for his love, and somehow, I will win it!"

She glanced at the clock over the mantel-piece. It was still not very late and she knew if she went to bed she would be unable to sleep until she had learnt the cause for Lord Colwall's rejection of love.

There was one person who could tell her, and she was certain that Nanny, having arthritis, would not be asleep.

Putting on a wrapper of heavy satin trimmed with lace, Natalia went to her door and opened it very quietly.

As she had expected, most of the candles in the silver sconces which lit the Hall and the passages had been extinguished.

But there was still enough light left for her to see her way towards the stairs up which the Housekeeper had taken her to the Nursery.

She climbed them quickly, feeling like a pale ghost flitting through the shadows of the Castle, and she hoped that no-one would see her.

She reached the next floor and, after considering a little, remembered exactly where the Nursery was situated.

She knocked lightly at the door, but there was no answer. After a moment she turned the handle and went in.

Nanny was sitting in an arm-chair in front of a brightly burning fire. There was some crochet on her lap, and she must have fallen asleep while she was working.

Natalia closed the door and the slight sound awakened her.

She sat up in surprise.

"Your Ladyship!" she exclaimed.

Natalia crossed to her side.

"I have come to see you because I want your help."

Nanny looked at her face and in the tone of one who was used to dealing with the problems of children, she asked:

"What has happened? Is anything wrong?"

"Yes," Natalia said frankly. "Something is very wrong and only you can help me."

There was a low stool in front of the fire-place and she sat down on it clasping her hands around her knees.

Nanny made no suggestion of getting her a chair but gave Natalia all her attention as if she knew she was in fact a child in trouble.

"I want you to tell me," Natalia said in a low voice, "the story of His Lordship's first marriage."

"Has he not spoken of it?" Nanny asked.

"His Lordship has said only that it was disastrous and there was no reason for me to know the details. But you will understand that I must know them! I cannot help him unless I know what happened."

"Help him?"

Natalia nodded.

"He needs help as you well know, but I did not realise it until this evening."

"I hoped that you would bring him happiness," Nanny said. "I hoped things would be different once you were married."

"Perhaps they will be in the future," Natalia answered, "but not until I can understand why he is . . . as he is."

"He should not have let you marry him without your knowing the truth," Nanny said.

Natalia shook her head.

"It is too late now for regrets. All I want is your help. Was he very much in love with his first wife?"

"He was crazy about her," Nanny replied. "She bewitched him as she bewitched every other young man in the neighbourhood. And she was wicked, really wicked!"

"I know nothing about her except her Christian name," Natalia said. "Tell me who she was."

"She was Lady Claris Kempsey, daughter of the Earl of Powick, whose home is on the other side of the Malvern Hills."

"So His Lordship and Lady Claris had been brought up together?"

Nanny shook her head.

"Nothing like that. Her Ladyship was five years older than Master Ranulf."

"Five years older!" Natalia ejaculated in astonishment.

This was something she had not expected.

"Yes, indeed," Nanny said, "with all the tricks and wiles of a sophisticated Society lady—and he as innocent as a new-born babe."

"Tell me what happened," Natalia asked breathlessly.

It was not difficult with a little imagination to paint in a picture of which Nanny gave the outline.

Lady Claris Kempsey had been beautiful, wild and completely unprincipled where men were concerned.

She had set the whole neighbourhood by the ears with her behaviour and went to London to gain a reputation which was looked at askance even in the licentious days of the Prince Regent.

She had returned to the country and met Lord Colwall, as he had recently become, when he was home from Oxford before his last term.

It was not surprising he had fallen madly in love with her. She tantalised him, teased him, humiliated him, and gave him half-promises of surrender which merely increased his infatuation.

Then strangely, unexpectedly she had told him she would marry him!

He was as surprised as everyone else, and although Lord Colwall's friends and relations begged him to do nothing so rash, and take a wife who could bring him nothing but unhappiness, he had laughed at their fears.

He was in love as only a very young and very vulnerable young man could be for the first time in his life and they were married only three weeks after the engagement was announced, in Worcester Cathedral.

Lady Claris made a very gay and very lovely Bride but, to everyone who knew them, they were an ill-assorted couple. Not only in age but in temperament, from the moment they walked down the aisle as man and wife.

They came back to the Castle after a short honeymoon, and Lady Claris immediately complained of it being dull.

It was not the right Season to be in London, so Lord Colwall had invited large numbers of guests to the Castle and there were entertainments from dawn to dusk.

Late one afternoon a month after their marriage, the guests from a luncheon party had left, when Lady Claris walked across the Salon to the window.

She wore the long, narrow, high-waisted Empire-style gown which was still fashionable and under which no lady wore corsets, and the sophisticates like Lady Claris no underclothes.

Her figure was silhouetted against the sunshine, and looking at her Lord Colwall exclaimed half jokingly:

"You are getting very fat, Claris. You will have to be more careful of what you eat."

She had turned to look at him, a mocking expression in her eyes, and he had felt as if a cold hand touched his heart.

"Can it be—p-possible?" he stammered. "No, it cannot be, and yet—are you having a—b . . baby?"

"But of course!" she replied. "Why else should I have married you?"

For a moment he could not understand what she was saying; then in a voice shaking as if someone had dealt him a body blow, he managed to ejaculate:

"Whose is it?"

She had shrugged her white shoulders.

"I have no idea," she replied.

Then before he could speak to her again, she had left the Salon, and gone up to her bed-room.

Lord Colwall had ordered a curricle to be brought to the front door, and while he waited for it he hated his wife with such ferocity that to prevent himself from murdering her, he knew he must put the greatest distance possible between them.

Taking only a groom with him, he drove towards London to get away from her, to escape from those mocking eyes, those jeering lips.

Fool! Fool that he had been! Dolt! Slaphead, not to have realised from the very beginning why she had been in such haste to be married!

Why had he never asked himself the reason why she should have suddenly succumbed to his love-making when he had least expected it.

Then, when he was some twenty miles from the Castle, Lord Colwall decided that having been a fool, he was behaving like one yet again. Why should he leave his house because his wife was unfaithful? Why should he leave her in possession of the Castle?

He would go back and turn her out. She could return to her family.

The arguments that must ensue as to whether he would accept the child as his own could be conducted between their lawyers decently and with formality.

Lord Colwall turned his horses round. They were tired from the speed at which they had been driven, and it took him some time to return.

It was nearly midnight when he arrived back at the Castle, but he was determined that he would see Claris and inform her that he would not keep her under his roof and she was to leave for her father's house at daybreak.

He walked into the Hall and saw the expression of surprise on the faces of the two footmen on duty. There was a cloak and hat lying on one of the chairs.

"Where is Her Ladyship?" he asked.

There was a moment's uncomfortableness before the flunkey replied somewhat hesitatingly:

"I believe—Her Ladyship is—upstairs, M'Lord."

He went up the stone staircase like a man possessed and burst open the door of the bed-chamber.

His wife was in bed, but she was not alone!

For a moment there was sheer unbridled murder in Lord Colwall's eyes. Then he seized the man who lay beside Lady Claris and dragged him from the bed onto the floor.

He was naked and when Lord Colwall recognised him as an older man of no social importance, someone whom he would hardly have considered worth a glance, he had laughed scornfully.

"I would not soil my hands by fighting you," he said. "But I intend to kick you out of my house."

He dragged the man just as he was down the stairs. The two servants were standing spell-bound in the Hall.

"Open the door," Lord Colwall commanded.

As they hastened to obey, there was a sudden cry from the staircase above.

Lady Claris was standing there. She had flung a diaphanous wrapper over her nightgown, her dark hair streaming over her shoulders.

"Stop, Ranulf!" she cried. "You cannot do this! You cannot behave in such a manner! It will cause a scandal, as you well know."

"You should have thought of that earlier!" Lord Colwall answered.

The man, whom he was holding tightly by his arms, made no appeal. He was obviously struck dumb by what was occurring.

"Ranulf! I command you to let Charles dress and leave decently."

"There is nothing decent about him or you!" Lord Colwall replied harshly.

He dragged the man towards the doorway and Lady Claris screamed furiously:

"Damn you! Will you listen to me?"

She began to run down the stairs.

Whether it was her nightgown which impeded her or the fact that she was heavy with child, it was impossible to determine, but she tripped and fell forward with a shrill cry which echoed round the walls.

She rolled over and over down the uncarpeted stone stairway to land in the Hall at the feet of her husband and her paramour.

Her neck was broken.

CHAPTER FIVE

Lord Colwall came down the steps of the Castle with a pronounced scowl on his face.

The black stallion waiting for him was being held with difficulty by two grooms and he swung himself quickly into the saddle.

"Her Ladyship's horse was a bit frisky, too, M'Lord," one of the grooms said, "and I was to tell Your Lordship that she's gone on ahead."

Lord Colwall looked surprised, and then a little way down the drive he saw a figure in a blue habit riding a roan mare and holding it under control with some difficulty.

He set off towards Natalia at a sharp pace. He had not slept well and had risen that morning feeling both apprehensive and angry.

'How,' he asked himself, 'could I ever imagine I would find myself in such an uncontrollable situation?'

At the same time he had to admit that in the circumstances Natalia had behaved in an exemplary manner.

She had neither wept nor berated him as another woman might have done. She had assembled her arguments well and had been logical in the manner in which she had presented them.

At the same time he was appalled at what the future might hold.

He reached Natalia's side and saw that she was wearing a sapphire-blue riding-habit of velvet which accentuated her small waist.

Her high-crowned riding-hat was encircled by a gauze veil which hung down her back and she looked very young and lovely.

"Good morning, My Lord," she said in a light tone as he approached. "I had hoped that you would invite me to ride with you this morning; but, as you did not do so, I presumed to order my own horse in the hope that I might be allowed to accompany you."

"I am delighted you should do so," Lord Colwall replied.

"And dare I suggest that I race you across the Park, which I feel will blow away some of the cobwebs?" Natalia asked.

She turned her horse as she spoke and rode off without waiting for his reply. Lord Colwall, pressing his top hat firmly on his head, set off in pursuit.

As she galloped ahead of him, he admitted to himself that she rode surprisingly well. He had expected her to be proficient, but himself an extremely experienced horseman he recognised that Natalia was in fact outstanding.

The sound of their horses' hoofs thundered in their ears as they sped across the Park and on through open fields.

Finally, when they must have gone for over two miles and Lord Colwall was two lengths ahead, they both drew in their horses and he turned to see Natalia's laughing face.

"You beat me fairly," she admitted, "as I had always hoped you would!"

He raised his eyebrows and she explained:

"When in my imagination Crusader and I were racing my Knight, I always permitted him to win! I felt it would lower his prestige to be defeated by a mere woman."

"You should not be so modest," Lord Colwall said. "You are, as I expect you well know, an exceptionally good horsewoman!"

"I am glad that one of my accomplishments finds favour in Your Lordship's eyes."

"It will be interesting to discover the others," he replied.

Their horses were walking side by side, sweating a little at the speed at which they had galloped.

"I thought last night that you were extremely surprised to find that I should have a will of my own," Natalia said with a smile. "You had me brought up in accordance with your wishes and then, unexpectedly, I disconcerted you."

Lord Colwall said nothing and Natalia went on with a look of mischief in her eyes:

"I wonder if you know the story that when Adam behaved so badly in the Garden of Eden, God protested about him to one of the Angels.

"'But, My Lord' the Angel replied, 'you gave Adam free will!'

"'I gave him free will to agree with me!' God answered. 'But when he disagrees, it is just darned impudence!'"

Lord Colwall laughed.

"Are you seriously comparing me with the Almighty?"

"Why not?" Natalia asked. "You are very autocratic."

"I have a feeling," he said, noting the dimple that had appeared at the side of her mouth, "that you are being deliberately provocative! If you are not careful, Natalia, I shall lock you up in one of the dungeons beneath the Castle, or perhaps incarcerate you in one of the turrets!"

"Oh, let it be a turret!" Natalia cried. "I can then let down my long hair to make a rope by which to escape!"

She glanced at him from under her eye-lashes and added:

"That is if I really wanted to leave . . ."

She touched her horse with a spur as she spoke and once again she was forging ahead and Lord Colwall had to exert himself to keep beside her.

They returned to the Castle in time for luncheon. Natalia chatted gaily all through the meal and when they had finished, she persuaded Lord Colwall to show her his home.

He was amazed at how much she knew about the pictures which hung on the ancient walls and the furniture which graced every Salon.

Natalia had expected the Castle to be impressive. What she had not known was that every owner for centuries had been not only an adventurer, but also a collector.

From the time the Castle had been built, the Colwalls had acquired valuables from all over the world by conquest, by piracy and from the sheer joy of acquisition.

There were scrolls and jade from China; mosaics and carpets from Persia, marble and bronze statues from Greece, pictures by all the great Masters from Italy, France and Holland.

Where the scenes depicted were mythological, Natalia was better informed than Lord Colwall had believed possible. He had expected to be the teacher, but found himself the pupil.

Finally, when they had inspected the magnificent Library which had so delighted the Reverend Adolphus, he unlocked a door which stood in a corner of it.

It was very heavily made. The hinges were of brass and so were the studs which were deeply embedded in the old oak.

"This is my Strong-Room," he explained.

When he pulled open the door for Natalia to enter, she gave a gasp of surprise.

It was a circular room, the windows were only narrow slits, and she realised she was in one of the turrets.

She could see that all round the room there were glass cases, rising one above the other, and they contained jewels.

There was a case in which reposed the magnificent diamond tiara she had worn for her wedding, surrounded by a necklace, earrings, bracelets and rings, all of the same design.

In another case there was a parure of emeralds, another of rubies, another of sapphires, and a fifth containing a diadem of pearls.

In other cases there were amethysts, topazes, turquoises, aquamarines, gold and silver necklaces of great antiquity set with un-cut stones.

Baroque pearls filled a bowl to overflowing, which Lord Colwall explained was treasure trove from the West Indies brought home by the Colwall who sailed with Drake.

There was also enamel work like the pendant which Natalia wore round her neck and which had been made by master craftsmen of Venice, whose work of two centuries earlier remained unrivalled.

Natalia ran like a child from case to case exclaiming excitedly and asking Lord Colwall to explain to her where the jewels had been found.

She listened while he related deeds of daring and sometimes of terror, the Colwall who had acquired them sometimes escaping death only by inches.

Finally he opened the cases and she took out the jewels one by one to touch them, to try them on her wrists and place them against her white skin.

She could see her reflection in the oval mirror which hung on the wall. It had come from India and was encrusted with emeralds the size of pigeon's eggs and diamonds seemingly too big to be real.

"Tell me more! Tell me about this!" she kept saying, until finally Lord Colwall protested:

"I think I have exhausted my stories. If you want to know more you will have to search through the Family Records which contain particulars of my ancestors' journeys and the battles in which they were engaged."

"Perhaps we could put them all together and make a book," Natalia suggested.

She was just going to add ". . . for future generations," when she realised what the words suggested!

Blushing she turned to the nearest case, took out an enormous tiara of sapphires and diamonds, and set it upon her head.

It became her fair hair, and the jewels echoed the light in her eyes as she turned towards Lord Colwall to say:

"Now I look like a Queen, fit to sit beside your throne!"

She was laughing as she spoke, and her voice seemed to echo round the room while a shaft of sunlight coming through an arrow-slit window made the great tiara glitter almost blindingly.

"Why not fit to grace my bed?" Lord Colwall asked.

His eyes met Natalia's as he spoke and somehow it was impossible for either of them to move.

Something passed between them until, as she saw a fire smouldering in his eyes, she took the tiara from her head and put it in his hands.

Then she walked away, leaving him alone amongst his jewels.

The following morning Lord Colwall returned from a meeting that he had been obliged to attend in Hereford.

There was no sign of Natalia as he came into the Hall, nor did he find her in the Salon.

He next tried the Library and had only just walked towards the fire-place to hold out his hands to the blaze, when the door opened and she came in.

She was still wearing a bonnet which framed her small face and the silk ribbons were tied under her chin.

She had not discarded the cloak she had worn, and it was obvious as she moved across the space between them that she was in a hurry.

She reached Lord Colwall's side and stood looking up at him, her eyes troubled, and he fancied in surprise there was something like anger in her expression.

"You have a threshing-machine!"

Lord Colwall raised his eyebrows.

"Why should it concern you?"

"I understand it has just been installed."

"It arrived on the Estate three days ago."

"How can you do anything so foolhardy at this particular moment?" Natalia cried, "and why indeed should you want one?"

"I consider myself somewhat remiss in not having one before," Lord Colwall replied. "Most estates of this size have moved with the times. I did in fact intend to purchase one last year, but I was not impressed with the performance of the ones I inspected."

"Do you realise what it will mean to the men you employ?"

Natalia asked, and now there was no doubt that her tone was angry.

"I cannot imagine why it should interest you," Lord Colwall answered.

"I have just come from a cottage where there are nine people living on the wages of one man."

"You have come from a cottage?" Lord Colwall repeated. "What right had you to visit one of my cottages without telling me?"

"I learnt this morning after you had departed for Hereford, that an Aunt of one of the under-housemaids was very ill," Natalia answered. "I took her some soup and food for the children and I found . . ."

She paused as if it was difficult to speak of what she had discovered.

"What did you find?" Lord Colwall asked harshly.

"I found a household on the verge of starvation!"

"It is not true. The labourers on my Estate are paid more than the average."

"I heard that," Natalia said. "You give them eight shillings per week. Do you really call that an adequate sum for a man to support his widowed mother, his wife and seven children?"

Lord Colwall did not answer and she went on:

"The only thing they can look forward to after the summer, and their only chance of survival, is by threshing through the winter by which they can earn just enough to feed them until the spring. At the moment they are existing on potatoes and roots."

"I cannot believe this is the truth."

"Of course it is the truth!" Natalia contradicted. "I have read about such things, but I had not seen the actual suffering myself. Those children are skin and bones, and the cottage . . . it looks decent enough on the outside, but the conditions within are indescribable."

"Dirty?" Lord Colwall asked.

"No! Poverty-stricken! They have hardly a blanket with which to cover themselves or a cup or plate on which to eat. Such things cost money."

"I will investigate your allegations concerning starvation."

"It will soon be worse if you bring a threshing-machine into use," Natalia cried. "Do you know what the labourers in other Counties are asking?"

"If you are referring to the rioters, I do not wish to hear," Lord Colwall replied.

"They are asking for justice," Natalia went on as if he had not spoken. "They want two shillings per day for each man and one shilling and sixpence for each child he has to support . . . Does that seem too much for a landlord who owns as much as you do?"

"That is not the point!" Lord Colwall exclaimed. "Let me make it clear once and for all, Natalia, I will not have you visiting the cottages on my Estate. I forbid it!"

"I can quite imagine why you do not wish me to do so!" Natalia answered. "The old woman, the grandmother of the children, told me that the last lady who visited her was your mother!"

There was silence. Then Natalia said in a very different tone:

"Please, My Lord, get rid of the threshing-machine! Send it away and tell your men you will not use it."

"Why should I do that?" Lord Colwall enquired.

"Because these machines have caused trouble in every County except this," Natalia answered. "You have read of the riots in Kent and Surrey, in Hampshire and even in Gloucestershire. Surely you do not want them to happen here?"

"I will take good care they do not!"

"And how will you prevent it?" Natalia enquired. "Do you imagine other land-owners have not regretted that their ricks were fired, their machines broken up? And what is much more important, good will between the employer and the employee disrupted to the point of violence?"

"I have told you it is not your business," Lord Colwall said. "I know quite well how to deal with my own men."

"The children are hungry," Natalia said in a low voice.

"I will make enquiries," Lord Colwall promised, but his voice was cold and she knew he was angry with her.

She went from the room to take off her bonnet and cloak before luncheon.

When they sat down in the large Dining-Room, she found that Lord Colwall was deliberately talking of other things.

There was a hardness in his voice and she knew that any progress she might have made in gaining his confidence had been lost because she had argued with him about the threshing-machine.

She felt despairingly that she had lost completely the little ground she had gained, because she had been so appalled at the conditions she had found on what had seemed to her a happy and prosperous Estate.

'What could I do but tell him what I think?' she asked herself.

She knew that it would have been impossible for her to pretend she had not seen the suffering in the labourer's cottage.

She had heard the despair in the women's voices when they talked of the difference the threshing-machine would make in their lives.

'What can I say? What can I do to help them?' Natalia asked herself desperately.

At the same time she longed to put out her hand to Lord Colwall and ask him to smile at her, to persuade him to laugh as he had done yesterday when she had teased him and they had joked together, not only through luncheon but also through dinner.

It had been a cosy and intimate occasion that she had never known before, when after dinner they had sat in front of the fire in the Library and Lord Colwall had shown her drawings by great Italian artists that one of his ancestors had brought from Rome.

There was even one by Michelangelo and several by Tiepolo, which had made Natalia exclaim with delight.

When finally it was time to go to bed, she had put away the portfolio almost reluctantly.

"There is so much more I want to know. So much more I have to learn about such things," she said.

"You have plenty of time," he answered with a smile. "You are very young, Natalia, but already surprisingly knowledgeable on such matters."

"Thanks to you, My Lord, although it was Papa who taught me most of what I know about Art."

"One day I will take you to Rome."

She looked at him with delight.

"That is one of the things I have longed to hear you say."

"You anticipated I might say it?"

"I have always wanted to visit Italy and Greece," Natalia answered, "and Papa suggested once that you might wish to take me to both countries. I cannot imagine anything more exciting than seeing the Acropolis with you to instruct me."

"It is very beautiful in the moonlight," Lord Colwall said, "and very romantic."

There was something in his voice that made her drop her eyes shyly before his.

Then as if he regretted what he had said he added:

"I am sure you would find the Colosseum equally fascinating . . . One can always imagine the Christians struggling against the wild animals for their lives."

"I assure you, My Lord, that is not at all the type of entertainment I should find amusing," Natalia protested.

"Then we can wait for the moonlight and visit the Forum," Lord Colwall suggested.

She felt he was teasing her, and at the same time she half suspected that he was being charming for his own ends.

He had only to sweep away her defences and then she would be all too ready to acquiesce in his wishes.

Natalia had risen to her feet with a little smile.

"I think, My Lord, we must for the moment concern ourselves with the present."

He took her hand in his.

"May I tell you I have enjoyed myself today?" he asked.

There was a note of sincerity in his voice which she could not misunderstand.

"I also found it very entertaining," she said. "Thank you, My Lord."

She curtsied as she spoke, and then as he opened the door for her she passed through it without looking at him again.

She had the uneasy feeling that if she did so she might throw herself into his arms, agree to do whatever he wanted, and promise not to oppose him any longer.

'It is going to be hard to be resolute, when he is so beguiling,' she told herself.

She loved him already more than she imagined it was possible to love anybody. She loved everything about him; the sound of his voice, his handsome features, the way his hair grew back from his forehead, his strong sensitive fingers.

She had only to see him walk across the room to feel her heart turn over in her breast.

Yet even as she thought about him, she remembered the tone of his voice when he had been talking with Sir James, when he had said so emphatically that there could be no possible mistake:

"I assure you, whatever Natalia looks like, it will not affect my resolve never again to love any woman, nor, if I can prevent it, to allow her to love me!"

When at last the Maids had withdrawn and Natalia was alone in her bed-room, she told herself that she must not be misled into thinking pleasantness was affection, nor that desire for his own way was love.

Now, because she was determined that somehow she would

make Lord Colwall love her, she knew it was stupid to antagonise him or incite him to anger as she had just done.

Yet she thought as they finished luncheon there was nothing she could have done but speak in defence of the men who would be facing incredible hardships during the winter because of the threshing-machine.

"This evening," Lord Colwall said in a distant voice which meant he was still incensed with her, "I have arranged that we shall dine with the Earl of Frome. He is a relative by marriage. His house is only the other side of Hereford so the drive will not fatigue you."

"I should like that," Natalia said.

"It is rather soon after our marriage to accept invitations," Lord Colwall said, "but His Lordship is departing for London the day after tomorrow, and is extremely anxious to make your acquaintance before he leaves."

"It is of course Lord Frome who speaks regularly in the debates in the House of Lords," Natalia said. "I should like very much to meet him."

"Then if that be your pleasure, we will leave here at about six o'clock."

Lord Colwall rose to his feet as he spoke and Natalia led the way from the Dining-Room.

When they were out of ear-shot of the servants and she realised that he was about to leave her she said:

"Please will you remember what I have said about the labourer's family? I will take them some food tomorrow, but there must be many more in the same state who need your help and consideration."

"I have told you, Natalia, that I will not have you interfering in matters that do not concern you," Lord Colwall said sharply.

He walked away and left her standing alone in the corridor beside a suit of armour.

The dinner party with Lord Frome was most enjoyable.

As they were supposedly on their honeymoon, Lord Frome had not invited more than four other guests, and with his own family of sons and daughters they sat down a mere twelve to dinner.

The house was delightful, the dinner well cooked, and Lady Frome was a kindly, motherly woman who made Natalia feel at home. Her daughters admired unreservedly her gown and her jewels.

Lady Frome had known Lady Margaret and had many tales of how attractive Natalia's mother had been in the old days.

She told Natalia how many ardent and important beaux had pursued Lady Margaret only to be refused when she gave her heart to the Reverend Adolphus and married him despite parental opposition.

There was so much to talk about and so much to hear, that Natalia was quite surprised when Lord Colwall said it was getting late and time they returned home.

It was very cold when they stepped out of the warm house.

There was however a foot-warmer in the comfortable carriage, which had His Lordship's Coat of Arms emblazoned on the panels, and there was a big fur rug to cover them both as they sat side by side against the soft cushions.

'We are in a little world almost of our own,' Natalia thought.

She wondered what she would do if Lord Colwall put his arms around her and kissed her.

Would she surrender herself to him?

She knew she longed above all things to feel his lips on hers, and then she remembered again the cold manner in which he had spoken to Sir James, and knew that nothing had changed as far as he was concerned.

They passed through the centre of Hereford and were just on the outskirts of the town, moving along a road that appeared to be empty of traffic, when the horses were pulled up with a jerk that almost flung Natalia onto the floor.

"What has occurred?" Lord Colwall enquired as he struggled to let down the window.

The footman opened the door.

"I'm afraid there has been an accident, M'Lord," he said. "We didn't see the child until we were right on top of him."

"What child?" Lord Colwall asked.

But even as he asked the question, Natalia had slipped from the carriage and out into the road-way.

The coachman had brought the horses to a standstill, but lying against the wheel she could see in the light of the lanterns a small boy.

She knelt down beside him, and as she did so she heard Lord Colwall say to the footman behind her:

"How did it happen?"

"The child must have been a-wandering about at the side of the road, M'Lord. We didn't see him until the horses were right upon him. We'd have run right over him if Mr. Hempton hadn't pulled them aside just in time."

"Is he dead?" Lord Colwall asked.

Before the footman could reply, Natalia, who was kneeling by the boy, said:

"No, I think he is unconscious but he has a very bad gash on one of his knees and his hand seems to be covered in blood."

"I wonder where he comes from," Lord Colwall said. "Perhaps we had better take him back to the town."

"I think, M'Lord," Hempton said from the box, "that he's a lad from the Orphanage."

"Which Orphanage?" Lord Colwall enquired.

"The Colwall Orphanage which was built by Your Lordship's grandfather."

"Oh, yes of course I remember," Lord Colwall said.

While he was talking, Natalia instructed the footman to lift the child into the carriage. He was laid on the small seat opposite the one on which she and Lord Colwall had been seated.

Now by the light of the candle-lantern inside the carriage she could see he was a child of only four or five years of age.

He had fair hair, a thin, delicate face and was very pale— presumably from the accident. There was a bruise on his forehead where he must have fallen against a stone.

Natalia felt his legs and arms and felt quite certain that owing to Hempton's skilful driving the carriage wheel had not passed over him but had simply knocked him down.

She lay the fur rug gently over the child as Lord Colwall climbed back into the carriage.

"Drive to the Orphanage," he said, "and go slowly."

"Very good, M'Lord."

Natalia was kneeling on the floor of the carriage holding the child on the small seat for fear he should fall off. The light gleamed on her fair hair and glittered on her diamond necklace.

Lord Colwall watched her, but he said nothing as they travelled slowly for perhaps half a mile.

When the carriage came to a standstill, Natalia said:

"The child is still unconscious. We must make it clear that he requires careful nursing and that they should send for a physician."

"I doubt if one will come out at this time of night to an Orphanage," Lord Colwall replied.

Then as a door opened in response to the footman's knock, he alighted.

As if she did not trust him to insist that the child needed urgent attention, Natalia followed Lord Colwall from the carriage and walked up a short stone-paved path.

She saw the building built of red brick was not large and it had small, gabled windows.

"That must have been Timothy in the road-way, M'Lord," she heard the woman say as she reached Lord Colwall's side. "He's always running away to go and look for his mother. He hasn't been with us long."

The woman looked harassed. The apron she wore over her gown was none too clean and there were strands of hair escaping from under her mob cap.

"I am Lady Colwall," Natalia said politely holding out her hand. "I am sorry that we have hurt one of your children."

"There's too many of them and that's a fact, M'Lady," the woman answered. "Over twenty I've got at the moment, and not a soul to help me."

"No-one to help you?" Natalia exclaimed in surprise.

"I think perhaps we should step inside," Lord Colwall said. "It is cold standing here and we have just come from a warm atmosphere."

"Yes, of course, M'Lord, excuse me," the woman stuttered, afraid she had done the wrong thing.

She held open the door while Natalia and Lord Colwall walked inside.

The Orphanage was austere, but they could see the room they entered was adequately furnished, although it was extremely untidy and badly in need of being dusted.

"I must apologise, M'Lord . . ." the woman began, but Lord Colwall interposed:

"Will you tell me your name?"

"Mrs. Moppam, M'Lord."

"And you have been in charge of this Orphanage for some time?"

"For over eight years, M'Lord."

"Then why are you so short-staffed?"

The woman looked embarrassed.

"I shouldn't have mentioned it, M'Lord, except that you finds me in such a mess. Of course, if I'd known Your Lordship and Your Ladyship were coming . . ."

"Why are you short-staffed?" Lord Colwall asked again.

"The truth is, M'Lord, there's not enough money these days. When Your Lordship's grandfather endowed the Orphanage it was enough and to spare, but the pound won't buy what it used to and that's the truth."

"You mean you cannot pay for adequate help?"

"No, M'Lord. I used to have two untrained girls—some of them as young as twelve or thirteen, most of them more trouble than they are worth—but I can't even get those now. There's too many places as wants 'em."

"You say you have twenty children here?" Natalia asked.

"Yes, M'Lady. They keeps asking me to take more, but 'tis impossible. But I has to do everything, except for old Mrs. Brown who comes in the morning to help me prepare a meal."

Natalia looked at Lord Colwall.

"We cannot leave the little boy here in the condition he is in. It would be too much to ask of Mrs. Moppam."

"It's not that I'm not willing, M'Lady, but what'd I do at the moment, with an injured child on my hands? As it is, there's eight children down with Whooping Cough."

"I suppose there is the Hospital . . ." Lord Colwall began.

"Not in Hereford, M'Lord. Worcester's nearest, and that's not much of a place to send a child, from all I hear."

"Then he will come home with us."

There was a firmness in Natalia's voice which told Lord Colwall without words she was determined in this matter whatever he might say.

His lips tightened as he said:

"That perhaps will be the best solution at least for tonight."

"Thank you, M'Lord. I am very grateful, and to you, M'Lady," Mrs. Moppam said, twisting her hands agitatedly in her dirty apron.

"Good-bye, Mrs. Moppam," Natalia said with a smile. "I am sure my husband will be able to make arrangements so that you can employ more help for the other children in your care. When the Orphanage was built it was certainly intended to be a model of its kind."

She moved towards the door as she spoke.

Mrs. Moppam followed her, bobbing and curtseying apprehensively up and down as first Natalia and then Lord Colwall went towards the carriage.

The child had not moved since Natalia had left him; now she sat down on the seat and said to the footman:

"Will you lift the boy into my arms?"

The footman looked surprised, and as he was about to pick up the child, Lord Colwall said:

"Is this wise? He is very dirty and the blood will undoubtedly stain your dress."

"That is of no consequence," Natalia replied.

She took the child from the footman and made him comfortable on her lap and pulled the rug over him.

Lord Colwall said nothing and they set off towards the Castle.

As they neared the lodges, the child's eyelids fluttered and he made a feeble cry.

"It is all right," Natalia said soothingly. "You are quite safe, Timothy."

He gave a little whimper because he was obviously in pain.

Natalia eased the rug from off his leg then put her arms around him again.

"It is all right," she said rocking him backwards and forwards.

"Mama . . . Mama," he murmured, just as they reached the Castle.

The servants came hurrying out and a footman lifted Timothy from Natalia's arms.

"Take him straight up to the Nursery," she instructed.

"Very good, M'Lady."

The footman carrying Timothy carefully went ahead, and when Natalia reached the hall she saw there was a great stain of blood on the skirt of her gown.

There was also dust and mud on her bodice, where she had held the child's body close against her.

She looked at Lord Colwall for one moment as she passed him to go towards the stairs.

"Thank you for letting me bring Timothy here," she said softly so that only he could hear.

His lips were twisted for a moment in a wry smile.

"Did I have any choice in the matter?"

"Not really!" she answered, and he saw the dimple at the side of her mouth as she walked away from him.

Upstairs in the Nursery, Nanny, who had not yet gone to bed, had forgotten her arthritis and was undressing Timothy by the fire.

"What happened, M'Lady?" she asked as Natalia entered.

"We knocked him down in the road outside Hereford," Natalia explained. "He had run away from the Orphanage to look for his mother."

"Poor little mite!" Nanny ejaculated. "Children of that age do not understand."

She pulled off the child's clothes that were little more than rags.

"You'll find a night-shirt which once belonged to His Lordship in the chest in the corner, M'Lady."

Natalia hurried to fetch it for her and then she helped Nanny wash the blood from the child's leg and hand.

Nanny bandaged him deftly, and now he was half-conscious and twisting his head from side to side, moaning and calling all the time "Mama . . . Mama."

Natalia soothed him with gentle fingers.

After he had drunk some warm milk they laid him in the small bed which still stood in the Night-Nursery beside the larger one occupied by Nurse.

It was then Nanny, looking at Natalia with a smile, asked:

"How did you persuade His Lordship to let him come here?"

"There was no alternative really," Natalia answered. "The Orphanage is desperately understaffed—only Mrs. Moppam to look after twenty children! Oh, Nanny, how could things have got into such a bad state?"

"It is always the same when there is no lady to see to things," Nanny answered. "When His Lordship's mother was alive, she knew everything that went on on the Estate."

"I learned today that she visited the cottages, but no-one had been near them since," Natalia murmured.

"Who was there to go?" Nanny enquired. "Lady Blestow only stayed here when there was entertaining to be done, and His late-Lordship was so sunk in his own sorrow he was not interested."

"I must try and help them," Natalia said almost to herself.

"That is exactly what they want!" Nanny said. "Someone like yourself to make them feel that they matter in the world. People get despondent when they are not wanted."

"That is true enough," Natalia said in a sad little voice.

Nanny glanced at her quickly and then she said:

"You go to bed, M'Lady. I'll look after Timothy and if he doesn't seem better in the morning, we'll send for the doctor. But if you ask me, there's nothing that a good rest won't cure. There's no bones broken—take my word for it!"

"I do, Nanny, and thank you!" Natalia said.

She went downstairs and to her surprise found as she reached the landing outside her bed-room that Lord Colwall was waiting for her.

"It is time you went to bed," he said. "You look tired."

"I am a little," Natalia confessed. "It was such a shock seeing the child lying there in the road and thinking we might have killed him."

"Is he all right?"

"Nanny says so."

"Then he will be!"

Natalia smiled.

"I am sure he will."

"Then go to bed and dream of pleasant things."

"I will try to," she said a little doubtfully.

Lord Colwall looked for a moment as if he wanted to say something else, and then he changed his mind and turned towards his own room.

"Good-night, Natalia."

"Good-night, My Lord."

She had a wild desire to run after him, to ask him if she could stay with him a little and they could sit by the fire talking.

Then she wondered if she was being sincere, if she really wanted to talk to him or did she in fact long for something very different!

CHAPTER SIX

Lord Colwall arrived at the Castle in his Phaeton.

He stepped down with a look on his face which made two of the younger footmen, who were less well-trained, glance at each other in consternation.

They knew only too well that His Lordship's "black look" meant that he was in a fault-finding mood.

His Lordship handed his high beaver hat to the Butler, who then helped him off with his overcoat.

As he drew his driving-gloves from his hands he asked:

"Where is Her Ladyship?"

"I think she is upstairs, M'Lord," the Butler replied. "I will inform her that Your Lordship has returned."

"I will tell her myself!"

Lord Colwall walked up the stone staircase, conscious as he did so of a feeling of intense annoyance that Natalia was not waiting for him.

He knew he was early and he was well aware that his meeting with the High Sheriff over County matters had put him in a bad humour.

But it added to his anger that Natalia was not waiting for him on his arrival.

He made it clear to her that when they could not go riding together in the mornings, he expected to see her as soon as he returned home.

Although he would not admit it to himself, he liked to see her eyes light up at his appearance.

He opened the door of her Sitting-Room and found, as he had expected, it was empty, and frowning, he climbed the minor staircase to the next floor.

As he approached the Nursery, Lord Colwall remembered that it was many years since he had visited this part of the Castle, which he had occupied as a child.

There was, he thought, the same smell about it and as he reached the Nursery door, it was almost disappointing not to find that homemade bread was being toasted in front of the open fire, or distinguish the sickly fragrance of toffee on the air.

Instead, he heard Natalia's voice saying:

". . . And then, just as the Dragon was coming nearer and nearer, fire coming out of his nostrils, his great scaly tail waving in the air, the Princess saw someone shining and silver coming through the green trees."

"'Twas the . . . Knight!" a little voice of one who obviously knew the story already cried excitedly.

"Yes, it was the Knight coming to rescue her!" Natalia said. "The Dragon had not seen the Knight approaching on his white charger, and now he opened his big, ugly mouth with its great big teeth to swallow the Princess up! But just as he was about to take a big bite, the Knight thrust his long lance down his throat."

"He killed him . . . He killed him!"

"Yes, he killed him, and it was a tremendous battle, but the Princess stopped screaming because she knew the Knight was going to win."

"What did the Knight do . . . then?"

The child's tone was breathless.

Natalia opened her lips to reply and a deep voice said:

"I, too, should be interested to know the end of the story."

She gave a little exclamation and saw Lord Colwall standing in the doorway.

He looked as usual, extremely elegant with tight pantaloons the colour of pale champagne, and the points of his collar very high against his firm chin.

"My Lord!" Natalia exclaimed with a tone of consternation in her voice.

She rose to her feet but not before Lord Colwall had seen her arms had held Timothy closely and his small head had been resting against her breast.

"You are early!" Natalia said with a glance at the clock on the mantel-shelf.

"Only a trifle," Lord Colwall replied loftily, "but as there was no-one to welcome me downstairs, I obviously had to come in search of you."

"I am sorry you should have been troubled," Natalia said in a low voice.

There was an accusing note in his voice which she knew meant that he was incensed.

"What happened? What happened?" Timothy begged, holding on to Natalia's full skirt with his small hands.

He had recovered from his accident, but he was still very thin. His face was almost ethereal with good features and large, blue, appealing eyes, which made him exceptionally attractive.

"I see that your protégé has returned to health," Lord Colwall said.

"He is better," Natalia replied, "and the scar on his knee is healed. At the same time he is very fragile."

"He looks well enough to me," Lord Colwall said, "and as Mrs. Moppam now has assistance in the Orphanage, I have arranged for him to return there this afternoon."

"Oh, no!"

It was a cry from Natalia's heart, and as she saw the expression on Lord Colwall's face, she said quickly:

"You have provided Mrs. Moppam with girls willing to assist her?"

"I have found two," Lord Colwall answered. "Or rather my Agent has discovered them in the village. They are not more than fifteen years of age, but they are glad to have the opportunity of working. I understand they both come from large families, so they will be used to dealing with children."

"That is kind of you," Natalia approved. "I know Mrs. Moppam will be delighted."

"She is!" Lord Colwall said, "and I have increased the annual income for the Orphanage, so that too should meet with your approval!"

There was a distinct challenge in his voice.

"I knew you would do what is right."

Lord Colwall looked away from the gratitude in Natalia's eyes.

"I am sure that, in the circumstances that now exist in the Orphanage, this child will find it impossible to run away at night, or at any other time and endanger his life."

"He is still not very . . . strong," Natalia said hesitatingly. "Could he not stay a . . . little longer?"

"No!"

The one syllable was firm.

"Why not?"

"Because it is a mistake for him to become used to a luxurious life when he will have to work his way in the world."

"That I can understand," Natalia agreed. "But at the same time he is only five years old and he misses his . . . mother."

She bent down as she spoke to lift Timothy up into her arms.

He clung to her and kissed her cheek.

"Another . . . story . . . Mama?" he pleaded.

"I see he already thinks you are his mother," Lord Colwall said. "A most undesirable illusion from the child's point of view."

"He calls every woman 'Mama,'" Natalia explained. "Nanny, Mrs. Hodges, and Ellen! In fact he is a child who needs attention."

"He is fortunate to get it," Lord Colwall said. "I myself find it in somewhat short supply."

"I am sorry," Natalia said simply. "It is nearly luncheon-time. I will wash my hands and be downstairs in a very few moments."

"And that child is to be taken back this afternoon," Lord Colwall said. "Is that understood?"

For a moment he thought Natalia might defy him. Instead she replied dully:

"I understand. I will take him . . . back."

Calling Nanny to come and look after Timothy, she ran downstairs hastily to her bed-room to find Ellen waiting for her.

As the Maid poured some warm water into a basin, Natalia said with a little sob in her voice:

"His Lordship has ordered me to take Timothy back to the Orphanage this afternoon. Oh, Ellen, he will be so unhappy again!"

"He'll miss you, M'Lady," Ellen said.

"And Nanny . . . and you," Natalia answered. "We have played with him, we have all tried to make him forget his mother, but now I feel that instead of crying for her, he will be crying for us."

"It's made all the difference to Nanny having him here, M'Lady," Ellen said. "I suppose you couldn't ask His Lordship if Timothy could stay a little longer?"

"I have asked him," Natalia answered, "and he has refused. I think His Lordship resents the time I spend in the Nursery."

As she spoke she knew that was the truth.

It was a continued irritant to Lord Colwall that she should want to be with the orphan child, when he felt she should be providing him with one of her own.

He had not said anything, but whenever she referred to the little boy, there was an expression on Lord Colwall's face which told her all too clearly what he was thinking.

"I've an idea, M'Lady," Ellen said suddenly.

"What is it?" Natalia enquired.

"My Aunt married the Blacksmith, M'Lady. His name's Turner. They lost their only child when he was nine years of age, and she's never been the same since. She can't have another and seeing how she's always been fond of children, it's been a bitter blow to them both."

Natalia's eyes were alight.

"Ellen, do you think they would adopt Timothy?"

"I'm almost sure of it, M'Lady, if you were to ask them to do so."

"I will take Timothy there this afternoon," Natalia said. "If she refuses to take him, then I must carry him on to the Orphanage. Oh, Ellen, how clever of you to think of it!"

"It's only just come to my mind, M'Lady," Ellen said, "but it does seem a wonderful opportunity for Timothy to have a home. That's what he wants—a home! With a father and mother to care for him."

"I shall pray that Mrs. Turner will agree," Natalia said.

She went down to the Salon to find Lord Colwall looking out of the window.

It was a grey, blustery day with a promise of rain in the sky. He turned as Natalia came into the room.

With her fair hair and gown of pale daffodil yellow, she looked like a shaft of sunlight.

She smiled at him and moved towards the fire-place.

"Have you had a busy morning?" she asked.

"An extremely disagreeable one," Lord Colwall replied. "If ever there was a self-confident, obstinate man, it is the High Sheriff!"

"I hope he is not thinking the same thing about you!" she said mischievously.

"I am quite sure he is thinking a great deal more. I defeated him in every argument, and the rest of those present supported me."

"I am sure they did," Natalia answered. "After all, you are so much cleverer than the average local Big-Wig."

"How do you know that?" he asked with a faint smile.

"I know only too well how dull and pompous County Gentlemen become when they discuss local affairs," Natalia answered. "Papa used to say that nothing seemed more dreary than when he had to go to a meeting with the Gentlemen of Cumberland pontificating for the good of their kind."

Lord Colwall laughed, and Natalia realised that his bad temper was evaporating.

"I wish we could do something interesting this afternoon," he said. "Unfortunately, I have to attend yet another meeting at Hereford."

"No-one could accuse you of not taking an interest in County matters," Natalia said, "but I would like above all things to hear you speak in the House of Lords."

"On what topic?" Lord Colwall enquired.

She was about to answer him and then she realised that this was not the moment to bring up the subject of injustice to the Labourers, cruelty to the climbing boys, or the horrifying abuses of the children working in factories.

One day, she promised herself, she would discuss it with him, but not until they had a better understanding between them and he would listen to what she had to say.

Instead she tried to amuse him during luncheon, telling him stories of Cumberland, and speaking of Art, which she had learnt by now was a subject which never failed to arouse his interest.

"When we go to London," he said, "you will have a chance of seeing the pictures at Buckingham Palace. The late King, for all his faults, had a taste with which it is impossible to find fault."

"I would love to see them," Natalia said, "although I think I should be too nervous to enjoy them properly as they are in the Palace."

"You would not be nervous with the new King, nor with his wife," Lord Colwall said. "King William is a blunt, good-humoured, jovial man, very like the Cumberland Gentlemen you have described to me, and Queen Adelaide is young, shy, but very anxious to be pleasant."

"You make them sound quite a homely couple," Natalia said.

"They are!" Lord Colwall replied laconically.

He hurried away after luncheon was over and Natalia went somewhat unhappily upstairs to put on her bonnet and cloak.

As she expected, Nanny was almost in tears.

"It's been like the old days, M'Lady, and that's a fact, having a child in the Nursery," she said. "It's made me feel young again."

It was true that Nanny seemed to have grown not only younger, but a great deal stronger since Timothy had been there.

She still limped as she walked, but she managed to bustle around as she made no effort to do before, and Natalia was quite certain that her rheumatism was partly due to being inactive.

As she had promised, she had made Nanny the herbal potion according to her mother's special recipe, but she knew that the best medicine she could possibly have would be a baby to look after.

'Just another reason,' Natalia said to herself, 'why I should give His Lordship an heir.'

She knew that she wanted more than anything else to have a child and know that it would grow up as handsome and attractive as its father.

Yet her whole body shrank with a kind of sick horror when she thought that, because Lord Colwall did not love her, she might produce a deformed baby such as she had seen lying on the grave of Sarah's step-father.

She would never forget, she thought, her feelings when she had seen it!

It had been a moment when repugnance and pity mingled with a fiery anger that such a thing should have happened.

She could remember her father saying quickly and almost harshly to her mother:

"Take Natalia away. I will deal with this."

Her mother had taken her arm and drawn her towards the Church, but she knew she could never forget, and what she had seen was seared deep into her memory for all time.

"See . . . horses?" Timothy was asking with a look of excitement in his blue eyes.

"Yes, two big horses," Natalia answered.

Nanny buttoned him into a warm coat which Ellen had gone to Hereford to buy for him. There was a woollen cap to cover his fair hair and new gloves for his hands.

When he was ready, a footman carried him down the stairs and set him beside Natalia in the comfortable brougham which she used when she went out driving alone.

There were two fine horses to draw it and two men on the box, and she thought as they moved down the drive how comfortable and secure her life was compared to what the future held for the little boy at her side.

He was so frail that she felt he would never survive if, when he was old enough, he was sent to a factory or apprenticed.

She had heard terrifying stories from her father of how badly apprentices could be treated. Some of them were little better than slaves, beaten and starved by their masters with no redress, unless they ran away.

Then, if they were caught, they could be brought back and beaten all over again.

'I cannot bear it for Timothy,' she thought to herself.

In the short time he had been at the Castle, she had developed a special affection for the child and she knew that he appealed to a maternal instinct which she had not known she possessed.

On her instructions the carriage stopped first at the Blacksmith's Forge.

There were a number of customers waiting outside holding their horses while there was the clang of a hammer on the anvil and the embers in the fire were glowing red.

The footman got down and opened the door.

"Your Ladyship wishes to speak with Mr. Turner?"

"No, to *Mrs.* Turner," Natalia replied.

"She lives in the house next to the Forge, M'Lady."

"Then see if she is at home," Natalia ordered.

The footman knocked at the door and when it opened, Natalia stepped down from the carriage.

She took Timothy by the hand and drew him into the Forge.

The Blacksmith looked up as she entered. He had hold of a horse's hoof and was nailing the shoe into place.

"Good afternoon, M'Lady!"

"Good afternoon, Mr. Turner!" Natalia said. "I wish to have a few words with your wife. Might this little boy, whose name is Timothy, stay and watch you?"

"He's welcome, M'Lady."

"Stay here, Timothy," Natalia said, "and do not get in the way."

She saw that the child's face was alight with interest as he drew nearer to the Blacksmith. He loved horses and did not remember his accident, so it had left no unpleasant memories in his mind.

Natalia left the Forge and went up the short path to the house.

Mrs. Turner showed her into the parlour.

"It's a great honour, M'Lady. I'd no idea you might be calling."

"Ellen has told me about you, Mrs. Turner," Natalia answered, "and I have a very great favour to ask of you."

"A favour, M'Lady?" Mrs. Turner cried, not believing that it was possible for her to do anyone so important a favour.

Natalia sat down on a chair and explained about Timothy.

She told Mrs. Turner how lonely the child was without his mother, how he had escaped from the Orphanage to go looking for her, and how he called every woman "Mama" in a pathetic effort to find the love he had lost.

By the time she had finished speaking, there were tears in Mrs. Turner's eyes.

"I have told you all this," Natalia said in her soft voice, "because I wondered if it would be possible for you and Mr. Turner to adopt Timothy? I cannot bear to think of him at the Orphanage. He is such a gentle, quiet little boy, I feel he will not hold his own with the other children, and I cannot contemplate what will happen when he has to earn his own living."

"You mean adopt him, M'Lady?" Mrs. Turner asked.

"Is it too much to ask?" Natalia answered.

"I don't know. I've never thought of it, M'Lady. I don't know if my husband would agree. It's been a bitter blow to him that we had no more children, and a better and kinder man 'twould be hard to find. 'Tis real miserable I am to feel that I've failed him."

"What I am going to suggest," Natalia said, "is that I leave Timothy here with you from tonight, and I will drive on to the Orphanage and explain to Mrs. Moppam that you are getting to know him. If Mr. Turner will not agree to keep him then perhaps you could take him back there tomorrow, or send me a message."

"We can manage that ourselves, Ma'am," Mrs. Turner said. "We has a gig."

"It does not matter which way it is done if Timothy has to go back," Natalia said, "but I am hoping and praying, Mrs. Turner, that you will find a place for him in your home."

She went back to the Forge to find Timothy entranced with the shoeing of the horses.

He had managed to get a streak of grease on his face and his hands were dirty, but he looked happy.

"Come with me, Timothy," Natalia said. "There is a lady who wants to meet you."

"Mama?" Timothy asked unexpectedly.

"Yes, Mama," Natalia said firmly.

She took the little boy into the house where Mrs. Turner was waiting.

"Why, he's beautiful!" she exclaimed.

"Mrs. Moppam will tell you all about him, should you wish to know," Natalia said.

She knelt down beside Timothy and said:

"Listen, Timothy, you are going to stay here today with Mama. Be a very good boy and I know she will tell you lots of stories. She had a little boy of her own once and he loved listening to them."

She saw the tears overflow in Mrs. Turner's eyes.

Then having kissed Timothy, she moved towards the door.

He did not seem to mind that she was leaving, as he was exploring the room. He liked a pretty shell he had found on a table near the wall.

The carriage carried Natalia on to the Orphanage.

There she explained to Mrs. Moppam what had happened and met the new assistants who had been sent from the village. She noted that the place was much cleaner.

The children seemed happy. Those who had been at the Orphanage for some time appeared well-fed.

At the same time, Natalia felt that Timothy wanted more than food and clothing. In contrast, the other children seemed very robust and coarser in appearance.

"What do you know about Timothy?" she asked Mrs. Moppam.

"His mother was a housemaid at a Gentleman's house," Mrs. Moppam replied. "She got into trouble and was turned out without a reference. She managed to keep herself and the child alive by hard work but gradually her strength gave out, I understand her lungs were affected."

"Who was the father?" Natalia asked.

"She'd never say, M'Lady, but I happens to know the house where she was employed and the son is a pleasant-spoken, handsome young gentleman."

She paused:

"The woman who brought Timothy here was with his mother when she died. She had told her that she had only ever loved one man in her life, and that he had loved her.

"'There was never any hope for us,' she said, 'but we loved each other.'"

"So Timothy was a love-child!" Natalia exclaimed.

It was, she thought, something she had known from the moment she had seen him. Only a child that had been born in love could have looked like Timothy.

She drove back to the Castle feeling she was leaving something of herself behind her, something she should have cherished and held on to.

Then she thought it was because she missed the affection she could expend on Timothy.

She longed to put her arms around Lord Colwall and tell him she not only loved him as a man, but as someone she could comfort and look after.

She found herself continually thinking of how much he must have suffered when he learnt of his first wife's deception and immorality. He was decent, upright, and proud and the shock must have been intolerable.

He was like a child that had been hurt. That was why she longed to give him a love he had never known.

Always he had been alone. Always he had had to control his feelings and perhaps when he was small like Timothy, he had called for a mother who was dead.

'I love him!' Natalia said to herself, 'but until he loves me I cannot give him what I know he needs.'

Lord Colwall had not yet returned when she went up to dress for dinner.

She chose one of the most attractive of her gowns, knowing that the pale blue satin and rosebud tulle made a perfect foil for her fair hair and white skin.

She wore a necklace of turquoises and diamonds and there was a bracelet and ring to match, so that when she went downstairs she felt that Lord Colwall would be pleased with her appearance.

She had heard him return while she was still dressing but the Salon was empty when she entered it.

As she walked towards the fire she saw that lying on the table were the day's newspapers.

She picked up the *Morning Post* and had been reading it for some minutes when Lord Colwall came into the room.

She put the newspaper down hastily.

"Is there any interesting news?" he asked. "I have not had time to read the papers today."

Natalia did not answer him for a moment fearing that what she had been reading might annoy him.

He was obviously waiting for an answer, and after a moment she said a little hesitatingly:

"I was reading that the Duke of Buckinghamshire has said that fifteen hundred rioters in Hampshire have threatened to attack any farmhouse where there are threshing-machines."

"I believe there are a few magistrates who are cowed into submitting to mob violence," Lord Colwall said sharply. "Sir Robert Peel is determined that a firm hand must be applied from the very onset."

"But the labourers are obeying this Captain Swing. It says that wherever he appears they listen to him bareheaded."

"If he comes here," Lord Colwall replied, "we will be ready for him. I have been discussing the matter this afternoon, and here we are prepared to quell the first sign of rebellion the moment it appears."

Natalia did not reply.

She longed to plead with Lord Colwall once again to dispense with the threshing-machine and not to incite the labourers to violence but she was certain he would not listen to her.

"The sentences are to be heavier than ever," Lord Colwall went on. "Any man who starts a fire or threatens a farmer will, in future, be transported for life!"

"They are only asking for . . . justice," Natalia faltered.

"That is not the way to get it."

Dinner was announced before he could say any more and because Natalia realised that argument would achieve nothing, she deliberately spoke of other things.

"I have something to show you after dinner," Lord Colwall said, "which I think will interest you."

"What is it?" Natalia enquired with some curiosity.

"I saw a picture this afternoon which I bought."

"A picture?" she exclaimed.

"It belonged to a gentleman who has lost a great deal of money at gaming," Lord Colwall explained. "He asked me if I would like to purchase two of his horses, but they were not up to my standard and I refused them. However when I was leaving his house I saw a picture which took my fancy."

"I am looking forward to seeing it," Natalia replied. "Who is it by?"

"Sir Joshua Reynolds," Lord Colwall announced. "Its owner was asking a somewhat fancy price for it—over two hundred pounds—but I thought it was worth it."

When dinner was over he took Natalia into the Library and showed her the picture.

It was of a very beautiful woman turning sideways, her hand outstretched, towards an urn on which was perched a small bird.

It had been painted exquisitely and Natalia gave a little cry of delight as soon as she saw it.

"It is lovely!" she exclaimed. "I am so glad that you bought it. The Lady has such grace!"

"I think that is why she reminded me of you," Lord Colwall said.

"Of me?"

She was surprised and the colour rose to her cheeks.

"I am very flattered that you should think me graceful," she said. "I have always thought that I was rather jiggety!"

"What do you mean by that?" he asked.

"Rather like a little bird which hops from twig to twig! I have always longed to fly slowly with great flapping wings as the larger birds do. That is what I think of as grace."

Lord Colwall put his arm on the mantel-shelf and looked down at her pointed face upturned to his.

"You are not like a bird," he said slowly. "You remind me of a small fawn. You have that same look in your large eyes that a fawn has! And you know how they scamper swiftly away, moving with a rhythmic grace which is almost indescribable."

"I am very pleased to be a fawn!"

She smiled at him, and then he said almost harshly:

"Of course, as an experienced hunter, I should not let the fawn get away."

"That sounds very primitive."

"Men are primitive!" Lord Colwall argued. "Have you not realised that by now? If I had behaved according to pattern, I should have dragged you away by force into my cave, just as my earliest ancestor would have done."

"Your earliest ancestor would have chosen his woman from a crowd of eligible females," Natalia replied. "He undoubtedly would have had to fight for her, and only when he had proved himself would he have been entitled to possess her."

Lord Colwall seated himself near the fire in the high-backed chair which he usually occupied.

"The trouble with you, Natalia," he said, "is you think too much! You use your brain, and brain in a woman is a nuisance and a hindrance to her femininity."

"I am sure you would much rather I was a simpering Miss who would agree with everything you said!" Natalia retorted. "But would you not find it rather dull?"

"I like women to comply with my wishes and be prepared to obey my commands."

Natalia gave him a little smile.

"I very much doubt it," she said. "You have too many brains of your own! Can you imagine anything worse than having to live permanently with someone who mouthed platitudes, never read a book, had no knowledge of Art, and would anticipate everything you wanted before you had time to formulate your needs to yourself?"

"That is exactly what I had hoped to find in my wife," Lord Colwall affirmed.

"If I believed you, I suppose that I should be humiliated into thinking how far I had fallen short of your ideal," Natalia replied. "But somehow I think that such an idea has no real substance."

She laughed.

"You wanted a doll, one of those wooden dolls I owned as a child, with a perpetual smile on its face! When you remembered to play with it, it would be there, and when you did not want it you would throw it in a corner and forget all about it!"

"Are you trying to tell me that it would be difficult to forget you?" Lord Colwall asked.

Natalia did not answer.

Herald had crept close to her as he always did, and she patted and caressed the great mastiff as he edged himself nearer and nearer in his delight at her touch.

"Did you take the child back?" Lord Colwall asked unexpectedly.

Natalia had a feeling he had been wanting all the evening to ask her this question and had been unable to bring himself to do so.

"Ellen had the wonderful idea," Natalia answered, "that her Aunt who is married to the Blacksmith might like to adopt Timothy. I have left him there for tonight, and if the Turners decide not to keep him, we can send him back to the Orphanage either tomorrow or the next day."

"You are determined he shall not go back," Lord Colwall said.

"He is such a sensitive little boy," Natalia explained, "not like the other children."

"Why should you think that?" Lord Colwall enquired.

Natalia did not answer and after a moment he said again:

"Tell me, Natalia, why should you think Timothy different from the other children?"

"There is . . . something about him," she faltered. "But perhaps they are all the . . . same, and it is . . . just that I have come to . . . know Timothy."

"What else is he?" Lord Colwall asked.

Natalia looked up at him.

"I see you . . . know already . . . My Lord, that Timothy is a . . . love-child."

"That is the answer," Lord Colwall said sharply. "That is why I wanted him out of the house. He was merely pandering to this ridiculous obstinacy of yours."

He paused and then continued:

"Now that you are no longer upset by what you overheard by

mistake, surely you realise that your ideas are exaggerated. Let us live a normal married life, Natalia, and then I can prove to you that we can find a great deal of satisfaction in each other, and perhaps a great deal of pleasure."

Natalia did not answer and he went on:

"It is not a bad foundation, as anyone would tell you, on which to base a successful marriage."

There was a note in his voice which Natalia found hard to resist.

She wanted desperately to put out her hand towards him, to tell him that she would do what he wished.

She thought how easy it would be to let him kiss her, to pretend to herself that he loved her enough for them to find some sort of happiness, even if it was not the one she had envisaged for so long.

Perhaps if she succumbed to his pleadings, if she did as he wanted, he would in time love her as she wished to be loved.

He would grow to rely on her, and she was sure that if she gave him the son he wanted, then he would be, if nothing else, extremely grateful.

But was that enough?

Would their children be strong and handsome? Beautiful of face and mind? Or would they reflect that ugliness, even perhaps that horror, that she was unable to escape?

Whatever she might say with her lips, she knew she would be unable to forget Sarah's baby.

Moreover, it was impossible not to remember the coldness in Lord Colwall's voice when he had spoken with Sir James after the wedding.

How, she asked herself, could she speak to him in moments of intimacy, of love, when he had said so scathingly:

"There is no place for that nauseating, over-exaggerated emotion in my life."

'Why can I not make him love me?' Natalia asked, in her heart.

She felt suddenly very alone, very helpless!

Without really realising what she was doing, she put her cheek down against Herald's head and held him even closer against her.

Lord Colwall was watching the picture she made in her blue gown, the diamonds glittering at her throat and her bare arms around the huge animal.

There was something weak and defenceless in her attitude, and yet Lord Colwall knew her will was strong enough to keep her emotions under control, to resist the desires and needs of her own heart.

Natalia had not answered his question and he knew it was because she could not find words.

Then suddenly, as if something snapped within him, he said furiously:

"Leave that damned dog alone! Do you not think I am aware of what you are trying to do? You are trying to beguile me into falling in love with you. You are deliberately attempting to attack me, but I can assure you I am well aware of your wiles and the way your mind is working!"

Natalia raised her head at the anger in his voice and stared at him, her eyes wide.

"You are like all women," he raged. "Because you cannot get your own way, you are tempting me. But I promise you that if you go on like this you will be sorry!"

Natalia was very still and now he rose to his feet, his eyes blazing with a fire from which she shrank visibly.

"You will drive me too far! I am endeavouring to behave like a gentleman and not to force myself upon you because you are young and because you are apparently sincere in this nonsensical, hysterical notion!"

He struck the mantel-piece with his clenched fist.

"But mark my words, Natalia, I will not be responsible for my actions if you continue to behave as you are behaving now."

"What . . . have I . . . done?" Natalia murmured, finding it hard to speak because Lord Colwall's anger had made her heart thump furiously in her breast.

"It is not only what you have done," he said angrily, "it is how you look, what you say! It is everything about you! For God's sake, give me a little peace, or else I swear to you I shall force you into behaving as my wife!"

He seemed almost to spit the last words at her.

Then as she still sat looking up at him in bewilderment, one arm still around Herald, her eyes large and frightened in her pale face, Lord Colwall went from the room.

He slammed the door loudly behind him.

Natalia was not asleep when Ellen called her the following morning. In fact she had been awake practically the whole night.

After Lord Colwall had left her alone in the Library she had gone very slowly upstairs to her room, and when her Maids had left her alone she had lain in the great four-poster feeling as if the whole future was dark.

For the first time since she had come to the Castle, she experienced a sense of hopelessness and depression which hung over her like a black cloud.

Even when she had first learnt that Lord Colwall did not love her, it was not the same feeling that she had now, of a despair for which she could find no relief.

All night long she had been haunted by the roughness in his voice and the violence with which he had spoken.

All night long she could see his eyes looking at her with an expression which she felt must be one of hatred.

'What am I to do?' she asked the darkness and found no answer.

She wanted above anything else to run to her mother, to seek the comfort and the understanding that Lady Margaret had always been able to give her.

Then she told herself it would be too humiliating to crawl home and confess that her marriage was a failure when she had been so confident, so absolutely sure it would be a success.

'What can I do? What can I do?' she asked again and again.

She felt she was in truth incarcerated in one of the dungeons below the Castle without light and without any hope of escape.

"It's a nice morning, M'Lady," Ellen said as she drew back the curtains. "There was a hard frost in the night but the sun's a-coming out."

Natalia did not reply and after a moment Ellen asked as she busied herself around the room:

"Will you be riding with His Lordship this morning?"

"No," Natalia replied, "I have a headache."

"Then I'll bring your breakfast to you, M'Lady."

Another housemaid came in to light the fire, and when it was burning brightly two Maids carried in the large bath-tub in which Natalia bathed.

They set it down in front of the fire so that it was ready for her when she wished to rise.

Breakfast, elegantly served on silver crested dishes with plates of Sèvres china, was as usual delicious, but Natalia felt that anything she ate would choke her!

She drank a little tea and nibbled one or two of the large purple grapes which came from the greenhouses.

When Ellen took away her tray she exclaimed reproachfully:

"You've eaten nothing, M'Lady. Do you think you've caught a chill?"

"No, I am all right," Natalia answered.

She rose from her bed and slipping her arms through her heavy silk wrapper walked to the window to look out.

It seemed almost incongruous that the sun should be shining so brightly through the morning mists, turning the frost on the trees and shrubs into a sparkling enchantment.

How could everything be so beautiful when she herself was so low and depressed?

Then in the Park beyond the garden she saw a figure on horse-back, and felt her heart quicken and come alive.

It was impossible not to admire the way Lord Colwall rode, the manner in which he sat a horse as if he was part of the animal.

In fact, only to see him was to love him.

Even at this distance, Natalia thought, she could see how handsome he was, could admire the manner in which he wore his high-crowned hat on the side of his head, and the slimness of his legs in his shining boots.

She felt as if her love welled up inside her, dispersing the darkness.

'I love him,' she murmured beneath her breath, and in that moment she knew what she must do.

'I have been absurd!' she told herself. 'Perhaps it was the shock of hearing he did not love me that made me behave as I did. If we are together, if I become his wife as he wants me to do, then I am sure that in time my love will evoke an answering response within him.'

She had forgotten, she now thought, in her obsession over Sarah's baby, that it had been born without any love, either from Sarah or from its father.

In her case it would be very different, because she loved Lord Colwall to distraction.

'I love him so much that I would die for him,' she thought. 'So why do I not live to please him?'

Quite suddenly the way seemed clear. Her love would be enough for both of them as far as their child was concerned.

If it was a son he would be strong and handsome, fine and noble like his father; and if it was a girl, there was plenty of time for them to have a son later, perhaps half a dozen!

'How stupid I have been! How foolish to have wasted so much time!' Natalia berated herself.

She moved across the room to tug at the bell-pull.

She wanted to be with Lord Colwall now—at once—to tell him that for the future everything would be different, that there would be no more reason for him to be angry with her—no reason to be incensed by her childish attitude.

'I have not been thinking straight,' Natalia excused herself.

But she knew that her father would be ashamed at her failure to think out everything carefully before she acted.

'If only I had not overheard that conversation,' she murmured. 'My wedding-day would have been different.'

It was too late now for regrets.

All she could do now would be to see that in the future Lord Colwall was happy as she wanted him to be.

'We have so many things in common,' she thought. 'We have so much to talk about, to discuss. When I am close to him, he will understand how deeply I feel about injustice and cruelty.'

She felt herself quiver with excitement at the thought of being in his arms, and when Ellen came into the room she said with a lilt in her voice:

"I want to get up, Ellen. Bring me my riding-habit."

"You're going riding, M'Lady?"

"Yes, order a horse. I will catch up with His Lordship. I know where he has gone."

She knew that Lord Colwall was trying out a new stallion which he had bought recently and she had already learnt that the best place to school an animal was where, some distance from the Castle, there was almost the equivalent of a race-course.

The ground was flat with no dangerous rabbit-holes in it, and the hedges had each been cut to a perfect height for a jump.

Natalia had already raced Lord Colwall on what was known as "The Course" on several occasions.

'That is where he will be now,' she thought to herself as she dressed. 'I will challenge him as I have done before.'

There was a sparkle in her eyes, and when she turned to look at her reflection in the mirror she saw that she was looking extremely pretty.

Ellen had produced a new riding-habit for her which she had not worn before. Of emerald-green velvet, it was warmer than the one she usually wore and was most becoming to her fair hair and white skin.

"Do you think you will be warm enough, M'Lady?" Ellen asked.

"I am sure I shall," Natalia replied.

But Ellen insisted on bringing her a satin scarf shaped almost like a cravat. She put it round her neck and tucked it into the front of her riding-coat.

"It is always hot when one is riding," Natalia smiled.

As she spoke she knew that she was glowing with the anticipation of seeing Lord Colwall and telling him that the gulf which had lain between them no longer existed.

She hurried down the stone stairs to find her horse was waiting for her at the door. It was the roan she had ridden before, and he responded immediately to her eagerness to be on her way.

"Is Your Ladyship sure you wouldn't like me to accompany you?" the groom asked.

Natalia shook her head.

"I am joining His Lordship."

Then she was trotting down the drive, eager to reach the Park where she could give her horse his head.

She galloped for some way and then as she turned from the Park onto a stubble field beyond, Natalia saw at the far end of it a crowd of men congregated around one of the big barns.

There were half-a-dozen of these built around a stockade where some of the cattle were kept in the winter.

Natalia was just going to hurry on when she saw a riderless horse and thought that it might be Lord Colwall's.

Accordingly, she turned her horse's head and as she drew nearer to the barn realised that the men whom she had seen had gone inside.

The horse, however, was left tethered to a post.

She looked at it as she approached and felt that it was not a fine enough animal to belong to His Lordship, and yet she was not quite sure.

She had not seen the new stallion of which he had spoken and she could not remember what colour he had said it was.

She rode up to the barn. The big doors were open and she could see a number of men moving about inside talking noisily.

Then she heard the sound of hammering and wondered what they could be about.

"Is His Lordship there?" she shouted but her voice seemed lost in the general confusion.

Because she felt that he must be there and at the same time, she was curious, she dismounted. Holding her horse by its bridle, she entered the barn.

For a moment, stepping from the sunlight into the darkness, it was difficult for her to see anything and then she realised there was a sudden silence.

All the men who had been talking so loudly had ceased speaking and had turned their faces towards her.

"Is His Lordship . . ." she began.

Then she saw that behind the men stood a huge piece of machinery.

Without asking she knew what it was! A threshing-machine! The monster of which she had read so much and which had aroused such violent feelings all over the country.

She stared at it and saw that a number of men were already standing on it and holding large hammers in their hands.

"What are you doing?" she asked and knew the answer even before she asked the question.

"May I enquire who this Lady is?" a cultured voice asked.

Natalia turned her head from the contemplation of the machine to see a man moving towards her among the crowd of labourers.

He was about medium height and fashionably dressed, but there was something pretentious and rather garish about him which told her he was in fact no aristocrat.

"This be Her Ladyship, Captain," one of the labourers said in a low voice.

"Indeed! Then you are Lady Colwall?"

"Yes, I am," Natalia answered, "and may I enquire your name?"

"I have many names," the man replied with an unpleasant twist to his thick lips.

He was in fact good-looking in a somewhat vulgar manner and

he had an air about him of such self-assurance that it implied a vast self-conceit.

"Many names?" Natalia repeated in perplexity.

Then she realised that one of the men had called him "Captain."

"You are . . . Captain Swing?" she said accusingly.

He bowed to her ironically.

"The evil genius who is behind the riots which are taking place in so many Counties!" Natalia went on.

"Your Ladyship flatters me!"

"I do not intend to do so," she replied fiercely. "You have no right to come here and incite our men to violence."

She saw the sneer on his lips and continued:

"You know as well as I do that if they break up this machine, they will be imprisoned and undoubtedly transported. How can you inflict such suffering upon them?"

"Us be only a-trying t'get our rights, M'Lady," one of the men muttered.

Natalia looked at their honest, rather stupid faces.

She knew several of the men by sight, and she was quite sure that they would none of them ever have taken such action if they had not been skilfully led into rebellion by this notorious Captain Swing.

"Listen to me," she insisted. "You know as well as I do that His Lordship will not tolerate the destruction of his property, or insurrection amongst his own people. Do not listen to what this man says—this outsider who has caused so much trouble in so many other Counties and achieved nothing."

"He says that a lot o'landowners have put up th' wages," one of the men remarked.

"That is true, Lady Colwall," Captain Swing interposed. "On a great number of farms we have been most successful."

"Not for the men who have actually taken the initiative!" Natalia retorted. "They are languishing in prison awaiting trial and you know the kind of sentence they will receive."

She turned again to the men.

"Have you thought if you are taken to prison how your wives and families will suffer? Perhaps His Lordship will not allow them to remain in his cottages."

She paused and added pleadingly:

"Let me speak to him on your behalf. Do not do anything so foolish as to destroy this machine or fire the ricks until you have spoken to His Lordship man to man about your problems."

"Proud words!" Captain Swing sneered. "But do you imagine that His Lordship will listen? The first man who opposes a landowner is clapped into prison before he can even open his mouth."

He looked around at the listening men.

"Only if we all act together, if we show these blood-sucking employers that we mean business, will anything ever get done!"

"You're right, Captain! That be true enough," a man shouted.

"It is not true!" Natalia cried angrily. "His Lordship has no idea that you are discontented. Your wage is above the average, but I agree it is not enough. I have already spoken to him, asking that you should receive more, and that extra money should be given for every child."

"If you've spoken to M'Master, what did he reply?" a voice asked from the back of the crowd.

"What I am suggesting," Natalia said, ignoring the question, "is that you speak with His Lordship before you do anything so rash as to render yourselves liable for transportation or even worse."

Captain Swing laughed.

"Can't you see she's trying to frighten you?" he asked the labourers. "It's the usual threatening talk. 'Lay one finger on my property, and you'll swing from the gallows'—you've heard it all before and in the meantime, men and women starve!"

"You certainly do not look as if you yourself are starving, Captain!" Natalia said sharply.

"You must not always judge by appearances, M'Lady," he replied suavely. "And now perhaps you should run along and leave us to get on with our business, which I assure you, is of National importance!"

"It is a business that might end up on the gallows," Natalia warned. "These men are my husband's employees and his responsibility. I will not allow you to encourage them to commit crimes that can only end in disaster."

"And how will you prevent me?" Captain Swing asked.

He asked the question with an amused note in his voice, and then, as he looked at her, his eyes narrowed.

"I have an idea," he said, "which I am sure will meet with Your Ladyship's approval."

"What is it?" Natalia asked, a little apprehensively.

For the first time since she had come into the barn, she felt afraid.

She knew now there was something evil about Captain Swing and had the idea too that he was slightly unbalanced.

She could understand how, because he was smart and glib and gave the appearance of being a gentleman, he could easily sway the poor, stupid labourers. They had never yet had anyone to speak on their behalf and were therefore easily inflamed by his recitation of their ills.

"I have thought of a better way to get what we want on this Estate," Captain Swing said slowly.

"What be that, Captain?" one of the men asked.

"Instead of breaking up His Lordship's machine, or even firing his ricks, we will take possession of something which I imagine is even more valuable to him."

"And what might that be?" a man enquired.

"We'll take a hostage," Captain Swing replied, "and who better than Her Ladyship?"

He moved towards Natalia as he spoke and instinctively she took a step backwards. A man standing near her took hold of her horse's bridle.

"Do not dare touch me!" she cried. "If any harm comes to me, His Lordship will bring Troops against you all."

Captain Swing took her arm and when she tried to shake herself free she found he did not release her.

She did not know what he was going to do and she felt a definite tremor of fear.

"Do not listen to him," she begged the men. "Can you not understand that when he has incited you to do something that is illegal, he will disappear. He has not been caught in Kent or Sussex, Surrey or Gloucestershire, but the labourers there paid the penalty for their crimes. Do not heed anything that he may say!"

"Fine words, M'Lady!" Captain Swing remarked. "But I have the feeling that, because you are far from unattractive, His Lordship will be extremely anxious to have you back, and our terms will be quite simple."

"Where're ye a-going t'put her, Captain?" a man asked.

"That's what you are going to tell me," Captain Swing replied. "It has to be somewhere where His Lordship'll not find her, and that rules out any buildings on the farm and your cottages."

"Do you really think," Natalia asked furiously, "that His Lordship will submit to blackmail?"

"He won't like to think of you hungry, cold and very uncomfortable," Captain Swing replied. "And doubtless he will be anxious for the return of his pretty Bride, not having been married long enough to have tired of you—as all men tire in time."

"Oi've thought of a place, Captain," one of the young labourers said.

"And where might that be?" the Captain asked.

"Th' ol' Mill."

There was a murmur from the others as if they approved the idea.

"No-un has used it for years. 'Tis derelict, and Oi doubt if the Master be aware it be still there. 'Tis supposed t'be haunted."

"The very place," the Captain smiled. "Are you afraid of ghosts, My Lady?"

"I am afraid of nothing! Not even of you!" Natalia replied. "But I am genuinely distressed that these foolish men should listen to you. You are evil, and they do not realise it."

"Now come along, my lads. There's no time to stand here talking," the Captain said. "What we want is action! How far is this place?"

"Less than half a mile, Captain, and if us goes along th'bank o' th'stream, no-un'll see us."

"A good idea!" Captain Swing approved. "Two of you come with me and see that our prisoner does not escape. The rest of you go back to work!"

"What about th' horse?" asked the man who was holding it.

"Keep it out of sight," the Captain commanded. "We'll return it later to the stables with a note for His Lordship, setting out our terms."

"Very good, Captain."

They hurried to obey his orders with a quickness which showed Natalia how much they stood in awe of him.

It was hopeless, she thought, to try to persuade them any further. They would listen only to him. He was their champion, their leader, and they were ready to obey him slavishly.

The boy who had thought of the derelict Mill went ahead and Captain Swing, still holding Natalia by the arm, followed while two others walked behind.

They kept in the shade of the willows bordering a small stream, which ran beside the farm and twisted its way through open fields.

The long grass beneath the willows was white with frost and soon the velvet skirt of Natalia's riding-habit was wet and she could feel the damp seeping through the short ankle-length boots she was wearing.

She was certain too that her white, lace-edged petticoat would soon also be soaked. But this was not the moment to worry over minor details.

What really perturbed her was how soon Lord Colwall would learn that she had been taken hostage, and what action he would take.

After they had been walking a little while, Captain Swing released her arm.

"I'm suggesting it would not be sensible to try to escape. I'm quite fleet of foot and I doubt if you could out-run any of us."

"I shall not do anything so foolish," Natalia answered proudly. "I shall merely wait for His Lordship to rescue me, which he will undoubtedly do. Then those poor idiots you have persuaded into agreeing to your nefarious schemes will be punished."

"Proud words, M'Lady!" Captain Swing said with a grin, "but before your husband receives you back into his manly arms, he'll agree to our terms—otherwise he'll not learn where to find you."

"Someone will undoubtedly tell him," Natalia said.

"You are being over-optimistic," Captain Swing replied. "I assure you that these men are loyal to me and to themselves. They know how much depends on their solidarity—how much they stand to gain, and how little to lose."

"Only their freedom!" Natalia snapped.

"Freedom to starve because a threshing-machine is taking away their livelihood?" Captain Swing asked.

Because it was difficult not to agree with him, Natalia pressed her lips together and made no reply.

They walked on in silence until a turn of the stream brought them in sight of the old Mill.

"It certainly looks dilapidated!" Captain Swing remarked.

Natalia's heart sank as she realised she had never seen it before and there was every likelihood that His Lordship had forgotten its existence.

The trees had grown up densely all round the building so that from a distance, she thought, it would be indiscernible.

Shrubs stood thick around the pool and the great wheel was rusted.

The boy walking ahead of them pulled open the door which was practically off its hinges.

"Th' room be at th'top," he said, pointing his finger. "'Tis where they used to keep th'grain."

Natalia looked apprehensively at the rickety stairway; one rail had broken away and some of the slats were missing.

"Is it safe?" the Captain asked the boy.

He was obviously referring to the stairway.

"Safe enough," the boy replied. "Oi often went oop there when Oi was a kid."

"Very well," the Captain said. "You go first and Her Ladyship will follow you."

"Th' only thing ye didna' want t'do is t'fall into th'pool. There be a current in it that'll suck ye down. Nothing that goes in ever comes oop again!"

"Then that is something we must all avoid. Come along, My Lady!"

Reluctantly, though there was nothing else she could do, Natalia climbed the rickety stair-way.

The boy who had gone ahead opened the door at the top and she saw a small, square room where the grain had been kept.

It was completely empty and the one window had been boarded up roughly so that only a few chinks of light came through it. But it was enough to show her that the room, unlike the approach to it, was strong and secure.

Captain Swing looked around him with satisfaction.

"I regret," he said, "that we cannot provide Your Ladyship with any furniture, not even the pallet to which prisoners are usually entitled! Let us hope that you will not have to linger here for long."

Natalia heard the boy rattling down the stairs again.

She was alone with Captain Swing and she turned to look at him, realising that in the dim light which came through the boarded-up window he looked even more evil and unpleasant.

"Let me beg of you, Captain," she pleaded, "to reconsider your actions. You must know what terrible retribution will be brought upon the men who work here. I agree with you that the wages are low, but this is not the way to improve their lot—not when dealing with a man like my husband!"

"I think we shall find that His Lordship will be amenable," Captain Swing replied with a leer. "You're a very pretty young woman, Lady Colwall, and he will undoubtedly find his bed a lonely place without you."

The impertinence of his words made Natalia draw herself up proudly.

"Then there is nothing more to be said, Captain Swing," she said coldly. "My husband, I am sure, will deal with the matter most effectively. I only hope you will be there when the moment comes!"

"Your courage does you credit."

The Captain bowed ironically, then went out through the door which led to the stairway, and Natalia heard a heavy bolt shoot into place.

She sat still listening to the sound of his footsteps going cautiously down the stairway.

There was a murmur of voices below as he gave the men some orders, and after a moment or two there was silence.

She walked across the room to pull at some of the boards which covered the window, but found it impossible to move them.

She then tried the door knowing even as she did so it was hopeless.

There only remained the shaft down to the floor below, but this too was boarded up. It was in fact, she had to admit, a very effective prison.

She would not suffocate as there was plenty of fresh air coming through the gaps in the boards.

She knew, however, that if she were to be cooped up here until late in the day, she would become very cold.

She began to walk up and down, realising that while she was warm now from the walk, she would need to exercise herself continuously when the sun began to set in the afternoon.

She told herself that she must be rescued before then, but she felt in fact far from sure of it.

She reckoned that the time was now about half past ten o'clock in the morning. It was doubtful if His Lordship would return to the Castle before noon.

Presumably Captain Swing's letter informing him that she had been taken as a hostage would be waiting for him.

She hardly dared to contemplate how angry Lord Colwall would be, and what was more, she told herself with a little sigh, he was certain to think it was her own fault!

Perhaps it had been stupid of her to have gone to the barn, but how could she have known that the horse was not his?

It was easy now to regret that she had not taken a groom with her, but she had been so sure that she had only to catch up with His Lordship and they would ride together for the rest of the morning, as they had done so often before.

She sat down on the floor and tried to think, but all she could remember was the sneer on Captain Swing's face, his mockery of her efforts to persuade the men to do nothing rash, the confidence he showed in his ability to cause trouble.

'He has been so clever,' she told herself. 'Everywhere he has been, he has incited the labourers to intimidate their employers by firing the ricks and breaking up the threshing-machines. Then he slips away and is never caught.'

There was no doubt in her mind that the labourers had been unjustly treated, but at the same time this type of revolution had no chance of success.

There might be a few farmers who would give in to threats, but the majority of landowners would fight back with the help of the Military and the magistrates. How then could a few uneducated labourers stand up against them?

Yet she could not help feeling that in a way Lord Colwall had brought this upon himself.

He could not have chosen a worse moment of all the times of the year to install a threshing-machine.

There was no doubt that the Government was taking the riots in Kent, Sussex and the other Southern Counties very seriously, and the fact that the unrest was spreading to other places would only increase their resolution to show no mercy to the rioters.

Natalia remembered how a man called Legge had been sentenced to death and she thought despairingly that Lord Colwall himself would show no mercy to any men who rioted on his Estate.

'I must escape! I must!' she said to herself.

She rose to pull again at the pieces of wood which boarded up the window, only to find as she had before that to move them was quite beyond her strength.

They were each held in place by several long nails.

She wondered if there would be any point in crying for help, but knew it was hopeless. She managed to peer through a slit in the boards and she could see fields stretching away into the distance but not a soul in sight.

At this time of the year there was little activity on the land and, even if there were any labourers within hearing, she felt quite certain that following Captain Swing's instructions they would make no attempt to rescue her.

There was nothing she could do but sit down and wait for His Lordship to give in to Captain Swing's demands, and when he had vanished, to wreak revenge upon the men who must remain on the Estate.

'I must pray,' Natalia told herself.

She sat down again, making herself as comfortable as possible in a corner of the room.

She prayed for a little while, then found herself thinking of her

Knight and how, when she had imagined a similar situation, he had always managed to rescue her in the face of impossible odds.

'Captain Swing is indeed a powerful Dragon,' she thought.

She remembered how she had held Timothy close in her arms and how much he had enjoyed the story of the Knight in shining armour who had attacked the frightening Dragon.

She had hoped this afternoon to learn that the Blacksmith and his wife would adopt Timothy.

At the thought of the little boy, she began to imagine the stories that she would tell her own children when she had them.

'How they would love the Castle,' she thought. 'What child's imagination would not be fired by the deeds of valour which had won the treasures hanging on the walls, performed by men who had worn the armour which lined the passages and corridors.'

To think of her children was inevitably to think of Lord Colwall. How handsome, how clever, he was!

'When I see His Lordship again,' Natalia promised herself, 'I will tell him why I was hurrying to find him this morning.'

She felt herself quiver with the excitement she had known when she had set out from the Castle.

When he understood why she had been trying to find him, she knew there would be a sudden light in his eyes, and the scowl would lift from his forehead.

He would kiss her, as she had always longed for him to do!

She wanted more than she could express in words the feel of his lips and the touch of his hands! She knew it would be like Heaven to be in his arms.

"I love him! I love him!"

She said the words aloud and heard them echo round the small room.

"I love him!"

There was almost a resonance in it as her voice struck the walls.

One day he would love her, one day she would make him happy and he would be able to forget Lady Claris and how she had made him suffer.

The hours seemed to drag on slowly. By the time it was afternoon, Natalia began to feel hungry.

She wished now she had eaten her breakfast, and she thought regretfully of the succulent dishes she had waved away because she had been feeling so depressed.

An hour later she knew the sun had gone and what light there was in the small room was fading rapidly.

Now the air was getting icy cold and Natalia walked up and down as briskly as she could—ten steps one way and ten steps back. But she could already feel the chill penetrate through her velvet jacket.

She was thankful now that Ellen had insisted on her taking the green scarf. She had pulled off her hat so that she could sit more comfortably in the corner, and she wondered if the gauze veil which encircled the high crown would bring her any warmth—but decided it was unlikely.

Backwards and forwards! Up and down!

She knew it would be stupid to stop, but after an hour she began to feel tired—tired of the confining space—tired of the smell of age, dust and mildew!

And tired of being alone, of wondering why she had not been rescued.

'Supposing,' she thought to herself in some consternation, 'His Lordship decides to defy the rioters? Supposing he refuses to give in to their requests?'

The idea had not occurred to her before. She had imagined that, incensed though he would be, Lord Colwall would not leave her unprotected in Captain Swing's hands.

She was suddenly still in apprehension.

Supposing, because she meant so little to him, he considered it more important to stick to his principles than to rescue her?

If he sent for the Military, it was unlikely they could arrive before late tomorrow, perhaps even the next day!

She was rather vague as to where soldiers were likely to be stationed in that part of the country, but she had a vague idea that she had heard someone say there were barracks at Worcester.

If Lord Colwall had received the letter at luncheon time, how long would it take a groom to ride to Worcester and the men to march back?

Natalia found it difficult to think clearly. So many new possibilities appeared to present themselves. So many problems she had not visualized before.

"Oh, come for me! Come for me," she found herself whispering.

She felt as if her need for Lord Colwall must wing its way across the fields and tell him how greatly she longed for him.

She was afraid now. Afraid he did not care enough to save her, and was indifferent to her suffering because she had angered him last night. Also he might well not realise the urgency of coming to her rescue.

Supposing she was left here indefinitely?

Then Natalia told herself sharply she was letting her imagination run away with her, as had happened so often before.

It was no use thinking such things. He would come—of course he would come!

He might be angered with her, but he would wish to protect his wife from unpleasantness.

"Come for me! I want you, I want you!" She found herself murmuring the words aloud and realised as she spoke that her lips were very cold.

'I must walk up and down again,' she told herself, and then felt it was almost too much trouble.

She wrapped her arms across her breast but her back was cold as ice, and now she could feel the chill of the frost on her ankles.

The room was becoming darker and darker. Now it was impossible to see anything.

'I ought to . . . walk about,' Natalia told herself again and knew she was afraid.

Afraid of being alone, afraid perhaps although she knew it was nonsense, of the ghost which it was said haunted the old Mill.

It was very quiet. The rooks which had been 'cawing' in the distance as they went home to roost were now silent. Somewhere there was a drip of water, and occasionally a sudden scuffle as if a rat ran across the floor.

Natalia felt herself shiver in horror at the very thought.

An owl hooted a long way off, so far that she could barely hear it.

Then suddenly, unexpectedly, as she sat shivering and afraid, she heard footsteps! Heavy footsteps coming up the rickety stairway!

She wanted to cry out in gladness that someone had found her—that she was saved!

But as the cry came to her lips, she bit it back.

Perhaps it was not Lord Colwall . . . but a labourer bringing her some food.

She heard the bolt being pulled back and as the door swung open there was the golden light from a candle-lantern.

For a moment she could not see who held it, until as she stared, trying to penetrate the darkness behind the light, a mocking voice said a little thickly:

"Good evening, Your Ladyship . . ."

CHAPTER EIGHT

Captain Swing came into the room and held the lantern high above his head.

Natalia thought that he was looking at her in rather a strange manner, and instinctively she took a step backwards and put her hand up to the collar of her jacket.

He gave a low laugh and pulled the door to behind him. Then looking around, he saw a large wooden nail protruding from a wall on which he hung the lantern by its ring.

"Have you heard from His Lordship?"

Even to her own ears Natalia's voice sounded rather frightened.

"Not a word!" Captain Swing answered. "So I thought, My Lady, we might pass the time while we are waiting for his surrender by getting to know each other."

There was something in the tone of his voice and the way in which he slurred his words which told Natalia that the Captain not only had been drinking but was dangerous.

His eyes flickered over her and she felt a sudden apprehension—a fear that she had never known before in the whole of her sheltered life.

With a tremendous effort she raised her chin proudly.

"I have nothing to discuss with you, Captain Swing, as you must well know. If His Lordship has not answered your threatening letter, then doubtless he has sent for the Military. Until they come to release me, I prefer to be alone."

"Brave words, My Lady!" Captain Swing said sneeringly. "But since your husband is treating me in such an arbitrary manner, it is up to you to make amends for his incivility."

He advanced across the floor as he spoke, and Natalia moved backwards until she was against the wall.

"I do not . . . know what you . . . mean," she faltered.

"I think you do," Captain Swing replied. "You are very pretty, and pretty women must learn to be generous with their favours."

By this time he was close beside her and put out his hand.

"Do not dare to . . . touch me!" Natalia cried.

Now that he had made his intentions plain, she managed to twist aside and rush to the other side of the small room.

The Captain had drunk too much to move swiftly, but there was no doubt that the liquor had inflamed him. His eyes in the light from the lantern were terrifying, as with a smile on his thick lips he pursued Natalia.

Again and again she avoided him, but she knew that because the room was small, she had little chance of escape.

Finally he pinioned her in a corner and laughed at her efforts as she twisted and fought against him.

"Let me go! Let me go!"

He was breathing heavily and she realised that his pursuit of her had excited him.

She made one tremendous effort to push him to one side, and then as they struggled he tripped her and she fell backwards on to the floor so violently that her head hit the bare boards.

For a moment it knocked her half-unconscious. Captain Swing flung himself upon her.

She felt nauseated by the brute force and the smell of him.

His breath exuded raw spirits, and his body pinioned hers as effectively as if she had been chained to the ground.

She wanted to scream, but she was breathless from fright and from her efforts to escape him.

Terrified she thought he would kiss her, and turned her face away, but instead he tugged violently at the front of her riding-jacket.

She put up her hands to prevent him—striking at him, trying to pull at his wrists.

But the buttons burst and now her jacket was open. He snatched the green scarf from her neck and flung it onto the floor.

The blouse she wore for riding was made of silk and tore easily beneath his fingers.

He was like an animal, plucking at the chemise next to her skin until her breasts were naked. It was then that Natalia screamed.

She screamed and screamed as his hands touched her and screamed again as he started pulling violently at her velvet riding-skirt.

It was tough and the waist-band resisted him, but brutal and primitive in his desires he had the strength of a wild beast.

Natalia was helpless beneath him.

She heard her own voice screaming and the sound of it echoing round the small room. Then she knew despairingly that her strength was failing and her efforts to fight off the maniac on top of her was of no avail.

She thought she must die of the horror of it. She thought she must go mad at the thought of what he was about to do.

"Help . . . me . . . God . . . help . . . me."

Suddenly there was a violent explosion which seemed to shake the whole building.

It was deafening in Natalia's ears, and Captain Swing collapsed on top of her, crushing her beneath his weight.

For a moment . . . everything seemed to go black . . .

Someone was pulling the Captain roughly from her body and she knew who it was!

She wanted to speak but her voice had died in her throat. She could only watch Lord Colwall—her eyes wide and terrified—as he dragged Captain Swing's body across the room by the collar of his coat.

For a moment Natalia was unable even to move her hands.

She felt paralysed from the rough impact when Captain Swing had fallen on top of her, and the fear which seemed to have numbed her mind.

Then as she heard Lord Colwall going down the rickety stairs dragging the body with him, she put her hands slowly and feebly, as if they hardly belonged to her, across her naked breasts.

It was difficult to breathe, difficult to think, and yet she found herself listening and waiting for Lord Colwall to return.

She heard a splash in the Mill pool and then he was coming up the stairs again.

With an almost superhuman effort, Natalia tried to raise herself from the floor. He reached her while she was still making the attempt.

"Come," he said. "I will take you home."

She was trembling and so weak that even when he had drawn her to her feet he had to support her.

He picked up her scarf and put it round her neck. Then taking from his shoulders the black cloak he was wearing, he covered her with it and fastened the buckle.

She stood quite still, her hands across her breasts, her eyes wide with shock.

"It is all over, Natalia, you are safe," Lord Colwall said gently.

She walked unsteadily towards the door, his hand supporting her arm. As he left the room he lifted the lantern from the nail, and it lit their steps down the stair-way.

As she reached the bottom something large and warm hurled itself against her, raising his great head to lick her cheek.

It was Herald!

"You must thank Herald for finding you," Lord Colwall said. "I felt certain that if anyone could track you down it would be he."

With his arm around Natalia he drew her outside the barn and she saw by the light of the half-moon climbing up the sky that there were two horses tied to a broken fence.

She knew one of the horses had belonged to Captain Swing, and that once he had reached the barn it would not have been difficult for Lord Colwall to guess where she was imprisoned.

His Lordship's horse was fidgeting a little, but the Captain's was quiet and apathetic.

Lord Colwall glanced at it.

"Wait one moment," he said.

He propped Natalia as if she was a doll against the doorway of the barn. She watched him without speaking as he went to Captain Swing's horse, undid the girths and lifted the saddle from the animal's back.

Then he slipped off the bridle and walking the short distance to the Mill pool threw them in. There was a loud splash as they hit the water and Lord Colwall chucked the lantern after them.

He retraced his steps, saw that Captain Swing's horse was unconcernedly cropping the grass, and picking Natalia up in his arms, he set her on the back of his stallion.

Just for a moment she balanced precariously, and then with the quickness of a man who is extremely athletic, Lord Colwall swung himself into the saddle behind her.

He put his left arm round her holding her close and picked up the reins.

Natalia turned her head to hide it against his shoulder and then, as if the closeness of him released the tension that had gripped her, she burst into tears.

She cried despairingly, tempestuously, her whole body shaken by the violence of her reaction as a child will cry who has been frightened beyond endurance.

"It is all right," Lord Colwall said soothingly. "You are safe."

His horse was moving slowly.

"You must forgive me," he went on, "if I was a long time in coming for you, but I returned home only just before dinner to find the note telling me you had been taken as a hostage."

His arm tightened around her and, although Natalia was still crying, she was listening.

"I had to make a quick decision," he continued, "whether to send for the Military, which would have taken a long time, to summon the farm labourers and force them—at pistol point if necessary—into telling me where that fiend had put you, or to try to find you myself!"

He paused for a moment as if remembering how hard the decision had been. Then he continued:

"I decided the best and quickest way would be to take Herald to the threshing barn where I guessed you had encountered the rioters."

Natalia was still crying. The tears were running down her cheeks and there was nothing she could do to stop them.

At the same time she was listening to Lord Colwall's deep voice, knowing that nothing mattered now he had found her and she was safe.

Even so, the evil from which she had so narrowly escaped still seemed to encompass her with a band of terror she could not break.

One of her hands clutched at the lapel of Lord Colwall's coat.

She wanted to be sure he was really there; she wanted to hold on to him; to know that she need not be stricken with that frantic, petrifying fear which had made her scream and scream as Captain Swing had lain on top of her.

"How could you have been so foolish," she heard Lord Colwall say, "as to ride alone without a groom?"

She did not reply and he answered his own question.

"They told me at the Castle you were coming to join me, and how should you know there was danger for you, of all people, in this quiet countryside?"

There was a note of fury behind his words, and as if the very word "danger" evoked again the agony through which she had passed, Natalia went on crying.

Yet at the same time she knew within herself that gradually the comfort of Lord Colwall's presence, the feel of his arms encircling her, was dispersing much of the nightmarish terror which had overshadowed her.

'I am safe with His Lordship,' she told herself, 'and he is holding me close to him as I have always wanted him to do!'

She tried to feel the rapture that she had always known she would feel if she was ever in his arms.

Yet while her mind told her it was what she had craved, her body still under the spell of Captain Swing's violence, she could only shiver at the memory of the experience.

Natalia had never known violence and had never seen it.

Now she thought she would never be able to forget the weight of his body on top of hers, the roughness of his hands, or the lust in his eyes which had contorted his face until he had seemed like the very devil incarnate.

Moreover it had been an abject humiliation to realise how helpless she was, to learn that against brute strength a woman was completely and hopelessly impotent.

"Herald picked up your trail almost as soon as we left the barn," Lord Colwall was saying. "I could not imagine why he should be leading me through the willows by the bank of the stream. Then when we came to the old Mill and I saw that swine's horse waiting outside it, I knew I had been right to come alone."

His arm tightened around her as he said:

"I killed that man, Natalia. Do you hear me?"

Natalia did not answer, but he knew by the manner in which she hid her face even closer against his shoulder that she was listening to him.

"I killed him," Lord Colwall repeated, "and I am not ashamed of it! It was not murder. It was simply the destruction of a rat who deserved to die."

His voice was sharp with contempt. Then he continued:

"Because to make an explanation to the Magistrates must involve you, and because I do not wish anyone to know that you have been in contact with a man of his depravity and reputation, we will, neither of us, speak of this again."

He paused then said insistently:

"Swing is dead. He is finished. The last trace of him is lost in the depths of the Mill pool and the world will be a better place."

By now they were approaching the Castle. Lord Colwall looked up at the lights in the windows and the great stone building rising above the skeleton branches of the trees before he said urgently:

"Forget what has happened, Natalia. Forget that he so grossly insulted you. In future I will protect you better. No-one, I repeat, no-one must learn that you have suffered in this manner."

There was so much solemnity in his tone that Natalia stopped crying.

She knew that they had reached the court-yard outside the front door because she could hear the sound of the gravel beneath the horse's hoofs.

"Leave all explanations to me," Lord Colwall commanded.

He drew the stallion to a standstill and now raising her head Natalia saw the golden light from the open doorway, and the Butler and a number of footmen waiting for them.

They would have assisted her to alight from the saddle, but Lord Colwall jumped to the ground and lifted her down himself.

Natalia dropped her head and folded the cloak tightly round her.

"You have brought back Her Ladyship!" she heard the Butler exclaim.

"I found Her Ladyship imprisoned in the old Mill," Lord Colwall replied. "She is very cold and it was an unpleasant place for her to be alone in at night. Send food and wine up to her room immediately."

"Yes, M'Lord—of course, M'Lord."

The servants hurried to obey Lord Colwall's orders, and with his arm around Natalia he helped her slowly up the stairs.

Ellen was waiting on the landing outside her bed-room.

"Get Her Ladyship to bed," Lord Colwall said. "She is cold and hungry."

"Oh, M'Lady, we have been so worried about you!" Ellen exclaimed.

She led Natalia into the bed-room.

Lord Colwall turned and went downstairs again.

Ellen helped Natalia off with her cloak and gave an exclamation when she saw the buttons were burst from her jacket and her riding-blouse was torn.

"I . . . struggled with the . . . men who were . . . shutting me up," Natalia said as explanation.

She felt that Lord Colwall must have forgotten the condition of her clothes and that Ellen would be curious.

"I've never heard of such a thing, M'Lady!" Ellen ejaculated angrily.

"Do not speak of it to . . . the others," Natalia begged. "His Lordship would not like it known that anyone has been . . . rough with me."

"No, of course not, M'Lady," Ellen agreed.

Natalia's voice was very low and hoarse and she knew it was the shock of Captain Swing's attempt to ravish her which still made it difficult for her to speak.

She realised she had not said a word to Lord Colwall as he brought her home. She wished now she had been able to thank him.

'He saved me!' she said to herself, 'just as . . . my Knight would have . . . done.'

Lord Colwall, returning to the Castle the following day just after noon, thought with satisfaction of what he had to relate to Natalia.

It was a cold day but fine, and Lord Colwall riding his big black stallion looked strikingly handsome as he entered the court-yard and glanced up at the great grey stone building that was part of his heritage.

He had intended to see Natalia the previous evening before she went to sleep.

He had in fact gone upstairs after his own lonely dinner in the great Dining-Room and had knocked on her bed-room door. Ellen opened it and slipped outside to speak to him.

"Her Ladyship is sleeping, M'Lord."

"Did she have something to eat?"

"Yes, M'Lord, and a little of the wine to drink."

"I think Her Ladyship's clothes were in a rather unusual state—" Lord Colwall began.

"Her Ladyship told me, M'Lord, that the men who imprisoned her treated her somewhat roughly. She asked me not to speak of it, feeling Your Lordship would not wish it known amongst the other staff."

"No, and I am sure I can trust you, Ellen."

"I would do anything for Her Ladyship, M'Lord, and that's the truth!"

"I am glad to hear that," Lord Colwall said. "Do you think you should sit up with her?"

"I did suggest it, M'Lord, but Her Ladyship said it would disturb her to have someone in the room. She is sleeping quite peacefully at the moment and is very glad to be home."

"That is all I wanted to know," Lord Colwall said. "There is of course a bell which Her Ladyship can pull if she needs you."

"It rings in my bed-room, M'Lord, and I could be with Her Ladyship within a few seconds of her wanting me."

"Have you made up the fire?"

"Yes, M'Lord."

Ellen looked at Lord Colwall wonderingly.

It was very unlike His Lordship to be so solicitous, and yet, she told herself, he had always been one for planning things down to the smallest detail.

"I think I have thought of everything, M'Lord, and as I said, Her Ladyship has only to pull the bell and I will be with her before it even stops ringing."

"Thank you, Ellen."

Lord Colwall went downstairs again and Ellen, watching him go, thought how handsome he was and how proudly he carried himself.

'If only they could be really happy,' she sighed.

And then something told her there had been a new kindness and consideration in Lord Colwall's voice.

She wondered as she went to her own part of the Castle what had occurred the night before to make her Lady seem so distressed that morning.

She had served Natalia long enough to know when she was unhappy, and it had been impossible for her mistress to disguise the misery in her eyes or the droop of her lips.

Then as she watched Lord Colwall across the Park, it had seemed to Ellen as if her mood had changed completely. She had been eager and excited at the thought of hurrying after him.

'She deserves happiness,' Ellen said to herself. 'And so does he— after all he has been through!'

Before he left the Castle after breakfast Lord Colwall had enquired if Natalia had enjoyed a good night. The Butler had gone in search of Ellen and returned to say:

"Ellen has asked me to inform Your Lordship that, not having been summoned by Her Ladyship at the usual hour, she peeped into her bed-room a short while ago, and Her Ladyship was still asleep."

"Then do not awaken her," Lord Colwall had commanded. "The longer Her Ladyship sleeps, the better."

"Yes indeed, M'Lord. There's nothing like it," the Butler agreed. "And I'll give Ellen Your Lordship's instructions."

Now on his return at mid-day Lord Colwall hoped that Natalia would be awake; for he had much to tell her.

A groom was waiting at the front door to take his horse. He swung himself from the saddle, patted the stallion on its shining black neck and walked up the steps.

He handed his hat to the Butler.

"Has Her Ladyship come downstairs yet?"

"No, M'Lord, but Ellen asked if Your Lordship would step up-stairs for a moment."

Lord Colwall looked at the servant in surprise. He seemed about to say something and then changed his mind. Instead he turned towards the stair-case and walked up it slowly.

Ellen was waiting for him on the landing.

She curtsied and said:

"Will you come into Her Ladyship's bed-room, M'Lord?"

She opened the door and Lord Colwall preceded her into the room.

He looked at the bed as if he expected to see Natalia lying against the lace-edged pillow under the great four-poster. But it was empty!

He turned sharply with a look of enquiry in his eyes towards Ellen.

"Where is Her Ladyship?"

"That is what I don't know, M'Lord."

"What do you mean, you do not know?"

"She is not here, M'Lord."

Lord Colwall stared at her as if she had taken leave of her senses.

"What are you trying to say to me?" he asked.

"It's like this, M'Lord," Ellen said in a nervous voice. "I received your orders to let Her Ladyship sleep on. I didn't go into her room until about twenty minutes ago."

She glanced at Lord Colwall as if she feared she had done wrong.

"I thought Her Ladyship might be needing me and perhaps something had prevented the bell from ringing," she said in explanation. "I opened the door very quietly thinking that, if Her Lady-ship was still asleep, I could creep out again. Then I stood and waited to hear her breathing. I could not hear her and so I pulled back the curtains."

"She was not there?" Lord Colwall asked.

"No, M'Lord. The bed was ruffled in such a way that it looked from the door as though there was someone in it, but Her Ladyship had disappeared."

"She must have gone downstairs."

"No, M'Lord, the footmen in the Hall would have seen her."

"She must be somewhere in the Castle—in the Nursery perhaps?"

"No, M'Lord, no-one has seen her."

"I cannot understand it!"

"Neither could I, M'Lord, but I went to the wardrobe to see if any of Her Ladyship's gowns were missing."

"And were any?"

"Look at this, M'Lord."

Ellen crossed the bed-room to the wardrobe which stood on the far wall.

She pulled open the door and Lord Colwall saw the rows and rows of beautiful and elaborate gowns that had so entranced Natalia when she first arrived at the Castle.

But Ellen did not concern herself with them.

Instead she pointed to something lying on the floor.

"Look at that, M'Lord!"

"What is it?" Lord Colwall asked in bewilderment.

He saw a heap of what appeared to be black ribbon and bows of velvet.

"They come from a black gown belonging to Her Ladyship," Ellen explained. "She had only one black gown amongst those which came from London, and it was a rather elaborate one. Almost too elaborate, I thought, for a funeral or if Her Ladyship was forced to wear mourning."

She paused and then as Lord Colwall made no comment went on:

"Her Ladyship has taken off all the trimmings. There they are, M'Lord, for you to see—the taffeta frills, the velvet bows. She must have cut them away leaving the gown very plain without them."

"Why ever should she do that?" Lord Colwall demanded.

"I cannot understand it, M'Lord. There is something else, too."

Ellen opened another door, and now, following the direction of her finger, Lord Colwall saw that lying on the floor was a heap of white fur.

He looked at Ellen for explanation.

"It's the ermine lining, M'Lord, of Her Ladyship's travelling cape."

"Her travelling cape!" Lord Colwall exclaimed.

"Yes, M'Lord. There's nothing else gone as far as I can ascertain, except for a few of Her Ladyship's intimate garments. Just enough, I should say, to fill a small bag that one could carry in one's hand."

"And is there a bag missing?" Lord Colwall asked.

"Yes, M'Lord. The smallest baggage was kept in a cupboard next door to this room. The trunks were taken upstairs."

"And one is missing?"

"'Twas only a small bag, M'Lord, rather a rough one, not as

smart as the others, but it was useful for last-minute objects when we were travelling."

Lord Colwall walked across the room.

"You think, Ellen, that Her Ladyship has left the Castle?"

"She must have, M'Lord. There is no sign of her."

"Have you spoken of this to anyone?"

"No, M'Lord. I merely asked the footmen if they had seen Her Ladyship come downstairs. They replied they had been on duty since early this morning, and there has been no-one about except Your Lordship."

"You did not tell them why you asked?"

"No, M'Lord."

"Then if Her Ladyship left the Castle, she could not have gone by way of the front door."

"No, M'Lord. It'd be easy though to get out any other way. There are half a dozen doors into the garden, and three or four in the kitchen quarters."

"Her Ladyship must have walked," Lord Colwall remarked as if he spoke to himself. "If she had ordered a carriage from the stable it would have come to the front door."

"Of course, M'Lord."

"I cannot understand it!" Lord Colwall exclaimed. "And where could she have gone?"

There was a knock at the door.

"See who it is," Lord Colwall said sharply, "and do not let anyone come in."

"Very good, M'Lord."

Ellen went to the door and passed through it, partly closing it behind her.

Lord Colwall could hear her voice speaking and one of the footmen answering her. Then she returned and there was a letter in her hand.

"It appears, M'Lord," she said, "that there was a note addressed to you, downstairs by the entrance to the Dairy. The boot-boy found it earlier this morning, but he thought it was only a bill left by one of the tradesmen."

Ellen saw the frown on Lord Colwall's face.

"He did not take it to the pantry until a few minutes ago," she went on, "and now, in case it may be urgent, it has been brought upstairs."

She handed the letter to Lord Colwall as she spoke, and he took it from her with an expression in his eyes which she could not fathom.

It would be difficult for anyone, he thought, except for some nit-witted scullery boy, not to realise that the envelope was of the thick, expensive vellum used only by himself and Natalia.

He sat looking at the note as if he was afraid to open it.

Ellen moved tactfully away to another part of the room, ostensibly to pat up a cushion and put straight an ornament on a side-table that needed no adjustment.

Lord Colwall walked across to the window.

He knew the note was from Natalia and he longed to know its contents, yet at the same time he was afraid.

Why should she have gone away? Why should she have left the Castle?

He thought last night that he had re-assured her and that after she had cried so bitterly against his shoulder the horror of what she had passed through had been expunged.

Now he could not understand why she had disappeared without any warning. If she had wished to return to her parents, surely she would have told him so?

Besides, why should she go on foot? Stage-Coaches stopped in the village once or twice a day, but why would Natalia, with a stable full of every type of carriage at her command, wish to travel by Stage-Coach?

She had been unpredictable, he thought, as he turned the envelope over in his hand, ever since he had married her. He had not realised that he could find any woman so incomprehensible.

He had imagined it would be so easy to manage a young girl, and yet Natalia had defied and confounded him from the first moment of their marriage.

He thought of how he had raged at her the night before last in the Library.

He could see now the startled surprise in her large eyes, the sudden tremble of her lips, and he had known even as the words poured from his lips that she had not understood the reason for his fury.

She had looked so lovely sitting there with her arms around Herald.

She had looked somehow unsubstantial, and yet, as he well knew, she had a will almost equal to his own and a determination that he had been unable to break.

Everything had gone wrong!

His plans had mis-fired. The scheme which he had devised more than three years ago had been completely disrupted by one unsophisticated and inexperienced girl.

And now he knew that she had left him and he was afraid to learn the reason.

It was somehow incredible that he, so decisive, so autocratic, so unbending, should stand with her note in his hand, unable to bring himself to open it and read what it contained!

He was aware that Ellen was waiting and her curiosity was understandable.

Yet he knew it was not curiosity that he himself felt, but an apprehension that was almost like the anticipation of a physical blow.

Slowly, very slowly, he slit open the envelope and drew out its contents.

He had never seen Natalia's hand-writing before, but he thought he would have known it was hers even if it had lain amongst a hundred others!

There was something beautiful in the way she wrote; in the way she formed her letters. There was an imagination in the curves of the S's, the tails of the G's and the Y's, as well as something upright and a little proud in the T's and the L's.

Because he was looking at her hand-writing, for a moment Lord Colwall found it impossible to understand what Natalia had written.

There just seemed lines and lines of words that had no meaning, until with an effort he forced himself to read:

"My Lord, I know now I was wrong not to obey Your wishes and become, as You begged of me, Your Wife. I was so foolish that I did not realise until yesterday that my Love would have been enough for us both. Later you might have grown a little fond of Me, but I think I would have been content if I could make You happy.

But now it is too late: when I overheard what Your Lordship said to Sir James, You stressed that your Wife must be "pure and untouched". I could not stay, loving You as I do, and know that You looked at me with disgust because I can no longer fulfil the second of these Conditions. So, My Lord, I am going away.

I shall not go home and You will not be able to find me. Also I think that where I am going I shall not live very long. Then You will be free again to find Someone who will not fail You as

I have done, and who, I pray, will give you happiness and a Son.

Please forgive me, My Lord, for all my faults and failings and thank You for saving me last night. I love You, as I have always loved You, so please sometimes think kindly of Your most reprehensible but penitent

Natalia."

Lord Colwall read the note through and then, as if the sense of it could not penetrate his mind, he read it again.

Holding the letter in his hand he moved nearer to the window to stare sightlessly out over the great expanse of garden and Park.

He stood there so long without speaking that Ellen, embarrassed, moved towards the door thinking she should leave him alone.

As she reached it, Lord Colwall said in a voice she hardly recognised:

"Her Ladyship has gone away for a short visit—but she will return. You can be certain of that!"

"Yes, M'Lord. Thank you, M'Lord."

Ellen curtsied.

She looked at him, his head and shoulders silhouetted against the brightness of the sky. There was something very strange about the look of him.

She had the remarkable feeling that he was a man bewildered and lost in an unfamiliar world.

Then she told herself she was imagining things and she left the room closing the door softly behind her. Lord Colwall was alone.

CHAPTER NINE

Nanny was sitting by the Nursery fire. She was not crocheting nor was she sleeping.

She was waiting.

Every evening for the last week she had sat late after the rest of the household had gone to bed, expecting Lord Colwall to visit her. Now at last she heard his footsteps coming along the passage.

She looked into the fire, her face compassionate, her eyes wise with the knowledge of grown-up people who still remain children in their hearts.

Lord Colwall opened the Nursery door and crossed the room without speaking to seat himself in the arm-chair on the other side of the hearth.

Nanny made no attempt to rise; she merely looked at him and waited.

After a moment he said:

"Where can Her Ladyship be? I went as far as the Orphanage in Gloucester today, but there was no sign of her there."

Nanny did not reply and after a moment he went on:

"I have visited every Orphanage in every adjacent town. I was so certain that she would go somewhere where there were children."

"I also should have expected that, M'Lord," Nanny murmured almost beneath her breath.

She realised that Lord Colwall had grown thinner in the last ten days.

He had lost, too, his aloof pride which had made him seem as if he stood apart from everyone with whom he came in contact.

'He now looks human,' Nanny told herself.

It was a fact that His Lordship's coldness and impenetrable reserve had been exchanged for an air of urgency, and his expression of habitual cynicism had vanished.

"Did you realise how unhappy Her Ladyship was?" Lord Colwall asked suddenly.

"I knew that she loved you," Nanny answered quietly.

"How could I ever have imagined," Lord Colwall asked almost savagely, "that a girl who had seen me once, when she was a child, had been in love with me for three years?"

Nanny smiled.

"It was not only your handsome face, Master Ranulf! It was because Her Ladyship is not an ordinary young woman. She's sensitive, romantic, imaginative, and I'm as sure as I'm sitting here that if she'd not loved you, she would not have consented to marry you."

"You are right! Of course you are right!" Lord Colwall said. "But I did not understand."

"And now you do—?" Nanny asked quietly.

"I have to find her—I will find her!" he said harshly.

"When that little boy Timothy was here," Nanny said, "I used to listen to Her Ladyship telling him stories. The one he liked best and the one Her Ladyship always seemed to want to tell him, was about a Knight."

She saw the expression in Lord Colwall's eyes and continued:

"There was something in the way Her Ladyship spoke of this Knight which told me he meant a great deal to her. She must have dreamt about him as girls do about someone they love."

Lord Colwall turned his head to stare into the fire, but Nanny knew he was attentive to every word she said.

"Her Ladyship used to describe to Timothy," she went on, "the dangerous situations in which the Princess found herself, but always she was rescued just in the nick of time by her Knight."

There was a pause and then Nanny said quietly:

"I've a feeling, Master Ranulf, that you have to rescue her in the same way. It's a test, so to speak. I don't know whether I am making myself clear?"

"You are making yourself very clear, Nanny, and you are making complete sense. I should be able to find her just as I found her, or rather Herald did, the other night when she was imprisoned in the old Mill."

"If you found her then, Master Ranulf, you can find her now. Did she ever say anything which might give you a clue as to where she was likely to go?"

"Something she said?" Lord Colwall replied. "I did not think of that. I was only so convinced in my own mind that because the little orphan-boy meant so much to her, she would go to him, or to another like him."

"There are children in other places besides Orphanages," Nanny said.

"Yes, of course there are," Lord Colwall agreed, "but how can I start looking for the sort of place that Her Ladyship would have heard about? And why should she have said that I would not be able to find her and that she thought that where she was going, she would not live very long?"

"Her Ladyship said that?" Nanny exclaimed incredulously.

"Yes, she wrote that in the note she left for me," Lord Colwall answered.

"It must be a place then, that she had heard about," Nanny murmured.

"Or she has read about!" Lord Colwall ejaculated suddenly.

There was a light in his eyes that had not been there before. He rose quickly to his feet and pulled at the bell which hung beside the chimney-piece.

"I remember, Nanny," he said, "that when I came down to dinner the night before Her Ladyship left, she was reading the newspaper as I entered the Salon. I asked her if there was anything of interest in it, and after a moment she spoke to me of further riots of the farm labourers and the measures to be taken against them."

"That need not have been all that she read," Nanny remarked.

"No, of course not," Lord Colwall agreed.

There was silence and Nanny knew he was deep in thought.

Again she appreciated the fact that the expression on his face had changed a great deal since Natalia had gone away. His jaw-line was sharper and she knew by the dark lines under his eyes that he had not slept much.

There was no doubt that he was suffering, but the fact that his emotions stifled for too long had now escaped his control improved rather than detracted from his looks.

'He has come alive again,' Nanny said to herself, 'and that's the truth.'

The door opened and a footman stood there who was obviously surprised at seeing His Lordship.

"You rang, M'Lord?"

"Bring me the newspapers for Wednesday, November tenth," Lord Colwall said.

"Very good, M'Lord."

The man had turned to obey him before Lord Colwall asked sharply:

"They will not have been destroyed?"

"Oh no, My Lord. The newspapers are always kept for a month in case Your Lordship should require a back-number."

"Then get them for me immediately."

The footman shut the door, Lord Colwall walked across the room to lay his hand on the piebald rocking-horse. He stroked its mane absent-mindedly.

And then he said in a voice in which there was no mistaking the pain behind the words:

"How can she look after herself? She is so inexperienced, so innocent. She has no knowledge of the world, and Ellen tells me she took no money with her."

"No money?" Nanny ejaculated.

"Perhaps a pound or two. That is all."

"Then how will she manage, M'Lord?"

"Do you suppose I have not thought of that?" he asked.

His voice was hard as he continued:

"I have been torturing myself night after night, imagining her in some dangerous situation, being insulted or hurt, crying for help, and my not being there to rescue her!"

There was agony in Lord Colwall's tone now and almost instinctively, as if he were still the child she had nursed when he was a baby, Nanny's hand went out towards him.

He did not see her gesture as he was still standing looking at the rocking-horse.

"It is all—my fault!" he said in a low voice.

As if she realised she must save him from his own despondency, Nanny said almost briskly:

"You'll find her, Master Ranulf. I'm sure of it. You must just use your brain and think where she could have hidden herself. I can't believe that Her Ladyship would deliberately do anything dangerous or foolish. She's too much sense for that!"

"But she does not know the evil and the dangers that lie in wait for someone as lovely as she is," Lord Colwall said hoarsely.

"We can only pray that God and his angels will protect her," Nanny said.

"—or her Knight," Lord Colwall murmured beneath his breath.

The footman brought the newspapers and put them neatly folded on a table which stood in the centre of the Nursery.

Lord Colwall crossed the room eagerly towards them. He picked up *The Times*. Then he said:

"I am almost certain it was the *Morning Post* Her Ladyship was reading when I entered the Salon."

He took the newspaper in both hands.

"Yes, here is what she must have read about the new penalties imposed by the Government on rioters."

He looked down the page and then he gave an exclamation.

"Nanny!" he said urgently, "listen to this!"

"ABNORMAL DEATH RATE
IN WORKHOUSES"

"In answer to a question in the House of Commons the Home Secretary agreed that last year's deaths in Workhouses all over the country were considerably above normal. It was due, he explained, to a new fever as yet unidentified, which had resulted in a sudden increase in mortality among work-house dwellers of all ages. Children had of course accounted for the majority of the deaths, although there was also a large increase of mortality amongst the aged. There was little that could be done about it, but the Charity Commissioners and Poor-Law Administrators were keeping close watch on their local Workhouses."

Lord Colwall finished reading the report aloud. Then he said with a sudden light in his eyes:

"I had forgotten that there are children in the Workhouses. To-morrow morning I will start a systematic tour of every one that is within a range of thirty miles."

"Do that, Master Ranulf!" Nanny exclaimed.

"Shall I go first to Hereford?"

"I have a feeling," Nanny answered, "although I may be wrong, that if Her Ladyship is hiding from you, she would not hide in Hereford where you have so many meetings. Also she might easily be recognised by one of the friends who came to your wedding."

"No, of course not. That is sensible," Lord Colwall replied. "And the Stage-Coach could have taken her to Malvern, or Worcester or any of the towns the other side of the hills. I will start first thing in the morning."

He threw the newspaper down on the table.

Then he walked to the fire-side and did something he had not done for very many years. He bent down and kissed his old Nurse on the cheek.

"Thank you, Nanny," he said.

The Workhouse was an ugly, bare building, built of grey stone with barred windows. There was a court-yard in front of it and a high wall with heavy gates, spiked on top, which Lord Colwall knew would be locked at night.

They were open now to allow his curricle, drawn by two horses, to pass through.

The gate-keeper was a very old man with white hair, quivering hands and bloodshot eyes that were running with the cold from the wind.

It appeared to Lord Colwall that the man's clothing was far from adequate for the duties he carried out.

His Lordship drew his horses up outside the somewhat forbidding entrance and handed the reins to the groom, who had jumped down from the small seat on the back of the curricle.

Without waiting, as he usually did, for his servant to knock at the door, Lord Colwall himself raised the knocker and rapped sharply.

At first he thought his request for attention had gone unnoticed. Then he heard slow, shuffling feet and the door was opened by another old man, so bent with age that his nose seemed to be half-way down his chest.

"I wish to speak with either the Mistress or the Master of this Workhouse," Lord Colwall said in a commanding tone.

The old man made a gesture which invited him in and he walked through the doorway into a paved passage.

The place smelled strongly of unwashed bodies, old age and drains, which Lord Colwall found very distasteful. The old man shuffled ahead of him and opened the door of a room.

It was obviously the private Sitting-Room of the Keepers of the Workhouse. It was furnished without taste, but there were faint touches of homeliness about it, including a fire burning brightly in a well-polished grate.

A door in the opposite wall opened and a woman came in. She was large, middle-aged and had an aggressive, authoritative manner which made Lord Colwall dislike her on sight.

She had however either been told that her visitor was important or she had seen his curricle outside, for there was an almost ingratiating smile on her thin lips as she said politely:

"Good day, Sir. What can I do for you? Are you a County Inspector, by any chance?"

"I am not," Lord Colwall answered. "I am making private enquiries as to whether you have recently employed or admitted a young woman to these premises."

He saw the look in the Mistress's eyes before she spoke, and ejaculated:

"You have!"

"I am not accepting, Sir, that you are right in your surmise concerning the presence here of the person you seek," the Mistress answered. "The inhabitants of this place come and go, and I assure you it is extremely difficult to find assistants."

"But you have found one," Lord Colwall said.

"I was left empty-handed when the last batch of children of over six years old were taken to the factories," the Mistress said, and her tone suggested that she thought Lord Colwall was finding fault. "Heaven knows, the little varmints weren't much help, but at least they could work better than those I've left."

"I am not suggesting that in seeking an assistant you were doing anything wrong," Lord Colwall said evenly. "I merely wish to know who she is. What is her name?"

"I thought there was something strange about her," the Mistress remarked viciously, "the moment I saw her, and I says to myself: 'You're either in trouble, or a run-away apprentice.' And that's the truth, Sir, isn't it?"

"I wish to see this girl," Lord Colwall answered. "Is she small and fair?"

"You can see her, Sir, and welcome," the Mistress said. "I suppose as usual I shall be left to do everything for myself. How can one woman cope with what we have in now? Three loonies; fourteen old people all getting on for eighty; four tramps and ten children. Ten! I tell you, Sir, it's too many!"

"I wish to see your new assistant," Lord Colwall said, interrupting the flow of complaints which he felt might go on endlessly.

"She'll be up on the top floor with the children," the Mistress replied. "I can't get her away from them, though I have told her again and again that I need her help downstairs with the decrepit and senile."

As she spoke the woman led the way out into the passage and started to climb the narrow stairs which led to the top floor of the Workhouse.

Lord Colwall had a glimpse of a room bare of furniture except for a few chairs, with two spinning wheels standing unused in the corner. The occupants were huddled around the walls, some of them sitting on the floor.

"Is there no heating?" he asked sharply.

"Heating?"

The Mistress turned her head to look at him incredulously.

"Where do you think the money comes from for that sort of luxury? The Parish provides for only the bare necessities and that's too good for most of them as is in here."

She spoke almost venomously and continued to climb the stairs, holding up her skirts with both hands.

The top floor was little more than a garret. The gabled windows that opened on to the tiled roof had several panes of glass broken in each of them. One or two of the apertures had been stuffed with rags.

There was a row of beds, some of them tied up with string, and on each there was one thin, tattered blanket.

At the far end of the room all the children were clustered in a little circle, except for one child who was lying on a bed.

The children were chattering and did not hear the Mistress approach, sailing down the centre of the room like a ship in full sail with Lord Colwall behind her.

Then as he neared them he could see that they were standing around a slender figure who was kneeling on the floor beside a bucket. She was scrubbing.

"Gray!"

The Mistress's voice, harsh and ugly, seemed to echo round the garret.

"How many times must I tell you not to do the work which that lazy little Letty should do? I told her to scrub the floor after she made a mess of it, and scrub it she shall! Get her off that bed and give her the brush, or I'll beat her into doing what she's told."

Natalia straightened her back and looked up at the Mistress who was now towering over her.

"Letty is only four, Ma'am, and she is feeling ill."

"She'll soon be feeling a good deal iller if she doesn't do what I've ordered her to do!" the Mistress replied sharply. "And here, Gray, is someone to see you. I don't suppose you expected your past would catch up with you so quickly."

The woman spoke spitefully and now Natalia saw Lord Colwall. Their eyes met and neither of them could move.

She was very pale, and it seemed to him that she had grown so thin that the skin was stretched taut over her bones.

Very quietly, almost as if he were afraid he might frighten her, Lord Colwall said:

"I have come to take you home, Natalia."

She rose to her feet and he saw that she was wearing a rough apron of sacking over her black dress; her fair hair was dragged back from her forehead and pinned into a bun at the nape of her neck.

She put the large scrubbing-brush she held in her right hand into the bucket of water and set the bucket against the wall. As she moved it, Lord Colwall saw that her hands were red and sore.

"There's no use putting that bucket aside," the Mistress said sharply. "Letty! Get off that bed and finish the floor and the rest of you children move out of the way, or it'll be the worse for you!"

Slowly Natalia took off her apron and hung it on a nail. Then she turned to one of the beds and picked up her cloak which had obviously been used as an extra covering.

She put it round her shoulders and as she did so the children began to cry:

"Don't leave us, Miss! Don't go away! Ye said ye'd stay!"

Their voices, shrill and protesting, rang out as they surged around her, hanging on to her cloak and her hands, their faces turned up to hers, their bodies pitiably thin under the rags they wore for clothes.

"I have to go now," Natalia said gently, "but I will come back to see you, I promise you I will."

"Ye promise? Ye promise? Ye won't forget?"

"No, I can never forget!"

Natalia disentangled herself from their clinging hands without looking at Lord Colwall. He stood watching her, in his elegance incredibly out of place in the cold barren garret.

As if something was happening which she did not understand, the Mistress turned angrily on the children:

"Get on with your work, you lazy little varmints! You've no right to be standing about doing nothing. You're paupers. Work, or you don't eat! This place is called a Workhouse and that's what it has to be, or I'll know the reason why!"

Lord Colwall saw Natalia wince at the woman's roughness, and then with a little helpless gesture as if she knew she could do nothing about it, she pulled her hood over her head and walked down the room towards the stair-way.

She did not wait to hear what Lord Colwall said to the Mistress, but proceeded through the front door and saw the curricle waiting for her outside.

Blindly, almost as if she were walking in her sleep, she stepped into it, and by the time Lord Colwall had seated himself in the driving-seat and picked up the reins, the groom had covered her with a fur rug.

"You will not be too cold?" Lord Colwall asked, as if they were setting out on an ordinary drive from the Castle. "I ought to have brought a closed carriage, but I knew that I could travel faster in the curricle."

"I am . . . all right," Natalia answered.

They were the first words she had spoken to him and he heard the tremor in her voice. He said nothing more, merely busying himself with driving as swiftly as horses could travel back around the hills to the Castle.

There was, he thought, nothing they could say to each other with the groom within hearing. In fact Lord Colwall knew that what was of primary importance was to get Natalia home.

He had been deeply shocked by the pallor of her face and her emaciation. She had grown so thin that it seemed as if she might float away in the mist and be lost to him forever.

It was with a sense of relief that he saw his home high above the trees, and soon they were climbing the long drive.

He drew up outside the front door and pulled the horses to a standstill.

The Butler ran down the steps to assist Natalia to alight.

"Welcome home, M'Lady."

"Thank . . . you," Natalia answered.

Her voice was very low, and now as she reached the hall she allowed her cloak to be taken from her, and almost automatically she walked towards the Salon.

A flunkey opened the door and she moved over the thick carpet towards the fire.

She had almost reached it when she heard the door close and turned to see Lord Colwall advancing towards her.

For a second he saw a sudden light in her eyes, and then as he drew nearer it faded and was replaced by an expression which he knew was one of fear.

She looked at him, made a little inarticulate sound and slipped down onto the floor at his feet.

He picked her up in his arms, and realising that she was unconscious he carried her from the Salon, across the Hall and up the stairs.

As he passed the Butler, he said sharply:

"Send for Nurse."

But when he reached the landing outside Natalia's bed-room, he found Nanny was there waiting for him and beside her was Ellen.

"You've found Her Ladyship! You've found her!" Ellen exclaimed ecstatically.

Lord Colwall did not answer. He carried Natalia into the room and set her down on the big four-poster, laying her very gently against the lace-edged pillows.

She looked so white, so frail in her black dress, dingy and dirty and so different from the elegant creation it had once been.

"Is she all right, Nanny?" he asked and there was a note of desperate anxiety in his voice.

"I think she's fainted, Master Ranulf," Nanny answered. "Leave Her Ladyship to us. We'll get her into bed and, judging by the looks of her, she needs something to eat."

"I will go and speak to the Chef," Lord Colwall said, as if glad to be able to take some action.

"Nourishing broth," Nanny said, and busied herself with Natalia.

"No . . . please don't touch her! . . . She is so small . . . she does not . . . understand . . ."

Natalia's words were a cry. Then someone said gently:

"Wake up, Natalia, you are dreaming. Wake up, it is only a nightmare."

She opened her eyes and saw Lord Colwall's face not far from hers. She felt a sudden surge of happiness at the sight of him . . . before she remembered and her eyes darkened . . .

"For God's sake, my darling, do not be afraid of me!"

The words seemed to burst from him. Then he said quickly, speaking as if he were ashamed of his lack of self-control:

"You are at home. You are safe, and nothing shall upset you, I promise you."

The fear in Natalia's eyes was replaced with surprise.

It seemed to him as if she held her breath.

"Nanny told me that when you awoke I was to give you some soup to drink. It is over here."

It was night-time, Natalia realised, as he moved away from the bed. There was only the light from the flames leaping high in the fire-place and of several candles to cast a warm glow around the bed and leave the corners of the room in shadow.

'It must be very late,' Natalia thought to herself.

She saw that Lord Colwall was wearing a robe of dark blue brocade, and she felt that had it been earlier, Nanny or Ellen would have been with her.

She must have slept for hours, and now she remembered vaguely that she had been awakened several times to be given something to drink, a soup that seemed to warm her body and make her feel alive again.

She had thought sometimes that she would never be anything but cold and hungry until she died.

Lord Colwall was busy at the table and she could see that he was pouring from a jug which stood on a silver tray heated by a candle-burner.

He carried the cup carefully across the room to her.

She raised herself higher on the pillows and he sat down on the bed facing her.

"I want you to drink every drop," he said as he handed her the cup, "and then I have something to tell you."

She looked at him enquiringly before obediently she raised the cup to her lips.

Her fair hair hung loosely over her shoulders and he saw that she was wearing one of the diaphanous nightgowns that had been part of her trousseau.

In the few short hours that she had been back at the Castle, sleeping with an exhaustion that was almost frightening, some of the tension and sharpness seemed to have gone from her small face.

She looked very young and very pathetic, Lord Colwall had thought, when Nanny had brought him into the room to see her asleep.

"She is all right, Nanny?" he had asked when the Nurse had come from the bed-room to find him waiting on the landing outside.

"Come and see for yourself, Master Ranulf."

Nanny had known without being told that Lord Colwall was ap-prehensive as he had followed her into the bed-room to stand look-ing down at Natalia, her eyelashes dark against her pale cheeks, her hair halo-ing her thin face.

"I don't think Her Ladyship's had a mite to eat since she left here," Nanny whispered. "She said it was impossible for her to swallow anything when the children were so hungry."

She saw Lord Colwall's jaw tighten as she went on:

"Heaven knows what sort of place she's been in, Master Ranulf, but there are bruises on her back which she says she received when trying to stop a child from being beaten."

Lord Colwall clenched his fingers together and his knuckles were white.

"It's my belief," Nanny said softly, "that Her Ladyship'll have no peace until something is done about those children."

She saw the expression on his face, then without a word he was gone from the room and she heard him running downstairs.

Now Natalia had finished her soup and handed the cup back to Lord Colwall.

"As you have been so good," Lord Colwall said, "I will tell you something which I know will please you."

She looked up at him expectantly.

"I sent two carriages this afternoon to collect all the children from the Workhouse and take them to our own Orphanage," he said. "I have promised Mrs. Moppam she shall have still further help, and I have sent practically all the food there was in the Castle to feed them in the meantime."

The light in Natalia's eyes seemed to transfigure her face.

"You did . . . that?" she breathed hardly above a whisper. "Thank you . . . Thank you."

She put out her hands as she spoke with a gesture eloquent of gratitude. Then as he took them in his, she saw how rough and red they were and would have taken them away, but he raised them to his lips.

She felt herself quiver at the touch of his mouth on her skin.

"You must rest," he said in a deep voice, "but first I have something more to tell you."

"What is . . . it?" Natalia asked.

"I have promised the men on this Estate ten shillings a week wages, with two shillings extra for every child and the same for any elderly dependent."

He felt Natalia's fingers tighten on his as he went on:

"They have agreed to work the threshing-machine, but they will receive two shillings each per day threshing money. Next year we will take one thousand acres more into cultivation, which will mean more work and more money for every man."

"Thank you . . . Oh, thank . . . you!"

There were tears on Natalia's cheeks but when her eyes met Lord Colwall's it was as if neither of them could look away.

With an obvious effort Lord Colwall said:

"You must go to sleep. I will leave the door open between our rooms so that if you cry out I shall hear you, but now there is no reason for any more nightmares."

He would have risen from the bed as he spoke, but Natalia held on to one of his hands.

"I do not . . . wish to be . . . alone," she said almost inaudibly.

"Then I will stay with you," Lord Colwall replied in his deep voice, "but oh, my dearest heart, get well quickly! There is so much more I want to tell you, so much more that we can do together, and you will never be alone again, if I can help it!"

"Do you . . . mean that?"

"You know I mean it," he answered. "Do you not realise by now, Natalia, that I love you? It has been an agony beyond words these past ten days when I thought I would never find you again."

"I thought you . . . would not . . . want me to . . . stay."

"How could you think such a thing?" he asked. "You know I want you. I have always wanted you, but I did not realise how much until that devil took you away as a hostage and I did not know where to find you. I knew when I brought you home in my arms that you meant everything to me."

"The night before . . ." Natalia faltered, "in the . . . Library, you . . . sounded as if you . . . hated me . . ."

"I was crazy!" Lord Colwall declared. "It was because I felt so frustrated at your refusal to be my wife. I was at the same time fighting against admitting to myself that I loved you."

He felt Natalia's fingers trembling in his and he said:

"I loved you really from the first moment I saw you, but I vowed to myself that I would never again suffer as I had suffered in the past. So I fought against the enchantment of you every inch of the way!"

He gave a little laugh.

"If I suffered in the past, I have forgotten now what it felt like. For these past days I have suffered all the agonies of hell wondering where you were, desperately afraid of what might have happened to you."

"I thought . . . you would soon . . . forget me."

"How could I do that?" Lord Colwall asked simply. "You have captured my whole heart. It no longer belongs to me, but to you."

"Is this . . . true?"

"It is true, my beloved, completely and absolutely true. I love you now and you must teach me to love you in the way you want to be loved."

He bent his head as he spoke and kissed her hands again.

"They are so red and . . . ugly," Natalia murmured.

"They are beautiful, my dearest, because they are yours, just as everything about you is all the loveliness I ever want of life."

He drew in a deep breath.

"I have realised these past days that I have been prizing all the wrong things. I know now that my possessions, even the Castle itself, are of no importance beside the fact that you love me! One day I hope to be able to make you understand what you mean to me."

He looked at Natalia as he spoke and saw the tears come into her eyes again.

"This has been too much for you," he said quickly. "You must go to sleep now, my darling, and we will talk about everything in the morning. I will not leave you alone. I will sleep on the sofa, so if you want me, I shall be here."

There was a moment's silence and then Natalia said hesitatingly:

"You might be . . . cold, and that . . . would worry me. Could you not . . . get into bed? . . . It is very . . . big."

For a moment Lord Colwall was absolutely still, until he said in a voice which strove to be normal:

"As you say—it is very big."

He rose and walked to the fire to put on more coal and logs. Then he blew out the candles behind the curtains beside Natalia and walked around to the other side of the bed.

There was only one candle burning there, and extinguishing it before taking off his robe, he slipped between the sheets.

As Natalia had said, the bed was very large and there was a wide space between them.

She lay against the pillows watching the flames leaping high over the new logs. She did not turn her face towards Lord Colwall, but she knew he was lying on his back, straight and still.

After a moment she said in a very small voice:

"There is . . . something I . . . want to ask . . . you."

"What is it?" he enquired.

She did not reply and as if he knew she was shy and embarrassed, he turned towards her, resting on his elbow to raise himself so that he could look down at her face.

"What is it?" he asked again.

"Do I . . . now that I have been . . . touched," she whispered, "disgust . . . you?"

For a moment it seemed as if Lord Colwall struggled to find

words with which to answer. Then he moved closer to her and putting out his hand he very, very gently pulled her nightgown off her shoulders.

She made no movement as he bent his head and kissed first one of her small rose-tipped breasts, then the other. He replaced the nightgown and said in a voice that was unsteady:

"When you will let me, I will kiss you all over your perfect body. That is the real answer to your question."

He drew in his breath.

"You must go to sleep, my precious, you have been through so much. I must not tire you."

He spoke as if he admonished himself rather than her.

"Will you . . . kiss me . . . goodnight?"

Lord Colwall hesitated and then slowly, holding himself in an iron control, bent forward.

His lips sought her cheek, but she moved so that it was her mouth he kissed. At first there was only the faint touch of their lips, until suddenly it seemed to Natalia as if the whole room was filled with a brilliant light.

She felt a sudden thrill run through her which was like a sword piercing every nerve in her body.

Then Lord Colwall's arms were round her and he was kissing her frantically, passionately, demandingly.

She had known this was what it would be like to be kissed with love. She knew an ecstasy, a rapture that was beyond anything she had ever imagined or had dreamt was possible.

She put her arms round his neck and as she did so he raised his head.

"I love you! God, how I love you!" he cried. "Be kind to me, Natalia, I did not know love was like this. But I would not frighten you, my darling. I must give you time."

She made a little sound that was half a laugh of unbridled happiness.

Then she drew his head closer until his lips once again were on hers.

She knew there was no need for time, or words, or explanations. This was love!

This was what she always knew they should feel for each other.

This was the wonder and glory of being not two people but one, of being close and indivisible, part of a joy and rapture not of this world, but of the Divine force which pouring through them, made them as gods.

The
Glittering Lights

AUTHOR'S NOTE

The background of this novel is authentic; the descriptions and gossip about the beautiful Lily Langtry, the Show at the Gaiety Theatre and its pretty Leading Ladies, the restaurants in London like Romanos, Rules, the Café Royal are all part of the history of the time.

CHAPTER ONE

1886

"I am back, Mama."

"Oh, Cassandra, I have been so worried! You are very late!"

"I had trouble with one of the horses," Cassandra said walking across the Drawing-Room to where her mother was sitting in a wheel-chair in front of the fire.

As she reached her, Lady Alice Sherburn looked up and gave an exclamation of horror.

Her daughter was certainly looking most disreputable. Her habit was splashed with mud, her hair had escaped from beneath her riding-hat, and she also appeared to be extremely wet.

Cassandra saw her mother's face and gave a little laugh.

"I am safe and sound," she said reassuringly, "but wet through! It is raining and I had a fall."

"Cassandra!"

The cry was one of horror.

Reaching her mother's side, Cassandra leaned down and kissed her cheek.

"Now do not worry, Mama, about something which has not happened. It was not a bad fall, and although I may be a little stiff tomorrow, there is no bone broken, and not too many bruises . . . not where they will show, anyway!"

"Cassandra, my dearest, if anything happened to you, I do not think I could bear it."

"I know that, Mama," Cassandra said in a soft voice, "and that is why I came in to tell you I was back before I went upstairs to change. Otherwise I would not have let you see me looking like this."

She saw the fear still lurking in her mother's eyes and said quietly:

"You know lightning never strikes in the same place twice! You have taken all the dangers of the family upon yourself, so Papa and I are likely to get off scot-free."

"If only you were not so reckless," Lady Alice murmured almost beneath her breath.

Cassandra kissed her mother's cheek once again.

"There is nothing you and Papa would dislike more than if I were a mouse-like little Miss, sitting at home with my tatting," she said. "And you, as the best horse-woman the County ever saw, would disown a daughter who trit-trotted along the roads and looked for gaps in the hedges."

Lady Alice smiled.

"I cannot imagine you ever being that kind of rider! Go and change, child, and when you are looking decent your father wants to see you."

"He will have to wait a little while," Cassandra replied airily. "I must have a bath, and while I am about it, I shall put on my evening-gown. So tell Papa, if he asks for me, it will be at least an hour before he can expect me."

"I will send a message to your father," Lady Alice replied. "Cassandra, I . . ."

But her daughter had already left the room and was running up the broad stairway to her own bed-room.

Her maid, Hannah, was waiting for her there and, like Lady Alice, she gave an exclamation of horror at Cassandra's appearance.

"Now do not start screaming at me," Cassandra admonished with a smile. "I took a toss this afternoon. It was all my fault. I tried a young horse at too high a fence and he refused at the last moment."

"You'll break your neck one of these days, Miss Cassandra," Hannah said in the scolding voice of an old servant whose affection allows her to take liberties.

Cassandra did not answer and she went on:

"And I should have thought that seeing your mother every day in her wheel-chair would be a warning to you. But no, you ride as if the devil himself was at your heels! But one day, you'll get what's coming to you."

Cassandra gave a little sigh.

She had heard all this before. At the same time, she understood her mother's anxiety and Hannah's.

For the last fifteen years, Lady Alice had been confined to a wheel-chair, having broken her back out hunting.

Yet, surprisingly, it had drawn she and her husband closer together.

There had never been, people said, a more devoted, considerate man than Sir James Sherburn, and Lady Alice's love for him was very evident every time her eyes rested on his handsome face.

The real tragedy lay in the fact that because of her incapacity they could have no more children.

Cassandra, who was five at the time of her mother's accident, was their only child.

That she was lovely, daring, reckless, and impulsive was to be expected in the off-spring of two such attractive and unusual people, and Cassandra had certainly lived up to their expectations of her.

To begin with, she was startlingly beautiful.

As Hannah took off her dirty riding-habit, she stood for a moment naked before stepping into her bath which was waiting in front of the fire. The perfection of her slender figure with its white skin made her look like a young goddess.

She released her hair from the last remaining pins that had not been dislodged while riding, and it fell over her shoulders reaching nearly to her waist.

It was a colour which drew every man's eyes when she entered a room. Deep red, it was highlighted with streaks of gold which appeared to ripple through it and shine tantalisingly, so that no-one was able exactly to describe it.

Cassandra's hair was a heritage from her father and he often said that "red hair ran like wine" in the Sherburn family.

But she had her mother's eyes and Lady Alice came from a long line of Irish nobility.

The O'Derrys had been Earls of Ireland for generations, and it was always said that the dark lashes which framed their blue eyes were a legacy from a Spanish ancestor.

He had, according to legend, been swept up on the South coast of Ireland from one of the wrecked galleons of the Spanish Armada and had married the pretty daughter of his captor.

The combination of red hair and blue eyes made Cassandra inevitably the object of attention. And it would have been a blind man who could resist the enticement of her smile or the way her laugh would ring out making everyone want to laugh with her.

She was naturally gay, invariably happy, and an irrepressible mad-cap which made some older members of Yorkshire society raise their eye-brows and look down their aristocratic noses.

But even they had to admit that Cassandra was irresistible, and they forgave her escapades which would have brought down the full weight of their disapproval on any other girl.

"I have had a really marvellous day," Cassandra said as having washed herself she lay back in the bath, feeling her stiffness ease away in the warm water.

She thought with satisfaction of the results she had obtained with the young horses her father had bought for her the previous week.

There was not another girl in the whole of Yorkshire who could have attempted to school her own mounts or to ride them over what was in effect a private steeple-chase course in the grounds of her own home.

"By the time hunting starts," she said, talking more to herself than to Hannah, "I shall have horses with which I shall out-ride and out-stay anyone else in the field."

"You'll do that—if you're alive to tell the tale!" Hannah said tartly.

She went from the room as she spoke, carrying the muddied and wet habit with her.

Cassandra laughed to herself.

She was used to Hannah fussing over her, but it hurt her if she knew her mother was anxious. That was why she had hurried in to see Lady Alice before she went upstairs to change.

At twenty Cassandra had lost her last remnants of adolescent awkwardness and to a great degree her shyness.

She was usually very sure of herself, and she would have been stupid—which she was not—if she had not been conscious of her own attractions.

There was hardly a young man in the whole neighbourhood who had not pursued her ardently and incessantly, and while she laughed at them for being immature, she was well aware there was a glint in the eyes of her father's old acquaintances when they looked at her and that the compliments they paid her were, for the most part, sincere.

"Thank goodness we are not dining out tonight," she thought as she stepped out of the bath.

The Sherburns lived in a very hospitable neighbourhood despite the fact that on the map it appeared somewhat isolated.

It was, however, excellent hunting country and that was what mattered, combined with the good fortune of having a large number of young people among the families of the big landowners.

When Cassandra finished drying herself, Hannah was ready to

help her into one of the exquisite gowns on which her father was only too happy to spend exorbitant sums.

Naturally they came from London and were the source of considerable envy, and sometimes a little malice, amongst the other girls of Cassandra's age.

But it was difficult for anyone to resent her for long.

She was as charming to women as she was to men, and apart from her shocking the older generation by behaving more like a boy than a girl in the hunting field and at other sports, there was no denying that she had been very properly brought up.

"Thank you, Hannah," she said now as she finished dressing. "Be an angel and call me at seven o'clock tomorrow morning."

"You're not going riding at that unearthly hour!" Hannah exclaimed. "Not after you've been out so late today."

"I am not going to let my horses forget what I have already taught them," Cassandra replied, "and tomorrow I will get Flycatcher to jump that fence. I am sure of it!"

"You're tempting Providence, that's what you're doing," Hannah said warningly.

But Cassandra only laughed at her once again.

"If I break my neck, it will give you so much satisfaction to say—'I told you so,'" she teased.

With her gown making a silky swish behind her she went down the stairs towards her father's Study.

She stepped into the room and he looked up from his desk, appreciating with the eyes of a man who was a connoisseur of beautiful women how lovely she looked.

Her dress was the pale leaf green of the spring buds that were just beginning to show on the trees, and a skilful hand had moulded it over the front of her body so that it revealed the perfect contours of her breasts and her tiny waist.

It was almost Classical in its simplicity to fall from the bustle in a cascade of frills which ended in a small train.

It was the dress of a young girl and yet every line proclaimed it to have been extremely expensive.

Cassandra wore no jewellery: with her white skin that had the texture of a magnolia she needed none.

Her hair was swept back from her oval forehead, and because she had been in a hurry, Hannah had simply arranged it in a large chignon rather than in the multiple curls which Sir James preferred.

But whichever way Cassandra wore her unusual and beautiful hair, it was always spectacular.

"I am sorry if I kept you waiting, Papa," she said as she walked across the large room and lifted up her face for him to kiss her.

"I forgive you," he replied.

When they were together, the likeness between father and daughter was very obvious, despite the fact that Cassandra was small-boned with delicate, very feminine features, and Sir James was a handsome, very masculine man.

He was dressed with an elegance which accentuated the lean and athletic lines of his figure.

His clean-cut features, his eyes which seemed to have a permanent twinkle in them, and his ability to make the most outrageous flattering compliments sound sincere, rendered him irresistible to women.

"I wish you had been with me, Papa," Cassandra exclaimed. "Those horses are outstanding! I cannot tell you how excited I am by their performance."

"I am glad they please you," Sir James said.

"You know they do," Cassandra answered, "and I think we have a real winner in Andora."

"I seldom make a mistake when it comes to horse-flesh," Sir James murmured.

Cassandra walked towards the fire.

It was the end of March, but the weather was still very chill and The Towers was a cold house, being not only very large but built on the summit of a hill with magnificent views over the surrounding countryside.

"Mama was worried because I was late," Cassandra said.

"I know," Sir James answered. "Try not to upset her, my dearest."

"I do try," Cassandra answered, "but Flycatcher threw me. I had to school him for at least half an hour afterwards—otherwise he would have thought he could get away with it."

Sir James, who had followed Cassandra to the fireplace, smiled at her gently.

"I think you now are as proficient with horses as I am and quite frankly, I could not pay you a bigger compliment."

"I would not like to suggest that you sound conceited," Cassandra teased. "At the same time I know that something has pleased you. What is it, apart from me?"

"You always please me," Sir James said with a note of seriousness in his voice, "but you are right as usual. There is something I have to tell you."

"What can it be?" Cassandra asked.

She had a feeling there was something unusual in the expression on her father's face.

Sir James hesitated for a moment and then he said quietly:

"I have had a letter from the Duke."

Cassandra was very still.

"I have been expecting it, as you well know," Sir James went on. "At the same time I began to feel that since he had come into the title he was no longer interested in the arrangements his father had made for him."

"It is over a year," Cassandra murmured almost beneath her breath.

"I know that," Sir James said, "and I should think it almost insulting if he had not prefixed his letter with 'Now that the period of mourning for my father has ended . . .'"

"And how does he go on?" Cassandra asked.

"He suggests that his visit here, which has been postponed for so long, should now take place," Sir James replied. "He asks if he would be welcome in two weeks' time, on the tenth of April to be exact."

Cassandra turned her head away to look at the fire. She held out her hands towards the flames as if she suddenly felt cold.

Sir James looked at her profile a little while before he said:

"You know, dearest, without my having to tell you, that I have always wanted you to marry the son of my old friend. We have not spoken about it for some time, but we are both aware it has been in the back of our minds."

'That is true,' Cassandra thought.

She and her father always knew what the other was thinking and it had been obvious these past months that they both deliberately avoided the subject of her marriage.

"It was all arranged and everything appeared to be straight-forward," Sir James continued, "until everything was upset by two, or should I say three, unexpected deaths."

'That also is true,' Cassandra thought.

It had been planned that she should make her *début* in the summer of 1884. She was to have gone to London and her father had planned a Ball at a house he had recently acquired in Park Lane.

She was to have been presented at Buckingham Palace and to

have been chaperoned, as her mother was unable to do so, by her father's step-sister, Lady Fladbury.

Then a week before they were due to leave Yorkshire, her mother's father, the Earl of O'Derry, had died and they had been plunged into mourning.

Queen Victoria had set a precedent for mourning long and ostentatiously every relative, however seldom one had met them and however slight the ties of affection.

It was therefore impossible for Cassandra to make her *début* then. All the arrangements that had been made in London were cancelled and they stayed in Yorkshire.

The following year the scene was set once again and Lady Fladbury who was only too willing to present Cassandra to London society, had actually sent out invitations to Receptions, Soirées and Balls to coincide with her arrival in London.

Two days before Cassandra and her father were due to set out from Yorkshire, Lord Fladbury died of a sudden heart-attack.

"That settles it!" Cassandra said. "I am obviously fated not to be a *débutante!*"

"Fladbury was only an Uncle by marriage," Sir James said, "but as the social world knows that my step-sister was chaperoning you, we can hardly ignore the fact that she is widowed and that we must wear black for at least a month or two."

"Cassandra cannot be presented in the circumstances," Lady Alice had said in concern. "I would take her to Buckingham Palace myself, despite the fact that I am in a wheel-chair, but how can I make an application before poor George is even in the grave. It would be in the worst possible taste."

"It does not worry me in the slightest, Mama," Cassandra said. "Quite frankly I would much rather spend the summer here in Yorkshire. You know as well as I do that I enjoy the races, and I find my own friends with whom I have been brought up far more agreeable than all the strange notabilities to whom I should be very small fry."

"Dammit! I wanted you to have a London Season," Sir James said irritably, "and I have made all the arrangements with the Duke."

That, Cassandra knew, annoyed her father more than anything else.

Sir James and the Duke of Alchester had decided many years ago that their children should marry each other.

The Duke wanted an heiress for his son—he made no bones

about it! His great estate was mortgaged, the house was in disre-pair, and the Marquess of Charlbury was well aware that he had to marry money.

"I had been half-afraid that I should have to put up with a damned American or a tradesman's daughter," the Duke had snorted to Sir James. "What could be better than that your girl and my boy should make a match, and we can see that they do things properly?"

The Marquess of Charlbury, who was six years older than Cas-sandra, had been abroad when it had all been decided.

"I have sent the boy to see the world," the late Duke said. "It will make him appreciate his position in this country. No-body, as you well know, Sherburn, has a better family tree or a finer family seat. It is just that we have not enough money to keep it up."

Sir James and the Duke of Alchester had been friends for some years. They had met at Tattersall's Sale-rooms where for some months they vied against each other in trying to acquire the finest horses.

It was after Sir James had out-bid the Duke and paid an exorbi-tant price for two particularly fine hunters, that he had walked up to the older man to say:

"It strikes me, Your Grace, that we are pouring a lot of unneces-sary money, not only into the pockets of the owners, but also into the hands of those who run this Sale-room."

The Duke looked at Sir James in surprise. Then he had suc-cumbed, just as so many other people had done before him, to the younger man's charm.

"What do you suggest we do about it?" he asked.

"Come to a sensible arrangement between us!" Sir James replied. "We can inspect the horses before the sales, pick out those in which we are personally interested, and agree as to which ones each shall bid for."

The same agreement applied to their race-horses. When they went to the Newmarket or to the sales which took place on the race-course, they were always seen consulting each other and if one of them was bidding the other was silent.

Because the love of horses is the closest bond that an Englishman can have with another, the Duke and Sir James Sherburn became close friends.

Cassandra was only twelve when she first saw the Marquis of Charlbury.

Her father had taken her to the Eton v. Harrow cricket match at

Lords. They had a Coach on the Mound, where an innumerable number of people of all ages drank champagne and ate raspberries and cream, usually with their backs to the cricket.

Cassandra however watched the boys in their white flannels fighting the annual battle of Eton College against Harrow School, and it had been impossible not to realise that the Captain of Eton was an outstanding young man.

He took four wickets and made sixty runs and had, it appeared, ensured almost single-handed that Eton was the winner.

He had been brought by the Duke to Sir James's coach during the afternoon and Cassandra, seated on the box, had looked down at him with interest.

She had not realised then that her future was already being planned for her by her father and the Duke.

In his long white flannel trousers, blazer and pale blue cap the Marquis had appeared extremely handsome. His hair was dark and he had grey eyes which she noticed immediately.

There was an expression of curiosity in them which made him, she thought, appear to look penetratingly at anyone to whom he spoke, as if he was searching for something.

He was tall and extremely thin, as if he had almost outgrown his strength, or else driven himself hard.

There was no doubt that he was popular with other Etonians, while older men spoke of what he had achieved at the match with a pride that told those who listened it was part of the nostalgia of their schooldays.

The Duke was talking eagerly to Sir James about a horse he had heard of in Suffolk and which he thought was worth their attention.

The young Marquis was surrounded by the young women who had been accepting Sir James's hospitality.

They were flattering him, hanging on his words, laughing at everything he said and doing their utmost, Cassandra thought with a little curve of her lips, to make themselves alluring.

'Today he is the hero of the match,' she thought. 'Tomorrow they will have forgotten him.'

But she was to learn as the years went on that the Marquis of Charlbury was not someone who was easily forgotten!

The newspapers were full of him, the illustrated journals went into rhapsodies over his looks, his charm and his rank.

She could never remember afterwards whether they had actually been introduced that day at Lords; but whether they had or not, she had certainly made no impact upon him, while she knew that as far as she was concerned her life had been changed that warm summer's afternoon.

It seemed to her inevitable and in a way part of a dream when her father told her that he and the Duke had planned that she should marry the Marquis.

"And supposing he does not like me?" she asked.

For a moment Sir James looked a little embarrassed.

"My dearest, you must understand," he said, "that in the social world marriages are arranged by the parents of those concerned."

"But could such a marriage ever be successful?" Cassandra enquired.

"They are successful," Sir James answered. "In the vast majority of cases the two people concerned fall in love with each other after the marriage and live in great contentment."

"Are you telling me that that is what happened with you and Mama?"

Sir James smiled.

"As usual, Cassandra, you have put your finger upon my Achilles' heel! I met your mother by chance. I fell in love with her as soon as I saw her. I think she will tell you that she also fell in love with me."

He paused and then he said:

"I was much older than she, Cassandra. I always intended to marry, but only when I was quite certain I found someone who would suit me."

"In other words," Cassandra said, "you meant to marry someone who had both breeding and an important place in the social world. You were rich, Papa, but you had no intention of not furthering your ambitions by your marriage."

"We have always been frank with each other," Sir James replied, "and therefore I can admit in all honesty, Cassandra, that that is more or less the truth. I had no intention, when I gave up my bachelor-hood, of making anything but a brilliant social marriage, something which I may add I had enjoyed very much."

Cassandra laughed.

"I have heard it said, Papa, that there has never been such a flirt as you, and that women pursued you like flies around a honey-pot!"

"You flatter me!" Sir James protested, but his eyes were twinkling.

"What you are trying to tell me," Cassandra went on, "is that you always intended to make a *mariage de convenance*. You would not have married someone unimportant, however much you loved her."

"I was fortunate in that the situation did not arise," Sir James said, "so I cannot tell you what I would have done in different circumstances. It was true I was enamoured with many lovely women and perhaps you are right in saying I broke a number of hearts! But the moment I saw your mother I loved her."

There was something rather moving in the simplicity with which he spoke.

"And I am not to have the same chance of finding someone I love," Cassandra said in a small voice.

Sir James made a gesture with his hands.

"My dear, you are a woman and how can a woman judge what is best for herself? Not a rich woman at any rate."

"You mean that, as soon as I am old enough, men will want to marry me for my money?" Cassandra said.

"Men will want to marry you because you are lovely, because you are sweet, intelligent and have a personality of your own," Sir James corrected. "And, to add to all that, you are also a very wealthy young woman!"

Cassandra sighed.

"So I have to allow you to choose my husband?"

"You have to trust me as you have always done, to know what is best for you."

"And what about the Marquis?" Cassandra enquired. "He is a man. He can have his own choice as you did."

"No! Charlbury has to marry for money," Sir James said. "There is no question of that. The Alchester Estate is in the red. Because I am the Duke's friend, he has confided in me that it will require a small fortune to set things to rights. The only chance Charlbury has of living in the home of his ancestors is to take a rich wife."

"He may . . . love someone quite . . . different."

Cassandra felt as though she forced the words between her lips.

"He is a gentleman," Sir James replied. "He will, I know, always show his wife courtesy and consideration. I have never heard anyone say anything unpleasant or indeed unkind about Charlbury."

Cassandra felt after this conversation that her father would arrange for her to meet the young Marquis. He so often went to stay at Alchester Park with the Duke or they met at one of their Clubs.

It seemed strange that no invitation for her came to The Towers and there was never any question of the Marquis being asked to stay for one of the innumerable Balls or functions which took place in Yorkshire.

When she was older she realised that this was deliberate on her father's part.

He did not wish the Marquis to see her when, as he put it himself, she was unfledged, half-grown, not quite as beautiful as she promised to be.

But there was no doubt they would have met when she went to London for her *début*, had not Sir James's plans been frustrated twice so that they had to remain in Yorkshire.

Then, as if fate had not finished putting obstacles in their way, the Duke died in 1885.

He had a stroke when he was watching one of his horses beaten at the post Epsom racecourse and only survived for twenty-four hours.

This was even a bigger set-back than Sir James had endured previously.

He had just arranged that the young Marquis should come and stay at The Towers for the local races and to take part in the County festivities which always coincided with them.

He had not pretended to Cassandra that this was not the auspicious moment in her life.

"You will meet Charlbury, he will propose to you, and you can be married at the end of the summer."

"Does he realise what has been planned for him?" Cassandra asked.

"Of course," her father replied. "The Duke has already invited us to stay at Alchester for Ascot, and by that time your engagement will be in the *Gazette*."

Cassandra had said very little. She felt as if she was waiting in a theatre for the curtain to rise and was not quite certain which play was being performed.

When she was alone a thousand questions came into her mind, a thousand fears and doubts and apprehensions seemed to encompass her like a cloud.

Then with the Duke's death, everything came to a standstill.

Sir James had travelled South to attend the funeral and he had not suggested that Cassandra should come with him.

Anyway she also was in mourning, and she was well aware it would not be right for her to meet her future husband at the death-bed of his father.

And so her second summer was spent in Yorkshire, while Sir James, she knew, waited at first confidently and then with some degree of anxiety for a letter from the new Duke of Alchester.

Cassandra waited too and for the first time in her life, she had not confided her thoughts and feelings to her father.

They were so close that she never had any secrets that he could not share.

"Who offered for you tonight?" he would ask as they travelled back from a Ball at which Cassandra had undoubtedly been the Belle and evoked the admiration of every male and the envy of every female.

"John Huntley, for the nine hundred and ninety-ninth time," she replied laughingly. "I am fond of him, but he does not seem to understand that the word 'No' exists in the English language."

"I admire his persistence," Sir James said.

"He is as heavy-handed as a suitor as he is with a horse," Cassandra had said.

"And what could be more condemning?" Sir James remarked with a smile.

"I know one thing . . . I could never marry a man who could not ride well and did not understand horses."

"There are plenty of good riders to be found," Sir James said mockingly.

"You know I also want someone intelligent," Cassandra said, "and that is more than I can say for Walter Witley. If you had heard him stammering and hesitating tonight, you would have been really sorry for him. I tried to prevent him coming to the point, but he had made up his mind to 'try his luck,' as he put it. But I do not think he will try again."

"Were you unkind to him?" Sir James asked curiously.

"No, but I have deflated his ego," Cassandra answered. "He thinks Lord Witley of Witley Park is too much of a catch to be turned down by the daughter of a mere Baronet!"

"Damn it all!" Sir James ejaculated. "The Sherburns were Squires in Yorkshire when the Witleys were nothing but sheepshearers."

Cassandra had laughed.

"Oh, Papa, I love you when you are proud of your ancestry and you give the *parvenus* a set-down! But Lord Witley is Lord Witley and he never lets anyone forget it."

"Well, I will tell your mother to delete him from her list of eligible young men," Sir James said, "and quite frankly, if you married a Witley, I should refuse to come to your wedding."

Cassandra laughed again and then linking her arm in her father's she said:

"The trouble is, Papa, that I find you so fascinating, so amusing, so clever, and so unusually intelligent, that all other men pale into insignificance beside you."

Sir James kissed the top of her head.

"You spoil me, Cassandra. At the same time, as you well know, I want the best—the very best—for you, and that is what I intend you to have."

It was now that the Duke's belated letter had arrived, that Cassandra found herself for the first time questioning her father's wisdom where she was concerned.

She knew that, had the Marquis of Charlbury come to stay as had been arranged the previous year, she would have accepted his proposal as her father intended, and by now they would have been married.

'But,' she told herself, 'in the past year I have changed.'

She was not a very young girl standing on the threshold of life, a little bewildered and uncertain of herself, and unsure of what she wanted of the future.

In simple words she had grown up.

At twenty she was no longer a *débutante*, and because she was far more intelligent than the average girl of her age, or indeed of most women at any age, she was prepared to look critically at her suitor and not accept him just because it pleased her father.

Sir James was perceptive enough to know that something was perturbing her, and while he was confident that in due course Cassandra would tell him what it was, he also was aware that he was no longer dealing with a child who would obey him without question.

There was no time to say much more to each other. Dinner was announced and they proceeded to the Dining-Room, Lady Alice being wheeled ahead of Sir James and Cassandra.

As might be expected, the meal was superlatively cooked by a French Chef, whose salary to keep him in Yorkshire was an extravagance which few other men would have contemplated.

There were flowers decorating the Dining-Room table from the huge green-houses which covered over two acres of garden, there were fruits forced in a manner which commanded the admiration of all the horticulturists in the North of England, and Sir James's gold racing trophies helped to decorate the table.

Sir James seated himself in his high-backed chair and remarked with satisfaction:

"How nice it is to have on either side of me two of the most beautiful women in the world, and to know that tonight I do not have to make polite conversation with a number of boring acquaintances."

Lady Alice laughed.

"You like having us alone because it is a novelty, but if it was something which occurred too often you would soon be yawning."

"How can you say anything so unkind?"

Sir James took his wife's hand and raised it to his lips.

"Have I ever appeared to be bored with you?"

"No, darling," Lady Alice answered, "but I take very good care that you have many distractions to amuse you."

It was true, Cassandra thought, watching them. Lady Alice would arrange for all the most attractive and beautiful women she knew to stay at The Towers and be their guests at luncheon, dinner and on every possible occasion.

She sometimes wondered if her mother felt jealous at the way in which they flirted outrageously with her father and obviously set themselves out to use every possible feminine allure to attract him.

Then she knew with that new instinct that she had discovered in herself that Lady Alice held her husband by not appearing to do so.

There was between them an understanding which seemed to enrich their lives, so that Cassandra knew that no-one, however beautiful, would ever take the place of her mother in his affections.

At the same time, she was well aware that Sir James had the reputation of being a Don Juan and that women found him irresistible.

"It is not surprising, Papa," she had told him once, "because I also find you irresistible and I am your daughter."

"I can return the compliment," he said, "and one day when you fall in love, Cassandra, the man to whom you give your heart will find it is possible to express your attraction in words."

When dinner was over they sat for a little while in the Drawing-Room talking in front of the fire, and then when Lady Alice went up to bed, Cassandra rose to follow her.

"I admit to feeling a little stiff, and also a trifle tired."

"Are you riding early tomorrow?" her father asked. "I think I might come with you."

Cassandra hesitated a moment before she replied:

"I think, Papa, I will go to London."

"To London?" Sir James exclaimed.

He realised that Lady Alice, being propelled towards the lift he had had installed for her, was out of earshot.

"I need some clothes, Papa."

"But of course! That is understandable. I want you to look your best, Cassandra, when Alchester arrives."

"I hope I will do that."

"Do you want me to come with you?"

"No, Papa, you know how much it would bore you if I was having fittings all day, and I do not expect I shall stay long."

"I know your Aunt is at our house in Park Lane," Sir James said. "I had a letter from her yesterday telling me she had engaged a new Cook."

The widowed Lady Fladbury had, after her husband's death, made her home in her step-brother's house in Park Lane.

It was convenient for Cassandra if she wished to go to London at any time to have a Chaperon on the premises, and it suited her Aunt, who had been left in somewhat impecunious circumstances, to live rent free.

"Aunt Eleanor never goes away!" Cassandra said. "So I was certain I would find her there."

"You will take Hannah?"

"Of course," Cassandra replied. "I know you would not like me to travel without her."

"Then the sooner you go to London and come back, the better," Sir James said, "and by the way, while you are there, have a photograph taken. We shall need it for the newspapers when your engagement is announced."

"Oh, Papa, you know I hate being photographed."

"I cannot abide the last one that was taken by that man in York," Sir James said. "I want an attractive likeness to console me when you have left home."

"Yes, of course, I had not thought of that. It would be awkward if you forgot what I looked like."

He smiled at her fondly.

"You know I could never do that. At the same time I want a very good one. Go to Downey's of Bond Street, who photographed Lily Langtry. I liked the last one I saw of her."

Cassandra was still for a moment and then she said:

"There is something I want to ask you, Papa. I would like to meet Mrs. Langtry."

"You would?" Sir James exclaimed in surprise.

"I have heard so much about her," Cassandra replied, "of her beauty, and the sensation she caused when she went on the stage. I was reading how when she returned from America last year, she was cheered as she stepped from the ship. There were crowds of people waiting on the quay to see her."

"I read that too," Sir James said.

"It shows what a place she holds in public affection," Cassandra went on. "Write me a letter of introduction, Papa, and I will go and see her new play."

"It is called 'Enemies' and it is on at The Prince's Theatre."

"Have you seen it yet?"

He shook his head.

"No. I saw the play she was in before. She was good—a little stiff —but she looked entrancingly lovely."

"Did you take her out to supper, Papa?"

"As a matter of fact, no, I did not," Sir James answered, "and, as you are so curious, I have not seen her since she returned to England from America last year."

"Then she will be looking forward to hearing from you again," Cassandra said. "Give me just a few words of introduction."

"I do not know her address. You will have to get the coachman to leave it at the theatre. At the same time, I am not really certain your mother would like you to meet an actress, even if it is Mrs. Langtry."

"We can solve that problem by not telling Mama. I expect she knows that at one time you were fascinated by the most beautiful woman in England, but she may now have forgotten all about it."

"Then we will not tell her," Sir James smiled, "and I would rather like you to meet Lily. You are as lovely in your way, Cassandra, as she is in hers."

He sighed.

"Let me think, she must be twenty-nine, and when I knew her first she was only twenty-two, and the most beautiful creature I ever encountered."

"You understand, Papa, why I want to meet her? I will just talk to her and see how she captivated the Prince of Wales and Prince Louis of Battenburg, and why the Prime Minister Mr. Gladstone is her friend."

"I cannot think who has been talking to you about such matters," Sir James said, but there was no reproof in his voice.

"If there is any scandal I have not yet heard," Cassandra said with a smile, "Aunt Eleanor will be full of it as soon as I arrive in Park Lane."

"You can be quite sure of that," Sir James agreed.

"Then you had best write me a letter now," Cassandra insisted.

"If I am going to London, I will catch the nine a.m. train from York, so it will mean my leaving early.

"Will you order the carriage for me, Papa, and as soon as I go upstairs I will tell Hannah to start packing. She will be furious at having to do it at what she will call the 'middle of the night'."

"And do not worry your mother," Sir James admonished. "You know she is rather anxious when you go to London without me."

"I am sure Mama will want me to look my very best when the Duke arrives," Cassandra said demurely. "Like every woman you have ever known, Papa, I literally have not a thing to wear!"

Sir James laughed at that and walking across the room went through the Hall and into his Study.

He sat down at the desk and wrote a short note in his strong, upright handwriting and put it into an envelope.

Sir James addressed it to: "Mrs. Langtry, The Prince's Theatre."

"Thank you, dear Papa," Cassandra said and bending, kissed his cheek.

She slipped the letter inside the bodice of her dress before she went to her mother's bed-room.

She said good-night to Lady Alice, told her that she was about to go to London, and found, as she expected, that her mother apparently understood her need for more clothes.

It was Hannah who protested when Cassandra, going to her bedroom found her there waiting to help her undress.

"Really, Miss Cassandra, you might give me a little more notice," she scolded. "How do you think I'm going to get ready by eight o'clock tomorrow morning unless I stay up all night?"

"You know you never go to sleep early," Cassandra replied, "and it is important, Hannah, it is, really, or I would not have made up my mind so unexpectedly."

"Are you up to some of your monkey tricks again?" Hannah asked. "Because if you are, you can take someone else with you. I shall not be responsible to Her Ladyship, and that's a fact!"

Cassandra paid no attention.

She had heard Hannah talk like this far too many times before to be taken seriously.

"I'll go and start packing," Hannah said when finally Cassandra was ready for bed. "It'll take me three hours. If I'm too exhausted to come with you in the morning, you'll understand what has happened."

"I have already told you, Hannah," Cassandra said, "I only want a few gowns, so do not pack half the wardrobe. I shall only be staying two or three days and I shall be shopping all the time."

"I can't think where we're going to put any more things. There's no room for what we have already," Hannah remarked as a parting shot.

As soon as she was alone, Cassandra jumped out of bed and put on the silk wrap which Hannah had left lying over a chair.

She tied the sash around her small waist and went from the bedroom into her Sitting-Room which adjoined it.

It was a lovely room and had been done up only two years ago by her father who had spared no expense.

Everything that Cassandra treasured, everything that meant something special to her was housed here in the room that was essentially her own.

She lit the lamp which had been turned out by Hannah before she left and found a key in its secret drawer which was indiscernible to anyone who did not know where it was concealed.

With it she opened the lower drawer of her desk in which reposed two large green leather Albums.

She took one out and put it on the table beside the lighted lamp.

For a moment she stared at it as if she was half-afraid to turn the cover with its silver edges and reveal what lay inside.

Then very slowly, with a strange expression on her face, she opened the Album.

CHAPTER TWO

Cassandra turned the pages.

On every one there were portrait-sketches, cuttings from newspapers and magazines, all referring to the Marquis of Charlbury.

She had started to collect newspaper reports of him after she had seen him at the Eton and Harrow Match. There had been quite glowing descriptions of the way he himself had batted and how expertly he had captained his team.

Cassandra had cut them out of the many newspapers her father read and from the *Illustrated London News*, the *Sporting and Dramatic*, and the magazines like *The Lady* which amused her mother.

Later she thought she had done it instinctively, because subconsciously she had known even then that the Marquis was to mean something in her life.

After her father had told her that he intended her to marry the Marquis she had bought the leather Album and stuck in the cuttings, starting with 1878 when she first met him and adding to them year by year until they had stopped abruptly in August 1885.

She had known then that her feelings towards him had changed.

It would have been different if their engagement could have taken place when she was seventeen and had made her *début* in London.

Then in her heart the Marquis had assumed the proportions of a hero, the ideal man who had already occupied her adolescent dreams for more than two or three years.

At times when she had gone to London to buy clothes and visit the theatre with her father, she was still in mourning and he had made no suggestion that she should meet the Marquis.

She had heard people talk about him, as of course, he was undoubtedly *jeunesse dorée* of society.

Despite the fact that the Duke was known to be spending more than he could afford, the Marquis from a matrimonial angle was nevertheless a much sought after catch.

Then last year, when it had been arranged for the Marquis to come and stay at The Towers and Sir James confidently expected to announce their engagement before Ascot races, Cassandra knew that her feelings were now not the same.

It was not that he did not continue to haunt her dreams, to linger at the back of her mind whatever she might be doing.

It was just that she knew that, unless things were very different than they appeared to be at the moment, it would be impossible for her to marry him.

Three months after his father's death and the Marquis had not suggested a visit to Yorkshire, Cassandra was saying to herself:

"I cannot marry him."

She had been idealistic enough to believe romantically that when they met they would fall in love with each other and live happily ever afterwards.

She was well aware that she was beautiful and it would be unlikely for her not to appeal to the Marquis's taste in women.

Then she discovered grounds for thinking that he would in all respects be quite unresponsive to her attractions.

When she visited London the Spring before the *début* was cancelled because of the death of her grandfather, Cassandra had somewhat shyly asked her Aunt whether she would be likely to meet the Marquis of Charlbury at the Balls she would attend during the Season.

"The Marquis of Charlbury?" Lady Fladbury had exclaimed. "Whatever makes you think that he might be a suitable partner?"

Her genuine surprise told Cassandra that the Duke and her father had kept their plans for their children a secret. If there had been any gossip about their intentions, her Aunt quite certainly would have heard of it!

Cassandra did not answer and after a moment Lady Fladbury went on:

"But of course, I forgot, your father races with the Duke. Well, I should not bother your pretty head over young Charlbury. He is far too interested in the footlights to dance attendance on any *débutante*, however attractive!"

"In the footlights?" Cassandra questioned.

"He is one of the many 'men about town' who hang around the stage-door at the Gaiety," Lady Fladbury explained. "There are a whole number of them making fools of themselves over pretty girls who have no breeding and who most certainly will not make them good wives."

"Good wives?"

Cassandra was aware that actresses were considered fast and extremely improper and were not accepted by any society hostesses.

"Kate Vaughan, who starred at the Gaiety, married the Honourable Arthur Wellesley, nephew of the great Duke of Wellington, last year," Lady Fladbury said. "A Billie Bilton is now the Countess of Clancarty. The Earl has made an idiot of himself and his mother is in despair, as you can well imagine."

"I did not realise that gentlemen actually . . . married actresses," Cassandra said.

"These women are very astute!" her Aunt replied. "They make the men who pursue them so infatuated that they cannot escape from escorting them up the aisle!"

"And you are saying that the Marquis of Charlbury is also . . . interested in these . . . actresses?"

"They do not do much acting—not on the stage at any rate!" Lady Fladbury snapped. "But they are very gay, their faces are painted like a herbaceous border, and their jewels glitter as my old Nurse used to describe it, 'like the devil's eye-balls!'"

She laughed:

"Oh well, do not worry, my dear! There are plenty of other men in the world besides those who are dazzled by the glittering lights in the Strand."

She did not see the expression on her niece's face because Cassandra had turned away, astonished and shocked by what she had heard.

When she had the opportunity she talked to her father, knowing that Sir James would tell her the truth. She only half-believed the gossip which came so easily to her Aunt's lips.

"Aunt Eleanor says that many young men are actually marrying actresses from the Gaiety, Papa. Is not that somewhat . . . unusual?"

Sir James had glanced at her quickly before he replied:

"Certainly not as many as your Aunt makes out. The majority of the men, Cassandra, find it amusing to take actresses out to supper and give them presents."

He paused to continue as if he sought for words.

"A man disports himself in the company of these ladies with a freedom which would not be permitted by any Chaperon and certainly not by any jealous husband."

"Are they very . . . pretty?" Cassandra asked.

"Extremely!" Sir James replied. "And they are easy-going, which young men find attractive in contrast to the stiff formality of more respectable occasions."

He spoke lightly and then as if he realised why Cassandra was questioning him, he said with a perception which surprised her:

"Have you been hearing stories about Varro Charlbury?"

Cassandra did not reply, and after a moment he said:

"I thought you might have. A young man, my dearest, has to sow his wild oats. In most cases he makes a better husband because of it."

"But . . . supposing he falls . . . in love?" Cassandra asked in a low voice.

"The word 'love'," he said after a moment, "reflects a multitude of emotions. What a man feels for an attractive woman of the type of whom we have just been speaking, is not really love, but desire."

He watched Cassandra's face, and went on:

"It gets dolled up in a great many pretty words, but he wants only to be amused by these women, but always to feel free, untrammelled, but unless he is very stupid, he has no wish to spend the rest of his life with a lovely face that has nothing behind it."

"Aunt Eleanor was saying . . ."

"Your Aunt is exaggerating a few isolated instances where men have married what are known as 'Gaiety Girls' thinking that what they were doing was worth the cost."

Sir James paused a moment before he went on:

"They pay a very high penalty for what you call 'falling in love.' A man who is in the Army must leave his Regiment. If he is in the Diplomatic Corps or in Politics, the same thing applies. His wife will not be accepted in most instances by his mother or by any of his relatives, and even if his men-friends visit him, their wives will refuse any invitation."

Cassandra gave a little sigh.

"It seems unfair."

"Society has to have rules, and the rules where a man marries a woman beneath his station, or one who is notorious because she is an actess or has been divorced, are very, very stringent."

Sir James looked at Cassandra's serious face and added:

"Do not worry over the tales you may hear about Charlbury. I am convinced it is all a passing phase, and when he marries he will settle down and be an extremely respectable and respected Duke."

But things had not quite worked out the way Sir James had expected.

When the new Duke of Alchester had not suggested after his father's death, that he should make his postponed visit to The Towers, Cassandra contrived in one way or another to make enquiries about him.

She had found, as she had anticipated, that he was incessantly in the company of the Gaiety Girls or of other actresses.

"Alchester is known as 'The Merry Marquis,'" one of Cassandra's hunting acquaintances told her. "Have you never met him?"

"No," Cassandra answered. "I was only interested because, as you know, Papa and the old Duke did a lot of racing together, and I was just wondering if the new holder of the title had kept up the stable."

"If he has, I expect he will soon have to sell up," her friend replied.

"Why?" Cassandra enquired.

"I believe he is badly dipped."

'If this was so,' Cassandra asked herself, 'why then did not the new Duke of Alchester fall back on the arrangements which had been made before his father's death and push ahead with the marriage which would bring him, through his wife, an enormous fortune?'

She could find only one reasonable explanation.

It was that, despite everything her father might say, the Duke was in love and had no wish to make an arranged marriage.

By the time the winter of 1885 had come and there was no word from him, she was convinced that her father's plans had finally and completely gone astray and that they were unlikely to hear any more from the Duke.

But Sir James was optimistic.

"There could be no question of your being married while Alchester is in deep mourning," he said. "He will wait the conventional year. Then I am sure we shall take up the negotiations where they were left off."

'I will not be treated in such a manner!' Cassandra told herself, although she did not say the words aloud to her father.

Every month that passed strengthened her determination. She would not marry a man whose heart was given elsewhere, and who wanted her for one reason and one reason only, that she was rich!

She saw now how childish her expectation had been that because she was pretty he would fall in love with her.

She might have far more brains and certainly be far more cultured than the women with whom he associated in London, but that was not to say that he would prefer such qualities.

She took to studying the photographs published of the actresses who were beguiling London audiences.

It was hard not to see that they certainly looked far more attractive and indeed more amusing than the stiff portraits of the society girls with whom they competed for the gentlemen's affections.

There were exceptions of course, if one compared them with the beautiful young Lady Warwick or the goddess-like Countess of Dudley.

'But who,' Cassandra asked herself, 'looks as attractive as Nelly Farran of whom the theatre critics say, "The Gaiety without Nelly is unthinkable," or Connie Gilchrist who has found fame with a skipping rope?'

Instead of cutting out from the newspapers pictures of the Duke of Alchester, Cassandra began to collect reproductions of the photographic beauties.

Photographs of them filled the shop-windows and were in many of the illustrated papers.

There had been loud criticism about one of the poses assumed by Maud Branscombe who was the first of the photographic beauties. She had figured in a study which portrayed "The Rock of Ages."

"Can you imagine that woman daring to display herself clinging to the Cross?" Aunt Eleanor had asked. "I cannot think why the Bishops do not protest about it!"

There were a great many other lovely smiling actresses whose photographs could be bought for less than a shilling.

Cassandra had been amused when her father, protesting about the photographs that had been taken of her in York, produced from a locked drawer in his desk some pictures of Mrs. Langtry.

"This is the sort of pose that I want," he said.

He showed her a picture of "The Jersey Lily" leaning gracefully on a high table, the shadow of her perfect features portrayed upon a plain wall behind her.

"She looks very lovely, Papa," Cassandra agreed.

Her father had shown her several other photographs and then he said:

"There is no need to mention to your mother that I keep these. It is just that I was trying to explain to you the way I want you to appear."

"I quite understand, Papa."

Sir James put the photographs away in his drawer.

"Photography may be a new art," he said, "but that is not going to stop every half-witted fool who can afford a camera thinking he is a photographer."

Turning over the pages of the Album which now covered no less than fourteen years of the Marquis of Charlbury's life, Cassandra told herself the whole thing was hopeless.

How could she marry a man who was interested in her only because she owned a fortune?

Her father might talk of a *mariage de convenance*. He might say it was usual in society, but there were still a large number of people who married for love, and she wished to be one of them.

She had been thinking about it for a long time—in fact for all the months that her father had been eagerly awaiting a letter from the new Duke. She had felt certain it would not arrive.

She had been wrong!

But she was sure that it had eventually turned up, not because the Duke wanted to see her, but because he had reached the stage where he needed money too desperately to procrastinate any longer.

She stared at an article giving a long description of Alchester Park which had appeared in the *Illustrated London News*.

It was not hard from the description to imagine the splendour of what was one of the most famous houses in England.

Covering several acres of land, the ancestral seat of the Dukes of Alchester, it had been built in the reign of Elizabeth I and had housed at some time or another almost every reigning Monarch.

It was magnificent, it was splendid, a little over-powering, and yet Cassandra could understand it was a suitable back-ground for the young man of whom the newspapers had written such glowing accounts even when he was a mere boy.

She turned the pages of the Album again. His face looked out at her from every one.

He was not so thin and so sharp-featured as he had been when he captained the Eton Eleven, but his hair still grew back in a straight line from his forehead.

Even in the rather harsh photograph sketches which were the nearest the illustrated papers could get to reproducing photographs, his eyes still seemed to hold that curious searching look she had noticed when she first saw him.

She had loved her memories of him, she had loved every scrap of information she could glean about him. But now she realised she no longer wanted to marry him.

Cassandra gave a little sigh.

'I would rather marry a man for whom I had no feelings at all,' she told herself.

That was indeed true.

It might be unpleasant, even a little frightening, to marry someone she hardly knew and for whom she had no affection, but to marry someone with whom she thought herself in love would be sheer unmitigating hell if he had no feeling for her except one of duty.

It would be his duty to touch her . . . it would be his duty to kiss her . . . it would be his duty to make love to her . . . to give her children . . .

Cassandra, like all her contemporaries, was very innocent and was not quite certain what that entailed. But she knew it must be something close and intimate.

"Mama, why do people who sleep in the same bed have babies?" she had asked Lady Alice once, when she was very young.

Lady Alice had hesitated before she replied:

"When you are married, Cassandra, your husband will explain such things to you."

Cassandra would have asked again, but sometimes she puzzled over it.

Now she knew she could not sleep in the same bed with a man she loved, as she loved the Marquis, but who did not love her.

"I couldn't bear it!" she said aloud.

She closed the Albums with a bang and put them back in the bottom drawer of her bureau.

Then she drew from the same secret drawer where she hid the key another book bound with leather, and started to write.

Ever since she had been quite young, Sir James had encouraged his daughter to keep a diary.

"You are growing up," he had said, "in a world of change—a world where everything will be very different from what we knew in the past. There are new inventions and new discoveries every day and new thoughts which should be recorded."

He smiled at Cassandra.

"You will also meet new people and have many contacts with

those who are famous. Put it all down. If nothing else, you will have the history of your own life to read when you are old. I have always regretted more than I can possibly say that I never recorded mine."

Obediently, because she always did as her father wished her to do, Cassandra kept her diary.

She wrote in it every evening before she went to bed, until there were already a number of volumes locked away, while the current book was kept at hand in her secret drawer.

She showed it to no-one, not even to her father, although occasionally when something happened which she had anticipated she would read him extracts.

Then he would admire her perspicacity and the fact that what she had expected had occurred, almost exactly as she had predicted.

Cassandra wrote now for only a short time, then put the book back in the secret drawer and shut it. Moving from her Sitting-Room she went into her bed-room.

As she walked across the thick carpet to the mirror over her dressing-table, she stared at her own reflection but she was thinking of something very different.

"I must see him first," she said aloud. "I want to be sure that I am doing the right thing before I upset Papa."

As if her thoughts moved from her inward preoccupation to her visual appearance, she looked critically at herself.

Her red-gold hair loosened by Hannah had been brushed until every strand, shining vividly in the lights of the dressing-table, seemed to dance tempestuously over her head.

Her blue eyes in vivid contrast stared back at her from between their long dark lashes.

"It is most unfair!" one of Cassandra's friends had exclaimed petulantly. "I spend hours trying to think how I can darken my eye-lashes without Mama being aware of it, and yours are as black as ink."

"They are quite natural, I assure you," Cassandra said laughingly.

"I am aware of that," her friend had replied. "That's just what makes it so unfair! If your white skin, your dark eye-lashes and your red hair owed their appearance to artifice, they would be easier to bear. As it is, Cassandra, you look deliciously, flamboyantly theatrical, without making any effort to do so."

Cassandra could hear the touch of envy in her friend's voice, but now she remembered the words.

"Flamboyantly theatrical!"

'It is true,' she thought and knew it was the same criticism which the older generation levelled against her.

"She is pretty, very pretty," she had heard one Dowager say disagreeably, "but far too theatrical for my taste!"

"Flamboyantly theatrical!"

Cassandra had often repeated the words to herself, and because she was given to telling herself stories and imagining situations which intrigued her just before she went to sleep, she had invented one in which she had become a Gaiety Girl.

Losing all her money, she had gone to London and approached George Edwards with a request that she might be in the chorus.

"You are too pretty for that, my dear," he would reply. "I will give you a part, and let us see if the audience will appreciate you as enthusiastically as the 'Stage-door Johnnies.' "

Of course in Cassandra's imagination, she had been a success over-night.

She had been applauded until the Gaiety Theatre had shaken with the noise of it, and there had been a queue of ardent admirers in their top hats, white ties and tails waiting to take her out to supper.

And naturally in her dreams the one upon whom she had bestowed her favour was the Duke of Alchester.

'A child's imagination,' she had told herself during the last six months, when despite every resolution the dream had returned to her.

Why should she not compete with the Gaiety Girls? Why should they have all the fun and collect all the men? Or was she worrying about only one man in particular?

There were a million questions which presented themselves and to which she could find no answer.

Now she knew that in some subtle and insidious way her adolescent dreams had become so much a part of her thinking that they were assuming reality.

It was mad! It was crazy! It was a recklessness that would excel anything she had ever done before, and yet she was determined to meet the Duke on his own ground.

She would see him as he was when he was not pretending, when he was not putting on an act for her father's benefit and for hers.

'I have to do it,' she told her own reflection in the mirror. 'I must do it! I cannot go on allowing Papa to live in a Fool's Paradise, thinking that I shall agree to his plans when I have no intention of doing so.'

She had been so sure ever since Christmas that the Duke would not write, and that sooner or later Sir James would have to realise that for once in his life he had lost a race.

It was just her father's proverbial luck, Cassandra thought, that now his horse should romp home at the last moment. It was the sort of thing that always happened to Sir James!

'But this time,' she told herself bitterly, 'there is going to be no gold cup for the winner.'

She walked across her bed-room restlessly, knowing it would be impossible for her to go to bed and sleep until everything was settled in her mind.

'Supposing,' her brain said to her, 'when you see the Duke you fall crazily in love with him—more in love than you have ever been?'

'I still will not marry him if he cares for someone else,' Cassandra answered.

Even as she spoke the words beneath her breath she wondered if they were true.

Would she be strong enough to refuse to marry the man she loved, to turn away from him, even if he was willing to marry her, because she could not endure the humiliation of loving where she was not loved?

'How could I be fool enough to think he would come to care for me in time?'

She knew she had more pride than that.

If she was convinced in her mind that he really loved someone else then she would be strong enough to say "No."

'I shall never be sure whether he is telling me the truth or not unless I see him when he is off his guard,' Cassandra said to herself.

She had in fact thought this all out quite a long time ago, and whilst she dismissed it as sheer nonsense, she knew that like her father she was merely planning ahead. All she had to do now was to translate her thoughts into action.

She would go to London. She had already decided that. And it was a genuine excuse for her to wish to buy clothes.

Somehow she must meet the Duke, not as Cassandra Sherburn, but as an actress, as the type of woman in whom he was interested.

She would be gay, amusing, sparkling with a *joie de vivre* which he could not find among simpering young girls or even the sophisticated society women who sought his company because he was the bearer of a noble title.

Almost like a puzzle, the pieces fell into place, making a complete picture that Cassandra could look at and know that, in its own way, it was faultless.

She had already told herself a long time ago that Lily Langtry would be a passport to the glittering world she was determined to enter.

To Cassandra her father's friendship with the Jersey Lily implied only a discreet flirtation. She had no awareness of physical passion, which had never intruded upon her sheltered life.

She thought she understood that her father, so handsome, so attractive to women and so masculine, must find it hard at times, to be tied to her injured mother.

He would in consequence occasionally escape from the conventional role he played to perfection to enjoy himself in London, to take a pretty woman out to supper and dance with her, as her poor mother could never dance again.

Sir James's love affairs never encroached upon his home.

There were numerous women in the County who pursued him quite shamelessly. He flattered them and paid them compliments, but he made quite certain that as far as he was concerned that was the beginning and the end of their association.

It would have violated his principles to go any further.

In Yorkshire he was the devoted husband, a man of integrity and responsibility, who had built up an impregnable position of authority in the County and was respected by all who knew him.

What he did in London was in fact nobody's business.

On his periodic journeys which involved attending race meetings and Tattersall's Sales, buying pictures and furniture, there were evenings when Sir James was certainly not dining in Park Lane with his Step-sister, nor was he at the Banquets, Dinner Parties or the Royal occasions graced by the Prince of Wales, to which he was invited.

If on his return home there was a flood of tinted envelopes, jauntily perfumed, and impetuous telegrams, neither Lady Alice nor Cassandra was aware of them.

But sometimes when her father was away, Cassandra thought her mother seemed a little more restless, and very occasionally she would protest against the fate which kept her tied to a wheel-chair.

At other times Lady Alice never complained. Never in front of her husband by word or deed did she ever draw attention to her helplessness or invite his sympathy.

Instead she made herself so attractive that when people stayed in the house or were entertained at The Towers, they would often say to Cassandra afterwards:

"You know, I keep forgetting that your mother is confined to a wheel-chair. She is so unbelievably brave and never makes anyone embarrassed by referring to it, that I always think of her as living quite a normal life."

"My father and I feel like that too," Cassandra would reply, and it had in fact been the truth.

But there was no disguising the unutterable gladness on Lady Alice's face when Sir James returned from London! Her arms would go out to him with a cry of welcome which to Cassandra was more moving and revealing than any words.

"Have you missed me, my darling?" Cassandra heard her father say once as he bent to put his arms around his wife.

"You know that every moment when we are apart seems like an eternity of emptiness," Lady Alice replied.

Cassandra had felt the tears come into her eyes as she recognised the throb of anguish in her mother's voice.

'That is love!' she told herself now. 'Love is when one can sacrifice one's own feelings so that the other person shall be happy! At the same time, Mama knows that Papa loves her with all his heart.'

It would be different where she and the Duke were concerned: he would have no love for her, only a sense of duty.

"I cannot bear it! I cannot bear it!" she said aloud again.

She decided that if her plan failed, if she learnt that the Duke's heart belonged elsewhere, then she would brave her father's anger and would refuse categorically to marry him, whatever the consequences.

Cassandra took off her silk wrapper and got into bed.

"I will give him a fair chance," she said aloud. "In fact he shall have more than a chance. I am giving myself a handicap in my efforts to be sporting about it!"

She tried to smile at the racing jargon but failed.

Instead she buried her face in the pillow and tried to think, not of the Duke of Alchester, but the part she must play in attempting to deceive him.

In the train to London Cassandra went over her plans a dozen times, and it seemed as if the wheels of the train sounded an accompaniment to what she was thinking.

"It is crazy—it is crazy—it is crazy!" the wheels were saying.

Cassandra had known it was crazy when she awoke in the morning and having dressed, had gone first to her mother to receive last minute instructions about taking good care of herself.

"Buy the loveliest gowns you can find, darling," her mother said. "I am sure Bond Street will be full of delectable confections!"

"I will certainly try to find some dresses you will like," Cassandra announced.

"But come back as soon as you can," Lady Alice admonished.

"I promise I will do that," Cassandra answered. "A little of Aunt Eleanor's gossip goes a very long way!"

Lady Alice laughed.

"I should not tell her the Duke is coming to stay. You know she can never keep a secret."

"I never tell Aunt Eleanor anything that I do not wish to be known all around Mayfair within the next half an hour," Cassandra laughed.

On the door-step she put her arms around her father's neck.

"I wish you were coming with me, Papa," she said. "But you know if you did I should never get anything done. Without you I shall concentrate on spending a large amount of your money."

"You have only to write a cheque on Coutts Bank and they will let you have everything you require," Sir James said. "You have enough with you now?"

"More than enough."

Cassandra kissed him again and got into the closed carriage where Hannah was already seated, stiff and still somewhat disagreeable about having to pack in such a hurry.

The horses set off and Cassandra waved to her father until a turn of the drive took them out of sight of the house.

Then she leaned back in the carriage.

"Hannah," she said, "we are off on a great adventure."

The maid looked at her suspiciously.

"What do you mean by that, Miss Cassandra?"

"You are going to help me to do something quite outrageous," Cassandra answered.

"I'm going to do nothing of the sort," Hannah said stiffly. "If you're up to any of your tricks, Miss Cassandra, I'm going back to Her Ladyship at this very moment."

Cassandra laughed.

"Oh, Hannah, I love to tease you! You always rise to any bait I cast under your nose. What I am going to do will not be too shocking, but I need your help."

"I'm not doing anything of which Her Ladyship would not approve," Hannah said stoutly.

But Cassandra knew that she could rely on her to help her as she had always done in other escapades however reprehensible.

It was a long, rather tiring journey to London, but Cassandra did not notice either the landscape speeding past them or that the hours seemed long drawn out.

She was planning, scheming, working out every detail of what she intended to do.

Her father had often said it was a pity she had not been a boy, and because he had no son he used to talk to her of his business schemes and developments.

He often tried out on her new ideas before he put them to a Board of Directors, or sounded her to find out whether a new approach to a difficult problem would get the response he intended.

Cassandra learned from him the importance of every tiny detail, when something new was to be put into operation.

"It is always the weakest link in the chain which can prove disastrous," was one of her father's favourite remarks.

Cassandra knew now that in her present scheming the weakest link in the chain would be the risk of exposure.

Hannah thought she was very quiet but said nothing. She did, however, look anxiously at her young mistress. She had been used to her chatter and was finding this serious mood almost frightening.

But Cassandra was smiling when finally they arrived at Sir James's house in Park Lane, where the bow windows on the ground and first floors overlooked the green trees of Hyde Park.

The residence was the acme of comfort, Sir James having even installed the new incandescent electric light which was the last word in sensational novelty, and a telephone, the first Exchange having been opened in London in 1879.

Lady Fladbury had in her youth been a pretty girl. She had however grown stout and heavy in her old age, and at sixty found it impossible to move quickly.

She was ten years older than her Step-brother but was devoted to him, and she had a real affection for Cassandra.

"I had been wondering when you would visit me again," she said when her niece appeared, "and I cannot tell you how delighted I was when I received your father's telegram this morning."

"It is delightful to see you, Aunt Eleanor. I have come to London to buy some new clothes. I have also a number of social engagements, so I shall not be a trouble to you."

"You are never that," Lady Fladbury replied. "At the same time, I was wondering if I should cancel the Bridge party I have arranged for tomorrow night."

"No, please," Cassandra begged, "do not cancel anything, Aunt Eleanor. I am practically booked up for the whole of the time I am here. In fact I was half-afraid you might feel offended that I can spend so little time with you."

"No, of course not. All I want is for you to enjoy yourself," her Aunt replied.

Cassandra sipped the hot chocolate which the Butler had set down by her side.

"Tell me all the gossip, Aunt Eleanor," she begged. "You know as well as I do that living in the wilds of Yorkshire we never hear any scandal until it is out of date."

Lady Fladbury laughed.

"I cannot believe that," she said, "but there are quite a lot of amusing incidents which are the *on-dit* of the moment."

She chattered away about a number of their acquaintances.

"To whom is the Prince of Wales attached now?" Cassandra asked.

"Far too many lovely women for me to enumerate," Lady Fladbury replied. "But one thing is very certain; since Mrs. Langtry, His Royal Highness's lady friends, even if they are actresses, are accepted in some sections of society."

Cassandra laughed.

"A crown can work marvels! But I see no reason why an actress should be treated as a pariah!"

Lady Fladbury appeared to be about to reply. Then changed what she was about to say to a question.

"What about you, Cassandra? Have you not any plans to marry?"

"Not yet," Cassandra answered. "I have yet to find someone who will capture my heart."

"It surprises me that James has no-one in mind for you," her Aunt said reflectively. "He always used to talk when you were a child as if he expected you to marry at least a Prince, and yet here you are over twenty and still a spinster."

"But not quite an old maid," Cassandra protested.

"I was wondering the other day who would suit you," Lady Fladbury remarked, "and I have quite a long list of eligible young men who would welcome a pretty, intelligent and of course wealthy young wife."

As Cassandra made no comment, she continued:

"I thought your father would be certain to bring you to London for the Season. He has not asked me to apply to Buckingham Palace that I might present you, so I assume he has done so himself."

"I expect so," Cassandra said indifferently. "The last Drawing-Room does not take place until the end of May. That gives us plenty of time."

"If you are to be presented, your father surely would have told you so."

"Perhaps he has not received an answer," Cassandra replied. "I feel I am too old to be a *débutante*."

"Nonsense!" Lady Fladbury exclaimed. "You will have to be presented sooner or later. It looks as if it will have to be on your marriage."

"When I find a husband!"

Cassandra hesitated a moment and then she said:

"Perhaps, as you told me some time ago, all the eligible bachelors have been caught by the Gaiety Girls. Are there any more heart throbs among the aristocracy?"

"Quite a number," Lady Fladbury replied. "There is a joke going around that the Duke of Beaufort, who is a Knight of the Garter, was asked by an inquisitive Frenchman what the letters 'K.G.' stood for after his name, and he answered 'Connie Gilchrist'."

Cassandra laughed.

"Are there many noblemen among the Stage-door Johnnies?"

"Too many of them for me to tell you about them all," her Aunt replied.

Cassandra took a deep breath. She realised she would have to risk being more direct to elicit the information she really wanted.

"What about the son of Papa's great racing friend, the Duke of Alchester?" She tried to make her voice sound casual. "Is the young Duke's name connected with anyone in particular?"

"During the Winter he was always with an actress," her Aunt replied. "I cannot remember her name. Betty somebody. But I do not think it was serious. Nevertheless there is no doubt he has a passion for Gaiety Girls. Lady Lowry was saying only last week that he refuses all invitations to any of the respectable parties."

"Do you think he will marry someone on the stage?" Cassandra asked.

"I should not be surprised," her Aunt answered. "Lady Lowry tells us that the men who are infatuated with these painted creatures are too stage-struck to be quite sane!"

"Perhaps that is the . . . explanation," Cassandra murmured despondently.

CHAPTER THREE

Cassandra woke early the following morning and, realising she had an hour before Hannah would come and call her, she rose to draw back the curtains in her bed-room.

She then took from the drawer in which she had placed it the night before the letter her father had given her addressed to Mrs. Langtry.

She looked at the envelope, then deliberately opened it.

Sir James had written in his strong, upright, hand-writing:

"Most Exquisite Lily,

I am so thrilled, as are all those who love you, by the huge success you have achieved on both sides of the Atlantic. I saw you in 'Peril' and thought you were not only brilliant but looking, if possible, more beautiful than ever.

This is to introduce my daughter, of whom I am very proud. Like so many other people she is longing to meet the most lovely woman in the world. I know you will be sweet to her, Lily, and I am grateful, as I have always been grateful to you for your kindness.

At your feet—as ever,
My Love,
James."

Cassandra read it through carefully. She thought it was very gushing, but she supposed that someone like Mrs. Langtry would expect a man to be effusive.

Taking a sheet of engraved paper which she had brought with her from The Towers, she started to copy her father's hand-writing.

She had done it before to amuse herself.

"You write so much better than anyone I have ever known,

Papa," she had said. "At the same time your writing is so clear and distinctive it would be easy for a forger to defraud you."

"Perhaps he would not be as skilful as you," Sir James had laughed, "but anyway I will be careful that you do not bankrupt me!"

Now Cassandra found that after a few efforts it would have been impossible for anyone who was not an expert to detect that the letter she had written had not been inscribed by Sir James himself.

She copied exactly the first part of his letter and then, where he had started: "This is to introduce . . ." she wrote instead:

"This is to introduce Miss Sandra Standish, a young actress who is the daughter of an old friend, and to ask you if, with your usual generosity, you would grant her a quite simple request. You are someone whom she worships from afar, but apart from the great honour of meeting you she is very anxious for an introduction to the young Duke of Alchester.

It is something as you know, I could easily do myself but unfortunately I cannot for the moment find time to visit London. So please, dearest Lily, help Miss Standish and when we next meet I shall once again be in your debt."

Cassandra finished the letter as her father had done and re-wrote the envelope. She tore into small pieces her father's letter and several mistakes she had made in her first efforts at copying it.

Rising to her feet she put the letter away. Then an idea struck her.

She crossed the room to the dressing-table and took from the bottom drawer the jewel-case with which she always travelled and which Hannah never let out of her hand.

It held a great deal of jewellery for someone so young, but Sir James liked his women to glitter, and both Cassandra and her mother received at Christmas and on their birthdays fabulous gems.

From the bottom of the case, Cassandra drew out a leather box which contained, reposing on a velvet lining, a large diamond star.

It was one of the few presents her father had given her which she had thought did not measure up to his usual exquisite taste. There was something a little garish and ornate about it.

The diamonds were too large and the setting not as delicate as the presents he usually chose, but she was aware that it was a valuable piece.

She thought as she looked at it that it would be a very suitable present for someone like Mrs. Langtry.

Cassandra had been surprised at the number and value of Mrs. Langtry's jewels, of which the papers gave long and elaborate descriptions every time she appeared.

The story of her climb to fame when she had appeared in London with her husband, so poor that she had only one black dress, had been reiterated over and over again, just as the Prince of Wales's infatuation had lost nothing in the telling, even to those who lived as far away as Yorkshire.

What was inexplicable was the thousands of pounds' worth of jewels Mrs. Langtry suddenly acquired, despite the fact that she was so poor she had to earn money by going on the stage.

'But of course, since she is so beautiful, people want to give her presents,' Cassandra told herself and the explanation seemed simple.

Cassandra thought it likely, because he rather enjoyed giving presents, that her father had contributed to the diamonds which had astounded America and even in England were referred to constantly in every newspaper.

She shut the box which contained the star, set it down on the writing-table, and closing her own jewel-case replaced it in the drawer.

She opened the letter which she had already sealed and added a postscript:

"To me you have always been the most glittering star in the Universe."

Once again Cassandra wrote the envelope and put the letter and the jewel box in a drawer of the writing-table which she locked.

When Hannah came to call her mistress she found her already half-dressed.

"Why didn't you ring the bell, Miss Cassandra?" Hannah enquired.

"I thought you might be having your breakfast," Cassandra answered, "and I did not wish to disturb you because we are going out as soon as you can be ready."

"At this hour of the morning?" Hannah asked in surprise.

"I have a lot to do," Cassandra answered. "I am sure, Hannah, you do not wish to stay in London any longer than is necessary."

She knew this was the best way of getting Hannah to do what

she wanted because the maid hated Sir James's town house and always longed to be back at The Towers.

It was however two hours later before Cassandra had managed to have her breakfast and leave her Aunt without appearing rude.

Lady Fladbury had a whole repertoire of gossip to relate about friends, and an endless flow of tittle-tattle about the Socialites who filled the newspapers; so that Cassandra could hardly get a word in.

She wished to pick her Aunt's brains without appearing to do so, and finally she managed to say:

"I would like to visit the theatre whilst I am in London. What is Mrs. Langtry's new play like?"

"Rather amusing!" Lady Fladbury replied. "It is a comedy-drama called 'Enemies.' Another of Coghlan's adaptions from the French."

"Is it exciting?" Cassandra enquired.

"The second act concludes with murder by strangulation of a country girl in a fit of passion by a deaf and dumb idiot," Lady Fladbury answered, "if that makes you laugh!"

Cassandra smiled as her Aunt went on:

"I have to admit that Mrs. Langtry acted quite well. Of course she was extremely refined and lady-like—that goes without saying—but everyone says it is the best part she has played."

"I would like to see it," Cassandra said.

"Of course the Prince of Wales was at the opening night," Lady Fladbury continued, hardly pausing for breath.

"I expect Mrs. Langtry's clothes are very beautiful," Cassandra hazarded.

"Of course!" Lady Fladbury answered. "Since she does not pay for them, she can naturally afford the best."

"I suppose the theatre management thinks the expense a good advertisement," Cassandra remarked. "But where does she buy them?"

"Most of her clothes come from Worth or Doucet in Paris, but Redfern of Conduit Street, where the Princess of Wales shops, makes some of them."

"I have often been to Redfern," Cassandra murmured, but her Aunt was not listening.

"Have you heard the story that Alfred de Rothschild said he would give her a dress from Doucet, and Mrs. Langtry ordered an extra petticoat with it? When the bill came he sent it on to her, saying he had offered her one dress but no more."

Cassandra laughed. She did not like to show her ignorance by revealing that she thought it very strange that Mrs. Langtry should allow a man to give her a gown.

"She must be the envy of every other leading lady," she remarked. "Where do they purchase their gowns?"

"In ordinary and much cheaper shops," Lady Fladbury replied, "and you may be quite sure they resent it. At the same time, I am told that Chasemore has done a wonderful job for George Edwards at the Gaiety. I have not seen the new show, but it caused a lot of comment that he gave them the chance to dress his new production."

Cassandra had found out what she wished to know.

"I must go, Aunt Eleanor," she said. "I am keeping the horses waiting, and you know how much Papa dislikes my doing that!"

It was an excuse to which there was no reply, and Cassandra got away while she could to find Hannah waiting for her in the hall.

Cassandra gave the footman an address and they set off down Piccadilly.

It was a cold, blustery day, and she was glad of the warmth from her fur-trimmed jacket.

"Where are we going, Miss Cassandra?" Hannah enquired.

"Shopping," Cassandra answered, "and do not be surprised, Hannah, at anything I buy. This is the beginning of the adventure about which I warned you."

In spite of the warning, however, Hannah was extremely surprised and said so in no uncertain terms when during the morning Cassandra purchased clothes of which the maid told her a dozen times her mother would not approve.

"You must have gone out of your mind, Miss Cassandra!" she said in horrified tones when the *vendeuse* had left the Dressing-Room to fetch a seamstress to alter one of the gowns.

There was no doubt the dress Cassandra was trying on was very different from the beautiful gowns she had previously worn.

They had been elaborate and many of them had had a decided Parisian chic about them. But what she was wearing now was glitteringly spectacular and accentuated her flamboyant red hair and dark-fringed eyes. It was also very theatrical.

"For goodness' sake, Miss Cassandra, why are you wasting your money on this trash?" Hannah asked.

"I have my reasons," Cassandra answered enigmatically. "What do I look like, Hannah? Tell me the truth!"

"You look like something off the Music Hall, and what your father would say about you dolled up like some fast hussy from behind the footlights, I don't know."

"Thank you, Hannah, that is exactly what I wanted to hear," Cassandra answered.

She paid no attention to Hannah's protests and went on ordering, to the delight of the saleswoman.

"We made some really attractive gowns for Miss Sylvia Grey," the woman volunteered.

"She is in 'Little Jack Shepherd' at the Gaiety," Cassandra remarked.

"Yes, and one of her gowns, not unlike the one you have on, Madam, was written up in several of the newspapers. But it is Miss Nelly Farran who gets the applause. She reallys pays for dressing, and she herself said she had never worn clothes which made her look better."

The woman recommended a milliner who had provided the bonnets for the leading ladies of 'Little Jack Shepherd,' and Cassandra bought shoes and handbags to match each outfit.

Finally Hannah announced it was long after her luncheon time.

"And you'll be fainting on my hands if you don't have something to eat soon, Miss Cassandra," she said sharply. "Come along, now. You've wasted enough money and a real waste it is too! I can't see you wearing one of those vulgar garments, and that's a fact."

"You will be surprised, Hannah!" Cassandra answered.

She took one of the gowns and an evening wrap with her, and arranged for her other purchases to be delivered if not that evening, first thing the following morning.

Then she stopped the carriage at a shop called Clarksons.

Hannah looked up in disgust and exclaimed:

"Theatrical wig-makers! You're never going to buy a wig, Miss Cassandra! If you do, I'll go straight back to Yorkshire and you'll not stop me."

"No, I want something quite different," Cassandra answered, "and you need not come in with me, Hannah. I can manage quite well by myself."

She went into the shop and found just inside the door there was a counter on which were displayed the grease-paint, lip-salves, powders and paints which were required by actors and actresses.

Such things were not obtainable in any of the shops she usually patronised.

She made several purchases and went back to the carriage.

"I want to know what's going on!" Hannah said. "If you want my help, Miss Cassandra, you'll have to tell me the truth."

Cassandra was as yet unwilling to reveal her secret plans even to Hannah.

She fobbed the maid off with excuses until finally they arrived back at Park Lane.

Lady Fladbury was not particularly interested in what her niece had been doing during the morning. She had more bits of gossip she wished to relate to Cassandra, and she chattered away all through luncheon hardly giving her time to reply.

"Are you never bored, Aunt Eleanor, living here alone most of the time?"

Cassandra could not help thinking that Lady Fladbury must be lonely—otherwise she would not be so vivaciously voluble when she had an audience.

"I have never been happier in my life!" her Aunt replied with all sincerity. "The truth is, Cassandra, I have never in the past had a moment to think about myself. My husband was a very demanding man, and my children, before they grew up and married, were always expecting me to do what they wanted—never what I wanted to do myself."

She laughed.

"It is the lot of all women! Sometimes I remember that someone once said: 'The best thing in life is to be born a widow and an orphan.' I think they were right!"

She smiled and added:

"Of course they meant a wealthy widow and orphan!"

"So you are now in that position," Cassandra remarked.

"I am not wealthy, but, thanks to your father, I am comfortable. I have a great many friends in London and as long as I can sit down at a Bridge table, then there is no more contented woman than I am."

"I am so glad, Aunt Eleanor."

"I suppose if I were a good Chaperon," Lady Fladbury went on, "I should be making enquiries as to why you are so busy, but I am not going to ask any questions."

"Thank you, Aunt Eleanor," Cassandra smiled.

"All I ask is that you do not get me into trouble with your father."

"What the eye does not see, the heart does not grieve over," Cassandra quoted.

Then she rose from the Dining-Room table and kissed her Aunt.

"You have always been very kind to me, Aunt Eleanor, and I am grateful."

"You are up to something, I know that!" Lady Fladbury laughed. "Run along with you! Everyone likes to keep their own secrets. I have three friends waiting for me at a green-baize table who will keep me occupied until it is dinner time."

To Hannah's mystification, Cassandra drove not to the shops but to a House-Agent's just off St. James's Street.

"What are we stopping here for?" the maid enquired.

"You wait in the carriage," Cassandra said and disappeared before Hannah could say any more.

An Agent in a smart frock-coat was suitably impressed by Cassandra's appearance and her expensive fur-trimmed jacket.

"I am looking for a flat or apartment for a friend of mine," she explained. "She is on the stage."

"On the stage, Madam?" the Agent exclaimed in astonishment.

Cassandra knew that he thought it almost inconceivable that someone who looked like her should be connected with a woman in such a disreputable profession.

"She is a leading lady," Cassandra explained sweetly, "and the same type of person as Mrs. Langtry. She therefore wants to live somewhere in the West End so that she will be near the theatre, but it must not be, you understand, in a building with a bad reputation."

"No, of course not!" the Estate Agent said in shocked tones. "But you'll appreciate, Madam, it is not every landlord who'll accept actors and actresses."

"Presumably because they do not always pay their bills," Cassandra said with a little smile. "But let me set your mind at rest. My friend has asked me to put down two months' rent in advance. That should annul any landlord's fears that financially he might be out of pocket."

"Yes, yes of course," the Agent agreed. "It'll make things very much easier."

He opened a large Ledger and looked through it with a little frown on his forehead.

Cassandra was quite certain that he was feeling embarrassed because he had so little to offer.

"You will understand," he said after a moment, "that we do not as a rule keep on our books the type of flat or lodgings which are patronised by your friend's profession."

"I understand," Cassandra said quietly, "but I remember hearing that at one time Mrs. Langtry had a flat in the Albany. Is there nothing available there?"

"I'm afraid not," the Agent replied, "but there's a flat in Bury Street. I don't know whether it would be suitable. The first floor flat was at one time occupied by Miss Kate Vaughan before she married."

"At least she is respectable now!" Cassandra exclaimed. "Her husband, I understand, is the nephew of the Duke of Wellington."

"Yes, Madam," the Agent answered, "and even when she was on the stage, Miss Vaughan would have been acceptable to most landlords."

"I am glad to hear that," Cassandra said. "I would not like my friend to feel uncomfortable when she comes to London or believe that she is unwelcome."

"I'm sure we will find her something which she'll like," the Agent said. "What about this flat in Bury Street?"

"You have the particulars?"

He consulted his Ledger.

"It has two bed-rooms, a sitting-room and a small kitchen."

"That sounds as if it would do," Cassandra said.

"It also was occupied at one time by someone of importance in the theatrical world," the Agent revealed. "And so the furnishings should be to your friend's taste."

"I should like to see the flat," Cassandra replied.

She and Hannah drove in the carriage to Bury Street while the Agent hurried after them on foot.

It was only a short distance and Cassandra stared up at the high building. Then having instructed Hannah to say nothing in front of the man, they climbed the staircase to the second floor.

Panting a little because he had been obliged to run in an effort to keep up with the horses, the Agent opened the door and ushered them into the flat.

It was with difficulty that Cassandra prevented herself from laughing.

It was in fact more gaudy and more theatrical than she could possibly have imagined.

The furniture was quite substantial but in poor taste. The sofas and chairs were upholstered in a vivid blue brocade and heaped with frilly pink cushions—most of them embroidered with beads or coloured silks.

Pictures of every sort and description smothered the walls, many of them cheap oleographs of Rome and Italy.

There were some photographs of actresses and a few actors. There were half a dozen framed posters and as they all starred a certain well-known Music-Hall personality, it was not difficult to guess the name of the flat's previous occupant.

"Where is the owner?" Cassandra asked the Estate Agent.

"As a matter of fact, Madam, she is in Australia," he replied. "She is on tour, it is her—friend—" he coughed apologetically, "who has asked me to find a tenant while she is away."

The bed-room was even more fantastic than the sitting-room.

Here the curtains were of sugar-pink, and held up at the corners of the palmettes with over-gilt angels.

The brass bed-stead was draped with material of the same colour, hanging from a half-tester decorated with artificial flowers.

There were bows, frills, fringes and tassels everywhere one looked, and the walls were almost completely covered with mirrors.

"The owner must be very fond of her own face," Cassandra remarked innocently.

She did not see the glint of amusement in the Agent's eyes.

"I will take the flat," Cassandra went on and tried not to laugh at Hannah's horrified and disgusted expression.

She paid two months' rent in advance as she had promised, and giving her friend's name as "Miss Standish" she took possession of the key.

A porter informed her that his wife would be willing to clean the flat on an hourly basis.

"Her has to stay longer, Ma'am, if the place is in a mess," he said frankly.

"I understand," Cassandra replied, "and my friend will be quite willing to pay by the hour."

"Will your friend, Madam, be moving in immediately?" the Agent asked.

"She should be arriving from the North this evening," Cassandra replied, "but if not, she will certainly be here tomorrow. I am so grateful to you for finding her somewhere to stay. She has a great dislike of Hotels."

"I quite understand that," the Agent said sympathetically.

He was delighted at having got the flat off his hands. He would never have sunk to putting anything so garish on his books, if the "friend" of the lady who had lived there had not been of social importance.

Cassandra bade him good-bye and then drove back towards Park Lane listening to a storm of protest from Hannah's lips.

"Now what's all this about, Miss Cassandra? I've never seen such a horrible place! It's not fit for someone like yourself even to enter, let alone to be living in!"

"It is for my theatrical friend," Cassandra answered.

"And who might she be?" Hannah asked. "You've never had any friends who are on the stage to my knowledge, and anyway the Master wouldn't allow it. You know that as well as I do."

"Her name is Sandra Standish," Cassandra answered.

"Sandra?" Hannah said suspiciously. "That's what the Master sometimes calls you."

"Yes, I know," Cassandra answered, "and that is why I have used it for my second self. It is difficult to answer to a Christian name you do not remember."

"What are you trying to tell me?" Hannah enquired sternly.

"That I am going to act a part," Cassandra answered. "Do not look so shocked, Hannah, I am not going on the stage. I shall play the part of a young and talented actress."

"An actress!" Hannah exclaimed in tones of horror.

"I only hope I am good enough to get away with it," Cassandra said.

"The only thing you'll get yourself into is a lot of trouble," Hannah said menacingly. "You're not going to stay in that ghastly place?"

"No, but I have to have an address," Cassandra answered, "and you are going to wait there for me, Hannah, in the evening. That is, if anyone takes me out."

"I don't know what's going on," Hannah said angrily. "All I know, Miss Cassandra, is that you're buying yourself a heap of trouble and no good will come of it, you mark my words!"

"I am marking them," Cassandra assured her.

At the same time she prayed that Hannah was wrong and that her plan would not fail.

The Stage-door keeper of The Prince's Theatre looked up in surprise when, at 7:30 P.M., a lady dressed in what seemed to him to be the height of fashion appeared at the glass window behind which he habitually sat.

"What d'you want?" he asked suspiciously.

He was an old man who had been at The Prince's for over twenty-five years and was known amongst the cast as "Old Growler."

"I would like to see Mrs. Langtry."

"Well, you can't," he answered. "She sees no-one until after the performance, and then not many of 'em can get in."

"I am sure she is very popular," the lady replied, "and that is why I wish to see her now."

"I told you. She don't see no-one at this time."

Cassandra put the letter down in front of him and laid on top of it a sovereign.

"Will you tell Mrs. Langtry that I have something very valuable to give her," she said, "and I cannot entrust it to anyone else, not even you."

"Old Growler" stared at the sovereign. There was a greedy look in his eyes.

He was used to tips from the top-hatted gentlemen who called after the performance, but it was not often the feminine sex was so generous.

"I'll see wot I can do," he said at length grudgingly, and pocketed the sovereign with a swiftness which came from long practice.

He picked up the note and Cassandra heard his footsteps echoing on the flagged floor as he went along a narrow passage and disappeared up a winding iron staircase.

She waited thinking that this was the first time she had ever been backstage and realised how unattractive it was. The walls had been written on in pencil and it must have been years since they had been painted.

There was the smell of dirt, dust and grease-paint and it was also extremely cold. Cassandra pulled her velvet wrap closer around her shoulders.

She wished she could have worn one of her furs, but she felt it would have seemed too extravagant for someone who was not a name in the theatre world.

She waited impatiently.

Supposing after all Mrs. Langtry would not see her? She felt quite certain that what she had said about having something valuable to give her would have been repeated by the door-keeper and would have made the lady curious.

After all, Sir James would undoubtedly have been very generous in the past. He always was.

She heard the footsteps of the door-keeper returning long before she saw him and finally he appeared to say gruffly:

"Come this way."

Cassandra, with a little throb of her heart, followed him down the passage.

The place seemed to get even dirtier as she progressed, but when they entered Mrs. Langtry's brilliantly lit Dressing-Room, it was to find it exactly as she had expected it would be.

She had read in one of the newspapers:

"Mrs. Langtry insists on having each Dressing-Room, in whatever theatre she is appearing, arranged as to furniture, etc., as nearly alike as possible. This is one of the first things her Stage-manager attends to on reaching a City. Most of the paraphernalia is carried with her when Mrs. Langtry is on tour."

The Dressing-Room, Cassandra saw, was not large and the most important piece of furniture was the dressing-table which was of white wood heavily enamelled in white.

It was elaborately ornamented with cupids and butterflies and festooned with old rose satin lined with muslin.

The mirror was electro-lighted and there was a tray on the table containing Mrs. Langtry's toilet set. The brush, comb, scent bottle and powder-box were of gold, each engraved with her initials, the monograms being surrounded by a ring of turquoises.

Cassandra only had a quick look at the dressing-table before she saw there were baskets of flowers all round the walls and a cosy sofa decked with cushions of every sort of design.

Then from behind a high painted screen which was pulled across a corner of the room Mrs. Langtry appeared, wearing a blue silk *négligée*.

Cassandra had expected her to be beautiful, but her photographs and pictures certainly did not do her justice.

At thirty-three Lily Langtry was breath-taking.

Her little Greek head and Greek features were so perfectly proportioned as to make one feel that one looked at an exquisite statue.

Her skin was transparent, so white and delicate that one could only stare and believe that every other woman must have a quite different covering to her bones.

As Mrs. Langtry moved towards Cassandra with her hand out-stretched she remembered that when he painted her, Sir John Millais had said:

"To see Lily Langtry walk is as though you saw a beautiful hound set upon its feet."

"How kind of you to bring me a letter from Sir James Sherburn," Mrs. Langtry said and her voice was low, soft and musical.

She smiled at Cassandra and walking to the sofa, settled herself comfortably against the cushions and patted the place beside her.

"Come and sit down, Miss Standish," she said. "You must tell me about yourself, but first I believe you have something for me."

Cassandra held out the jewel box which she had wrapped in tissue paper.

"Sir James said I was to give this into your hands, Mrs. Langtry, and entrust it to no-one else."

It seemed to her as if Mrs. Langtry took the box almost eagerly and, pulling off the tissue paper, opened it.

The large star glittered in the lights from the dressing-table.

"It is charming!" she said and Cassandra felt the words were almost a purr of appreciation.

She took the brooch out of the box, examined it and replaced it on its velvet bed.

"And now," she said with a smile. "I understand you wish me to do something for you. Are you acting in London at the moment?"

"No, I have come South to have singing lessons," Cassandra answered. "I have been promised a part in a Musical play if I can improve my voice, and so I intend to spend a month in London just working with a teacher."

"How very sensible," Mrs. Langtry approved. "And while you are here you are anxious to meet the young Duke of Alchester?"

"I should be very grateful if you could introduce me to him," Cassandra said.

Mrs. Langtry raised her eye-brows and Cassandra saw the curiosity in her eyes.

"Varro is a friend of mine," she said. "Do tell me why you are so anxious to meet him?"

Cassandra dropped her voice.

"I have a message for him from someone who is now . . . dead."

"Then your meeting can be quite easily arranged," Mrs. Langtry assured her. "As a matter of fact, I am going to a party this evening where it is almost certain he will be present. It is being given by Lord Carwen and he will not mind in the least if I take you with me. That is, if you have no other engagement?"

"No, none," Cassandra replied, "although I was hoping to see you act."

"Then that of course is something you must do. I have a friend who always sits in the stage-box. You shall watch the play with him and afterwards we will take you with us to Lord Carwen's party."

"How kind . . . how very kind you are," Cassandra said in heart-felt tones.

She noticed that while Mrs. Langtry was speaking her eyes had flickered over her evening-dress and noted that not only was it new and expensive, but also the diamond brooch she wore pinned to the bodice was real as was the bracelet she wore over her kid gloves.

She could not help feeling that Mrs. Langtry might not have been so kind had she in fact been an impoverished, badly dressed young actress.

Nevertheless, Mrs. Langtry gave another glance at the star-brooch, doubtless appreciating the largeness of the diamonds, before she walked across to her dressing-table to place it in a drawer.

"Have you not to change?" Cassandra asked. "Would you like me to wait in the theatre?"

"No, you cannot go there alone," Mrs. Langtry said. "You must wait for Mr. Gebhard to arrive, and then he will take you to the Box. In the meantime, sit in that chair in the corner and keep very quiet. I have about fifteen minutes to rest before my dresser will begin to get me ready."

The next three-quarters of an hour was to Cassandra one of the most interesting experiences she had ever had.

When Mrs. Langtry rose from the couch where she had lain with closed eyes, her hair-dresser had arrived to arrange her hair, and the dresser to get her elaborate gowns ready for the performance.

Cassandra saw that the mirror was electro-lighted to Mrs. Langtry's own special design, and an ingenious arrangement of colours such as blue, red and amber could be obtained at will.

"This makes it easy," Mrs. Langtry explained, "for me to tell how my gowns will look when I am on the stage."

It was continually reiterated in the Press that Mrs. Langtry wore no make-up, but that, Cassandra saw, was untrue.

She deliberately contrived a very pale appearance by using only the faintest touch of rouge on her cheeks, and a powder which was sold in the shops with her name on it.

She out-lined her eyes, darkened her eye-lashes and eye-brows, and finally used a lip-salve sparingly on her mouth.

Cassandra was particularly interested because in the carriage on the way to the theatre, despite Hannah's horrified protests, she had added a touch of colour to her lips and also used powder on her cheeks.

"Whatever are you doing, Miss Cassandra?" Hannah had exclaimed in a tone of horror. "What will people be thinking of you if they see you painted like an actress."

"I am supposed to be an actress," Cassandra had answered.

"And that's nothing to boast about!" Hannah snapped.

"I have an uneasy suspicion that your sentiments are echoed by the majority of the public," Cassandra answered.

Then she closed her ears to the long impassioned recitation of Hannah's disapproval.

Now she noted how skilfully Mrs. Langtry enhanced her appearance while remaining both lady-like and overwhelmingly beautiful.

Finally, a quarter of an hour before the curtain was due to rise, Mr. Frederick Gebhard arrived.

Cassandra remembered reading that this young American had returned with Mrs. Langtry from New York.

Some of her father's more disreputable papers which she was not supposed to read, such as *The Sporting Times*, known as "The Pink 'Un," had made some pointed remarks concerning the amount of money the man they called a "Boudoir-Carriage Romeo" had spent on Mrs. Langtry.

Freddy Gebhard who had been bowled over by Lily Langtry's beauty the first night they met, was four years younger than she was.

He was the son of a dry goods businessman, who had left him a yearly income of between eighty and ninety thousand dollars.

Tall, clean shaven and elegant, his Fifth Avenue tailors rated him as New York's "Best Dressed Man," but he bought most of his clothes, which were always dark in colour, in London.

Freddy Gebhard had made the headlines by not only giving Lily Langtry his cheque book, but defending her physically against any admirer who tried to force his acquaintance upon her.

He had knocked out a man who had tried to introduce himself to Lily in St. Louis, and he was lionised by the local bloods during the rest of the week.

He had almost as much Press coverage in the American papers as Lily herself, and by the time Gebhard had gone with her on tour in a private railway-car he had built to her design, he was determined to marry her.

The railway-car advertised his infatuation. It was seventy feet long, painted blue, emblazoned with wreaths of golden lilies, encircling the name "Lalee." Brass lilies decorated the roof.

The bath and bathroom fittings were in solid silver.

Lily had returned to England three years earlier in 1883 to try to persuade Mr. Langtry into giving her a divorce but her husband had categorically refused.

She had re-crossed the Atlantic to discover Freddy Gebhard still adored her. He installed her in a luxurious house in West 23rd Street, where they threw riotous parties which were headlined in all the newspapers.

Cassandra thought Freddy Gebhard had a rather weak face. At the same time he was undoubtedly good looking.

He shook her hand politely when they were introduced, but it was obvious that he had eyes only for Mrs. Langtry and was in fact wildly and overwhelmingly in love.

"Lily, my darling, you look more wonderful than I can tell you," he said softly and bent his head to kiss her hand.

'How sad they cannot be married,' was Cassandra's first thought.

Then she thought it strange that a married woman, even if she was an actress, could be on such intimate terms with another man.

Mrs. Langtry appeared, however, to be concerned only with her own appearance and her audience which awaited her in the theatre.

"Every seat is sold out!" Freddy announced.

"But of course!" Lily replied. "They told me when I arrived that people have been queueing since twelve o'clock this morning."

She was already wearing the dress in which she was to appear in the first act.

Cassandra noticed how tightly it was moulded over her bosom and how the bustle at the back accentuated her tiny waist.

"You are so lovely," she said impulsively. "It is not surprising everyone wants to see you."

Mrs. Langtry smiled.

"Thank you," she said with the ease of a woman who takes her compliments for granted.

Then turning to Freddy she said:

"Take Miss Standish to the Box, Freddy. She will sit with you during the performance, and then I have promised her we will take her with us to Lord Carwen's party."

"Yes, of course—delighted!" Freddy agreed.

Cassandra felt that he was disappointed that he would not be alone with his adored Lily, and resented the fact that she would accompany them even the short distance from the theatre to where the party was to take place.

"I hope I am not being a nuisance," she said humbly.

She knew even as she spoke that she did not care if she was, for she had every intention of going to the party where there was a chance she would be introduced to the Duke.

"No, of course not," Freddy said politely but with an obvious insincerity.

He kissed both Lily's hands and whispered something in her ear, before he escorted Cassandra down the long draughty passages and through the pass-door, which lay behind the stage, at the side of the auditorium.

An attendant ushered them into the stage-box.

For the first time Cassandra wondered apprehensively if there was anyone in the audience who might recognise her.

It was unlikely. Nevertheless, if any of her friends had come to London from Yorkshire, they would undoubtedly wish to see Mrs. Langtry's play.

Cassandra was well aware of the scandal it would arouse if she were seen alone with a man in the stage-box of a theatre—most of all if she was accompanied by someone as notorious as Freddy Gebhard.

She solved the problem by moving to a seat against the partition so that, while she had the best view of the stage she was almost invisible to the audience.

If Freddy Gebhard thought it strange that she did not wish to make herself conspicuous, he did not say so.

He was only too pleased to take the centre of the Box.

He stood in the front of it looking at the audience, waving to a friend or two in the Stalls, looking up at the Gallery, until finally the people in the cheap seats realised who he was and started to clap.

This was obviously what he was waiting for; for he bowed, waved his hand and was almost childishly elated with his reception.

He sat down and said to Cassandra:

"They are beginning to know me as well over here as they do in New York. I have often said to Lily—we make a splendid pair!"

Cassandra smiled at him.

There was no need for her to say much. He was clearly content with his own appreciation of himself, and once again he bent forward so that the audience could have a good look at him.

Cassandra was glad when the curtain rose.

The play was well-written, thoroughly dramatic and depicted a feud between two older members of a respected aristocratic family and a reconciliation brought about by the love of two younger ones.

In the fourth Act Mrs. Langtry had to go on her knees and plead with her father to abandon his foolish schemes and save the old house.

Here, almost to Cassandra's surprise, Lily Langtry proved herself a quite moving actress and she certainly carried the sympathy of the audience with her.

She was very touching when she cried:

"Help us! Help us! You are our last and only hope. We give up everything—but save, oh save my brother Percy!"

The applause rang out, the women in the audience wiped their eyes and there was curtain call after curtain call.

A great number of bouquets were carried onto the stage. Lily held in her arms one of the yellow roses which Cassandra guessed had been given her by Freddy.

After "God Save the Queen" Freddy hurried Cassandra back through the stage-door and they waited in the Dressing-Room, while Mrs. Langtry changed.

She came from behind the curtains wearing a grey satin evening-gown which made her look like a goddess. There was a necklace of enormous diamonds around her neck and diamonds glittered in her ears and round her wrists.

"Do I look all right?" she asked Freddy.

Cassandra saw him draw in his breath before he answered:

"You are more beautiful every time I look at you!"

"Then let us go to the party," Mrs. Langtry exclaimed gaily. "Everyone who matters in the theatre world will be there and I have no wish for any of them to eclipse me!"

"No-one could do that!" Freddy said.

He kissed her shoulder passionately as if they were alone and Cassandra was not watching and feeling somewhat embarrassed.

She had sent her own carriage with Hannah to the flat she had rented in Bury Street.

"I'm not going to that place," Hannah said angrily.

"Yes, you are!" Cassandra replied, "unless you wish me to come home alone in a hired cab, and goodness knows then what might happen to me!"

There was nothing Hannah could do after that but agree.

"Send the carriage away," Cassandra told her. "We shall have to find a cab, but doubtless there is a night-porter who will get one for us."

She had also told Hannah to wait for half an hour after she had gone into the theatre before driving away. There had always been the chance that Mrs. Langtry would accept the present and make arrangements for her to meet the Duke some other night.

Cassandra could only hope the meeting would not be too long delayed, but it seemed, she thought excitedly, as if everything was falling into place.

It was just luck there was a theatrical party that evening and that Mrs. Langtry had been pleased with the present which she thought had been sent to her by Sir James.

In Freddy Gebhard's comfortable carriage, as they moved down the Strand, Cassandra said to herself:

'This is where my play begins! The curtain is rising and I can only pray that I shall give a convincing performance.'

CHAPTER FOUR

Lord Carwen's house was in Arlington Street and overlooked Green Park.

It was extremely impressive with a porticoed front-door and iron railings dividing the short drive-in from the pavement.

Cassandra entered behind Mrs. Langtry, and as she saw the brilliantly-lit chandeliers and the luxurious furniture which decorated the hall, she wondered a little apprehensively if there would be anyone at the party who would recognise her.

As she followed in the wake of Lily Langtry, she could see them both reflected in huge, gilt-framed mirrors, and she thought it would be difficult for them to remain unnoticed however large or important the party might be.

Mrs. Langtry's grey gown from the front made her look like a Greek goddess and at the back she had a huge bustle supported by a satin bow which formed the small train.

Despite the wealth of diamonds around her neck and glittering in her hair and on her bodice, she looked both dignified and a lady.

Cassandra could not think the same about herself.

Her dress from Chasemore was lovely in its own way, but she knew she would never have dared to wear it as Cassandra Sherburn.

Of vivid green, almost as deep as an emerald, it was fashioned of tulle, ruched round the extremely low neck and over her shoulders.

The colour made her skin look strikingly white, whilst the very tight bodice revealed the curves of her young figure and her very small waist.

Tulle fashioned the enormous bustle even bigger than Mrs. Langtry's—which billowed out behind her, cascading down in frill upon frill to the floor.

But what made the dress different from the type of gown Cassandra would have worn as herself was the fact that the tulle was strewn with tiny silver and green sequins which glittered and shimmered with every move she made.

It was also caught up at one side with an enormous bunch of artificial water lilies, and these too were speckled with sequins which looked at a distance as if they were dew-drops glistening in the light.

It was a gown that a leading lady could have worn for her entrance in the first Act, and would undoubtedly have stimulated a round of applause.

Cassandra had with some difficulty persuaded Hannah to arrange her hair in innumerable curls on top of her head, and amongst them she wore three diamond combs.

She also wore diamond ear-rings which she had been left by her Grandmother, but which on a young girl Sir James had thought too sophisticated.

There was the sound of music and then, just before they reached the Reception-Room, Cassandra had a last glimpse of herself in the mirror and smiled.

Her red lips certainly contributed to the flamboyance of her appearance. She had applied a little more salve to them in the dressing-room while she was waiting for Mrs. Langtry to change after the performance.

Her eyes did not need any additional artifice since her lashes were naturally so long and dark, and because she was excited at what was happening her eyes shone even more brightly than the sequins on her dress or the diamonds in her hair.

"Lily! Shall I say how overjoyed I am to see your beautiful face?" a deep voice exclaimed.

A man of about forty, rather large and overpowering, was raising Mrs. Langtry's hand to his lips.

"I have brought a little friend with me," Mrs. Langtry said. "I hope you do not mind?"

Cassandra felt the man's eyes take in every detail of her face and her sensational gown.

"But of course, I am delighted," Lord Carwen said. "Will you introduce me?"

"Miss Sandra Standish," Mrs. Langtry said. "And this, dear, is your very kind and generous host—Lord Carwen!"

Cassandra made a graceful curtsey.

"I hope Your Lordship will forgive me for coming uninvited to your party," she said with a smile.

"I am prepared to forgive you anything, if you will dance with me later," Lord Carwen replied.

He held out his hand to Freddy Gebhard.

"Delighted to see you, Freddy. I hope my party measures up to some of those which I hear you gave in America."

Cassandra did not listen for Mr. Gebhard's reply.

She was staring round the Ball-Room, her eyes alight with curiosity.

It was a beautiful room with huge chandeliers and decorated with fabulous pictures and very valuable mirrors.

It was in fact the type of room Cassandra had seen often enough in the homes of her father's friends, but it was the occupants on this occasion who were unusual.

The men were all gentlemen, the majority of them of Lord Carwen's age.

Many of them were obviously distinguished and they had an elegance which could be achieved only by an Englishman in evening-dress.

But the women were to Cassandra's eyes quite fantastic!

'It is extraordinary,' she thought, 'to see so many pretty women all together!'

Then she realised it was because, using cosmetics, they looked far prettier and far more attractive than their contemporaries in the social world who dared not employ such means to beautify themselves.

Eyes enlarged with mascara and eye-shadow, very pink and white skins, and laughing red lips made a picture which Cassandra could understand most men would find alluring and desirable.

Their gowns too were fashioned to attract attention.

Never had she seen so much naked flesh, such yards of tulle, so many sequins, or such a profusion of artificial flowers.

The majority of the women wore jewellery which Cassandra could tell at a glance was not real.

Nevertheless, it added to the glamour of their appearance.

She was so amused and interested in everything she saw that she gave a start when she heard Mrs. Langtry say beside her:

"As I expected, I see the Duke of Alchester over there. Let me introduce him, otherwise we may become separated in the crowd and then I should not have been able to keep my promise to you."

Cassandra drew in her breath.

Mrs. Langtry swept ahead of her, and once again she followed in the wake of the grey bustle, moving through the throng of guests who seemed to be talking animatedly at the tops of their voices, or laughing with a kind of wild gaiety which almost shook the chandeliers.

For a moment Cassandra felt that she could not look at the Duke.

She felt a sudden shyness creep over her. She wanted to run away. Then she told herself she was being ridiculous.

This was what she had planned—this was what she had schemed and dreamed about. Now it was up to her! It was certainly not a moment for shyness or embarrassment. She had to convince the Duke that she was a gay, rather pushing young actress.

She had to amuse him . . . to make him notice her!

Mrs. Langtry had stopped, and now Cassandra saw him, the man who had been in her thoughts ever since she was twelve.

He was far better-looking than his pictures suggested. He was no longer the thin, rather cadaverous boy she remembered in his white flannels and Eton-blue cap at Lords.

He was tall, broad-shouldered, and had an almost commanding presence which she had not expected.

She had somehow not imagined that he would have such natural dignity or would have a pride in his bearing which she sensed immediately.

It was obvious even in the grace with which he rose from the chair on which he was sitting to greet Mrs. Langtry.

"I expected to find you here, Varro," Mrs. Langtry said.

"I am honoured that you should think of me," the Duke answered.

As he spoke, Cassandra knew that she remembered his voice. There was some quality in it which she had never heard from anyone else—something she, in particular, found strangely moving.

"You have not been to see me in my new Play," Mrs. Langtry said accusingly.

"I assure you that it is only because I have found it impossible to obtain a seat," the Duke replied.

Cassandra watching him realised that his eyes twinkled as he spoke and when he smiled there was a dimple on the left side of his mouth.

'He is wildly, overwhelmingly attractive,' she told herself, 'much more so than I had imagined! There cannot be a woman in the whole of London who would not try to marry him if he so much as looked in her direction!'

"You should not be so popular!" the Duke was saying to Mrs.

Langtry. "They tell me there have never been such long queues as I see outside The Prince's day after day."

"You should have seen them in America," Freddy Gebhard interposed, who had followed Mrs. Langtry and Cassandra across the room.

"Hello, Freddy!" the Duke exclaimed. "When are you going to find time to come and have a drink with me at White's?"

"The next time that Lily doesn't want me," Freddy Gebhard replied.

"But I always want you," Lily Langtry said softly.

"Then I withdraw my invitation," the Duke said. "Who am I to interfere between two people who obviously enjoy each other's company?"

He spoke quite seriously, but Cassandra could see that his eyes were laughing.

"And now, Varro," Mrs. Langtry said, "I have someone with me who is very anxious to meet you. She has something to tell you which I expect you will find interesting."

She turned towards Cassandra.

"Miss Standish, may I present the Duke of Alchester? Varro—this is Miss Sandra Standish, who I understand, is an extremely talented young woman."

Cassandra put out her hand and, as the Duke took it, she had the strangest feeling that all this had happened before.

She could not explain it to herself. It was as if they were enacting an episode which had taken place, not once, but a dozen times, all down the ages.

"You have something to tell me?" the Duke said raising his eyebrows.

"Yes," Cassandra answered and she was relieved to hear that her voice did not quiver. "But at the moment it would be impossible to make myself heard."

Even as she spoke, the Band which had been playing when they first arrived in the hall, started up again.

It was a waltz and Freddy Gebhard said to Mrs. Langtry:

"This is one of our tunes."

He did not wait for a reply, but put his arm round her and led her on to the centre of the room.

The Duke and Cassandra stood alone, facing each other.

"Will you dance with me first?" he asked.

"I would like that."

She felt herself quiver as he put an arm round her and hoped he would not notice. Then he was swinging her round the floor and she found he was easy to dance with and they seemed to be perfectly matched.

If she had wanted to talk to him, it would have been impossible.

The noise and laughter from the other guests were quite deafening, and the Band played louder than was usual at other parties which Cassandra had attended.

The dance was by no means decorous even for a waltz. It was in fact quite riotous and as it ended Cassandra moved from the floor to the other end of the room which seemed a little less crowded.

"Let us find somewhere where we can sit down," the Duke suggested.

He put his hand under her arm with a lack of formality in which she knew he would not have indulged at a more formal Ball.

He led her out through a door, and she saw there were various Drawing-Rooms and Ante-Rooms leading off the room in which they had been dancing.

There was one which she guessed was a Writing-Room, beautifully decorated in soft colours with French furniture which must have been worth a fortune.

There was a sofa in front of the curtained window, the lights were discreetly low and there was the fragrance of hot-house flowers to scent the atmosphere.

The Duke led Cassandra to the sofa, and when she had seated herself he sat beside her, turning a little sideways so that he would look into her face.

"Who are you?" he asked, "and why have we never met before?"

"Surely that is a very conventional remark for someone like you?" Cassandra replied.

"Why for me in particular?"

"Because you have the reputation of being original, dashing and very intelligent."

"Good Heavens!" The Duke held up his hands in pretended horror. "Who has been telling you such a lot of lies about me?"

"In my profession," Cassandra replied, "they chatter about you almost as much as they do about the productions in which they hope to appear."

"I think you are being rather unkind to me," the Duke said accusingly, but his eyes were twinkling. "Have I done anything to offend you?"

"On the contrary," Cassandra said. "As Mrs. Langtry told you, I was very anxious to meet you."

"Why?"

Cassandra hesitated a moment and then she said:

"For one frivolous reason and one serious one. Which will you have first?"

"The frivolous one!" the Duke replied. "At this sort of party one never wants to be serious."

"Well . . . the frivolous reason is that I have often wondered why someone as gifted as you are should find the theatre more amusing than anything else."

She realised as she spoke she was being deliberately provocative. Yet she knew she had to hold his attention, to make him curious about her, or else she might lose him as quickly as she had found him.

"How do you know that?" he asked.

Cassandra laughed.

"Are you really surprised that I can read?"

"You mean the newspapers! You should never believe all you read in those scurrilous rags."

"Nevertheless, they cannot invent all the things they say about you," Cassandra said. "I read for instance that you attained a First Class Degree at Oxford and that at one time you considered a career in the Diplomatic Service. That must mean that you are able to speak several languages."

"That was a long time ago," the Duke answered. "I suppose I was ambitious once, but then I decided it was all too much trouble."

"I think people are happier when they are working at something which interests them."

"Is that what you find?"

"I am always interested in what I am doing," Cassandra answered truthfully.

"Tell me about yourself."

"What do you want to know?"

"Are you acting at the moment?"

"No, I have come South to London for singing lessons. There is a chance of my getting a good part in a Musical Comedy, but my voice is not yet strong enough and I have to work hard at it for at least a month."

"Who has arranged all this for you?"

It was a question Cassandra had not expected and she had to think for a moment before she replied:

"A . . . friend has given me an introduction to a good teacher."

As soon as she spoke she saw the Duke's eyes glance at the diamonds in her ears and in her hair and she wondered if he thought a man had paid for them.

She felt the blood rising in her cheeks and a little ripple of fear run through her in case the Duke should be shocked.

Then she told herself not to worry: it was what he would expect from anyone in the theatre-world. Had her father not said that men liked giving presents to actresses they took out to supper?

"So you are spending a month in London," the Duke said reflectively. "Will you be very busy all of the time?"

She smiled at him.

"I am always ready to be . . . tempted into playing truant."

"They tell me that is a part I play extremely well," the Duke said. "Will you come to the theatre with me one night?"

"I would enjoy that," Cassandra said simply. "I had not been to a theatre in London for a very long time until tonight when I saw 'Enemies.' "

"What did you think of it?"

"I think Mrs. Langtry was magnificent in the part."

"She is extremely adaptable," the Duke said.

Then, as if Mrs. Langtry did not particularly interest him, he went on:

"Now will you tell me the serious reason why you wanted to meet me?"

Cassandra had her story ready. She had thought it all out coming down to London in the train.

"Do you remember a groom your father once had with the name of 'Abbey?' "

There was a little frown of concentration between the Duke's eyes.

"Do you mean a man who was at Alchester many years ago when I was a child?"

"That would be Abbey," Cassandra replied. "I knew him when he was very old. I used to visit him in the cottage to which he retired."

"Of course, I remember old Abbey!" the Duke exclaimed. "Even when I was a child his face was like a withered walnut. He must have been a hundred when you knew him."

"He was eighty-seven before he died," Cassandra said. "He asked me, just before his last illness to tell you, if we ever met, that he still had the horseshoe that you gave him."

"Good Heavens!" the Duke exclaimed. "I remember the incident well! Abbey was an inveterate gambler. He never had a penny to his name and he was always full of stories of how his horse had been 'pipped at the post.' "

"Yes, I heard them too," Cassandra said with a little smile.

"One day when he was taking me out riding," the Duke went on, "we stopped for a rest and I was running around, as small boys do, and found a discarded horseshoe.

"'Look, Abbey,' I cried, 'I have found a horseshoe.'

"'So you have, Master Varro,' he replied. 'It'll bring you luck.'"

"I remember debating with myself for a moment, because I wanted to take the horseshoe back home to show my father, but then I said:

"'I think you need luck more than I do, Abbey,' and I gave it to him."

"That is exactly the same story that he told me," Cassandra said with a little cry of delight. "The horseshoe stood on his mantelpiece right up to the day of his death. It was in the place of honour and I think it did bring him luck."

"I have not thought of Abbey for years," the Duke said. "I have an idea he went to work for a racehorse owner called Sir James Sherburn. Is that right?"

"He may have," Cassandra said lightly. "When I knew him he was far too old to work. He talked of nothing but horses."

"And what could be a better subject?" the Duke enquired. "Except of course, beautiful women!"

There was no disguising the expression in his eyes.

"I believe you are an acknowledged judge of both," Cassandra answered.

"Again you flatter me," the Duke answered. "Shall I tell you I cannot resist a fine horse or a lovely woman, and you are very lovely, Miss Standish!"

Cassandra could not prevent the blush rising in her cheeks, and for a moment her eye-lashes flickered shyly. Then she forced herself to say:

"Your Grace is obviously also an expert flatterer."

"You say that with a cynical note in your voice which I do not like!" he said accusingly. "How can I convince you that I am sincere? Surely in the North, or wherever you come from, there must be men who have eyes in their heads and are not completely blind?"

"They can see with their eyes," Cassandra answered, "but perhaps they are not quite so glib with their tongues as you gentlemen in the South!"

The Duke threw back his head and laughed.

"You have an answer to everything. Come, let us go and dance and I hope that as you are a stranger to London you do not know many other men here tonight."

"As a matter of fact, I am throwing myself on your mercy," Cassandra answered, "as I do not wish to keep bothering Mrs. Langtry for introductions."

"There is no need for that," the Duke said firmly. "I will look after you, and that is something at which I can assure you, without boasting, I am very proficient!"

The dance-floor was even more crowded than when they had left it, but the Duke skilfully steered them round the room and Cassandra wondered how she had ever enjoyed dancing in the past.

It was something quite different to be held in the Duke's arms; to feel her hand in his and know the tulle trimming her *décolletage* brushed against the satin facing of his evening-coat.

"You dance divinely!" he said. "Do you dance on the stage?"

"I am a better . . . actress," Cassandra replied.

The party was getting even noisier than it had been in the earlier part of the evening, and now as the dance came to an end the Band started up the loud gay music which heralded the Can-Can.

"We will watch this," the Duke said. "It is always amusing."

Cassandra had read in her father's sporting papers of how the Can-Can had startled London some years before.

Brought from Paris by a *troupe* consisting of two men and a girl, who were brothers and sister, they appeared at The Oxford Music Hall, and packed the place night after night.

The Can-Can was considered the very height of impropriety and even *The Sporting Times* had some very scathing things to say about it.

Cassandra did not read this paper bought by her father, because she was interested in the "Seamy" side of London, nor in the broad jokes which she did not understand.

She read it because so often the Duke, as the Marquis of Charlbury, was mentioned in it.

Every few months or so *The Sporting Times* gave a list of what they called "The Young Bloods About Town."

It also referred to the "Mashers" who haunted the stage-door of the Gaiety and were to be found at "the promenades" of all the Music Halls.

Cassandra added cuttings which mentioned the Marquis to her Album, but when she was searching for his name it was impossible not to be interested in the theatre gossip with which she realised he was so closely connected.

The Can-Can was later to lose The Alhambra its licence because of the slim legs and high kicks of a young lady called "Wiry Sal."

Cassandra had often wondered exactly what it was like and now she was to find out!

Quite a number of Lord Carwen's female guests considered they were proficient at the dance which had been denounced even in Paris because it revealed what women wore under their skirts—and what they did not wear!

It was obvious that the ladies of Lord Carwen's party wore extremely frilly and lacy underclothes.

Amid the roars of applause from the Gentlemen guests present, they kicked their legs and went on kicking them round and round the room.

Cheeks became flushed, hair became loosened, but the high kicks went on with more and more frothy underclothes being revealed until, despite every resolution, Cassandra found herself really shocked.

The Duke was looking amused, but he was not cheering and shouting like the other men, who endeavoured to incite the girls to kick their legs even higher and be even more daring than they were already.

She felt she could not go on looking at members of her own sex making such disgusting exhibitions of themselves. She felt as if she too was degraded because she was a woman.

"It is very . . . hot," she murmured and turned away from the dance floor towards a window.

The Duke followed her.

Cassandra stood looking out into the darkness of the Park. She could just see the branches of the trees silhouetted against the sky.

"You have never seen the Can-Can before?" the Duke asked.

"No, no."

"You are surprised? It is not what you expected?"

"No."

"I have the feeling you are shocked," he said, his eyes on Cassandra's averted face.

"It . . . seems somewhat . . . abandoned," she faltered.

"I understand. I do not expect that such extravagances have yet reached the North."

"No."

Behind them the dancers had collapsed into chairs around the Ball-Room and even onto the floor itself, panting and exhausted. Now the Band changed from the exuberant music to a soft, dreamy Waltz.

Cassandra looked at the Duke expecting him to invite her once again onto the floor, when a voice beside her said:

"You promised me a dance, pretty lady!"

She glanced up and saw Lord Carwen standing beside them.

"I hope Varro has been entertaining you," Lord Carwen said, "while I was regretfully too busy to do so."

"He has been very kind," Cassandra murmured.

"And now I must see if I can equal or even excel his kindness," Lord Carwen said.

He drew Cassandra into his arms and they began to dance.

She realised that he was holding her too closely and too tightly. When she tried to move a little further away from him, he merely laughed down at her.

"You are very lovely, Sandra."

She felt herself stiffen at his familiar use of her Christian name, then told herself it was out of character.

"You have a lovely house, My Lord."

"I am not interested in my house, but in the loveliest person in it," he replied. "Lily Langtry tells me you have just come to London. You must allow me to show you some of the amusements."

"Thank you," Cassandra answered, "but I am afraid I shall be very busy with my singing lessons."

Lord Carwen laughed.

"It does not matter whether you sing or not," he said. "You only have to look as you look now and you will fill the theatre for a thousand nights!"

He paused and added:

"That is, if the theatre is really important to you. I can think of more interesting things to do."

"And what could they be?" Cassandra asked without really considering what his answer was likely to be.

"That is something I can explain to you in great detail," Lord Carwen said tightening his arm around her waist.

As he did so Cassandra realised that she disliked him.

It was not only because he was treating her in a familiar manner —that was her own fault; she had invited it upon herself.

But there was something unpleasant about him as a man, and she was a good judge of people.

Even as a child she had seldom been wrong in judging the character or the characteristics of the people who came to The Towers and Sir James had encouraged this perceptiveness.

"How did that man strike you?" he would ask when someone had come to luncheon or for dinner. "What did you think of that fellow?"

Sometimes Cassandra would say:

"He is all right. Rather stupid, I thought."

But occasionally she said:

"Have nothing to do with him, Papa. I am sure he is crooked! There is something about him I mistrust."

Over the years Sir James found she was invariably right.

Once he came to her to say:

"You remember that man you warned me against, who came here about six months ago? His name was Bull."

"Yes, I remember," Cassandra answered. "There was something about him I mistrusted."

"He has just received a sentence of eight years at the Old Bailey for fraud."

Cassandra knew that she was not wrong now. There was something about Lord Carwen which made her involuntarily wince away from him.

"Will you dine with me tomorrow night?" he asked. "I want to talk to you."

There was something in his tone which told her that conversation was not his main objective.

"Thank you, but I have an engagement."

He smiled.

"Are you playing hard-to-get, little Sandra? I assure you I am very persistent, and I know we are going to see a great deal of each other."

"Do you give many parties like this?" she asked in an effort to try and change the conversation.

"I will give any sort of party you wish me to give," Lord Carwen replied. "Ask Varro. He will tell you I am a very agreeable Host, and very generous to those I—like."

The Band stopped playing.

"Thank you for our dance," Cassandra said.

She would have been unable to move away from him because Lord Carwen still kept his hand around her waist, if at that moment some new arrivals had not diverted His Lordship's attention.

Quickly Cassandra hurried away.

She was relieved to find that the Duke had not taken another partner but was standing alone, leaning against a pillar at the far end of the room.

She almost ran towards him.

As if he knew instinctively that she had not enjoyed her dance he said:

"Shall we go and find the Supper-Room? Or better still, shall we slip away and I will give you supper somewhere else?"

Cassandra's eyes looked up into his.

"Could we do that?"

"Why not?" he answered. "Come with me. I know another way of reaching the Hall so that we need not embarrass our Host by bidding him good-bye."

Like two conspirators they slipped out of the Ball-Room and the Duke led Cassandra through several Reception Rooms back to the Hall where guests were still arriving.

"You are not leaving, Varro?" a pretty woman cried putting out her hand towards the Duke.

"I am afraid so."

"How disappointing!"

Two red lips pouted very invitingly.

"I will doubtless be seeing you in the next day or two."

"Come to my Dressing-Room in the interval and have a drink."

"I will," the Duke promised.

Cassandra stood on one side feeling for the moment forgotten.

Yet she could understand why the Duke found this gay, informal life he had chosen amusing.

So much more so than the type of entertainment to which he received an embossed invitation card and where he must make desultory and stilted conversation.

Also being a Duke, he would always have to escort an old Dowager into supper because she would be of higher social importance than the pretty young girls he would have preferred.

'Of course he finds this more fun,' Cassandra told herself.

She felt despairingly that nothing she could say or do would ever make him think differently.

Outside the house the Duke said:

"Do you mind if we take a hansom? I have only one coachman in London, and he is getting old, so I send him home at about twelve o'clock."

"I would love to go in a hansom," Cassandra answered.

She was well aware it was considered very fast to travel in what Disraeli had called "London's Gondolas."

Her father had once taken her for a drive in one when she was only fifteen, but no young man of her acquaintance would have dared to suggest such a thing.

As the Cabman closed the glass front over them, there was something very intimate in being so close to each other in a tiny, isolated world of their own.

The Duke reached out and took Cassandra's hand.

"I am so glad that you agreed to come away with me," he said. "I want to talk to you! I want to listen to you teasing me with that provocative note in your voice which tells me that you are not quite as impressed with me as you ought to be!"

Cassandra felt herself quiver. The touch of his hand sent little shivers down her spine.

She was thrilling to the warmth of his fingers; to the knowledge that their shoulders were in contact and their faces were very near to each other's.

"You are lovely! Ridiculously and absurdly lovely!" the Duke said and she thought that his tone was sincere. "How could you possibly have blue eyes with that strange, half-red half-gold hair?"

"There must be Irish blood in me somewhere!"

Cassandra felt as if it was difficult to speak. Her throat was contracting so strange little feelings were rippling through her. She could not help wondering if the Duke felt the same.

"Your eye-lashes. Do you darken them?"

Cassandra shook her head.

"They are natural."

"If you are lying to me, I shall wash them and see."

"You can do that. They are what the Irish call 'Blue eyes put in with dirty fingers,' and I promise you they will resist rain and tempest. Water is completely ineffective."

"I would still like to try," he said softly.

By the lights shining into the hansom as they passed through Trafalgar Square she could see the look in his eyes.

They had that curious searching expression that she remembered so well.

"There are so many things I want to ask you and so much I want to hear, and I am delighted beyond words that you did not wish to stay at that noisy party."

As he spoke, he drew her kid glove very gently from her right hand. Cassandra did not speak because she did not know what to say.

The Duke turned her hand over, as if to look at the palm.

"Such a small and very pretty hand," he said.

As he spoke he pressed his lips on her palm.

Cassandra told herself she ought to stop him; she ought to protest that he must not do such a thing to her! But her voice dried in her throat.

It was a wonder such as she had never known to feel the warm persistence of his mouth and to know deliriously and incredibly her dreams had come true.

Then she remembered it was all play-acting. She was acting and so was he!

This was amusement—this was fun! This was just the bubbles one found in a glass of champagne! Nothing real, nothing serious, nothing permanent about it, and to forget the truth for one moment would be disastrous.

The Duke released her hand.

"Here we are!" he said. "I thought you would like to go to Romano's."

They seemed to have reached the Strand very quickly.

Cassandra was well aware of how famous Romano's Restaurant was; she had heard it spoken of so often, but she had never expected it to be as gay as it was.

The oblong room with its dark-red draped curtains and plush sofas was filled with men and women eating supper after the theatres were closed.

Cassandra guessed that many of them were Gaiety Girls, simply because they seemed more attractive, more alluring and far better dressed than the other women.

Nearly every one of them wore flowers in her hair, their *décolletage* was extremely low, their waists so tiny it seemed as if a man's two hands could easily meet round them.

They all appeared to have perfect complexions; they all appeared to be laughing until the whole Restaurant was filled with their gaiety.

Romano himself, a dark, suave little man, greeted the Duke with respectful delight and led them to a sofa underneath the balcony.

As she walked towards it, Cassandra realised that at least three-quarters of the women in the Restaurant knew the Duke and waved and smiled at him whenever they could catch his eye.

There appeared to be flowers everywhere, and she was to learn later that the Gaiety Girls had special tables kept for them which their admirers decked with flowers. Some sat under a veritable canopy of blooms.

Some had bells of blossoms with their names emblazoned on them suspended over their heads.

It was quite unlike any Restaurant that Cassandra could have imagined, and once again she could understand why the Duke found it amusing.

The sofa on which they sat close together was very comfortable.

The Waiter brought them a hand-written menu and the Wine-Waiter hovered behind him.

"What would you like to eat?" the Duke asked.

"Very little," Cassandra answered. "I am not hungry, but please order for me."

The Duke gave the order and then chose from the wine list a bottle of champagne.

It seemed that the champagne was almost compulsory in Romano's, for huge silver wine-coolers stood beside every table.

Before the night was out, Cassandra saw what she had often read about but hardly believed: champagne being drunk from the white satin slipper of a beautiful young woman whose table was festooned with the most expensive orchids in the room.

Her admirer poured champagne into her shoe and stood up to toast her. The other men in the party raised their glasses.

"Who is that?" Cassandra asked.

The Duke looked at her in surprise.

"Do you really not know?"

"I have no idea."

"That is Connie Gilchrist. You must have heard of her."

"Yes of course I have," Cassandra replied. "I recognise her now from the portrait sketches of her in the illustrated papers, but she is far prettier in real life."

"She is very attractive," the Duke answered, "as half the men in London will tell you."

"Are you in love with her?" Cassandra enquired.

As she spoke she was astonished at her own daring, and yet she felt that in some way she had to arrest his attention by keeping him amused, if only by her boldness.

"No!" he answered.

"Then with whom are you in love?" Cassandra enquired. "Or is that an impertinent question?"

He looked at her, his eyes twinkling.

"You are very direct. You have asked me a lot of intimate questions, and yet you have not answered one of mine. I think it is my turn."

"Very well," Cassandra answered, "what do you want to know?"

"The thing is," the Duke said in rather a strange tone, "I want to know so much that I cannot put into words. I have a feeling there is a great deal behind everything you say. Behind everything we have talked about this evening there is something I do not understand."

Cassandra did not answer and he said:

"I am not explaining myself well, and yet I have the feeling you know what I mean."

"I think you are curious," she said. "When you look at people, you have a curious look in your eyes."

"How do you know that?" he asked sharply. "People have said something of that sort to me before, but we have only just met."

"Yes . . . I know," Cassandra answered.

"I know what you are thinking," he said unexpectedly, "and I believe you feel the same way I do, that we are not strangers to each other."

"Why should we feel like that?" Cassandra answered, without attempting to deny his assertion.

"I do not know," he replied, "but it is something I am determined to find out."

CHAPTER FIVE

Cassandra and the Duke sat talking and time seemed to speed by so quickly that it was with genuine surprise she found it was after two o'clock in the morning.

She had never before had a meal alone with a man except her father.

She realised now how much more interesting and indeed entrancing it was to talk intimately with the Duke, to feel the stimulus of his mind and above all, to know that their eyes were saying so much more than their lips actually spoke.

There was no mistaking the admiration in the Duke's expression.

There was something very personal in their conversation, something which made even the most banal subjects somehow seem special to them both.

They talked of horses and the Duke said:

"You sound as if you have ridden quite a lot."

"I have," Cassandra answered.

She saw a question in his eyes and added:

"Perhaps it is easier when one is living in the North than it would be in the South."

"Maybe it is less expensive," the Duke conceded. "At the same time I am sure wherever you are there will always be men who will wish you to ride their horses."

Cassandra knew he was thinking that an actress would not be able either to afford horses or to have much time for hunting! So she excused herself by saying:

"My father keeps horses."

"Your father lives in the North?"

"Yes."

"I would like to see you on a horse," the Duke said.

Then with a different note in his voice he said:

"Will you come with me to Tattersall's tomorrow?"

"To the Sale-Rooms?"

He nodded.

"Tomorrow is Friday," Cassandra said. "I thought as the sales are on Monday, one could only inspect the horses on Sunday."

"That is true for the general public," the Duke answered, "but my horses are arriving at Knightsbridge Green tomorrow morning from my stables in Newmarket and from Alchester Park."

"You are selling them?" Cassandra exclaimed.

"I am selling the last twenty of my father's stud."

She heard the pain in his voice and said impulsively:

"But you must not do that! Your father's horses are famous."

"I have to sell."

"But why?"

There was a twisted smile on his lips as the Duke replied:

"Is not the reason obvious? Why does one have to sell anything that one treasures except for money?"

Cassandra was silent. She could not understand what was happening.

If the Duke thought he was going to marry the rich Miss Sherburn, why should he dispose of his precious horses? She knew from the expression on his face that they meant as much to him as they had to his father.

The Alchester Stud was famous, and the late Duke in the last years of his life had won a great number of races.

He had also been a notable Patron of the Turf, a member of the Jockey Club, and was so popular that whenever he appeared on a race-course he was cheered by the crowds.

It seemed incredible to Cassandra that the new Duke should dispose of the Stud that had taken his father a life-time to build up and on which he had expended not only money but loving care.

She was finding it difficult not to ask the questions that were trembling on her lips when the Duke went on:

"I would like you to see my horses. It will be the last time that I shall look at them, except perhaps when they are racing under someone else's colours. I could not bear to attend the sale on Monday."

"I can understand that," Cassandra said. "But surely if you need money so badly, there is something else you can sell?"

"Do you suppose I have not thought of that?" he asked almost sharply. "No, there is nothing."

It seemed to Cassandra as he spoke that he withdrew from her, so that for the first time that evening they were no longer close and friendly, but strangers.

Then the party which included Connie Gilchrist rose to leave the Restaurant.

The women's voices were so loud and shrill as they said good-night to each other that it was impossible to go on talking until they had moved down the Restaurant towards the door.

Connie Gilchrist however turned back and walked towards the Duke.

He rose to his feet as she approached.

"How are you, Varro?" she asked. "I've not seen you this last week."

"I have been out of London as it happens," the Duke replied. "I only returned this evening—too late to come to the Theatre."

"We all wondered what had happened to you," Connie Gilchrist said.

She was blonde, very pink and white and attractive, Cassandra thought, but her voice was not as pretty as her face. There was something slightly harsh about it, and just a touch of commonness in the way she pronounced some of her words.

"I'll see you tomorrow evening, I hope," Connie said. "Good-night, Varro."

"Good-night, Connie," he replied.

She hurried after her friends, an exaggerated bustle of pink satin rustling behind her.

The Duke re-seated himself beside Cassandra.

"I did not introduce you," he said. "Did you wish to meet her?"

"I am quite content to admire her from afar," Cassandra answered.

"She is a great draw," the Duke said. "I will take you to the Gaiety one evening; it will amuse you."

"Thank you," Cassandra replied.

The Duke signalled to the Wine-Waiter who filled up their glasses.

Cassandra began to think that she ought to suggest leaving, and yet she could not bear the evening to come to an end.

Perhaps tomorrow the Duke would regret the various invitations he had given her. Perhaps he would not find her so interesting or so attractive as he had appeared to do earlier in the evening.

Since they had talked of his horses it seemed as if his mood had changed.

"I must try to think of a way to amuse him," Cassandra told herself.

Then as she was frantically searching for a new subject, the Duke said:

"What do you think about when you are acting?"

Cassandra considered for a moment.

"When I am playing a part," she answered, "I am trying to think of the effect it will have on the people who are listening to me."

This was the truth, she thought. For she had not thought of herself during the evening, but solely of the impression she was making on the Duke.

"That is not the answer most actors and actresses give," the Duke said. "They usually say that they think themselves into the rôle they have to play so that in fact they become the person they depict."

"I suppose that is how it should be," Cassandra said.

"They are lucky!" the Duke exclaimed. "Actors and actresses can play a rôle, and then discard it. When they leave the stage, they can become themselves. They do not have to go on pretending!"

There was a note in his voice that told Cassandra that he was speaking personally.

"I think what you are trying to say," she said slowly, her eyes on his face, "is that the people who are not on the stage have to go on acting indefinitely."

She smiled and continued:

"Have you forgotten that Shakespeare said—'All the world's a stage and all the men and women merely players?'"

"That may be true," the Duke said, "but the trouble is the play goes on too long. There is no escape. Only actors and actresses can change their rôles and, as I have said, are free to be themselves."

"Do you really think that is so desirable?" Cassandra asked. "I think actors and actresses are mimics and, if they are really professional, they have to subordinate their own personalities to the part they are playing. If not, they become even on the stage, like so many of our famous actors, themselves . . . very thinly disguised."

"What do you mean by that?" the Duke asked.

"If an actor has any personality," Cassandra answered, "he is not Julius Caesar, Bottom, or, if you like, a Crossing-Sweeper or a Policeman. Instead, he is Martin Harvey, or Beerbohm Tree in that particular part, and one can never really forget the person beneath the trappings."

She paused and went on:

"Just as when I watched Mrs. Langtry tonight, I was not thinking of the miserable, unhappy woman trying to save her brother, but how skilfully Lily Langtry was pretending to be her."

"I have never thought of it that way," the Duke said slowly.

"Can you not see that a good actress should have as little character or personality of her own as possible?" Cassandra continued. "Then when you watch her in a part you are not distracted by the knowledge that she herself is doing it."

"You are destroying my illusions about the stage," the Duke said accusingly.

"I think that you are envious merely of actors because you are bored with your own part," Cassandra said daringly.

"Who would want to play the Duke?" he asked bitterly.

"A great number of people," Cassandra answered, "and actually it is a hero's rôle. How much you make yourself a real hero is up to you."

"Do you really believe that?"

"Of course I believe it! If we are assuming as we have been, that we each have in life a special part to play, a Lawyer must be a Lawyer, that is his profession. But whether he is a good or bad one is up to him!"

She went on:

"The same applies to a Salesman or Labourer or a Duke! I think in life we cannot often alter our rôle, but we *can* improve the performance!"

The Duke looked at her for a long moment and then he said:

"You are a very remarkable person, Sandra. You have given me a lot to think about. Something I certainly did not expect to happen this evening!"

"What did you expect?"

The Duke paused for a moment as if he considered his words.

"I expected to be amused, beguiled, captivated. You are, as you are well aware, one of the loveliest people I have ever seen."

"Again you speak as an expert?" Cassandra smiled.

"Of course!" he answered. "But now you have opened new vistas, unlocked doors that I had thought were closely shut. How shall I describe the effect you are having upon me?"

There was an expression in his eyes that made Cassandra feel shy.

She saw that while they had been talking the Restaurant had been emptying and now there were only a few couples like themselves left, and the waiters were yawning.

"I think . . . I should go . . . home," she said.

"I suppose we must," the Duke answered reluctantly.

He asked for the bill.

Cassandra sent for her wrap and they walked towards the entrance. Romano was waiting with a bunch of pink roses in his hand.

"May I ask you to accept these?" he said to Cassandra. "His Grace has brought many beautiful women to my Restaurant, but tonight you have eclipsed them all."

"Thank you," Cassandra said a little shyly.

She took the roses, a doorman called a hackney-carriage and the Duke assisted her into it.

"Tomorrow, if you will dine with me," he said, "I will try to produce a vehicle more worthy of you. I am ashamed that tonight I must treat you in such a shabby fashion."

"It has been a wonderful evening," Cassandra said softly.

The cab smelt of hay, old leather and horse.

But it was close and intimate to be sitting next to the Duke and she knew as he put his arm around her shoulder that he was thinking the same thing.

She felt a thrill run through her! Then as he drew her closer and she realised he was about to kiss her, she turned her head away.

"No!"

"No?" he questioned. "I want to kiss you, Sandra, I want it more than I can possibly tell you."

"We have . . . only just . . . met," Cassandra murmured.

It was difficult to speak sensibly with his arm touching her. She had a feeling of weakness she had never known before, a weakness combined with a kind of wild excitement which made it hard to think clearly.

"I feel I have known you for a very long time," the Duke said in his deep voice. "I feel too that we were meant to meet. There is something inevitable about it."

Cassandra did not speak and after a moment he said:

"You are so lovely, and so completely and absolutely different from anyone I have ever met before."

He gave a little laugh.

"You will tell me that it sounds banal, and yet it is true. I cannot explain it in words, but I know that this is different."

"In what . . . way?" Cassandra asked.

"That is something I intend to explain to you, but not tonight."

The Duke's arm tightened.

"You tell me not to kiss you, but I have the feeling, Sandra, that if I insisted you would not resist me."

Cassandra felt a little quiver run through her at his words. He felt it too.

"But because this *is* different," he went on, "because I want you to think of me in a very special way, I will not kiss you until you allow me to do so. But do not keep me waiting too long."

He was silent for a moment and then he cried:

"Time is short. I cannot explain, but the sands of time are running out as far as I am concerned."

"What do you mean?" Cassandra asked.

"You would not understand," he answered, "but I can only beg you, Sandra, to let me grasp what little happiness I can. I need more desperately than I can explain the happiness of knowing you."

"You speak as . . . if you were . . . going away," Cassandra managed to say.

"That is in fact what will happen," the Duke said. "But until I do, I have to see you. I must see you!"

His arm drew her close. Then unexpectedly he released her and sat back in the corner of the cab.

"I sound almost hysterical," he said, "and I cannot explain."

"Why not?"

"Because, as you just reminded me, we have only just met, because you do not wish me to kiss you, and because—how do I know that you are feeling as I am feeling tonight?"

"What . . . are you . . . feeling?"

"Do I have to answer that?" he asked. "I think you know that something entirely unusual has suddenly happened to me, and I am almost conceited enough to hope it has happened to you too."

He paused and then he said:

"Look at me, Sandra."

She turned her head and by the lights of the street lamp that were shining on both their faces, it was easy for her to see the expression in his eyes.

"You are so lovely," he said hoarsely, "so incredibly, unbelievably lovely! Oh God! Why did I have to meet you at this particular moment of my life?"

The Duke called for Cassandra on the following morning at half past twelve.

She had begged him not to come earlier, knowing that it would take some time for her to explain to her Aunt that she was out to luncheon, get to the flat and change her clothes.

The most difficult person to deal with was Hannah who, having sat up until three o'clock the night before, was in a thoroughly disagreeable mood.

It had however not been such a hardship as she had tried to make out.

When Cassandra let herself into the flat, she had found Hannah fast asleep on a bed in the small bed-room, and it had been quite difficult to awaken her.

The Night-Porter had called them a cab, and they had driven back to Park Lane with Hannah not only grumbling every inch of the way but threatening to return to Yorkshire and tell Sir James what was going on.

Cassandra had managed to pacify her, but it had been difficult this morning to get her to return to the flat and help with her change of clothing.

The gown Cassandra was wearing when the Duke arrived was very attractive. At the same time it was a little too gaudy to be anything other than theatrical.

Of bronze silk trimmed with velvet, the skirt was draped at the front and swept behind into a bustle. The little jacket which ended at the waist was trimmed with fur and buttoned down the front with imitation topazes.

Because she had real jewels to match, Cassandra could not resist wearing a topaz brooch, bracelet and ear-rings—a set which her father had given to her the previous year.

He had told her not to wear the ear-rings until she was married, but she thought now they made her look more sophisticated. They were also very fetching, with a bonnet trimmed with topaz-yellow feathers, which was tied under her chin with velvet ribbons.

Cassandra was only just ready and was waiting in the Sitting-Room when the Duke knocked at the door of the flat.

She let him in and she could not disguise the amusement in her eyes as she watched him glance around at the over-decorated, vulgar Sitting-Room.

"Is this yours?" he began with an incredulous note in his voice.

Then he exclaimed:

"But of course not! This is Hetty Henlow's flat! I have been here once before, many years ago."

"Then you know my landlady?" Cassandra laughed.

"I know old Lord Fitzmaurice who pays for it," the Duke

replied. "He is a member of White's and he has been keeping Hetty for years!"

Cassandra stiffened.

She had never heard the expression before, but she could guess what it implied.

She suddenly felt ashamed that the Duke should see her in such a place.

Before, the flat had merely seemed common and gaudy, but now, being deeply in love, she could not bear him to associate her with anything crude or immoral.

"Let us go," she said quickly.

Without waiting for him to answer, she pulled open the door and started to descend the stairs.

Carrying his top hat and silver-headed cane, the Duke hurried after her.

When Cassandra reached Bury Street, she saw waiting outside a very smart Phaeton drawn by two horses.

"Are these yours?" she asked.

"About all I have left," he answered.

Once again she saw a cloud pass over his face.

"Surely you are not selling your carriage-horses or your hunters?" Cassandra said as she stepped into the Phaeton.

"Most of them have already gone," the Duke replied abruptly.

Cassandra had lain awake the best part of the night wondering exactly why the Duke wanted money so urgently.

Why, having written to her father, making it obvious that he was prepared to go on with the marriage as planned, was he now making what appeared to be an unnecessary sacrifice?

'I cannot understand it,' she had told herself again and again, and she thought the same now.

The Duke drove down Piccadilly with an expertise that she could not help admiring.

"You are looking very lovely," he said, as if forcing himself to change the subject. "I know that every man who sees us is filled with envy of me."

It was the sort of glib remark he would have made if she had in fact been an actress, and Cassandra resented it.

Then she realised that she was being very foolish.

She had set out to amuse and intrigue him, so that she could learn the truth. And that was what she must continue to do.

She turned her face to look at him. With his top hat set at an angle on his dark hair, he looked slightly raffish and extremely handsome.

"Shall I tell you I am very honoured to be in such distinguished company, and with such an exceptionally attractive Duke?" she asked.

"Should I be flattered?" he asked. "Or suspicious that you have a hidden reason for being so kind to me?"

"Must I have a . . . reason?"

"No," he answered, "but I am half-afraid to put into your mind or mine the thoughts I really want you to think."

They were back again where they had been last night, Cassandra thought, fencing with words, hinting at what might or might not be below the surface.

She had the feeling that while they had been apart the Duke had thought about her as she had thought of him, but that he had decided that their relationship should be gay and amusing but by no means serious.

Accordingly she tried to play up to the mood he desired, but underneath everything they said, she felt there was a streak of seriousness which neither of them could ignore.

The Duke took her to The Café Royal in Regent Street which was a popular place for luncheon and dinner.

It had not been open for many years but it had been a huge success from its very beginning. It was the first restaurant in London where an excellent and really French meal could be eaten.

Cassandra found it fascinating. It had atmosphere, and the big room with long, red, plush-covered seats contained a mixture of celebrities from all walks of life.

"Tell me who everybody is," she begged.

Amused by her interest and curiosity, the Duke pointed out the actors, crooks, jockeys, confidence-men, trainers, owners and professional backers who were all eating the superlative food and drinking wine from a cellar which was acknowledged to be one of the best in London.

When Oscar Wilde came in looking pale, elegant and extremely pleased with himself, Cassandra exclaimed excitedly:

"I have always wanted to see him. I have enjoyed his poems so much. But my father has always said he is a terrible *poseur.*"

"He is," the Duke answered. "Nevertheless he undoubtedly has great talent."

There were of course a number of women in the Restaurant who were either actresses or quite obviously of a class with which Cassandra had never come in contact.

However, after her initial interest in the other guests, she found it difficult to notice anyone but the Duke.

Once again, she found it easy to talk to him, to discuss so many different subjects. It seemed they could hardly pause for breath before they were arguing, discussing, exclaiming over something else!

When finally they drove away in the direction of Knightsbridge Green, Cassandra's eyes were shining and she was feeling as happy as she had felt the night before. Never had she enjoyed a meal more.

She had been to Tattersall's with her father on a Sunday some years previously, and she remembered the great grass-covered yard where the horses were shown off to prospective buyers.

She knew there were seventy-five open boxes and twenty-five stables for brood mares, above which there was a Gallery served by lifts for storing carriages and harness.

When she had been there before, the yard had been filled with top-hatted gentlemen and elegantly-dressed ladies, while grooms had trotted the horses up to the Auctioneer's box and back.

Today there were only the grooms in their shirt sleeves, moving amongst the stalls, carrying buckets of water, whistling through their teeth as they rubbed down their charges.

For the first time Cassandra saw the Duke in a very different guise. It was almost as if he had forgotten her very existence.

His head-groom reported to him on the way in which the horses had travelled, telling him that one was nervous after the journey, another seemed a little off-colour, but the majority were settling into their new quarters.

"Keep them as quiet as you can," the Duke said.

"I'm seeing to that, Your Grace! A nervous horse never gets the best price."

"That is very true."

The Duke then went with Cassandra to look at the horses, one after another. There was no doubt they were magnificent animals.

"I have put a reserve of one thousand guineas on this one," the Duke said. "He has already won three races and seems sure to win the Gold Cup at Ascot."

"Would you not be wise to keep him then?" Cassandra asked, knowing the Gold Cup brought in a large amount of prize money.

"I cannot afford to wait," the Duke answered and went on to the next stall.

Cassandra asked for a catalogue of the sale on Monday.

A member of the Tattersall's staff brought it to her, and she looked through it wondering as she did so if her father had seen a copy.

Almost as if he read her thoughts the Duke said:

"I only decided to put my horses in the sale a week ago. You will therefore find they have been added at the last moment and listed all together at the end of the catalogue."

"But surely that means that the addition has not gone to many of the people in the country who receive it regularly before every sale," Cassandra said.

The Duke shrugged his shoulders.

"Perhaps. But I am sure there will be no lack of bidders. My father's Stud is well known in racing circles."

"Yes, of course," Cassandra answered.

She was however thinking that Sir James being in Yorkshire could not have heard that the Duke's horses were in this sale.

If he had, she was quite certain he would have mentioned it to her. This meant that there was no time for her to communicate with him, unless she sent him a telegram.

If she did that, she argued to herself, he would undoubtedly come to London, in which case she could no longer go on acting her part of a young, unknown actress.

Besides, if Sir James was in London, there was every likelihood that he would introduce her to the Duke. It would be so easy for it to happen, even if she did not go with him to the sale.

An idea came to her. When they left Tattersall's she took the sale catalogue carefully with her and sat with it on her lap in the Phaeton so that she would not forget it.

"You are dining with me tonight," the Duke said.

It was a statement rather than a question.

"If you still want me to do so," Cassandra answered. "Are you quite certain you have not had enough of my company?"

"You are fishing for compliments," the Duke replied with a smile.

He looked at her and added:

"You know I want to be with you—to see you. Do not play with me, Sandra. I cannot bear it."

There was something almost desperate in his voice, and again Cassandra did not know what was happening.

She only felt that she was being carried along on a tide which was moving too quickly for her to have any clear or coherent thoughts about herself or her relationship with the Duke.

She knew only that he overwhelmed her, that it was a joy beyond words to be with him, to know that he was beside her, to listen to his voice speaking to her and to see his eyes looking into hers.

And because she felt it was all too wonderful to put into words or even to contemplate, it was dangerous.

Dangerous because she might forget that it was only a performance, that their relationship had no substance, no foundation in reality.

She was an actress he found pretty and attractive, and he was a Duke who was about to become engaged to a rich heiress.

Cassandra felt as if she had embarked on a journey the end of which she could not foresee.

Her plan of meeting the Duke, of finding out the truth about his interests, and most of all whom he was in love with, appeared to be going well.

Yet there were so many new depths to it, so many hazards and difficulties which she had not anticipated.

The whole idea had been, she thought, a fairy story that she had told herself.

She had imagined it for so many years that to put it into operation had been easy.

Yet now she was afraid, uncertain of what might happen next.

She only knew there was in her an uneasiness, a kind of growing fear that lay beneath the excitement and the sheer delight of being with the Duke, of knowing that she loved him more every minute they were together.

Cassandra was ready a quarter of an hour before the Duke called for her at Bury Street.

Because she could not bear him to see her again in the garish Sitting-Room which belonged to Hetty Henlow, she watched from a window until she saw the carriage arrive.

Then she ran downstairs.

She met him in the Hall and he raised her hand to his lips.

"I have not kept you waiting?" he asked in surprise.

"No, but I thought I would save you climbing two flights," Cassandra answered.

"You are very considerate."

She was wearing tonight a white gown which, like the one she had worn the previous night, sparkled with sequins and was ornamented with bunches of artificial flowers.

It was elaborate, beautiful and theatrical.

Hannah had set two white roses in her hair and tonight Cassandra discarded her ear-rings and wore instead a two-string pearl necklace which belonged to her mother.

It was very valuable and she hoped the Duke would think the pearls were artificial, but when she saw him notice them while they were having dinner, she realised he was not deceived.

He took her to dine at Rule's, a much quieter place than Romano's. It was small and intimate and the other diners were mostly, like themselves, couples who were intensely interested in each other and who wanted to talk in low voices.

"If it seems dull, there will be many more people here after the theatres close," the Duke apologised.

"I am very content with it as it is," Cassandra answered.

"That is what I hoped you would say."

They sat talking over their meal, and afterwards Cassandra found it difficult to remember what they had discussed.

She only knew that the Duke not only made her quiver when his hand touched hers, but he stimulated her mind so that her brain responded to his and everything they said seemed to have a special meaning.

"I have never known a Sandra before," he said to her one moment during dinner. "I suppose it is a diminutive of Alexandra?"

Cassandra parried the question by saying:

"I hope Your Grace lives up to your name?"

"What do you know about it?" the Duke asked with a smile.

"I know that Marcus Terentius Varro was the greatest scholar of the Roman Republic. He is said to have written more than six hundred books on a wide range of subjects."

"Where did you look that up?" the Duke enquired. "The British Museum?"

"You know as well as I do that I have had no time to visit Museums since I arrived in London," Cassandra answered, "but I find the name rather fascinating."

"And what about its owner?" the Duke enquired.

His eyes looked down into hers and once again she knew he was searching for something. Because his scrutiny made her feel shy, she looked away from him.

"What are you thinking?" he asked in a low voice.

"I am thinking about you."

"And what conclusions have you reached?"

"Perhaps I was . . . trying to read your . . . thoughts."

"Can you do that?"

"Sometimes."

"Then tell me what I am thinking."

"You are worrying," Cassandra answered. "I think that you are standing, one might say, at a cross-roads in your life. You have made a decision and you are not certain if it is the right one."

The Duke stared at her in astonishment.

"How could you know that?"

"Is it true?"

"Yes, it is true. But what you have not seen, is the reason why I am worried."

"Will you tell me what it is?"

"That is not difficult—it is you!"

She turned to look at him and again his eyes held hers so that she felt something quiver within her and come to life. For a moment they were both spell-bound.

Then, as they looked at each other quite oblivious of their surroundings, a voice said:

"What a pleasant surprise to find you both here!"

Cassandra looked up to see Lord Carwen standing by their table.

"Good-evening, Sandra," he said and held out his hand.

She did not wish to touch him but she could not help but put her hand in his.

He kissed her fingers lightly, then he put his other hand on the Duke's shoulder as he would have risen.

"Do not get up, dear boy," he said. "I have just written to you as it happens, and sent my letter round to White's."

"Is it anything of importance?" the Duke enquired.

Cassandra thought there was a worried note in his voice.

"No, it is only an invitation to ask you to stay tomorrow until Monday. Lily will be coming after the theatre tomorrow evening, and there will be various other mutual friends whom you should find amusing."

"It is very kind of you," the Duke began, "but . . ."

"Of course," Lord Carwen interrupted, "the invitation includes the beautiful Miss Sandra Standish."

He smiled at Cassandra in a manner which was somehow distasteful.

"I would, pretty little lady, have written to you direct," he went on, "but you omitted to say good-night to me last night, and so unfortunately I was unable to ask for your address."

"I am sorry if we seemed . . . rude," Cassandra murmured.

"I missed you," Lord Carwen said, "and so to assuage my disappointment at not being able to dance with you again, will you come with Varro and stay at my house in the country?"

Cassandra was about to refuse. Then the thought came to her how wonderful it would be to drive into the country with the Duke.

They would be together and be able to see more of each other than was possible just by meeting for meals.

As she hesitated, Lord Carwen said to the Duke, with an insistent note in his voice:

"You must come, Varro. I will not take 'No' for an answer!"

"Then we have no choice," the Duke said. "That is, if Sandra will agree."

"I cannot believe that Sandra would be so hard-hearted as to cast me into the depths of despair by refusing my hospitality," Lord Carwen said.

He picked up Cassandra's hand as he spoke and kissed her fingers again.

"I must go back to my party, but I shall expect you both about tea-time tomorrow. Varro will doubtless explain what clothes you will find necessary. I promise you a very entertaining time!"

"Thank you," Cassandra said in a small voice.

As Lord Carwen walked away, she felt he had cast a shadow over their evening.

Although they stayed for another hour or so, Cassandra was aware of him all the time. He was on the other side of the room surrounded by his friends, yet she felt as if he was eavesdropping at their table.

As if he felt the same, the Duke asked for the bill.

"Do you want to go and stay with him?" he asked.

They both knew to whom he was referring without his mentioning a name.

"No," Cassandra answered, "but I would like to be in the country with you."

"Then we will go," the Duke said decisively, as if there had been a question in his mind about refusing the invitation.

Cassandra had the strange feeling that he was in some way compelled to do what Lord Carwen wished.

Because she wanted to make things easier for him she said:

"It will be nice to see Mrs. Langtry again. Do you think Mr. Gebhard will come with her?"

"But of course," the Duke replied, "you do not imagine that she would go anywhere without him?"

Cassandra had not thought that it would be possible for a married woman to take another man with her to stay in a country house as if he were her husband.

Then she told herself there were special rules for actresses.

Nevertheless Mrs. Langtry was a lady, and she wondered what her mother would have thought of such behaviour.

The Duke having paid the bill rose and Cassandra preceded him across the room.

So many people had arrived since they had come in that she thought they might have difficulty in finding the velvet wrap that matched her white dress.

Rather than sending a waiter for it, she herself went to the cloak-room.

There were dozens of wraps, cloaks and coats in the charge of a woman wearing a black dress and a white, frilled apron.

"I'm not quite certain which is yours, Madam," she said apologetically.

Cassandra was helping her find it when there was a little sound behind her. She turned to see a young woman who had just entered the cloak-room collapse slowly onto the floor.

She hurried to her and recognised that she was one of the guests in Lord Carwen's party.

With the help of the cloak-room attendant Cassandra assisted her to a couch.

"I think the lady has fainted," she said.

"I'll get some brandy, Ma'am," the attendant murmured and hurried away.

Cassandra rubbed the woman's hands which were very cold and after a moment her eyes fluttered open.

She was pretty in a rather obvious manner, with very fair hair and gold-specked, hazel eyes which held a frightened look.

But Cassandra thought that, unlike Connie Gilchrist, she was obviously wellbred and a lady.

"It is all right," she said. "You have only fainted. Lie still."

At that moment the cloak-room attendant came back with a small glass of brandy and Cassandra persuaded the girl to take a few sips.

The spirit brought the colour back into her cheeks, and after a moment she took the glass from Cassandra's hand and drank a little more.

"It was . . . stupid of me," she said, "but I have been feeling . . . ill all the evening."

"Perhaps you had better go home," Cassandra suggested. "Is there anyone of your party who will escort you?"

"No, no-one. Lord Carwen invited me to supper last night when I was at his party, and his carriage was waiting for me after the theatre."

"Shall I send him a message?" Cassandra asked.

"No! No! I do not want to worry him. I do not know him well. He was just filling up the party which he was giving for Sylvia Grey, who is in the cast."

Cassandra realised she had not recognised the Gaiety star in Lord Carwen's party, but then she had not looked at them very closely.

"Well, perhaps my friend and I could take you home," Cassandra said doubtfully. "Do you live far away?"

"No. It is quite a short distance behind Drury Lane."

"Then that would be the best solution," Cassandra said. "Are you sure we should not inform Lord Carwen that you are ill?"

"No! All I want to do is go home to bed and lie down. I should not have come. I found it difficult enough to get through the per-formance."

"It must have been very hard, feeling as you do," Cassandra said sympathetically.

Still very pale, her hands shaking a little, the young woman rose to her feet.

"Are you quite sure," she asked as the cloak-room attendant brought her wrap, "that you do not mind taking me home? I can easily go alone."

"You are not well enough," Cassandra answered, "you might faint again."

"I think—I am all right."

"Then come along," Cassandra smiled. "The sooner you are in bed the better. What is your name, by the way?"

"My name is Nancy—Nancy Wood."

"Then if you are certain you do not wish to say good-bye to Lord Carwen, we will leave a message with the Head-Waiter."

Cassandra was sure it was best to take the young actress away. She looked so ill that she would be a damper on the gaiety of any party.

Putting an arm around her to support her, she helped her outside to where the Duke was waiting. He looked surprised as they appeared.

"This is Miss Nancy Wood," Cassandra said. "She is performing at the Gaiety and you may have seen her. She is feeling very ill and I said we would take her home."

"But of course," the Duke replied.

It was nice of him, Cassandra thought, not to ask questions, not to fuss, but to assist Nancy Wood out through the door and into the carriage.

She sat back in a corner and closed her eyes.

Cassandra sat down beside her and the Duke seated himself opposite them.

Nancy gave her address in a far away voice which made Cassandra think she might faint again at any moment.

They drove in silence and, as Nancy Wood had said, it was not far to go.

The streets at the back of Drury Lane were narrow, squalid and dirty. The house at which they stopped was certainly far from prepossessing.

"Have you a key?" the Duke asked.

With some difficulty Nancy Wood found it in her reticule.

The Duke opened the door and with Cassandra's assistance they got the sick woman out of the carriage and onto the pavement.

"I had better take her inside," Cassandra said in a low voice.

"Can you manage?" he asked.

She smiled at him.

"I am sure I can."

She put her arm around Nancy Wood and took her inside the house which had a straight staircase running up almost perpendicular to the first floor.

The place smelt of dirt, gas and cooking. As they laboriously climbed the staircase, Cassandra could not help thinking how squalid it was.

The stairs could not have been scrubbed for years and the linoleum which covered them was full of holes.

Nancy Wood had another key which opened the door of a back room. She lit a candle which revealed an unmade bed and a terrible state of untidiness.

There were clothes hanging on the outside of a broken wardrobe. There were stockings, underclothes, petticoats and gowns thrown on a chair and also on the bed.

Shoes were scattered along the side of the wall and the dressing-table was littered with paraphernalia of every sort.

There were hair-brushes that needed washing, combs without teeth, grease-paint, mascara and artificial flowers which looked as if they should have been thrown away years ago.

"It is in rather a mess," Nancy Wood said weakly.

"Never mind about it now," Cassandra answered. "Get into bed. You will feel better in the morning, and if not, you must see a doctor."

"There is . . . nothing a doctor can do for . . . me," Nancy said.

She sat down on the crumpled bed and her whole body seemed to sag dejectedly.

"Why? What is wrong with you?" Cassandra asked.

"I'm having a baby," Nancy Wood answered and burst into tears.

CHAPTER SIX

Cassandra came down the steep stairs and saw the Duke waiting for her below.

He looked up at her with a worried expression on his face.

"You have been a long time."

"She is . . . ill," Cassandra answered, "and I do not . . . know what to . . . do."

She spoke hesitatingly. When she reached his side he asked:

"What is wrong with her?"

Cassandra did not answer. Then, as she realised he was waiting, she said uncomfortably, a blush deepening the colour in her cheeks:

"I . . . cannot . . . tell you."

"I suppose she is having a baby?"

The Duke's words brought the colour flooding into her face and her eyes widened as she exclaimed in surprise:

"How did you . . . guess?"

"There is nothing you can do," he said sharply.

"But she is so . . . distressed."

The Duke seemed to consider for a moment. Then he said:

"Did you leave her any money?"

"I did not think of it," Cassandra replied.

"Wait here!"

He started up the staircase.

"No! you cannot go to her!" Cassandra cried. "She is . . . in bed."

The Duke appeared not to have heard her. Before she could say any more, he had reached the landing, and she heard him knock at Nancy Wood's door and walk in.

Cassandra waited irresolutely, not sure what she should do.

She was shocked at the idea of the Duke going into the untidy, squalid room where she had helped Nancy into bed, but she was much more shocked at having spoken to him of her having a baby.

No lady would have thought of saying anything so intimate to a man. Even with her contemporaries, a married woman would only talk of being in an "interesting condition" or of "expecting an addition to the family."

To discuss such personal matters with anyone but her mother or her husband, was to be incredibly coarse and crude.

The actual arrival of a child into the world was to Cassandra, as to average young women of her age, wrapped in as deep a mystery as the manner in which it was conceived.

The fact that Nancy Wood had blurted out her condition had struck her with almost the same effect as a bombshell!

She did not know what to say! While Nancy wept bitterly, she could only offer some practical assistance in helping her to undress and mutter words of consolation which even to her own ears sounded ineffective.

It seemed incredible to Cassandra that the Duke should have guessed so quickly what was wrong, and when in a few minutes he came down the stairs, she found it hard to meet his eyes.

He did not speak. He merely took her by the arm, opened the front door, and when they were outside assisted her into the carriage.

He gave Cassandra's address to the Coachman and the horses set off at a good pace, since the streets, although narrow, were at this hour of the evening empty of pedestrians.

"I did not think of giving her . . . money," Cassandra said after a moment. "It was stupid of me, but in any case I had none with me."

"There is nothing else you can do," the Duke said firmly.

"I must try to help her," Cassandra argued. "She cannot go back to her family."

"Why not?"

"Because she ran away from home to go on the stage. Her father, who is a Parson, is Vicar of a Parish in Wiltshire. She has not communicated with him since she came to London."

"There is nowhere else for her to go," the Duke said in what Cassandra thought was a hard voice.

"There must be . . . somewhere," she answered desperately.

"You cannot entangle yourself with this chorus girl. You never saw her before tonight, and it is just unfortunate that you should have happened to be there when she fainted."

"I think you are being hard-hearted, and perhaps rather cruel," Cassandra said. "She is in trouble and someone has to help her."

"I have left her some money," the Duke replied, "and I will take her more tomorrow."

"That is very kind of you," Cassandra said, her voice softening. "When she can no longer . . . act, she will have to live somewhere. I doubt whether, even if she wished to keep her . . . baby in that terrible little room, the Landlord would permit it."

The Duke was silent and after a moment Cassandra said:

"I thought that the . . . father of the child would help her. But she said . . . something I did not . . . understand."

"What was that?"

"She said she did not . . . know who he . . . was! How could it be . . . possible that she does not . . . know?"

The Duke did not reply.

He turned to look at Cassandra's profile in the light from the street lamps. Her straight little nose was etched against the darkness of the carriage, as was the soft curve of her lips and the firm line of her chin.

"How old are you?" he asked unexpectedly.

Cassandra thought he was deliberately changing the subject, and she did not know what to reply.

To say she was only twenty would, she thought, make her seem too young to have played many parts on the stage. On the other hand she felt a strong reluctance to lie to the Duke.

She had already told him so many falsehoods, and she wished now she could be frank and that there were no secrets between them.

"I have always been told," she answered at length, in what she hoped was a light tone but which sounded very immature, "that it is extremely . . . rude to ask a lady . . . her age."

"You must accept my apologies," the Duke said.

They drove on in silence and it was not long before they reached Bury Street. The footman on the box of the carriage alighted to arouse the night-porter.

As they waited for the man to open the door the Duke said:

"Try not to worry, Sandra. I will call for you tomorrow at twelve o'clock and, if it pleases you, we will go to see this woman before we proceed to the country."

"I would like to do that," Cassandra said. "Thank you."

The night-porter had opened the door and Cassandra put her hands down to lift her skirt so that she could step out on to the pavement.

"You will be all right?" the Duke asked. "I do not like to think of you alone in that flat."

"I am not alone," Cassandra answered without thinking.

She did not notice that he stiffened, nor did she see the strange expression on his face.

Cassandra was ready just before twelve noon the following morning, but it had been a tremendous effort.

First of all she had had to explain to her Aunt that she was going away until Monday. Lady Fladbury was curious.

"Who are these friends with whom you will be staying?" she enquired.

Cassandra thought it best to tell the truth.

"I have been invited to Lord Carwen's house, which is only about three-quarters of an hour out of London."

"The Carwens'?" Lady Fladbury exclaimed. "I thought Her Ladyship was seldom in England. She prefers Paris, being half-French. I have never met her, but I heard she is a beautiful woman and Lord Carwen has the reputation of being extremely gay."

"He is quite old," Cassandra said, thinking that made it sound more respectable.

"He is only about forty!" Lady Fladbury retorted. "Of course that seems old to you, but I dare say there will be a number of young people in the house-party. Enjoy yourself, my dear!"

"I am sure I shall," Cassandra answered, feeling she had jumped the first fence.

Hannah had been far more difficult.

"If you're staying in a decent house, Miss Cassandra, why aren't you taking me?" she demanded angrily. "You know as well as I do that where you have been invited before it has always been understood that you bring your Lady's-Maid."

"Yes, I know, Hannah," Cassandra answered, "but this is a large house-party and I think they find visiting maids a nuisance."

"I don't know what your mother would say, I don't really! Going off alone like this!" Hannah said. "And if it's all above-board and respectable why can't His Lordship fetch you from here?"

"Please, Hannah, help me," Cassandra pleaded. "I told you I was acting a part, and I promise you there is nothing wrong in the place where I am going. Aunt Eleanor knows all about Lord and Lady Carwen, and if there was anything wrong she would have told me about it."

"Well, I don't like it and that's a fact!" Hannah said positively. "While I'm able to keep my eye on you, I know you can't get into any real mischief, but to stay in a strange place without me—Heaven knows what might happen!"

"What could happen?" Cassandra asked. "And it is only for two nights. Come to the flat on Monday morning and wait for me. If I am not there before luncheon, I shall certainly arrive soon afterwards."

Grumbling, muttering to herself, and being extremely disagreeable, Hannah began to pack the clothes she thought Cassandra would require.

Then they took the trunks to the flat in Bury Street and she packed Cassandra's theatrical clothes under protest.

On one thing Hannah was adamant and made such a scene that Cassandra was obliged to give in to her.

She insisted that Cassandra should travel to the country in one of her own gowns covered with a cloak which was both warm and decorative.

"You'll catch your death of cold in these new flimsy garments in which no respectable young woman would be seen," Hannah said aggressively. "Besides, you'll look a figure of fun arriving to stay at a country house in something that's only fit to be worn on the other side of the footlights."

Finally, because it was too exhausting to argue further, Cassandra gave in and wore the gown of sapphire blue velvet which had cost her father a large sum at Jay's.

It had a velvet bonnet in the same colour trimmed demurely only with little bows of ribbon.

It made her look very young, but it also threw into prominence the dazzling whiteness of her skin and accentuated the gold lights in her red hair.

Cassandra remembered consolingly that people thought she looked theatrical without the addition of the gowns she had bought at Chasemore's. She doubted if the Duke would notice any appreciable difference from her appearance on the previous day.

Besides the difficulties of getting ready, moving her trunks to Bury Street, and keeping Hannah from open rebellion, she had a very special letter to write.

Once again she forged her father's hand-writing on the engraved writing-paper she had brought from Yorkshire, as she wrote to Tattersall's Sales-Room instructing them to buy all the Duke's horses when they came up for sale on Monday.

As she signed her father's signature, Cassandra knew that this action put a time limit on the length of her stay in London.

She would have to arrive home before he received a notification from Tattersall's of their purchases for him together with the bill for them.

She was quite certain in her own mind that she was only anticipating her father's wishes in buying the Duke's horses; but at the same time she was well aware she would have some explaining to do, and that she would have to do it in person.

Even to herself, she would not face up to what she expected to happen between today and Tuesday morning when she must go back to Yorkshire.

Once again she was conscious of being swept along on a flowing tide. Once again she was aware that something tremendous was happening, but she could not formulate it to herself.

She only knew that she loved the Duke overwhelmingly.

Every hour she was away from him seemed to pass so slowly that it might have been a year, a century. But when she was with him, time flashed by so that the moment of parting seemed always to be upon them.

He had said that for him "the sands were running out," and Cassandra felt the same expression was true for herself—and yet what did she hope or fear for the future?

She despatched a footman from Park Lane to Tattersall's Sales-Rooms before she travelled to the flat in a closed carriage with Hannah.

"I can't imagine what the Coachman'll be thinking of us going to such a place," Hannah said sourly.

"I hope you told the servants that I had a friend I visited in Bury Street."

"I'm not soiling my mouth with a lot of lies, Miss Cassandra," Hannah said tartly, "and I've always believed 'least said, soonest mended.'"

It was true that Hannah was not a gossip, Cassandra thought, but she too had taken a violent dislike to the flat and she knew she would be extremely glad when she could see the last of it.

She left all her trunks but one in the Hall. The porter carried up only the round topped piece in which she wished Hannah to pack the gowns from Chasemore's.

Hannah sniffed and muttered all the time she was folding them, and just as she finished, Cassandra, who had been watching from the window, exclaimed:

"The carriage is here! Oh, I think there are two of them."

She had not told Hannah who was fetching her, and now she hurried down the stairs to greet the Duke as he stepped into the Hall.

"I am ready," she said with a lilt of joy in her voice.

She saw that his eyes rested on her admiringly and was glad that after all she had conceded a victory to Hannah by wearing the sapphire outfit.

"I see you have a warm cloak," he said. "I am glad about that, because as it is a fine day I suggest that we drive in my open Phaeton. If it rains, there is a hood we can raise. I have also brought a brake for our luggage. My valet will see to yours."

"I shall enjoy being in the fresh air," Cassandra replied.

She noticed that today the Duke had a different Phaeton from the one he had used the day before, when there had been a groom seated behind them.

Built for speed, there was room for only two people in it.

She saw a man climb down from the brake which was driven by a Coachman wearing the Alchester livery and a cockaded tall hat.

She thought, as she saw him enter the flat, that she had been wise to tell Hannah to put the trunk that had been packed upstairs outside on the landing and close the door.

She did not want Hannah to meet the Duke's servants.

The Duke helped her into the Phaeton, and as they set off down Jermyn Street, Cassandra said:

"You have not forgotten that we are going to see Nancy?"

"I have already been there."

"You have?" Cassandra ejaculated in surprise. "How was she?"

In reply the Duke held out an envelope which she took from him. There was a grim expression on his face which made her exclaim:

"What has happened? What did she say?"

"She was not there," the Duke said quietly.

Cassandra stared at him in surprise then she looked at the envelope he had given her.

Written on the outside was just her name: "Sandra."

She opened it. Inside was a brief letter written in an educated, tidy handwriting, but in pencil.

"You were so kind, but there is nothing you or anyone else can do for me. I would rather face God than my father! He is more likely to forgive me.

Nancy."

Cassandra read it through. Then she said fearfully:

"What does she mean? Where had she gone? I do not . . . understand."

"I went up to her bed-room," the Duke answered. "The door was unlocked and she was not there. On the dressing-table I found this letter and the money I had given to her last night."

"But what had she . . . done?" Cassandra cried.

"I think it is obvious," the Duke answered, "that she has taken the easiest way out of her dilemma. She really had little alternative."

"You mean she has . . . killed herself?"

"I imagine she will be one of the unidentified bodies that are fished out of the river every day," the Duke said. "Many of them are in fact in the same condition as Nancy Wood."

"But we must do something . . . find out for certain!"

"It would involve you with the police," the Duke said, "and I do not think that is at all desirable."

At the thought of the police Cassandra was suddenly still.

"After all," the Duke went on, "all we have to show them is this note left for you. We do not know how to find her father, his name may not even be Wood."

"No . . . of course . . . not," Cassandra agreed.

"It would cause a scandal for you and for me to be involved publicly in this tragedy," the Duke continued. "And we are too late to help her."

"But will not the . . . police, or Nancy's landlord make enquiries?"

"I doubt if either of them will trouble themselves unduly," the Duke replied. "The police will find it difficult to discover who she is. The landlord, when she does not return, will pocket the money which we left behind in lieu of rent and dispose of her belongings."

Cassandra sat stunned by shock. At the same time she knew that if the police discovered that she and the Duke were the last people to see Nancy alive, her subterfuge would be revealed.

Her father would be furious if this happened, and she was well aware what a story the newspapers would make of it.

But she was at the moment very appalled at the thought of what had happened to Nancy.

"It is horrible! It is cruel! How could she have . . . done such a . . . thing?" Cassandra cried.

The Duke did not reply but concentrated on driving his horses. After a moment she went on in a low voice:

"She told me last night that her father would never . . . forgive her. It seems . . . un-Christian and . . . wicked to punish her so . . . severely."

The Duke still made no answer. Cassandra stared ahead seeing only Nancy Wood's white, frightened face, hearing the despairing note in her voice which had been followed by a flood of hopeless tears.

After they had driven for some distance, the Duke said:

"I want you to try to forget what has happened. It is something that you should not have experienced. Dwelling on it will help no-one."

He paused as if he searched for words before he continued:

"I cannot help thinking that from her own point of view Nancy Wood did the best thing possible. What future could there possibly be for her or her child?"

That was a sensible view, Cassandra had to agree, and yet she could only feel almost physically sick at the thought of the wretched girl going out, perhaps at dawn, to seek oblivion in the dark cold waters of the Thames.

But she told herself that the Duke was right.

To keep thinking about it, to wonder if she could have prevented such a tragedy, to reproach herself for not having given Nancy Wood more help than she had been able to do, would only make her miserable to no purpose and would ruin this lovely day alone with the Duke.

She could quite understand that he found this whole subject distasteful, but in a way, she wished she could have asked him more questions.

She wanted to understand how a Vicar's daughter, brought up in a decent household, could have got herself into such trouble, and why there was no man to marry her, thereby making the child legitimate.

There were so many questions to which Cassandra could not find an answer, but she knew that she must not pester the Duke with them.

In any case, in all probability he would refuse to reply.

It all seemed to her very mysterious, but at the same time, she had only to think of the dirty boarding-house and Nancy Wood's untidy, squalid bed-room to see that for his sake she must try to forget.

With an effort, Cassandra told herself to think of the Duke. He wanted to be amused, to be gay. This situation could do nothing but irritate and embarrass him.

She could almost feel it putting a barrier between them. So, desperately, because she felt her own happiness was slipping away from her, Cassandra tried to talk of other things.

As if he understood the effort she was making, the Duke talked of his horses.

He told Cassandra the pedigrees of the ones he was driving, described some of the sales he had visited in his father's time.

The old Duke had gloried in visiting Horse-Fairs all over the country, always hoping, as many owners had hoped, before him, to discover a Derby winner being sold for a few pounds.

"Some men collect horses, as other men collect pictures and 'objets d'art'," the Duke smiled.

"Is that what you would like to do?"

"I have no opportunity of doing either at the moment," he replied. "If I had the chance, I would be greedy and collect both!"

"I am sure you have some very fine pictures at Alchester Park," Cassandra said.

"The family collection is unique," he said. "Every head of the family and his wife all down the ages have been painted for posterity—some by great artists—some by what my father used to call 'the village carpenter'."

He laughed.

"But they are all there: first the Earls and Countesses of Alchester, and—then after the Dukedom was created, every Duke and Duchess."

"Has your portrait yet been added to the others?" Cassandra asked.

"No," the Duke replied. "It is traditional that the owner of the title waits until he is married."

As he spoke Cassandra saw a shadow cross his face.

She knew he was thinking of the marriage that had been arranged for him years ago and to which today he was committing himself.

She had an impulse to tell him the truth—and then quite suddenly she was afraid.

When she had planned this wild escapade, she had known that at the back of her mind lay the idea that if after all the Duke was not in love with someone else she might be able to attract him.

Then as in a fairy story, she would only have to throw off her disguise and reveal her true identity.

Now for the first time she had the feeling that the Duke might well resent being tricked and imposed upon.

Her dreams had all been concerned with what was really a cardboard figure of a man. The pictures and portraits of the Marquis had filled her adolescent dreams.

But they were not of a man who was flesh and blood; a man who had kissed the palm of her hand and wished to kiss her lips; a man who had said that only actors and actresses were free to be themselves.

'I have made a mess of it!' Cassandra admitted to herself frankly.

And her brain was busy with how she could extricate herself from a position that she felt now might so easily be misinterpreted.

They had been driving into the country for some time before Cassandra asked where they were going.

"Lord Carwen's house is only three-quarters of an hour's drive from London, I thought," she said. "Surely we shall arrive too soon? He did not ask us until tea-time."

"I have no intention of turning up one moment before we have to," the Duke answered. "I am taking you to luncheon at an Inn which I think you will enjoy. It is on the river and later in the year is very popular, but I do not think today we will find it very crowded."

The Duke was right in his assumption. The Inn was charming.

Having arranged stabling for the horses, he escorted Cassandra to the Dining-Room and they were seated at a table in the window, overlooking the slow-moving silver Thames.

The Inn was old, with great oak beams and a huge open fireplace in which a log-fire was burning.

The Duke ordered wine, and the meal, though simple, was well-cooked and palatable.

It was easy as they faced each other across the small table in the window to forget the tragedy of Nancy Wood and to pick up their discussion where they had left off the night before.

Cassandra realised she had been right in thinking that the Duke was extremely clever.

She knew that she herself had an intelligence superior to many of her contemporaries. There was no doubt that they stimulated each other's mind, capped each other's quotations, and were able to argue as equals.

"How dare you be beautiful as well as clever?" the Duke demanded at one moment when he found some argument of Cassandra's unanswerable.

"You do not make that sound as if it were a compliment," Cassandra replied.

"It is not!" the Duke said. "Most men dislike clever women. They are frightened of them."

"And you?"

"I find you very interesting, Sandra, but it perplexes me why, being so intelligent, you have chosen your particular profession."

"There are not many careers open to women," Cassandra replied.

"That is true," the Duke answered. "Who would want to see women Members of Parliament, women lawyers, women stockbrokers, or worst of all—a woman Judge!"

"Why would that be so horrifying?" Cassandra asked.

"Because women are always prejudiced. Their minds are supremely illogical."

This was a provocation Cassandra could not let pass, and once again they were arguing fiercely with each other, until the Duke threw himself back in his seat to say:

"I take back all I said! You are a blue-stocking! If you were my daughter I should pack you off to Oxford and see how you fared at Somerville amongst the student feminists."

Cassandra smiled and he added:

"You see, it is really not fair when you look like that with your lips curved in a smile. No man could refuse you anything, whatever the odds against him!"

They sat for a long time after luncheon was over.

There had been few other guests in the Inn besides themselves, and when they had departed the waiters seemed to disappear too, and Cassandra and the Duke were alone.

"I wish we did not have to leave here to go on to this boring house-party," he said suddenly.

"Will it be boring?" Cassandra enquired.

"There will be other people there," he replied, "and I want you to myself. I want to talk to you; to listen to you; to be with you. Anyone else, whoever they may be, will be an interruption which I shall resent."

"I, too, would . . . much rather be just with . . . you," Cassandra murmured.

"Do you mean that?" he asked.

He leaned forward as he spoke and took her hand in his.

Once again she felt herself quiver because he was touching her. As their eyes met, he said in a low voice:

"Do you know what has happened to us, Sandra?"

She did not reply and after a moment he went on:

"I think I fell in love with you the moment we were introduced. It was not only that I thought you more lovely and attractive than anyone I had ever seen before, but there was something else. Did you feel it too?"

It was impossible for Cassandra to speak, her heart was thumping so wildly in her breast. Then the Duke released her hand and stood up.

"There is no point in talking about it," he said harshly. "Come! If I take you by a somewhat round-about route so that you can see the countryside we should arrive at exactly the right time at His Lordship's residence."

For a moment it was difficult for Cassandra to move.

She felt as if by his abruptness he had slapped her in the face. Then suddenly she realised she faced a new and even worse dilemma.

The Duke had admitted loving her, but he was not prepared to do anything about it!

His head would rule his heart! Money was more important to him than love!

Because Cassandra loved him so that her whole being vibrated with it, she could not bear the thought that his love for her was something he could set aside for mercenary reasons.

Now she knew that she had brought upon herself an agony that was almost impossible to contemplate.

He loved her!

He had fallen in love with her just as she had hoped he would, but he was quite prepared to give her up for a rich heiress he had never seen, but who would bring him the millions he needed.

It had been bad enough to envisage the Duke, her ideal man, the hero of her girlish dreams, being in love with someone else.

But that he should be in love with her, and yet not have the courage to do anything about it, was a pain beyond anything she had imagined she might endure.

As she rose from her seat at the table, she felt as if she could not go on with the farce any longer.

Then she knew that having once embarked on this crazy adventure, she must continue playing her assumed part at least until they returned to London.

She could not face him now with the truth!

She could not bear either the contempt with which he might treat her or worse still, his delight in finding that he could have for the asking both the woman he loved and the money which he needed so desperately!

'I cannot bear it,' Cassandra whispered to herself.

She knew that if she had thought it difficult to act in the past, it would be far more difficult to act now as if nothing of any consequence had occurred.

The horses were harnessed to the Phaeton once again, and by the time they set off it was growing late in the afternoon.

The country was very beautiful. There was no wind and it was therefore comparatively warm. There were primroses under the hedgerows and the daffodils were showing their golden trumpets among the young grass in the meadows.

Cassandra was telling herself that she almost hated the Duke, when he turned his head to look at her and say softly:

"When I look at you, I think you are spring and in some magical manner you can disperse for me the darkness of winter."

There was a note in his voice that made her heart seem to turn over in her breast. She longed to move closer to him, to rest her head against his shoulder.

'What does it matter what happens tomorrow?' she asked herself wildly, 'as long as we can have today?'

He was near her, and when he spoke to her with just that note in his voice and that particular expression in his eyes, the only thing that mattered was that they were together.

They travelled for miles down twisting lanes, along cart-tracks and through woods to the top of a hill where they could look over the valley towards the Chiltern Hills.

They spoke of many superficial things, but Cassandra knew that they were conscious only of each other's hearts.

Something magical had happened! Something which drew them closer to each other every second, until she felt, although he had not touched her, she was in his arms, and that with every word he spoke, he kissed her lips.

Then all too soon the sun was beginning to sink in the West, the sky was a kaleidoscope of colour and below them was a huge stone mansion, its roofs impressively ornate above the trees which surrounded it.

"Is that the house?" Cassandra asked.

"It is," the Duke replied briefly.

Cassandra thought as they drew nearer that it was typical of Lord Carwen to own a place which seemed to symbolise importance, pomposity and wealth.

The green lawns with their stereotyped flower beds; the gold-tipped iron gates; the yew hedges fashioned by topiary work into travesties of nature, seemed to her to reveal the character of their owner.

She was sure of this when they entered the huge Hall, where half a dozen footmen in a grandiose livery bedecked with gold braid were in attendance.

"His Lordship lives in style," Cassandra commented as she and the Duke followed an imposing Major-Domo down wide corridors hung with valuable pictures.

They reached a large Drawing-Room and Cassandra saw Lord Carwen detach himself from a small group of people centred round the mantel-piece at the far end of it.

He advanced towards them.

Taking Cassandra's hand in his he raised it to his lips.

"May I welcome you to my home, pretty lady?" he said with a look in his eyes which she particularly disliked.

She curtsied and withdrew her hand from his with some difficulty.

"Varro, my dear boy," Lord Carwen said to the Duke, "you know you are always welcome. I think you know everyone who has arrived so far, but I must introduce Sandra."

By the time Cassandra was able to go upstairs for a short rest before dinner more guests had arrived. They were mostly men, with a few exceptions of Lord Carwen's age and on intimate terms with him.

He chaffed them in a manner which Cassandra felt was vaguely insulting to her and the other women present.

It was not the way she would have expected her father to speak in a lady's presence, and then she realised that to Lord Carwen she was not a lady!

She was not certain, either, how to place His Lordship's other female guests.

There was a very attractive woman of about thirty-five, obviously well-born, who was flirting with sophisticated expertise with the Earl of Wilmere.

He was a middle-aged man and responded with bursts of loud laughter. The innuendo in most of the things he said were lost on Cassandra.

They kept referring to episodes when "we did this" and "we did that," and seemed so intimate that Cassandra innocently thought they were man and wife.

When she accompanied the other ladies upstairs to find their bed-rooms, she said, making polite conversation:

"Do you and your husband live in the country?"

The woman, whom Cassandra later found was called Lady McDonald, laughed derisively.

"He is not my husband!" she exclaimed. "I only wish he were, and poor old Jimmy wishes it too! But unfortunately he has a dragon of a wife and six extremely tiresome children!"

Cassandra's eyes widened in astonishment.

"How is your husband, Julie?" one of the other women asked.

"As boring as ever," Lady McDonald replied, "wrapped in tartan and his pride in the frozen North."

"He still refuses to divorce you?"

"He is adamant about it!" Lady McDonald answered. "Says there has never been a scandal in the family since Robert the Bruce liaised with the Spider!"

Her laughter at her own joke echoed round the Hall.

Cassandra was shocked. Then she told herself that it was exactly what she might have expected.

After all, both Lord Carwen and the Duke thought that she was an actress, and an actress would certainly not have been invited to a house-party together with someone like her mother or indeed with any lady of her acquaintance.

'It will be amusing to see how these sort of people behave,' she told herself.

At the same time she knew that the manner in which the gentlemen had joked not only amongst themselves, but with Lady McDonald and the other women downstairs had made her feel embarrassed.

She learnt that more guests would be arriving much later in the evening after the theatres closed.

There would be Lily Langtry and Freddy Gebhard besides, judging by what Lord Carwen said, several well-known figures from the Gaiety and the leading lady of Daly's Theatre.

"We shall be quite a packed house," Lady McDonald said as they reached the top of the staircase. "Now, let us see where everyone is sleeping."

Lying on a table on the wide landing was a plan of the bed-rooms.

Cassandra looked at it and thought she had never before seen such a thing at any house at which she had been a guest.

There was always a plan of the dining-table so that guests could

go straight to their places without having to wander around the
table looking for the card on which their name was inscribed.

But to have the bed-rooms planned in such a manner was something new!

She saw that the majority of rooms were arranged in suites; her
own, which was named "The Blue Room," had a Boudoir and
Dressing-Room attached.

She saw it was not far away from "The Master-Suite," and that
the Duke was only just round the corner in what was entitled "The
Red Room."

Lady McDonald was commenting on the rooms which had been
allotted to two people called Rosie and Jack.

"Jack will have to go out in the corridor," she giggled, "and if
there is one thing he dislikes, it is having to do that!"

They all laughed, and Cassandra wondered why it should upset
anyone to have to go into the corridor, especially one as well-
heated and well-furnished as those that she saw on either side of
the staircase.

But a great deal of the women's chatter was incomprehensible,
and she was glad when she could retire to her own room and find
that Lord Carwen's housemaids had unpacked for her.

She rang the bell and a maid came to undo her gown.

"Will you rest on the bed, Miss, or on the chaise-longue?" she
enquired.

"On the bed," Cassandra answered.

She put on the silk wrap which Hannah had packed for her, and
the maid having removed the bedspread, she settled herself against
the pillows and was covered by a satin eiderdown.

"I would like my bath an hour before dinner," she told the maid
and shut her eyes.

She thought she might be able to sleep, because having been up
late last night she was in fact a little tired.

Instead she found herself thinking of the Duke and the moment
that he told her that he had fallen in love with her! She had
known, even as he held her eyes spellbound, that he was speaking
in all sincerity.

He was in love as she was in love!

They were drawn to each other and there was no escape.

'I want him to love me,' Cassandra admitted to herself. 'But I also
want him to think that nothing else, not even money, is of importance beside our love.'

She thought of the bitterness in his face when he told her that his horses were to be sold at Tattersall's.

She wondered what else he had disposed of, and thought that Alchester Park must be filled with treasures that would fetch enormous sums of money in the London Sale-Rooms.

'I want him to tell me the truth,' she thought. 'I want him to admit to me that he is marrying for money, and then perhaps I can tell him who I am.'

Yet again there came that little tremor of fear that he might be angry because she had deceived him.

She was still thinking of the Duke when the maid came back to light the gas-lamps, make up the fire, and bring in the bath in which Cassandra could bathe by the fire-side.

Lady Carwen might be in Paris, but she certainly provided every expensive luxury for her guests.

There were three different oils from which Cassandra could choose to scent the bath-water, and the towels, which were embroidered with a huge coronet, smelt of lavender.

She noticed also that throughout the house there were bowls of pot-pourri obviously made, as her mother made hers at home, from the flowers in the garden.

The sheets and pillow-cases were edged with lace and there was an ermine rug lying on the chaise-longue.

The desk contained every possible facility for writing a letter. There was a jewel-studded pen-holder, a blotter with gold corners, a writing-paper box in red leather. There was a clock with a face encircled by diamonds.

There was an onyx pen-tray, a tortoise-shell letter-opener, a calendar framed in polished silver, and innumerable other objects, all of which were designed to make letter-writing an Art.

There were also carnations and a profusion of yellow daffodils to decorate not only the bed-room but the adjacent Boudoir into which Cassandra peeped before she went downstairs.

"Which gown will you wear, Miss?" the maid enquired.

Quite suddenly Cassandra knew she could not go down flaunting one of the low-cut theatrical dresses she had bought from Chasemore's.

She had a revulsion for the women who were already staying in the house.

There was no need for her to look at their exaggeratedly fashionable clothes to know that they were not the type of whom her mother would approve.

The way they laughed, the boldness of their eyes, their hands which seemed to be always reaching out to pat a masculine arm or to hold on to the lapel of a coat, were more revealing even than anything they said or wore.

Cassandra looked with distaste at the glittering green gown she had worn on the first night to Lord Carwen's party, at one of jonquil yellow and another of coral pink satin.

She pointed instead to one of her own gowns which Hannah had packed regardless of her protests.

It was exquisitely styled. The very soft lace which was draped over the front of the full skirt, swept backwards into quite a small bustle at the back, to fall in frills to the floor.

The *décolletage* was much higher and indeed correct for a young girl, but it revealed Cassandra's tiny waist and the perfect symmetry of her white arms.

Tonight she did not even attempt to open her jewel-case, and she asked the maid to arrange her hair in the exact manner in which Hannah had done it before she left London.

The long tresses of fire-touched gold were swept around her head to make it small and almost Grecian in shape.

But however subdued Cassandra might wish to appear, there was nothing she could do to conceal the brilliant blue of her eyes or the dark lashes which seemed too long to be natural.

Because she felt it might cause comment if she left her face untouched, she flicked just a suspicion of powder onto her cheeks and put the faintest touch of salve on her lips.

"You look lovely, Miss, if I may say so!" the maid remarked.

"Thank you," Cassandra smiled.

"I have never seen a more lovely dress," the maid went on. "When I unpacked it, I thought it might be a wedding-gown!"

Cassandra turned towards the door.

"Thank you for helping me to dress," she said and walked downstairs.

She felt a little nervous as a footman opened the door of the Drawing-Room.

It was a very attractive room lit by a great Chandelier in the centre while candles in huge carved Italian candlesticks illuminated the rest of the room.

Lord Carwen had already said before dinner that he thought gaslight was ugly and that women looked their best by candlelight.

He was standing in front of the fireplace as Cassandra entered and she realised as she moved towards him that she was the first guest down to dinner.

"It seems I am a little early," she said quickly.

"You could never be too early for me."

As Lord Carwen spoke he took her hand and held it close against his lips.

Cassandra felt herself shiver from the warm possessiveness of his mouth, and she disliked even more the way his eyes looked at her. She thought she saw a touch of fire in them.

"You are very lovely," he said, "and I cannot tell you how happy it makes me to have you here in my own house. We have a lot to say to each other, little Sandra."

Cassandra was concerned with trying to take her hand from his grasp but he would not relinquish it.

"Please," she said insistently, a flush coming to her cheeks.

"Are you afraid that the others will come in and see us?" Lord Carwen asked. "In that case, Sandra, later we will go somewhere quiet where we can get to know each other."

He let her hand go as if reluctantly, and Cassandra walked quickly away from him towards the fireplace.

"I know," Lord Carwen said following her and standing too close, "that we are going to mean a great deal to each other, you and I."

"I think you are mistaken, My Lord," Cassandra answered firmly.

"I am never mistaken where a pretty woman is concerned," Lord Carwen said. "I knew as soon as I saw you, Sandra, you were someone I wished to know well—very well."

Cassandra turned her head away from him to look into the flames.

"I have a present for you which I know will please you," he said softly.

He looked at her bare neck and she felt as if he touched it with his fingers.

"You may tell me which is your favourite stone," he went on, "but I have already decided that diamonds become you best."

There was no mistaking the insinuation behind his words and Cassandra moving away from him said formally:

"I never accept presents from—strangers, My Lord."

"We will not be strangers for long," Lord Carwen smiled.

She thought there was a confidence about him that was unassailable. He was so sure of himself; so completely convinced that he could say or do as he wished and she would not rebuff him.

"I am afraid you are under a misapprehension," Cassandra said. "I am here because I am a friend of the Duke. You invited us together and it was a great pleasure to drive here with him in his Phaeton. I hope that is clear?"

She wondered as she spoke if she had been too rude, considering that Lord Carwen was her host.

To her surprise he laughed!

"I like your spirit," he said, "but I assure you you will find me very much more generous than Alchester can afford to be, and the more I see you the more I am convinced that we shall get along very well together."

"You are mistaken, My Lord," Cassandra said sharply.

Then to her relief the Drawing-Room door opened and the Duke came in.

She turned to him with what was almost a little cry of gladness and if she had not restrained herself, she would have run down the room to meet him.

She wanted to hold on to him to make sure he was there, to know that he would protect her, although she could hardly say that Lord Carwen's advances had been actually menacing.

And yet she was afraid!

She knew that, even as the Duke came to her side, for some inexplicable reason she was really very frightened.

CHAPTER SEVEN

Dinner was not so noisy or so gay as Cassandra had expected.

Since there were extra men, some of them had to sit together and they instantly began to talk sport. Even the Earl of Wilmere's normally unrestrained laughter seemed more subdued than it had earlier.

Cassandra was glad to find that she was not next to Lord Carwen.

Instead she was on the right of the Duke with a middle-aged man on her right. He was engrossed in talking about the shooting prospects for the coming year with the gentleman on his right.

Cassandra found herself thinking that the Duke was very quiet, and she fancied that when he was not actually speaking to her there was a frown between his eyes.

She wondered if it had anything to do with the conversation that had taken place when he had come into the Drawing-Room and found her alone with Lord Carwen.

She had been glad and relieved to see him, but she fancied that, as he advanced across the room, there was a grim expression on his face.

"I want to speak to you, Varro," Lord Carwen said as he reached the hearth-rug.

The Duke did not answer. He merely looked at his host expectantly.

"De Veet has arrived and I want you to be nice to him."

"I do not like him," the Duke replied in an uncompromising voice.

"That is immaterial!" Lord Carwen retorted.

"On the contrary, I think it is very pertinent to the matter in question," the Duke contradicted. "I am quite convinced that he is not to be trusted."

"That may be your opinion," Lord Carwen said, "but I have gone into the matter very thoroughly, and I can assure you, Varro, that your apprehensions are quite unfounded."

The Duke walked nearer to the fireplace and stood holding his hands out towards the fire as if he felt cold.

Then he said quietly:

"I am still not interested, Carwen."

Cassandra saw an expression of anger in Lord Carwen's eyes.

"Now look here, Varro—" he began, but before he could say any more the door opened to admit a number of other members of the house-party.

Several new guests appeared to have arrived while they were changing for dinner. Among them was Mr. De Veet, who, Cassandra learned, was a South African.

He was a heavy, coarse man, flashily dressed, who spoke with a decided accent. Looking at him perceptively, Cassandra was certain the Duke was right and he was not to be trusted.

She wondered why Lord Carwen was so anxious for the Duke to be nice to Mr. De Veet.

She came to the conclusion there must be some matter of business involved, because Lord Carwen himself went out of his way to be almost over-effusive to his guest.

At dinner Mr. De Veet had two of the prettiest women in the party on either side of him.

Later, when Lord Carwen's theatrical guests arrived from London, it was obvious that the party was to be paired off, every man being more or less allotted a particular woman in whom he either already had, or was expected to take, an interest.

Dinner was so long drawn out with many courses, and the gentlemen lingered so long over their Port, that there was in fact little time to wait before Lily Langtry arrived with Freddy Gebhard.

They were followed shortly by the ladies of the theatre who, Cassandra learned, had been conveyed to the country by Lord Carwen's fastest horses.

Mrs. Langtry was looking very beautiful.

She arrived wearing full evening-dress with magnificent jewellery, and she looked so elegant without a hair out of place that she might have stepped from behind the footlights into the Drawing-Room.

Everyone present paid her extravagant compliments and she

greeted Cassandra with a charming smile, although it was obvious she was surprised to find she was staying in the house.

"I am grateful to you, Lily, for introducing me to the entrancing Sandra," Lord Carwen said. "But then your taste has always been impeccable."

"I understood it was Varro she wished to meet," Mrs. Langtry replied, with what Cassandra felt was a hint of mischief in her eyes.

"Varro is also here," Lord Carwen remarked.

"How kind of you," Mrs. Langtry said with a little smile.

Cassandra thought there was a suggestion of sarcasm in her voice.

As soon as everyone had arrived, a room off the Drawing-Room was opened to reveal a roulette table, in addition to which the guests could play Baccarat or Bridge.

It was obvious, Cassandra noticed, that the women were carrying no money with them and that the gentlemen were expected to act as their backers.

A great number of golden sovereigns were soon lying on the green-baize tables.

"Do you want to play?" the Duke asked.

Cassandra shook her head.

"I hate gambling!"

"Then let us sit by the fire," he suggested, and they remained behind in the Drawing-Room while the rest of the party clustered round the tables in the Card-Room.

"I think I shall go to bed soon," Cassandra said. "This is my third night of gaiety and I feel rather tired."

"You certainly do not show it," the Duke answered.

He looked at her sitting in a chair which framed the soft ivory lace of her gown. The golden lights in her red hair glittered in the candlelight and her eyes were very blue.

It seemed as if there was little they had to say to each other, and yet Cassandra knew it was a joy beyond words to be with him; to feel that they were together, although they were surrounded by other people and in the house of a man she disliked.

She had a feeling the Duke was thinking the same thing.

Suddenly feeling shy of the expression in his eyes, she turned her head away to look into the fire.

"I was very happy today," the Duke said softly.

"It was . . . something I have never done . . . before," Cassandra said without thinking.

"What have you never done before?" the Duke enquired.

"Driven alone with a man and had luncheon at an Inn."

She was speaking more to herself than to him, and then she feared he might think it strange that as an actress she should not find such occasions quite ordinary.

He was about to say something when Lord Carwen came back into the Drawing-Room.

"I wondered what had happened to you both," he said.

His tone was not accusing but perfectly pleasant.

"I do not gamble," Cassandra said quickly.

"Perhaps you do not know how to do so," Lord Carwen suggested. "Let me be your instructor."

"No, thank you," Cassandra replied. "Quite frankly I think it is a silly way of passing the time, when one might be talking or reading or doing something else more interesting."

"There I agree with you," Lord Carwen smiled.

He turned to the Duke.

"Varro, if you are really determined not to do as I have asked you with regard to De Veet, will you have a word with him? He has just told me that he is counting on you, so, if you have really changed your mind, I feel it would be a mistake to leave him in ignorance."

"I have not changed my mind," the Duke answered. "I told you from the beginning I did not wish to be associated with him."

"I am afraid I did not understand that," Lord Carwen said. "In fact I told De Veet that you would represent me on his Board."

"That is something I have no intention of doing," the Duke said sharply.

"Then, my dear fellow, you must make your attitude clear to De Veet. He is suffering under the same misapprehension as I was, that you were definitely interested in his proposition. I think you had better tell him now—at once—before things go any further."

"I should have thought tomorrow would be soon enough!"

Lord Carwen shook his head.

"If you are not prepared to play ball, dear boy, then I have every intention of asking Wilmere. He has been badgering me for some time to put him in touch with just such a chance to make money."

The Duke rose slowly to his feet.

"Very well, I will speak to De Veet. Are you coming with me, Sandra?"

"Yes, of course," she answered.

She rose and moved towards the Duke, then as he turned towards the door into the Card-Room, Lord Carwen said:

"One moment, Sandra, I have something to show you."

Both Cassandra and the Duke stopped still.

"What is it?" Cassandra asked.

"Nothing more sensational," Lord Carwen replied with a twist of his lips, "than a plan of my Estate. You were talking to Colonel Henderson about it at dinner, I believe."

"Yes, I was," Cassandra answered. "Did he tell you so?"

"He told me that you were interested in my Point-to-Point Course that has been spoken of as a model of its kind. It certainly commanded a great deal of attention last week when we had our first meeting."

"Colonel Henderson described it to me," Cassandra said. "He told me your horses won two races."

"I should really thank Varro for that," Lord Carwen said agreeably. "He sold me the hunters and I was very pleased with their performance."

Cassandra glanced at the Duke and knew without his saying anything how much he must have disliked having to part with his precious hunters. Once again he must have been in pressing need of the money.

"I have the plans here on my desk," Lord Carwen said. "Let me show them to you."

There was nothing Cassandra could do but agree, and reluctantly the Duke walked away from her and into the Card-Room.

Cassandra had no wish to be alone with Lord Carwen, but she felt she could not refuse to look at his plans without being extremely rude.

Moreover it was unlikely that he would try to be over-familiar when the rest of the party were in the next room and might interrupt them at any moment.

Lord Carwen drew from the drawer of a bureau inlaid with ivory a plan which was headed "The Lord Carwen Point-to-Point, March 15th, 1886."

"Now let me show you why this is different from the usual Point-to-Point Course—" Lord Carwen began conversationally.

He spread the plan out as he spoke, and Cassandra with her experience of her father's private Steeple-Chase Course at The Towers realised that it was in fact very well planned.

"Unlike most Point-to-Points," Lord Carwen continued, "the

Judges here can keep an eye on the Competitors the whole way round, and of course it is more interesting for the spectators."

"What you have really devised," Cassandra said, "is a race-course."

"I suppose that is true," Lord Carwen said, "but I am not particularly interested in racing as such. It is Varro who thinks only of the 'Sport of Kings.'"

"His father's horses were famous," Cassandra said, almost as if she were defending the Duke.

"Would you like to own a race-horse of your own?" Lord Carwen asked.

"Not particularly," Cassandra answered.

She wondered what Lord Carwen would say if she told him that her father owned a large number of race-horses and had promised her that as soon as she was twenty-one that she could race under her own colours.

"I wonder what you would like to possess," Lord Carwen said.

Cassandra did not answer.

She was aware that he was looking at her with that expression in his eyes which she most disliked. So she merely bent her head over the plans on the desk.

She traced with the tip of her finger the course the riders would follow; noted the height of the jumps; and was certain that they would prove of little difficulty as far as her new horses, Firefly and Andora, were concerned.

Lord Carwen suddenly set down in front of her on the plan an open jewel-case.

In it lay a broad diamond bracelet glittering in the light from the Chandelier.

For an instant Cassandra was still. Then she said coldly:

"I have already told you, My Lord, that I do not accept presents from strangers."

"I am not a stranger," Lord Carwen answered, "and you know as well as I do that diamonds are something every sensible girl should collect, besides being vastly becoming to a skin as white as yours."

"Thank you," Cassandra replied, "but my answer is no."

She would have turned away, but Lord Carwen caught her by the wrist.

"When you are as sweet to me as I wish you to be," he said softly, "I will give you a necklace to match the bracelet."

"You seem to find it very difficult to understand plain English," Cassandra replied. "How can I make you realise, My Lord, that I will not accept a gift of any sort from you? No diamonds, however large, however expensive, will tempt me to alter my decision."

"I suppose you fancy yourself in love with Varro?" Lord Carwen said, and now there was something like a snarl in his voice.

"That has nothing to do with it!"

"I think it has," Lord Carwen insisted. "But let me inform you that Varro can give you nothing while I am a very generous man!"

Cassandra tried to release herself but his fingers were still clasped tightly around her wrist.

She was not really afraid. She could hear the voices of the other guests as they crowded round the tables in the Gambling-Room, and she knew Lord Carwen would not risk her calling out or making a scene.

"Let me go!" she said firmly but quietly.

"I cannot credit you are serious in refusing my presents," Lord Carwen answered making no motion to release her.

"You do not appear to listen to what I say."

"You are entrancing! You attract me more than any woman I have seen for years. It is not only that enticing red hair of yours, but the curl of your lips, the way your eyes glint under those long dark lashes."

"I do not wish you to say such things to me," Cassandra said. "I am here as your guest and I must ask you to treat me with courtesy."

Lord Carwen laughed.

"I have no desire to be courteous to you, Sandra. I want to make love to you; to kiss you; to awaken a response in that perfect little body of yours!"

He paused before he added:

"I cannot believe that anyone with hair the colour of yours would not be passionate in response to the desire you arouse in me."

"Again you are mistaken," Cassandra said, holding her chin high. "How can I make it clearer to Your Lordship? You simply do not attract me."

"But you attract me!" Lord Carwen retorted. "And as far as I am concerned, that is all that matters!"

"I see I made a mistake in accepting your hospitality," Cassandra said. "It would clearly be best if I asked His Grace to take me away tomorrow morning."

"You fascinate me by the challenge in your voice," Lord Carwen said, apparently quite unabashed. "You bewitch me with every word you say and every movement you make! You are adorable and very exciting, little Sandra!"

Once again Cassandra tried to free herself from the tight hold he had on her wrist.

"Shall I tell you something?" he asked.

She did not reply and he went on:

"Women always change their minds and I will make you change yours. I want you, Sandra, and I intend to have you! And let me tell you I am a very determined fighter."

"Then I am afraid, My Lord, that on this occasion you have met your Waterloo!" Cassandra answered coolly.

She twisted her arm unexpectedly and was free. Without another word she turned her back on him and walked away across the room.

She knew he was watching her and heard him laugh very softly beneath his breath.

'Why should I be frightened of him?' she asked herself. 'At the same time, I shall leave tomorrow morning.'

She found the Duke talking to Mr. De Veet in a corner of the Card-Room. They were both looking cross, Cassandra thought, and the Duke's eyes lit up when he saw her.

She went to his side, resisting an impulse to hold on to him as if she needed his protection.

"I think it is time I went to bed."

"I quite agree," the Duke answered. "You have had a long day."

He turned towards Mr. De Veet.

"You must excuse me, De Veet. There is really no point in discussing it any further."

"Let me try to persuade Your Grace," Mr. De Veet answered in a gutteral voice.

"It will be a waste of time!" the Duke said quietly.

He took Cassandra's arm and led her towards the door into the Hall; but before they had reached it they encountered Mrs. Langtry.

"I have lost a lot of Freddy's money," she said to the Duke, "and so the sooner I retire, the better. I never was a good gambler!"

"I dislike gambling in private houses," the Duke answered.

"I quite agree with you," Freddy Gebhard said, "and we are both tired. It must be very late."

The first move having been made, it appeared that most of the other people in the party were ready to do the same, and Cassandra walked up the stairs with Mrs. Langtry and most of the other ladies in the party.

It was impossible for her to have a last word with the Duke or even to say good-night to him with everyone listening.

She wanted to tell him how Lord Carwen had behaved, but there was no opportunity.

The same maid came to her room to undo her gown, and when she was alone she brushed her hair and finally was ready to get into bed.

It was then a thought struck her and she walked to the door to turn the key in the lock. But there was no key!

She stared in perplexity remembering distinctly that she had noticed the key before she went down to dinner because it had been gold.

Gold keys and gold locks to the door, she had thought, were ostentatiously opulent! She had never in fact seen them before in any house in which she had stayed.

Now the key had gone!

She looked around apprehensively and went into the Boudoir next door.

'Perhaps,' she thought hopefully, 'the key for that door will fit the one in the bed-room.'

But once again there was no key!

Cassandra tried to tell herself:

'I must have been mistaken in thinking I saw a key before dinner.'

Yet she knew she had definitely noticed it because it had been ornate and in rather an attractive design.

She looked around the bed-room. There were two upright chairs that appeared to be fairly substantial despite the fact that they were covered in pale blue damask, with their frames carved and gilded.

She placed the back of one of the chairs under the handle of the door which led to the corridor, the other against the door which led into the Boudoir.

She remembered her Nanny doing the same years ago because she had always been afraid of burglars. At the same time the chairs Nanny used had always been heavy and of solid wood.

Cassandra hoped that the gold frames of these chairs would be just as effective.

'Anyway,' she told herself, 'I am being unduly apprehensive. I cannot believe that anyone would try to come into my room.'

With a sense of relief she remembered the Duke was not far away in "The Red Room" which she had seen on the plan she had examined with Lady McDonald.

He was sleeping just around the corner from the suite she occupied and she could, if necessary, reach him quite easily.

She got into bed and realised when she put her head down on the pillow that she was in fact very tired.

It had been difficult to sleep the night before because she had lain awake thinking about poor Nancy. The night before that it had been her thoughts of the Duke which had kept her awake until it was dawn.

Now she felt the soft warm waves of slumber creeping over her and in a very short while she was unconscious.

She awoke suddenly with a start, aware that some sound had awakened her.

She heard it again—a distinct knock on the door!

She sat up in bed. The fire had burned low but there was still enough light to see across the room and to realise that the doorhandle was being turned and only the chair was preventing the door from opening.

The door however did open a crack and she heard a voice say: "Sandra, let me in!"

It was hardly more than a whisper and yet there was no need for her to guess who it was that spoke.

She felt as if she was unable to move. She could only sit staring at the crack in the door; seeing the chair shake as it withstood a violent assault upon it.

Then suddenly she was terrified!

She was sure that the chair might give way at any moment.

"Sandra, let me in! I wish to talk to you."

There was no mistaking a command in the words, even though the voice was still kept low! Cassandra knew she must get away! She must escape while she still could!

It seemed to her that the crack was getting wider. She thought the legs of the chair might break or it might slither across the carpet and be no longer an effective obstacle.

She was hardly conscious of what she was doing, but driven by a fear that was like a sword piercing through her she sprang from the bed.

Running across the room, she pulled aside the chair that she had placed in front of the door into the Boudoir.

She slipped through it and then passing the unlocked door which led into the passage opened the outer door on the other side of the room.

She could see her way by the light of a fire burning low in the grate and beyond the Boudoir she found a Dressing-Room.

It was in darkness but she sped across it, being just able to discern a door facing the one by which she had entered. She realised that this opened not on to the main corridor but on to a side passage, and desperately she pulled it open.

Opposite she saw by the faint light of a gas-bracket "The Red Room."

Without thinking, without knocking, she turned the handle and went in . . .

The Duke had found his Valet waiting for him when he went upstairs to bed.

The man had been in his service for a long time; in fact he had been with the Alchester family since he was a boy.

"Your Grace's early. I wasn't expecting you for some hours," he remarked as the Duke entered the bed-room.

"You need not have stayed up, Hawkins."

"I always wait up for Your Grace."

"You have had to put up with a lot of discomforts in the past year," the Duke remarked, "but this need not be one of them."

"I know m'duties, Your Grace!"

"And you have carried them out magnificently, despite the difficulties."

"I've not minded that, Your Grace," Hawkins said. "'Tis only we've all of us hated to see the house being run on a skeleton staff and the young ones having to leave the Estate."

"I know," the Duke said with a deep sigh, "but there was nothing I could do about it at the time."

"And now, Your Grace?"

"Things may get better—I am not certain."

"That's just what I says to the others, Your Grace, when they grumbles," Hawkins said. "'Things'll get better,' I tell 'em, 'you mark my words. Master Varro won't let us down.'"

"I wish I could be sure of that," the Duke remarked in a strange tone.

He watched the Valet open a cupboard in the panelling and put his shoes inside. Then the man went to the large wardrobe and hung up his evening-jacket.

"Well, there's money to burn in this place," Hawkins remarked. "But it's not a happy house, Your Grace."

"Why not?" the Duke enquired.

"I've always said, Your Grace, for a house to be a home, it needs a lady to run it. From what I hears, Her Ladyship's never here, and His Lordship fills the place with all sorts and kinds. Not that I intend to be disrespectful, if you take my meaning."

"I take your meaning, Hawkins. You always were one to call a spade a spade!"

"Yes, indeed, Your Grace. At what time do you wish to be called?"

"At about eight o'clock," the Duke replied.

"Very good, Your Grace," Hawkins said. "Good-night to you."

"Good-night, Hawkins."

The Duke, wearing a long robe of heavy silk frogged with braid, picked up the *Times* which was lying on a side-table and sat down in an arm-chair by the fire.

He opened the newspaper but he did not in fact read it. Instead he laid it on his lap and sat staring into the flames.

He was thinking of what Hawkins had said. He knew the man was speaking the truth when he said that the employees at Alchester Park were relying on him to restore to them the comfort and security they had known all their lives.

No one resented more than the servants that the house was in a dilapidated state, repairs were not done, damp was coming in, and the whole place looked shabby and unkempt.

There had been a reason for Hawkins saying Lord Carwen's house needed a mistress to look after it and his meaning had not escaped the Duke.

He sighed again, a deep sigh that seemed to come from the very depths of his being.

Then, almost as if he forced himself away from his own thoughts, he opened the *Times* again to read the leading article.

He was almost half-way through it when the door opened.

He glanced up casually thinking that Hawkins must have returned and saw Cassandra!

She stood for a moment looking at him. Then hastily she shut the door behind her and he saw that her hands were trembling.

She wore only her night-gown which was of very fine lawn trimmed with lace.

It was the type of night-gown she had worn all her life, buttoned demurely to the neck, with a small flat collar, and long sleeves which ended in lace-trimmed frills that fell over her hands.

Her hair was loose and fell in red-gold waves over her shoulders. She looked very young, little more than a child, and her face was white with fear.

The Duke rose to his feet.

"What is it? What has upset you?" he asked.

He realised she was finding it difficult to reply.

"L . . Lord Carwen . . . he is t . . trying . . . to get into . . . my b . . . bed-room!" she stammered breathlessly.

Then with a little cry she turned towards the door.

"He will r . . realise I have c . . come . . . here. I . . . left the door of the . . . Dressing-Room o . . . open."

For a moment they looked at each other. Then Cassandra whispered:

"Hide me . . . he must not . . . find me . . . !"

"No, of course not," the Duke said, and his voice was calm and matter-of-fact.

"Shall I g . . get into . . . the w . . wardrobe?"

Even as she spoke they heard footsteps, and swiftly the Duke opened the cupboard in the panelling into which Hawkins had put his shoes.

Without making a sound, Cassandra slipped past him and he closed the door behind her.

He hardly had time to take the few steps back to the hearth before the door of the room opened and Lord Carwen stood there.

He too was wearing a long robe over his night-shirt. The dark red of it seemed to echo the flush on his heavy face, and to accentuate the suspicion in his eyes.

"Hello, Carwen," the Duke exclaimed in a surprised tone. "Is anything wrong?"

Lord Carwen looked around the room.

Then as if he spoke deliberately choosing his words with care he replied:

"I came to see if you were quite comfortable, Varro. I hope you are being properly looked after?"

"I have my Valet with me."

"Yes, of course," Lord Carwen said. "But my staff are often extremely careless about details. I suppose there are hangers in your wardrobe?"

As he spoke he pulled open the door and glanced inside. Then he shut it again and moving across the room looked behind the heavy damask curtains which covered the window.

"I am always finding sash-cords broken and—blinds which do not work," he muttered.

"I have always thought that everything in your house was perfection," the Duke remarked.

Lord Carwen came and stood beside him in front of the fire.

"If there is any—suggestion of your leaving tomorrow," he said, "I hope you will remember that I particularly want you here for dinner."

"But of course," the Duke answered. "I thought Sandra and I were staying until Monday."

"You are!" Lord Carwen said positively.

He looked at the Duke for a moment. Then he said:

"By the way, Varro, I rather fancy little Sandra, and quite frankly, my dear boy, you cannot afford her!"

The Duke did not answer and after a moment Lord Carwen went on:

"Soiled doves of her type prove very expensive, as I am sure you know. I am prepared to offer her a house of mine which has recently become vacant in St. John's Wood, and of course her own carriage."

"Have you suggested to Sandra that she should become your mistress?" the Duke asked and there was a steely note in his voice.

"She is at the moment showing a provocative reluctance," Lord Carwen admitted, "which, needless to say, has exactly the effect she intends! It increases my ardour and my determination to possess her in the end!"

He laughed and it was not a pleasant sound.

"Women are all the same, Varro. They all believe that to play 'hard-to-get' increases their price, and in the majority of cases it does!"

"You sound very sure of yourself," the Duke said. He spoke slowly with an intentional lack of expression.

"I am sorry to cut you out, dear boy," Lord Carwen smiled, "but I can assure you that your interest in this little butterfly was bound to be short-lived."

He paused to say impressively:

"Diamonds are expensive, but very rewarding, as our friend Lily knows! Sandra is well aware on which side her bread is buttered and I feel quite certain you will not put any obstacles in my way."

"Are you so certain of that?" the Duke asked.

"Quite certain!" Lord Carwen replied positively. "I could make things very difficult for you, Varro. Like the villain in a melodrama, I can always foreclose on the mortgage, or refuse to extend your loan!"

He laughed again.

"But I do not think there need be any dramatics between us. Just fade out of the picture where Sandra is concerned! I shall take your place very ably and with an expertise which at your age you undoubtedly lack."

"Perhaps the lady in question might have something to say about it," the Duke suggested.

"She may prevaricate a little," Lord Carwen replied. "She was astute enough this evening to refuse a diamond bracelet I offered her —doubtless holding out for the necklace, the ear-rings and the brooch to go with it! However, I consider it to be worth my while to pursue the matter. So as far as you are concerned, Varro, it is good-bye."

"You have made yourself very clear," the Duke said.

There was an ice in his voice that Lord Carwen did not pretend to misunderstand.

"Look elsewhere," he said putting his hand on the Duke's shoulder, "and you will find me as accommodating in the future as I have been in the past. I am a good friend, Varro, but a bad enemy! Good-night!"

He walked across the room as he spoke, opened the door and closed it behind him.

The Duke waited. Then, as he saw the door in the panelling open, he held his fingers to his lips.

He stood quite still until some seconds later he heard footsteps going down the passage.

Only then did he cross to the door and turn the key in the lock.

He turned round to see Cassandra, having come from her hiding-place, standing white-faced and trembling, her eyes on his.

Then she moved towards him and hid her face against his shoulder.

"Take me . . . away! Take me away now . . . at once!" she pleaded.

The fear in her voice was very obvious and the Duke could feel her body trembling beneath the fine lawn of her night-gown.

He put his arms round her and heard her whisper, her voice muffled against his shoulder:

"I did not . . . know . . . I did not . . . understand . . . that anyone could be . . . like that . . . could say such . . . things!"

The Duke reached out towards the bed and pulled off the silk coverlet.

Wrapping it round Cassandra's shoulders like a shawl, he moved her towards the fire and sat her down, almost as if she were a child or a doll, in the wing-backed arm-chair.

She looked at him wide-eyed, her face very pale, and her hands which had clasped the bed-spread around her were shaking.

"Take me . . . away!"

"I will do that," the Duke answered, speaking for the first time. "But there are some questions I want to ask you."

"Q . . questions?"

Her eyes were dark with fear.

"Yes, and I want the truth, Sandra."

She did not answer, surprised by the sternness of his face and the manner in which his eyes looked into hers. He seemed to be seeking, searching into the very depths of her heart.

"What is . . . it?" she asked, more frightened than she had been before.

"Who was with you in your flat last night?"

"My . . . maid."

"Is that the truth?"

"Yes . . . Hannah was with me . . . she is always with me . . . when I am in the . . . flat."

"Have you ever had a lover?" The Duke's words seemed to vibrate through the air.

For a moment Cassandra did not comprehend what he meant. Then the colour flooded over her pale face, rising from her chin up to her forehead to recede again, leaving her paler than she had been before.

"N . . no . . . of course not . . . how c . . could you think such a . . . how c . . could you i . . imagine . . . ?"

The words came brokenly between her lips. It seemed to her that he thought of her as if she were Nancy.

There was an expression on the Duke's face which she did not understand. Then he said, although now his tone was not so fierce:

"Where did you get your jewellery? Who gave it to you?"

"My father . . . except for the pearls . . . they belong to my . . . mother."

The Duke looked at her for a long moment and then he said quietly:

"I believe you! Oh, my darling, you do not realise what I have been imagining, how much it has tortured me!"

He saw that she was so bemused by what had occurred that she did not really take in what he was saying. Then in a tone of voice which was now kind and comforting, he said:

"I will take you away, but not tonight. We will leave first thing tomorrow morning. Have you brought a riding-habit with you?"

"Y . . yes."

"Then we will rise early, borrow two horses from His Lordship without asking his permission, and ride across country. There is something I wish to show you."

"Could we go . . . now?"

The Duke shook his head.

"It is too late and might cause comment amongst the servants. But I promise you we will leave before anyone else in the house-party is awake."

He saw a light come into Cassandra's eyes. Then like a child who was still frightened of the dark, she said frantically:

"I cannot . . . go back to my . . . room . . . I cannot . . . sleep . . . there."

"No, of course not," the Duke answered. "Wait here a moment."

He walked to the side of the bed, lit a candle and carrying it in his hand opened another door.

He was gone only a moment or two. When he returned he said: "Come with me!"

She rose to her feet, still clutching the bed-spread around her. The silk of it rustled as she walked towards him.

Without touching her he led the way across the Sitting-Room which she had suspected was next to his through another door which led into a Dressing-Room.

There was a large comfortable bed, but it was not so impressive as the one in the room which the Duke was using.

The Duke set the candle down on a bed-side table, then walked across the room to turn the key in the door which opened onto the corridor.

"Now listen, Sandra," he said. "When I have gone, lock the door behind me. Do you understand? You will be quite safe here and no-one can possibly disturb you until the morning."

Cassandra glanced around as if to convince herself that he was speaking the truth. Then she said nervously:

"Will you . . . leave the door of your . . . room open, just in . . . case I am . . . frightened?"

"It will be open," the Duke promised with a faint smile.

He looked at her.

In the candle-light she was very young and very vulnerable.

"You will be quite safe," he said reassuringly. "Tomorrow morning I will knock on the door at about half-past six. When you are dressed, we will go down to the stables, get our horses and be away long before anyone else has been called."

"Can we . . . really do . . . that?"

"We will do it!" he promised. "But we have a long ride ahead of us, so try to sleep. For I do not want you to collapse on the way!"

"I will not do that," Cassandra answered.

"Then good-night," the Duke said, "and lock the door behind me."

For a moment they looked into each other's eyes. Then abruptly he turned away and without saying another word left the room.

In the Sitting-Room he stood listening until he heard the sound of the key turning in the lock.

With a sigh he walked on into his own bed-room.

CHAPTER EIGHT

'We have escaped!' Cassandra told herself triumphantly as she and the Duke rode their horses away from the Stables, and, keeping out of sight of the house, moved into the Park.

The morning was sunny and fresh and the horses were frisky, so for the time being there was no chance for conversation.

But Cassandra was exultant to know that she was again alone with the Duke and free from the menace of Lord Carwen.

She had thought it would be impossible to sleep last night. But she had been already very tired when she went to bed, and the shock of what occurred later naturally had taken its toll of her strength.

Instead therefore of lying awake as she had expected, fearful and apprehensive, she had slept dreamlessly until she was awakened by a knock at the door.

For one second her fears came flooding back over her, and then she realised that day-light was coming through the sides of the curtains.

"Are you awake, Sandra?" she heard the Duke ask softly.

She got out of bed and picked up the silk counterpane in which he had wrapped her the night before. She put it once again round her shoulders and going to the door unlocked it.

He was standing in the Sitting-Room fully dressed and wearing riding-breeches.

"It is half past six."

She smiled at him and he wondered how many other women of his acquaintance would have been quite unselfconscious about their looks at that hour of the morning.

Cassandra's red hair was tumbled; her eyes were still sleepy; and there was a faint flush on her cheeks.

"I have looked into your bed-room," the Duke said quietly,

"and you can feel quite safe. Will it take you long to get dressed?"

"I will be as quick as I can," she answered breathlessly.

The Duke opened the door of the Sitting-Room and she saw that it led into the same passage that she had crossed the night before from her Dressing-Room to his bed-room.

The gas-lights were extinguished and the empty passage was dim, but it was still easy to see the way to the open door of the Dressing-Room.

Cassandra, with a sense of urgency, ran to the bed-room she had left so fearfully the night before.

The door into the corridor was closed but she could see that it had been opened. The chair had been moved and was standing a little away from the door, its gilded frame damaged from the manner in which it had been thrust aside.

Because she was so anxious to get away quickly, Cassandra did not try to think now what had happened.

She washed quickly in cold water, found her riding-habit in the wardrobe and put it on.

It was a little difficult to fasten it herself because Hannah had packed her very latest and smartest habit from Busvine.

It was the habit-bodice which was widely advertised as being extremely becoming to the female figure and made so that no fastenings were visible.

It was in fact a riding-dress rather than a skirt and jacket, and was what all the fashionable lady riders had taken to wearing in the warmer months of the year.

The plain black of the material, with just a touch of white at the throat and wrists, was severe and yet extremely becoming to Cassandra.

As she dressed herself hastily, she had no time to notice the translucent whiteness of her skin or how her red hair, braided neatly around her head to wear under the black topper, glowed in the morning sunshine.

Instead she tucked a handkerchief into the pocket of her skirt, and only as she turned to run back to the Duke the way she had come did she wonder what she should do about her clothes and jewellery.

As if he anticipated that this was the question she would ask, or perhaps their minds were so attuned to each other that he knew what she was thinking, he answered the question as soon as she reappeared in the Sitting-Room.

"You have been very quick," he said approvingly. "Do not worry about your other things. I have left a note with my Valet to have them all packed and taken to London with mine."

"Then can we go?" Cassandra asked.

"At once," he replied with a smile.

Despite the fact that she supposed everyone must still be sleeping so early in the morning, Cassandra tip-toed along the corridor behind the Duke.

He ignored the wide staircase which led down into the Hall and instead led the way down several corridors until they came to another narrower staircase.

Descending it, the Duke continued through less formal parts of the house until finally they emerged into the open through a door off the kitchen, finding that it was only a few minutes away from the stables.

The Duke ordered the horses he required with an authority which Cassandra thought would have infuriated Lord Carwen if he had known what was happening.

Two magnificent horses, one a black stallion, the other a roan, were saddled and brought by the grooms into the yard.

The Duke said nothing, but Cassandra seeing the expression on his face exclaimed:

"They were yours!"

"Yes," he answered briefly, "they were mine."

The grooms were listening and Cassandra could say no more.

She wondered why the Duke had sold his animals to Lord Carwen rather than put them up at Tattersall's.

She could not help feeling that if her father had seen either of these horses and known to whom they belonged, he would have been willing to pay a very large price for them.

But what was important at the moment was that they should be clean away from the house and its owner.

Once they were out of the Park, the Duke led the way over the fields into the open countryside. Since their horses were fresh, they both realised without words that the first thing was to give them their heads.

They must have galloped for nearly two miles before the horses automatically slowed their pace and Cassandra looked at the Duke with laughter in her eyes.

"That has swept away the morning mists!"

"And your fears?"

"For the moment."

He looked at her shining eyes and flushed cheeks, as he said:

"You ride better than any woman I have ever seen. I was half-afraid that Juno would be too strong for you to hold, but I see I need have had no anxiety on that score."

"Where are we going?" Cassandra asked.

"To my home," the Duke answered. "I want you to see it."

"I would love that!"

As she spoke with a little lilt in her voice, she remembered the long article about Alchester Park that she had cut out from an illustrated magazine and stuck into the Album.

Now at last she would see the house of which she had read so much, and which was the birth-place and the background of the man she loved.

When they had ridden for another hour the Duke said:

"Do you see that Inn ahead of us? I think we would both enjoy breakfast. I know I am hungry!"

"So am I," Cassandra agreed.

The Inn with a thatched roof stood on the edge of a village green.

The Landlord was not unnaturally surprised to receive such obviously important guests so early in the morning, but ushered Cassandra and the Duke into a small private parlour where a maid-servant quickly kindled the fire.

There was a mirror on one wall of the room, and going towards it Cassandra took off her hat and tidied away the small tendrils of red-gold curls that had escaped from the tidy plaits.

Then she sat down at the round table opposite the Duke and the Landlord came hurrying in with eggs and bacon, home-cured ham, and a huge pork-pie, besides newly-baked bread, honey in the comb and a huge pat of golden butter.

"Oi'm afraid we've only simple fare to offer ye, Sir," he said to the Duke.

"It looks very palatable," the Duke replied agreeably.

He refused ale or cider and instead drank the fragrant coffee that had been brewed for Cassandra.

"Food always tastes good when one has taken exercise," Cassandra said. "I have not eaten such a big breakfast since I was last out hunting."

She realised as she spoke that it was hardly in character for an actress to hunt. But the words were spoken and she could not unsay them.

To cover the slip she had made she went on hastily:

"I think perhaps I am hungry mostly because I am so relieved to get away from that horrible house and those even more horrible people. I thought when we arrived last night that it would be interesting to study them and see what they were like. I know now that I never want to see any of them again."

"Why were they such a surprise?" the Duke asked.

"I suppose I did not realise . . . before that women who are born . . . ladies, like Mrs. Langtry and Lady McDonald, would go everywhere with a man who was . . . not their . . . husband."

The Duke did not say anything but his eyes were on her face.

After a moment Cassandra said almost as if she was talking to herself:

"My father told me that gentlemen liked to take pretty actresses out to supper and give them presents. I thought it was just because she was . . . beautiful that Mrs. Langtry had so many . . . diamonds but . . . perhaps that is not the only . . . reason."

"Why did you think Lord Carwen was offering you the diamond bracelet?" the Duke asked quietly.

Cassandra tried to meet his eyes and failed.

Looking down at the table she said:

"I heard you asking him . . . last night if he had . . . suggested to . . . me that I become his . . . mistress."

Her voice trembled before she went on:

"I did not . . . understand that was . . . what he meant."

"What does your father do?" the Duke enquired.

Once again it seemed to Cassandra that he was changing the subject for some reason of his own.

She wondered wildly what her reply should be. It was obvious the Duke did not suppose her father was a gentleman of leisure as were the majority of his acquaintances.

"Father has some . . . land," she answered at length.

It was not a very adequate way of describing the 20,000 acres that Sir James Sherburn owned.

"So he farms?" the Duke said.

Cassandra nodded. That at least was true.

"Then you did not go on the stage because you needed the money. Was it because you found the country dull and you wanted excitement?"

Cassandra did not answer. She had suddenly felt ashamed of the part she had acted to deceive the Duke. She wanted to tell him the truth and yet she could not bring herself to do so.

He had said yesterday that he was in love with her but he had not said it again.

Last night when she had been so frightened, he had treated her as he was treating her now, as if he were her brother rather than a man in love.

She rose from the table and walked across the room to the mirror, picking up her hat as she did so from the chair on which she had left it.

"I think we should be going," she said. "You said we had a long ride. I suppose we are returning to London tonight?"

"Were you expecting to do anything else?" the Duke asked.

"No, of course not," Cassandra said quickly.

The Duke paid for their breakfast and they mounted their horses in the yard and set off again.

There was no more beautiful time of year, Cassandra thought, than Spring. The buds on the trees were vividly green, and were echoed in the colour of the young grass in the meadow-land.

They rode through woods where there were violets shyly showing their purple and white heads from under the dark-green leaves, and primroses on the mossy banks were sunshine yellow.

There were anemones so fragile they seemed like fairy flowers against the trunks of the dark pine or the white of the silver birch.

They rode beside streams winding their way beneath weeping willows. Sometimes there were purple hills in the distance, and at others flat lush valleys where fat cows grazed contentedly.

Just as Cassandra was beginning to think it was time for another meal, they rode between two high iron gates with heraldic stone lions rampant on either side of them. Ahead lay a long drive lined with ancient oak trees.

It was obvious that the drive was untended, half-covered with moss, and no-one had swept away the broken branches which had fallen in the winter gales, or cut the grass beneath the trees.

The trees ended and ahead of them she saw Alchester Park!

It had appeared large and awe-inspiring in its pictures, but in reality it had a warmth that could not be translated into pen and ink.

The brown red bricks with which it had been built in the reign of Queen Elizabeth had mellowed with age and glowed rosy in the sunshine.

There were towers and chimney-pots silhouetted against the sky, glittering diamond-paned windows and a wide flight of ancient stone steps led up to the great oak door with its huge ornamental hinges and studded with iron nails.

"It is lovely!" Cassandra exclaimed. "Far lovelier than I expected."

The lawns surrounding the house were not as smooth as they should have been and were badly in need of cutting, but Cassandra realised that if they were tended they would look like velvet.

The almond trees were in bloom as were the yellow jasmine flowers climbing over the red brick walls of what she suspected might be an herb-garden.

The Duke had drawn his horse to a standstill, but he made no effort to dismount.

He sat for a moment looking at the house and then he said:

"I think we had best take our horses to the stables. It is doubtful if anyone will have heard us arrive. Most of the few servants I have left are deaf anyway."

He turned the stallion's head as he spoke and trotted ahead of Cassandra until they came to the stables situated on the west side of the house.

Here there were long rows of stalls which Cassandra could see were empty.

When the Duke shouted, an old groom emerged from one of them. His eyes lit up when he saw the Duke and he touched his forelock respectfully.

"'Morning, Ye Grace. Oi did not know ye were a-coming home today."

"Neither did I," the Duke replied, "and I am not staying. See to these horses, Ned. We shall be needing them later this afternoon."

"Why, 'tis Juno and Pegasus!" the old man exclaimed delightedly, "'tis fine to see'm again, Ye Grace."

"I am afraid they will not be staying with us," the Duke said, and his voice was hard.

He helped Cassandra down from the saddle and for a moment she was in his arms, but she knew he was thinking not of her but of his horses.

Because she could not bear to see the pain in his eyes, she walked ahead of him towards the house.

They went in through a side door which was open and the Duke led her down a passage which led into the main Hall.

The panelling was the beautiful silver-grey of oak that has matured over the years. The sunshine coming through the heraldic coats-of-arms on the glass windows cast strange shadows on the floor.

It gave the place a mystic appearance and the whole house seemed to Cassandra to have an atmosphere that was sweet, calm and happy.

She looked at the exquisitely carved oak staircase curving up to the floor above.

The heraldic newels on the staircase had once been painted in brilliant colours. Now they were scratched and faded, but they still had an inescapable charm that nothing new could have equalled.

"I expect you would like to wash," the Duke said. "You will find a bed-room at the top of the staircase. I will go and order something for luncheon."

Cassandra walked up the staircase. It was so beautiful that she felt she should be wearing a gown of satin with an Elizabethan ruff high against her red hair, and long strings of huge pearls.

The bed-room too was lovely.

Beneath a painted ceiling a carved four-poster bed was hung with embroidered curtains. The walls were papered in a Chinese design and the pelmets above the curtains had strange golden birds rioting amongst exotic flowers.

It was, however, impossible not to notice that the carpet was threadbare and the curtains were torn and faded at the sides until there was no colour left.

There seemed also to be a sparsity of furniture which Cassandra guessed had once stood against the walls.

She took off her hat and washed her face and hands in the china basin which stood on an elegant wash-stand carved in peach-wood.

As she did so she suddenly realised that in her hurry to be away from the house she had put no colour on her lips, nor had she used any powder.

'I doubt if he will notice,' she told herself.

At the same time when she looked in the mirror she realised that she now looked younger than when she had been using cosmetics.

She was still looking at herself when she heard a knock at the door.

"Come in," she said, thinking that it might be a house-maid.

But it was the Duke.

"I thought you might like to take off your riding-boots," he said, "so I have brought you a jack."

Cassandra saw that he held in his hand a wooden jack which every horseman used to facilitate the removal of high boots.

"Oh, thank you!" Cassandra exclaimed.

The Duke set the jack down on the floor, and then as Cassandra walked towards it she exclaimed:

"But I have no slippers with me!"

"I did not think of that!" the Duke said, "but I am sure I can find you a pair."

He disappeared. Cassandra pulled off her long boots and knew she would be more comfortable without them.

At the same time she thought she would feel embarrassed at walking about without any slippers on her feet.

She had been waiting for several minutes when the Duke returned. He walked in through the open door holding in his hands a pair of heel-less black slippers with a little rosette on the front of them, very similar to a pair Cassandra owned herself.

"I am sure these will fit you," he said confidently.

Then as she looked at them Cassandra suddenly wondered to whom they had belonged. He was a bachelor and the behaviour of the women in the house-party last night came flooding into her mind.

She felt suddenly that she could not . . . she would not wear the shoes of some other woman, perhaps an actress whom the Duke had brought to his home.

"I do not want them!" she said turning her head away.

The Duke looked at her averted face in surprise.

"Why not?" he asked.

"I do not . . . wish to wear . . . them."

He dropped the shoes into the seat of a chair as he advanced towards Cassandra. He took her by the shoulders and turned her round to face him.

"Why do you speak like that?" he asked. "What are you thinking?"

Then suddenly he gave a little laugh.

"You are jealous! Oh, my foolish, ridiculous darling, you are jealous! But I promise you there is no need for you to be."

He pulled her close against him until as he tipped back her head, his mouth was on hers.

Just for a moment Cassandra was still with surprise.

Then as her lips were soft beneath the hardness of his, she felt something strange and wonderful flicker into life and rise into her throat so that it was almost impossible to breathe.

It was an ecstasy, a wonder like nothing she had ever imagined, she felt as if the sun flooded into the room and enveloped them in a blinding light.

She could think of nothing except that the Duke was kissing her, and that was what she had always known it would be like.

It was a moment so ecstatic, so glorious, so utterly and completely wonderful that when at last he raised his head and looked down into her face, she was unable to move.

"I love you!" he said in his deep voice. "Oh, my sweet, how much I love you!"

She felt that she vibrated at the sound of his voice and then with a little inarticulate murmur, she turned her face and hid it against his shoulder.

"I feel as if I have loved you through all eternity," he said, "as if you have always been there in my life. Look at me, Sandra."

She was unable to obey and very gently he put his fingers under her chin and turned her face up to his.

"Why are you shy?"

"I always . . . thought that if you . . . kissed me it would be . . . wonderful," she whispered, "but not so . . . unbelievably . . . glorious!"

He looked at her searchingly and yet the expression in his eyes was very gentle.

"I would believe, if it were not incredible, that this is the first time you have been kissed!"

"The . . . only . . . time!" Cassandra whispered.

"But why?" he asked.

As if the question was superfluous his lips found hers again, and he kissed her demandingly, insistently, and with a passion that made her feel as if he drew her very heart from her body and made it his.

Then as she felt herself quiver with the thrills which ran through her like quick-silver, the Duke released her.

He took his arms from round her so quickly that she had to hold on to him to steady herself.

She had no idea how beautiful she looked; her eyes wide and excited; her lips soft and trembling a little from his kisses; a faint flush on her cheeks; her neck very white against the severity of her riding-habit.

The Duke looked at her for a long moment and then he said almost harshly:

"For God's sake do not look at me like that! I have a lot of explaining to do, but first let us have something to eat, and then I want to show you the house."

His tone was so different from when he had spoken of his love, that Cassandra felt as if she had suddenly been shaken into wakefulness.

The Duke picked up the slippers from where he had dropped them into a chair.

"You can put these on," he said. "They belonged to my mother!"

"I am . . . sorry," Cassandra murmured, and he knew she referred to the fact that she had been suspicious of a previous owner.

"You could hardly think anything else," he said almost savagely, "seeing the type of company with which you had to associate last night."

Cassandra put the slippers on and followed the Duke down the staircase and into the Hall.

She felt as if he had suddenly erected a barrier between them, and yet in a way she knew it was inevitable and that sooner or later they both had to face the future.

A very old Butler served their luncheon in a long Elizabethan Dining-Hall with a minstrels' gallery and an oriel at one end of it.

They ate at a refectory table that was as old as the house itself and sat on high-backed carved oak chairs which had come into the family in the reign of Charles II.

The old servant apologised that there was not much to eat.

But a golden-brown omelette filled with fresh tomatoes was followed by pigeons stuffed with mushrooms. There was no pudding, but a big round cheese was served, which the Duke told Cassandra was a local speciality.

They talked of quite ordinary things while the old Butler shuffled round the table waiting on them, but they neither of them seemed very hungry, and Cassandra knew she was avoiding the Duke's eyes.

It was impossible, when she thought about it, not to thrill with the memory of how he had kissed her.

At the same time she had heard the harshness in his voice when he pushed her away from him, and she knew she was waiting in an agony of apprehension for what he would say to her when they were alone again.

She was afraid as she had never been afraid before that he would tell her that they must say good-bye to each other; that their love could mean nothing because he must marry a woman for her money.

'How can I bear it?' Cassandra whispered to herself.

When finally they rose from the table and left the Dining-Hall, she felt as if every nerve in her body was tense in anticipation of what lay ahead.

But first the Duke took her round the house.

He showed her small, panelled Salons, the Great Chamber where once the Manorial Courts were held, the Armoury filled with flags and ancient weapons that had been collected over the years.

There were flags captured at the battle of Worcester; others by an Alchester who had fought with Marlborough in his campaigns; one by an Alchester who had fought with Wolfe in Canada and two more by another Duke who had served at Waterloo.

But there was a sparsity of furniture, no tapestries, and in the Drawing-Room few *objets d'art*. When they reached the long Picture Gallery, it was to find the walls were bare.

The Duke said very little.

He only led Cassandra through room after room until finally they came to the Library, and only there were the walls fully covered.

"The valuable editions have been sold," the Duke said sharply. "What is left is not worth the expense of carting them away."

She knew he was suffering and as she turned towards the fire which she saw had been newly-lighted, she said softly:

"Will you explain to me what has . . . happened?"

"Sit down," the Duke said abruptly, "because that is exactly what I am going to do."

Obediently Cassandra sat down in a chair by the fireplace. The Duke stood in front of the fire not looking at her but staring across the room.

"I do not know quite where to begin," he said, "but I want to make you understand that I was brought up to believe that this house and the Estate in which it stands was a great heritage."

"Indeed it is," Cassandra said.

"It was drummed into me almost from the moment of my birth," the Duke went on. "I was told it was my destiny and my duty to expend my whole energy, my whole enthusiasm, my whole life, on being the ninth Duke."

Cassandra looked at him, remembering their conversation of the other night.

"So inevitably you . . . hated the idea."

"Not exactly," the Duke answered, "but it made me long for freedom, to be myself, to be allowed to have one independent thought, apart from what was almost a strait-jacket into which I had to live my life."

Cassandra gave a little sigh. She was beginning to understand so many things the Duke had said to her.

"At first it did not seem quite so constricting as it did later," the Duke said. "I had the idea of going into the Foreign Office, believing I could have there a career of my own. Then I learnt that it was impossible: I had too many responsibilities here. Moreover it infuriated my father to think I should have any interests outside the sacred circle of the Alchester domain."

"So there was no escape?"

"None," the Duke answered in a hard voice. "I was also told that in the pattern of Royalty I had to marry money, so that the Estate could be kept up and I myself could live as befitted my rank."

"And you agreed?" Cassandra asked.

"My assent was taken for granted," the Duke replied. "My marriage was arranged by my father and I accepted it as something inevitable that must happen to me at some time in the future. Then I went round the world."

"That was important to you?"

"I realised that in other countries men of my age were making money by using their brains and their energy. In England it is considered degrading for gentlemen to work for a living. But that does not apply elsewhere."

His voice deepened.

"In Australia I saw a chance of making a fortune, and I found even greater opportunities when I reached South Africa."

He paused for a moment and Cassandra saw he was looking back into the past, recalling perhaps his enthusiasm at what he had discovered.

"I came back to England with ideas that I was certain could be the foundation stone for restoring the family fortunes."

"What . . . happened?"

"My father laughed at me, refused to invest one penny either in the mining possibilities I had envisaged in Australia or in the prospecting for gold that I was sure would prove to be a success in South Africa."

He was silent and Cassandra saw the bitterness on his face.

"So you could not do what you wanted to do."

"But I did!" the Duke answered. "I borrowed the money!"

Cassandra looked up at him.

"From . . . whom?" she asked, her voice hardly above a whisper.

"Need you ask?" the Duke replied. "From Carwen. He offered me anything I wanted. He is a very rich man."

"And you trusted him?"

"He made himself very pleasant," the Duke said. "He listened to my ideas, he flattered and encouraged me. That was something I needed desperately at that particular moment."

"What happened?"

"I was making up my mind to tell my father the truth and to ask him to reconsider his decision and be my sponsor, when he died," the Duke said. "It was then I realised I was my own master—until I learnt how utterly impoverished the Alchester coffers were!"

Cassandra saw that it had been a shock, but she did not speak and after a moment the Duke went on:

"There were death duties, and my father had spent far more than he could afford on his horses—banking, I suppose, on being able to pay off all his debts through the rich marriage he had arranged for me."

There was so much sarcasm in his voice that Cassandra drew in her breath.

"I realised that if I was to stand on my own feet I had to have money. I mortgaged part of the estate to Carwen. I sold everything that I did not consider a family heirloom. Then when the money was invested Carwen began to show himself in his true colours."

"What did he do?"

"He began to manipulate me as I had been manipulated all my life by my father. He used my name to further his own interests and insisted that I should be his representative on Boards which I considered to be shady. He also asked for security against the loans he had made me in my father's life-time."

"What did you give him?" Cassandra asked.

"Horses, among them those we rode today, a large amount of furniture and the family pictures," the Duke replied. "He deliberately took them off the wall so that every time I looked at the spaces where they had been I should feel under a deeper obligation to him!"

"He is despicable!" Cassandra cried.

"He is a sharp-headed business-man," the Duke replied, "and I was a fool to get into his clutches."

He was silent for a moment before he went on:

"I know that in a few years the money I have invested in Australia and South Africa will increase a thousand-fold. Already the reports from both countries are fantastic, but I cannot wait."

"Why not?" Cassandra asked.

"Because I cannot maintain the estate and pay the wages. Because I refuse any longer to be beholden to Carwen!"

He paused to say slowly:

"Now there is only one thing I can do."

"And what is that?" Cassandra asked and her voice seemed almost to have died in her throat.

"I can sell the house," the Duke answered, "pay off the mortgage and the monies that Carwen has loaned to me. That will leave enough to pension off the old retainers and provide cottages for their old age. What part of the estate is left will, in time, pay its way."

"Is there not . . . another alternative?" Cassandra asked hesitatingly.

"Of course there is," the Duke answered. "I can marry the heiress that my father procured for me. She wants my title—I want her money. A very sensible arrangement, you might say."

Cassandra did not speak and after a moment the Duke went on:

"I was prepared to do it. I had made up my mind that it would be better to be beholden to a woman—any woman—than to Carwen. And then you know what happened."

"What . . . happened?"

"I met you!"

For the first time he turned to look at her.

"Oh, God! Why did this have to happen to me now at this moment? And yet would I have it any different?"

His eyes showed her the anguish he was suffering.

He put out his arms and drew Cassandra from the chair.

"I love you!" he said. "I love you and I know that really nothing else matters. Will you be poor with me, my darling—for a few years at any rate?"

"You mean . . . ?"

"You will have no pretty gowns, no gaiety, just a rather dull life in a small house, but we shall be together."

He held her close in his arms. His eyes were looking into hers as if he was searching once again for something that was of the utmost importance to him.

Cassandra tried to speak but the words would not come to her lips.

"I am asking you to marry me," the Duke said very softly. "What is your answer, my beloved?"

He saw the sudden light in her eyes and there was no need for words.

His mouth came down onto hers, holding her captive.

"I love you . . ." she tried to say but he was kissing her wildly and it was impossible to speak.

Only inside herself Cassandra felt waves of happiness like white doves flying up to the Heavens.

She had won! He loved her!

He loved her enough to sacrifice everything that had mattered to him in the past.

He loved her and she felt his lips demanding her complete surrender.

No-one she thought, could know such happiness and not die of the wonder of it!

CHAPTER NINE

Cassandra shut her eyes so that Hannah, thinking she was asleep, would stop grumbling.

"I have never in all my life known such a carry-on!" Hannah had exclaimed last night.

She said it not once but a dozen times when Cassandra had returned to Park Lane to inform the old maid that they were leaving for Yorkshire by the seven o'clock train the following morning.

"There's a good train, stopping only a few times, that leaves at nine-thirty," Hannah said.

"I know that," Cassandra answered, "but I wish to leave at seven. If you cannot be ready, Hannah, I will go alone and you can follow later."

She had known this was the surest way to make Hannah get the packing done and be sure that they left together.

Listening with her eyes closed to the rumble of the wheels on the track, Cassandra found herself reliving the wonder she had felt when she knew that the Duke loved her enough to give up his ancestral house so that they could be married.

She was well aware of the immensity of his sacrifice and how despite his complaints about being tied to the Alchester Estate, it was in fact a part of him, and to sell it would be like losing an arm or a leg.

"Are you . . . sure?" she had asked him later when they were seated together on the sofa so that he could still hold her in his arms.

"Sure that I want to marry you?" he asked. "I am more sure of it than I have been of anything else in my whole life."

"But we have . . . known each other such a . . . short time," Cassandra murmured.

"I feel that you have always been there in my heart," he answered. "The woman I have always been looking for, the wife I have wanted beside me, but whom I could never find."

There was a depth of sincerity in his voice that told Cassandra he spoke the truth.

"I love you!" he went on. "I love everything about you. Your absurdly red-gold hair, your little nose, your blue eyes! But more than all these I love the quickness of your brain and the kindness of your heart."

"You are . . . flattering me!" Cassandra demurred.

"I am telling you what I believe to be the truth," the Duke answered. "But I forgot to mention something else which I love."

"What is that?" she asked, lifting her face a little to look up at him.

"Your lips!" he answered.

Then he was kissing her again and it was difficult to say anything more . . .

A long time later Cassandra looked at the clock on the mantelpiece and realised it was time they returned to London.

It was then she could not help asking the question which had trembled on her lips for some time.

"What are you . . . going to do about . . . the girl you were supposed to . . . marry?"

The Duke rose from the sofa to stand with his back to her looking into the fire.

"I admit that in some ways I have been a cad," he said. "Our engagement should have been announced two years ago, but she was in mourning for her grand-father and we did not meet. Then, after my father's death, I decided to make it clear that I did not intend to go on with the arrangement he had made with the girl's father. But I was afraid—"

"Of what?"

"That my business commitments would fail and I should be left at the mercy of Carwen! I had begun to find out the sort of swine he was."

The Duke paused to add:

"So I did nothing."

"And now?" Cassandra asked, her eyes on his broad shoulders and his head bent to look into the flames.

"I must behave decently," he said speaking as if to himself. "I will go to Yorkshire tomorrow and see Sir James Sherburn. After all, he was my father's greatest friend. If nothing else, I owe him a personal explanation."

"And what will that be?" Cassandra asked.

The Duke turned round.

"I shall tell him the truth," he said, "that I have fallen in love with someone so utterly adorable that not all the gold in the world could prevent me from marrying her!"

'He loves me!' Cassandra said to herself now. 'He loves me! And everything I ever wanted or dreamed of in life has come true!'

At the same time she was aware of a real fear within herself that the Duke might be angry when he learned the truth.

She had known she could not confess her deception while they sat in front of the fire in the Library at Alchester Park.

It had also been impossible to do so when they had ridden back to London, arriving late at the stables of Alchester House where the Duke kept his horses.

The house was closed because he could not afford to live there, and in the stables, which could accommodate a dozen horses, there were only the pair which they had driven to the country.

The Duke saw them in their stalls and said to Cassandra:

"Your luggage will be waiting for you at the flat."

When Cassandra and the Duke arrived at Bury Street, it was in fact waiting for her in the Hall, and the porter had charge of her jewellery case.

"I was told to give it only into your own hands, Miss," he said.

"Shall I come upstairs with you?" the Duke asked.

"No," Cassandra answered. "I am tired and I am going straight to bed. Thank you for a wonderful day."

She put her hands in his and he raised them to his lips.

It was impossible to say more because the porter was within earshot.

The Duke had already promised as they rode towards London that he would return from Yorkshire on Wednesday and they would dine together that evening.

As soon as he had departed in his carriage in which they had driven from his stables to Jermyn Street, Cassandra asked the porter to find her a cab and place her luggage on it.

When he had done so she handed him the key of the flat.

"I shall not be returning," she said. "Here is the key and I should be grateful if you would get in touch with the Agent."

The porter thought it strange, but it was not for him to argue with the tenants.

As Cassandra drove away, she knew how glad she was that she would never again have to enter that horrible vulgar flat.

She wondered how she had ever allowed herself to rent such a place, but at the time she had not understood as much about the theatrical world as she did now.

As the train carried her home to Yorkshire it was a satisfaction in itself to know that she was going back to security, to her parents who loved her and had protected her, and cosseted her from the crude realities of the world outside her home.

She had never dreamt that there would be women who suffered as Nancy Wood had, or women who could flout the conventions like Lady McDonald and in a different manner even Mrs. Langtry.

'I have learnt a lot,' Cassandra told herself, but she knew her father would not consider it particularly desirable knowledge.

She was well aware that there was every likelihood of his being extremely angry at her behaviour. But what was more important at this moment was what the Duke would say when she told him the truth.

'I will make him understand . . . he must understand!' Cassandra told herself.

She was conscious all the same of a little quiver of fear and a number of questions in her mind which would not be silenced.

Now that she knew him, she was well aware that he would dislike being beholden to his wife as much as he had resented being beholden to his father and Lord Carwen.

He was a strong character and to a man who was as masculine as he was, it would be humiliating to know that his wife held the purse-strings.

Then Cassandra told herself it was only a question of time. The Duke had said that eventually he would be rich in his own right and she was sure he would be.

She had never yet heard him exaggerate or boast about anything, and he had been absolutely certain in his own mind that in perhaps only a few years the investments he had made in Australia and South Africa would bring him the fortune he so ardently desired.

Yet at the moment the house had to go, and that he should be willing to sell Alchester Park with the whole history of his family behind it because he loved her was to Cassandra so perfect, so utterly marvellous that she could only pray that she herself would be worthy of such a love.

She loved him so overwhelmingly that she thought now that, if he had in fact been in love with anyone else, she would not have wished to go on living.

She loved everything about him—not only his outstanding good looks but his air of authority, his charm, his pride and his sense of humor.

Because she was jealous she could not help saying to him:

"You must have . . . spent a lot of . . . money on the pretty . . . ladies from the Gaiety?"

"Are you suspecting diamonds?" the Duke asked.

His eyes twinkled.

"Dare I be conceited enough to tell you that I did not have to give anything more expensive than a few flowers for any favours I received?"

He had kissed her and added:

"That at least is one economy I can make in the future!"

Cassandra had sent a telegram first thing in the morning to The Towers to say that she and Hannah were arriving at York at 2:00 p.m.

It was nearly an hour's drive to her home, and she knew that, even travelling by the faster train, it would be impossible for the Duke to arrive until after five thirty.

That would give her time to prepare her father for the shock of what he had come to say.

But in her own mind Cassandra was not decided as to how she would let him learn the truth.

She somehow felt desperately shy at the thought of just letting him walk in and find her there.

The carriage was waiting at York Station and all the way to The Towers Cassandra was very quiet. She was thinking apprehensively of what lay ahead, and though Hannah tried to talk she only answered in monosyllables.

The Butler was at the door to greet her.

"Welcome home, Miss Cassandra."

"Is Sir James in?" Cassandra asked as she walked into the Hall.

"No, Miss, Sir James and Her Ladyship had left before your telegram arrived."

"Then my father did not know I was coming back?"

"No, Miss. Sir James and Her Ladyship were having luncheon with Lord Harrogate and going on afterwards to a Reception given by the Archbishop of York."

"Of course!" Cassandra exclaimed. "I remember that engagement."

She also had been invited.

"Sir James has ordered dinner a little later than usual," the Butler went on, "but he and Her Ladyship should be back before seven o'clock."

"Is there another telegram?" Cassandra asked.

"Yes, Miss. It also arrived after Sir James had left, so I opened it, as he has always instructed me to do."

"What did it say?"

"It is from the Duke of Alchester, Miss Cassandra, to say he is arriving by the train which reaches York at three twenty-five. I have arranged for a carriage to meet him."

Cassandra considered a moment.

"Now listen, Hudson," she said. "When His Grace arrives I want you to inform him that Sir James is unfortunately not here to greet him and that as I have a bad cold I will receive him in my Sitting-Room. Is that clear?"

"Yes, Miss Cassandra."

"Just show him into the room and do not interrupt us until I ring."

"Very good, Miss."

The Butler looked slightly surprised at the instructions, but Cassandra knew he was too well-trained not to carry them out.

She then ran up the stairs to her own room—she had a lot of preparations to make.

The train must have been late because although Cassandra was ready and waiting by half past four, it was after five o'clock when she heard footsteps coming along the corridor towards her Sitting-Room.

Although it was not yet dark outside she had drawn the curtains and there was a fire in the grate, the flames flickering over wood logs.

She had put a screen around an arm-chair which had its back to the windows as if to furnish protection against draughts, and she had extinguished all the lights in the room with the exception of one cut-glass oil-lamp.

It stood on the circular table in the centre of the room and on the table Cassandra had laid the two Albums she had treasured for so many years.

Because she was determined to keep her secret a surprise until the last possible moment, she wore a pair of dark glasses and held a fan in one hand as if to protect her face from the heat of the flames.

She knew it would be difficult for the Duke, coming from the light in the rest of the house into the dimness of the room, to recognise her at first sight.

She also had the feeling that because he would be embarrassed at what he had to say, he would not look at her very closely.

'It will be a surprise—a wonderful surprise for him when he knows who I am!' she told herself.

But her words sounded more convincing than the feeling they evoked within her. She was still afraid he might be angry!

It seemed to her while she waited that every moment was an eternity. The clock ticking softly on the mantelpiece seemed to pause between every second, her heart beat feverishly in her breast, and she kept moistening her lips because they were dry.

'Why should I be afraid?' she asked herself, and yet she knew she was.

Then at last, when Cassandra had begun to fear that something had gone wrong and that the Duke had missed the train and was perhaps trying to get in touch with her in London, she heard the door open.

"His Grace, the Duke of Alchester," Hudson announced and Cassandra felt herself tremble as the Duke walked across the room towards her.

He put something down on the table by the lamp, then he came nearer to the fire.

"I hear you have a cold," he said courteously. "I am sorry if you stayed up to receive me when you should have been in bed."

"It is . . . not too . . . bad," Cassandra managed to say.

She had intended to sound hoarse, but there was really little need to disguise her voice because she was so nervous it sounded strange even to herself.

The Duke did not look at her. He stood for a moment holding out his hands to the flames. Then he said in what seemed to Cassandra a hard voice:

"I intended to speak to your father, but as he is not here perhaps we can speak frankly with each other?"

It was a question.

Cassandra managed to murmur:

"Y . . yes."

"Then I think you know why I am here," the Duke said, "and what was arranged between your father and mine before he died? Their plan was that we should be married."

He paused, Cassandra said nothing and after a moment he went on:

"So, Miss Sherburn, let me put it very simply—I shall be deeply honoured if you will consent to be my wife!"

Cassandra was frozen into immobility. She could not believe that what she had heard was not a product of her imagination.

He could not have said it! He could not!

Then through her dark glasses she looked at his profile clear in the light of the fire, and saw the square, determined set of his chin and the hard line of his mouth.

He meant it! He had said it and he meant it! He had changed his mind after she had left him yesterday and decided that love was not worth the sacrifice of his heritage, of the house which had meant so much in the history of his family.

It was impossible for her to speak or to move.

She could only stare at the Duke as the tears began to run from her eyes down her cheeks, and her hand which still held the fan to shadow her face trembled.

She felt as if the whole ceiling had crashed on to her head; that everything she had ever believed in had fallen in pieces around her.

And now the numbness of her body was replaced with an agony that was like a thousand knives being driven into her heart.

The Duke turned towards her.

"Come," he said. "I have something to show you."

He put out his hand as he spoke and taking hers he drew her unresisting from the chair in which she had been sitting across the room towards the table.

She went with him because he compelled her and because she was quite incapable of speech.

They reached the table and Cassandra saw there was now a magazine lying beside the two Albums.

"I want you to look at this," the Duke said. "Perhaps you would be able to see more clearly without those glasses."

He took them off as he spoke and now with her heart palpitating Cassandra tried to understand what was happening; tried to look at what lay on the table in front of her.

It was a copy of *The Sporting and Dramatic* and on the open page there was a portrait sketch of herself!

Although it had been copied from the photograph which had been taken by the photographer in York which her father had disliked, it was quite unmistakable.

Underneath it was written:

"A NOTABLE LADY RIDER TO HOUNDS AND BELLE OF THE YORKSHIRE BALLS—MISS CASSANDRA SHERBURN."

She stood looking at it and the Duke said:

"I could hardly fail to recognise you, could I?"

His voice was harsh and now Cassandra managed to say through dry lips:

"I . . . could not . . . tell you . . . yesterday . . ."

"Why not?" the Duke asked in an uncompromising tone, "or need I ask such a foolish question? You wished to extort from me the last vestige of humiliation—to force me down on my knees in front of you."

"No . . . No!" Cassandra whispered. "It was not . . . like . . . that."

"Of course it was," the Duke retorted. "Do not deceive me any further. Not content with my title—you wanted my heart also. It was very clever!"

"No! No!" Cassandra cried again. "I . . ."

"You were determined to manipulate me," he interrupted, "as I have been manipulated all my life. First by my father, then by Carwen and now by you. Well, you have been most successful, and I can only congratulate you on being an even better actress than you pretended to be!"

His voice cut like a whip and Cassandra cried frantically:

"You must listen to me . . . you must! It was . . . nothing like . . . that . . . look, I have . . . these to show . . . you."

She threw open the Albums as she spoke.

The Duke looked down at the newspaper cuttings stuck neatly in the pages, but the expression on his face did not change.

"There is . . . something . . . else," Cassandra said.

She ran across the room to her writing-desk. With hands which trembled so much that she could hardly control them she found the key of the secret drawer, opened it and drew out her Diary.

Then she went back to the Duke.

He had not moved from the table. He still stood there with the two open Albums and Cassandra's picture in front of him.

There was nothing in the Diary after the last entry written on March 29th, which she had made before she left for London.

She held it out to the Duke.

"Read this . . . read . . . it," she begged.

The Duke did not look at her and she thought for one moment he would refuse to take the Diary from her.

Then he took the little book and held it towards the light, so that he could see better.

In Cassandra's neat and elegant hand-writing he saw written:

"Papa has just told me that after all this time he has received a letter from the Duke of Alchester. I had been certain, since his father's death, that the young Duke had changed his mind about the arrangements that were made so long ago for our marriage. Now because I understand he is desperately hard-up, he is prepared to go through with it.

"But I know this is something I cannot and will not do! It has been Papa's dream that I should marry the son of his old friend and that also I should be a Duchess.

"If we had become engaged two years ago when I was only seventeen-and-a-half, I should have accepted Papa's judgment in this as I have done in so many other things.

"But now I am older and I know that it would be a travesty of everything in which I believe and which I hold sacred for me to marry a man I love but who, I am convinced, loves someone else.

"I had also thought because I have loved him so deeply ever since I was twelve years old and saw him at the Eton and Harrow cricket match, that he would come to love me and that we could find happiness together.

"But I know now that was merely a child's dream.

"My love for him has prevented me from marrying anyone else or caring for any of the men who have proposed to me.

"But I would rather be an old-maid and remain unmarried for the whole of my life than suffer the humiliation and degradation of being married to the Duke who wants only my money.

"I am certain it would be easier to marry, if I must, someone for whom I have no affection, rather than to know that Varro kissed me and touched me because it was his duty. That I could not face.

"In fact I would rather die than be tortured by my longing for something very different.

"I wanted to tell Papa this but then I thought he would merely brush my arguments aside unless I can prove irrefutably that the Duke is in love with someone else.

"I am sure he is, and that she is an actress from the Gaiety Theatre. But because he would not be likely to admit it to Papa, I have to find out the truth for myself.

"I have therefore decided that I shall go to London and try to meet the Duke through Mrs. Langtry. I shall pretend to be a part of the world which he enjoys and which obviously means so much to him.

"People have always said I look theatrical. If I can act the part of an actress sufficiently well to convince him, I feel sure I can find out the truth.

"There are other heiresses in the world who would be only too willing to give him their money in exchange for his coronet, but all these years it has not mattered to me whether he was a Duke or a pauper.

"I have loved him because the first time I saw him I lost my heart!

"It sounds so stupid put down on paper, but that is what happened.

"Now I must find out the truth and I will then tell Papa that I cannot marry the Duke. He will not force me in those circumstances.

"But I know that however long I live, even if I never see him again, I shall never love anyone as I love Varro."

The Duke reached the bottom of the page. Then as he stared at what he had read with an almost incredulous look in his eyes, a very low, broken voice said behind him:

"You are . . . not on your . . . knees, Varro . . . I am! Please . . . please . . . will you . . . marry me? I love you so . . . desperately."

The Duke turned round slowly, Cassandra was kneeling on the floor behind him. Her hands were clasped together, she had thrown back her head to look up at him and the tears were streaming down her cheeks.

She looked into his eyes, and seeing no softening in the hardness of his expression, she gave a pitiful little sob as she whispered:

"If you . . . will not . . . marry . . . me, will you . . . make . . . me your . . . mistress?"

For a moment the Duke was still. Then he bent down and putting his arms round Cassandra pulled her roughly against him.

"How dare you say such a thing?" he asked and his voice was still angry.

But as if he could not help himself, his mouth sought hers.

For a moment his lips were hard and rough. Then as he felt her body soft and yielding against his and as he knew that a flame had been ignited in them both, his kiss became more tender and at the same time more demanding.

It seemed to Cassandra that the room whirled round her and she was dizzy with the wonder of it.

Then the Duke was kissing the tears from her cheeks, her wet eyes and again her mouth with a passion that made her quiver and tremble. Yet her whole being responded to the fire that consumed him.

When finally he raised his head to look down at her she turned her face and hid it against his shoulder.

"I am . . . sorry," she whispered.

"How could you have done anything so crazy, so reprehensible, so incredibly naughty?" he asked.

She did not answer and he went on:

"God knows in what sort of trouble you might have found yourself, if I had not been there to protect you."

"But you were . . . there!" she murmured. "And I . . . had to find . . . out the . . . truth."

"There would have been better ways of doing it than acting a part though having no conception whatever of the type of woman you were pretending to be."

"You . . . were . . . deceived!"

"I was completely bewildered," the Duke replied. "I fell in love with you when you were shocked by the Can-Can that first evening at Carwen's house, but I could not understand what was happening. How anyone who looked as you looked with your painted face could be so innocent and so obviously ignorant of the world was beyond my comprehension!"

"I . . . thought I was rather . . . clever!" Cassandra murmured.

"As a performance it was lamentable! And let me tell you another thing: if I ever catch you reddening your lips again, I will beat you! Do you understand?"

He held her very closely against him, and Cassandra said in a small hesitating voice:

"Does that . . . mean that . . . you are . . . going to . . . marry me?"

He looked down into her eyes and there was a smile on his lips.

"I suppose I shall have to!" he said. "After all, the fact that you slept in my suite is extremely compromising."

"I locked . . . the door."

The Duke laughed.

"Because I told you to! Oh, my darling, when I think of how badly you have behaved and what wild, crazy chances you have taken, I am appalled! It terrifies me even now to think of what might have happened to you!"

"I knew I was . . . safe with . . . you."

"You will always be safe with me in the future," the Duke said firmly, "for the simple reason that I shall never let you out of my sight! How could I, when you are so ridiculously lovely? But I am going to punish you because you have deceived me and because you have behaved so badly."

"How?" Cassandra asked rather apprehensively.

"We are going to be married almost immediately," he said, "but you are not going to have the pleasure of flaunting yourself in London as the lovely young Duchess of Alchester. We are going on a very long honeymoon trip first to Australia and then to South Africa."

"How wonderful!" Cassandra cried, her face radiant with happiness.

"When we return," the Duke went on, "I anticipate it will be time to put our house in order for the future generations."

For a moment Cassandra did not understand his meaning, then she blushed.

"You mean . . ." she began and hesitated.

"I mean exactly what you think I mean," the Duke answered, "and how, when you blush like that, you ever expected anyone to think of you as a hard-boiled, tough little actress, I do not know!"

He kissed her again.

"I love you!" he said after a moment. "I love you so much that I can think of nothing but you."

"That is what I have felt about . . . you for years."

"Have you really been in love with me for so long?" he asked wonderingly.

"Ever since I first saw you," Cassandra answered. "I felt we were meant for each other. Did you not feel the same?"

"I thought it from the first moment I set eyes on you at Carwen's party," the Duke confessed. "I was depressed, worried and very apprehensive about the future. Then I saw you standing in front of me and everything was changed from that moment."

"And nothing else . . . matters?" Cassandra asked.

He saw the meaning in her eyes and knew what she asked.

"Nothing, my precious," he said. "Titles, money, rank are unimportant compared with a love like ours! A love which will last all through our lives."

"I love . . . you!" Cassandra whispered. "I love you . . . agonisingly."

Then the Duke's lips were on hers fiercely, passionately demanding they asked her complete and absolute surrender.

She knew he would always be her Master and gloried in his strength.

She felt that he swept her away into a sunlit, perfect world where there was only themselves.

He raised his head.

"Do . . . you really . . . love me?" she whispered.

"I worship you—my wonderful darling."

"For . . . ever?"

"For eternity and beyond."

Cassandra gave a sigh of sheer happiness, then the Duke's lips blotted out thought.

She could only thrill and thrill at the rapture and ecstasy of a love which was part of the Divine.

ABOUT THE AUTHOR

BARBARA CARTLAND, the celebrated romantic author, historian, playwright, lecturer, political speaker and television personality, has now written over 150 books. Miss Cartland has had a number of historical books published and several biographical ones, including that of her brother, Major Ronald Cartland, who was the first Member of Parliament to be killed in the War. This book had a Foreword by Sir Winston Churchill.

In private life, Barbara Cartland, who is a Dame of the Order of St. John of Jerusalem, has fought for better conditions and salaries for Midwives and Nurses. As President of the Royal College of Midwives (Hertfordshire Branch), she has been invested with the first Badge of Office ever given in Great Britain, which was subscribed to by the Midwives themselves. She has also championed the cause for old people and founded the first Romany Gypsy Camp in the world.

Barbara Cartland is deeply interested in Vitamin Therapy and is President of the British National Association for Health.